Keep You Like a Secret

Also by Jeannie Choe

Best I Never Had Series

Best I Never Had

No Place Like You

Keep You Like a Secret

TAKE ME BACK TO THE START
Book Two

JEANNIE CHOE

To anyone who's been told they're too hard to love.

Keep You Like a Secret

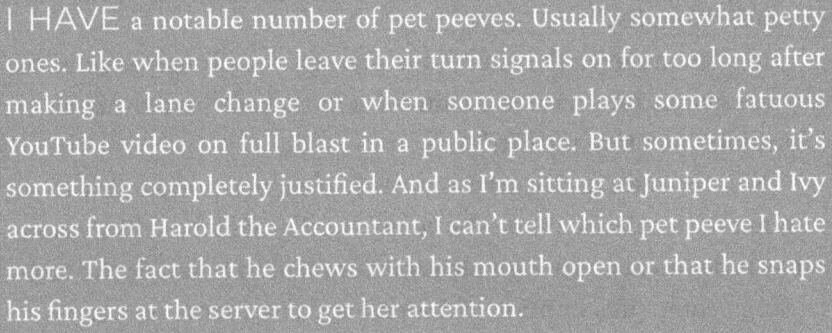

CHAPTER ONE

Grace

I HAVE a notable number of pet peeves. Usually somewhat petty ones. Like when people leave their turn signals on for too long after making a lane change or when someone plays some fatuous YouTube video on full blast in a public place. But sometimes, it's something completely justified. And as I'm sitting at Juniper and Ivy across from Harold the Accountant, I can't tell which pet peeve I hate more. The fact that he chews with his mouth open or that he snaps his fingers at the server to get her attention.

"Your mother said you're a social worker?" Harold asks, a set of narrow reading glasses perched on the bridge of his nose. He has his phone screen lit up in his hand, and he's reading off this detail about me, along with my age and height, as if my personal demographics have been registered online.

"Yes, and I believe she mentioned you're an accountant," I counter. I really don't know much else about him, aside from the fact that, according to my mom, he may or may not have a pet dander allergy.

He nods. "I'm glad your mother prepared you for tonight." I don't miss that this is the second time he's said "mother" with his nose pointed in the air.

"Hmm," I hum. I take a long soothing sip of my wine, wondering how desperate I must've been to agree to this blind date. Was it desperation? Or was it more likely guilt? When my mom came to me with the prospect of an "optimal match," along with the reminder of my continuously ticking, hard-to-ignore biological clock, I think it was my easily swayable conscience more than anything else. Although that biological clock feels more like an hourglass at this point, the grains of sand dwindling as my age remains a constant factor in my quest for what my mom considers a perfect husband.

He continues scrolling through his phone while managing to spear an oily asparagus stem and place it on his awaiting tongue. With a full mouth, the contents pushed aside to one cheek, he asks, "Then I'm assuming she mentioned my list?"

I pause mid-sip, using the moment to suppress a disgusted grimace. "Your list?"

He eyes me over the rim of his glasses, the obtuse edge of his jawline giving him an extra chin with it tucked toward his chest. "She didn't mention my list?"

"No, she didn't." I clamp my teeth over my pursed lips in an attempt to hold back a sarcastic comment that will most likely come off as rude or crass. Though pleasantries seem to have left the table, leaving behind presumption on his end and impatience on mine.

He sighs as if the mere thought of having to explain his "list" inconveniences him. He taps away at his screen, a third chin appearing as his lips turn down into a frown, and he thrusts his phone in my direction. I take it from him, though I do so with a towering reluctance, and peer at the screen.

"Read it over," he instructs, or rather demands, returning to his grilled duck.

It's a list, all right. Bullet points on what makes the perfect partner for Harold the Accountant. Reputable job. Comes from a good family. Dresses nicely. Good cook. Of childbearing age. Decent health. Not overweight. Preferably Chinese. Is respectful to his mother, no matter the situation.

This isn't real. I'm getting *Punk'd*, right? Or I'm on an episode of *Impractical Jokers*. My mom's behind this. And maybe even my sister, Jade. They're trying to give me a laugh. That has to be it.

"Now, I know one of the items on the list is that you have to be of childbearing age," he adds. "And considering you're...thirty-seven?"

I turn the phone back to him where my demographics are neatly typed, showing him where he input my age. "Thirty-nine."

He draws in a concerned breath. A ruminant wince. "Well, as long as you're willing to have kids right away, I can look past that."

"That's so considerate of you," I say flatly, though he doesn't seem to catch onto my sarcasm.

He smiles. It's brusque and cursory, and by how clumsily his lips move, I can only assume he's smiled about a handful of times since he was born. "And I know you're only half-Chinese, but again, I'm willing to overlook that. As long as I talk to my parents first. They prefer their first grandson to be raised traditionally Chinese. Speaking the language, follow our customs."

I need more wine.

This isn't a date. It's a business transaction. We aren't asking questions pertaining to the getting-to-know-each-other variety. We haven't once grazed over personal details that don't define my worth. I feel like livestock put up for auction. There might as well be a bid caller at my side, answering questions to hash out a deal. Whatever happened to asking about my favorite color or what I do for fun?

Harold takes his phone back, a smug look of pride on his lips as he takes another look at his list. It's clear he's thought it through and most likely won't sway from it, not that I had any plans to convince him my age is merely just a number or that the half-Korean part of my heritage is one that can be tossed aside. No one can be that desperate.

But as I consider the other prospects in my life, along with my mom's more recent and unusual helicopter-parent-like tendencies, I can see how my standards are gradually lowering. Singledom is starting to feel like a death sentence I never thought I'd sign up for. I mean, in all honesty, in this day and age, who cares if you're single? There are plenty of men and women who live a fulfilling life without a partner. Would it be so bad if I did too?

The short answer is, yes. As much as I admire those who aren't on a lifelong search for their other half, it's not the life I'd choose for myself. But the long answer? I want to spend the rest of my life with someone who wants me the same way. I want a partner. I want a family. I want all those yearly traditions I grew up with along with a noisy home and memories. I know a person's relationship shouldn't define them, but is it so bad that this is what I want?

I grit my teeth through the rest of the dinner. I maintain a polite, neutral air, and by the time the server has brought our check, my hand is already firmly gripping my valet ticket.

"So, your half is...112.07." Harold is reading over the check, those reading glasses back over the oily bridge of his nose. He looks up at me expectantly, and I reach into my purse for my card. He takes it with another stiff smile and adds, "Actually, it's about 115.07." He tucks my card right alongside his in the leather check holder. "Tip," he explains, and I make note of how he's not only uptight but also cheap.

He informs the server that it'll be a split bill when she picks it up, completely oblivious to her raised brow and wordless nod. I catch her eyeing me with disbelief, and I give her a look of equal perplexity. By the time we're leaving the restaurant, I'm counting down the seconds until I'm in my car.

"That was nice." Harold has his hand extended in my direction, offering a stiff handshake. I should be thankful he doesn't assume I'd do something that requires more physical contact like a hug or, God forbid, a kiss. He seems satisfied, like he's grading the firmness of my grip and the respectful way I don't go beyond the etiquette of handshake rules by lingering for longer than necessary. "I'll give your mother a positive report of our date."

I respond with a curt nod and a pursed-lipped smile. "Take care, Harold."

His car arrives first, and he slides into the driver's seat. He takes his time adjusting the seat and mirror, disapproval marking his terse movements as if he's annoyed the valet had to adjust anything at all. When he's finally satisfied with the orientation of everything, he drives off, not bothering to check if my own car made it to the front of the valet line.

My body sags the second he turns onto the road, and I can't help the sudden shudder that runs up my spine. I feel gross. Like by being in the same air as that man makes my pores ooze a pungent body odor that's equally offensive and foul. I need to wash this date off my body as if it left a sticky, slimy film in the wake of Harold's offensive appraisal. That cattle-like feeling returns, making me wonder if I dodged a bullet by leaving the restaurant sans tag. More specifically, one that would've been clipped to my ear with my going rate.

"Brrrr," I mutter, shaking my arms out while the repulsion rattles my entire body. I reach for my phone in my purse, quickly tapping along the screen to call my sister.

"Hello?" she answers through the video chat. Her tired smile fills up the screen through the dim lighting in her living room. Her hair's disheveled, and I can see that she's a little distracted.

"Hey," I respond. The frustration that was climbing up my throat dies when I realize I shouldn't be adding onto her already chaotic life by complaining about our mom and her horrible setup skills. So instead of venting to her or even asking her if she and my mom recently were in cahoots to prank me, I ask her about my niece. "How's Avery?"

"She's right here." She hefts baby Avery onto her lap and what little remaining anger I was holding on to out of spite melts as soon as I see her chubby cheeks and glistening drooly chin.

"Hi, Av!" she squeals, and I wave at her. "I miss you, baby girl!"

Another squeal, and I've all but forgotten my date from hell.

Well, almost. It's hard to forget a wife list and all the ways I'm falling short in the marriage market.

"So, how was the date?" And just like that, my sister pops my small, very temporary, balloon of happiness.

I sigh.

"Uh-oh, that bad?"

"Can we just never let Mom set me up again?"

She laughs but quickly covers it with a hand clamped over her mouth. "I think the only way to do that is for you to actually meet someone."

"What's so funny?" I hear through the speaker. The screen suddenly fills with a third face lined with curiosity and a small case of FOMO. It's Jade's husband, Trevor.

"Grace and her horrible blind date," Jade explains.

"Oh, no!" he exclaims. "Did he show up, see you, and leave?"

Jade smacks his arm. "Why would you say that?"

He shrugs, his cluelessness the epitome of honesty. "Because that's a pretty horrible blind date."

Though that would've been a pretty discouraging outcome, I can't help preferring it over the night I had. "I wish he didn't show up."

"That bad?" Jade asks through a wince.

"He came to dinner with a 'wife list.'" The flat tone of my voice measures equal amounts of annoyance and disbelief. I'm still in shock a wife list exists, and that I was graced with it tonight.

"What's a wife list?"

"A list of Harold's requirements to be his wife," I say, answering Trevor's question. "And he made me split the bill."

Avery chooses that moment to wail, and a part of me thinks my blind date nightmare story is what caused her outburst. Which would actually be a valid response. Trevor takes Avery from Jade's arms, and Avery's crying fades into the background. While I miss the sight of my adorable niece, I'm relieved to have my sister all to myself.

"So, what was on this wife list?"

I reluctantly scour through my memory. "Um, decent health, not overweight. Preferably Chinese. Of childbearing age."

If I weren't so baffled as I recounted said list, I'd probably laugh at the amount of disgust distorting Jade's face.

"I think I actually threw up in my mouth a little bit."

"I *did* throw up in my mouth a little bit," I counter, though it's an exaggeration since it seems my gut decided it didn't want a good meal—that I paid for by the way—to go to waste.

"What the hell does he mean, 'childbearing age?' I thought this was a date, not some livestock sale."

"That's what I said!" I exclaim, relieved my completely rational analogy wasn't irrational at all. Maybe my standards aren't as low as I thought.

"I'm sorry you had such a horrible night," she says, knowing there's really nothing else to offer.

"Eh," I say, brushing off her apology. "At least I'll have an interesting story to tell."

"Don't let Mom off that easily."

"You know it doesn't matter if I get mad at her," I argue. "She's just going to tell me that if I could find my own dates and if I hadn't stayed single so long after my divorce, she wouldn't be forced to find my dates for me."

"It's not like you asked her to."

"Still."

"We'll talk to her together," she offers. "I'll hold your hand, and we'll calmly tell her this is why she needs to stop meddling in your love life."

I roll my eyes. "Whatever. It's not like she's wrong. I've been single for so long, I'm going to need a broom to untangle the cobwebs between my legs." I look up and notice the very nosy valet's brows shoot up. I turn toward a row of bushes for more privacy.

Jade laughs. "Maybe I can help her screen them before setting you up then," she offers.

7

I shrug. "Yeah, I guess." While I appreciate my sister's sentiment, I wonder what good it'll do. With every date I go on, whether it's set up by my mom or a meddling relative or through a very unreliable dating app, I feel parts of me chip away. My confidence is at an all-time low, as is my hope. Maybe I can be one of those women who has a bunch of plants and goes to book club meetings and fills their time doing crafts. They look happy and content. The afterthought of living out my life alone forces a ball of anxiety to tumble low in my belly, and I say, "Did you know that you're thirty-two percent at higher risk of an accidental death if you live alone? Forty-seven percent if you're a woman."

"Grace, don't do this."

"What?" I argue. "I'm just telling you a fact."

"A fact that you probably made up."

"I didn't." I may have.

"Don't go all morbid on me because you think you're going to die alone. What about Buster?" she asks, referring to my beloved dog at home. I guess that's the silver lining.

"Yeah, true."

I hear Trevor call for her, his voice distorted in the background of their home. "I gotta go," she tells me. "You're going to lunch on Sunday?"

"Yeah."

"Okay, you can tell me more about this date. Trevor's going to want all the details too."

"Don't worry, I'll have plenty to fill you in."

"And Grace," she adds. "You're going to be fine. Stop this whole dying alone spiral you do every time you meet some douche-y mama's boy."

"Yeah, yeah. I'll see you Sunday."

It's so easy for her to offer a string of reassuring words with nothing to back them. Sure, this overthinking blob I tend to spiral into isn't healthy either, but neither is lying to myself. It's so easy to be bright and rosy when you're not the subject of said spiral.

This feels so fucking lonely. There, I said it. I'm going to die alone, most likely while choking on a piece of sweet and sour pork, and my plants will all die. And no one will take care of Buster, so he'll spend the rest of his life looking for me. He'll be like that dog who stayed at the train station for years and years after its owner died, living off scraps given by strangers while he waited for a ghost.

Okay, so maybe spiraling is as bad as Jade says.

I stare at my blank phone screen, thinking about how Jade and Trevor are probably wrestling Avery down for her bedtime. All while I'll be going home alone. I'll walk into my empty two-bedroom condo, with nothing but a bottle of wine and binge-watching Netflix to help me fall asleep. The morose frown on my face lingers while my reflection stares back at me.

The thought of scolding my mom or letting her off easy starts to totter in my brain. She meant well, and if I explain to her the reasons why a man with a "wife list" ironically isn't parallel to my own hypothetical "husband list," then she'll be able to weed out the losers better. And if I completely turn her off from being my own personal matchmaker, I may completely miss my chance to find a soulmate. Who knows? Maybe one of them will be a diamond in the rough. The golden treasure she finds in the battlefield of love using her nifty Mrs. Han metal detector. It can't hurt, right?

"Grace?"

I look up, only to come face-to-face with the last person I expect to see. "Andrew?"

Andrew Cohen. One-fourth of the Cohen siblings, one of which is Teeny, my best friend. And being the youngest, Andrew always seems to carry with him the buoyancy that comes with the lack of responsibility while adding on the baggage of always having someone watch over his shoulder and correct his mistakes.

He tucks his hands into his pocket where the bottom hem of his blazer gives a drapery-like effect. I see his watch glint off the overhead lights past the sleeve of his shirt. Such a small expression of assurance. Combined with a slight saunter as he steps closer to me, he creates a guise over him, shielding away the image of Teeny's brother and putting in its place Andrew fucking Cohen.

"What are you doing here?"

"I was, um, on a...I was having dinner," I vaguely explain, though given that we're standing in front of a restaurant, it seems obvious. A wave of diffidence tumbles through me, making me clumsy and unsure, but I plow through it, reminding myself the date from hell isn't something to be embarrassed about. If anything, Harold should be embarrassed for treating me like the next candidate in a meat market lineup. Andrew eyes me with a bit of skepticism, but I brush past it by asking, "You?"

"I had a work thing," he tells me, his answer carrying the same vagueness I did.

We stay quiet, lingering in this slightly awkward silence, when Andrew cuts into it with a charming laugh.

"I just saw you last year. Why does it feel like forever?"

I mentally fact-check his timeline, confirming that Teeny's wedding was almost a year ago. It's odd how much can change in a year. That boyish charisma he wore so proudly in his early twenties disappeared long ago. I noticed it at the wedding. How his black tux and slicked back hair, and even the calla lily pinned to his lapel, instantly replaced the college boy I met over a decade ago.

"Yeah," I confirm. "It was your sister's wedding. I guess the year's just...dragging."

"You look great," he comments, eyeing me from head to toe. Though I didn't opt for anything risqué or revealing, what I chose to wear tonight looks nice, somewhat modest. I picked a deep navy dress with short-capped sleeves and a hem that reaches just below my knees. The back has an opening, exposing a sliver of my shoulder blades, and that small show of skin has me feeling confident and sexy. I put some effort into tonight. I took the time to do my makeup and hair, and I even shaved my legs. Too bad it was all for nothing.

"So do you." It's not even a lie or a knee-jerk response to his compliment. He looks good. Annoyingly good. Especially his hair. It's thick and wavy, pushed back with the kind of fade I find irresistible in most men.

"So, was this dinner thing a date? Or..." His sharp jawline softens for a moment, his subtle five o'clock shadow rolling with the curves of his errant smirk. The corners of his eyes, the tawny color of honey, crinkle, making the small mole below the tip of his brow disappear in the wrinkles.

I smile, the mask I put on to hide my embarrassment slipping just the tiniest bit. "How did you know?"

He shrugs. "Just an educated guess." I roll my eyes, just as he adds, "And since you're leaving the restaurant alone, I'm going to make another educated guess and say it didn't go well?"

I cast aside my attempt to save face. I peer up at him, noticing how far back my neck has to crane to meet his eyes. "It was a blind date."

He grimaces. "Do I want to hear about it?"

"I don't know," I answer, sarcasm edging its way into my voice. "Do you know what a 'wife list' is?"

His grimace deepens. "Do I want to know?"

"It's probably best if you don't."

"His loss."

He throws it out there so aimlessly, I don't know whether to take it as a compliment or a show of sympathy. I choose the former and say, "That's probably the nicest thing anyone's said to me all night."

Pity lines the creases on his forehead. "I'm sorry," he offers.

"Nothing you need to apologize for, Andrew." I pat his chest, letting him off the hook, just as I see my car pull up out of the corner of my eye. I grip the cash in my hand to slip to the valet when Andrew stops me.

"You want to grab a drink? It could help you forget about this 'wife list.' You can complain all you want about your blind date." His thumb is pointed toward the entrance to the restaurant where I saw a sleek bar surrounded by more stiff suits and polished footwear.

The valet holds open the door for me, and it's my answer to

Andrew's offer. A sign I should say "no, thank you" and go home, wash off this night with a hot shower and some warm cuddles from Buster. I push aside the temptation to take him up on his offer and walk toward the driver's side.

"Maybe another time," I tell him, throwing a cheeky smile over my shoulder. "I'm sure I'll have plenty of dates I need to drown in alcohol in the near future."

Andrew smirks and nods, taking a step back to wait for his car. I slip in, watching how he stands there, his hands in his pockets and his shoulders hunched with an air of stress settling over him. I start to wonder if his offer for a drink is for him just as much as it is for my own need to erase the last hour of my night. Maybe a nightcap can't hurt. One drink. How much damage could that do?

I unbuckle my seat belt and open my door. "Hey, Andrew."

He looks up, and his eyes round with curiosity.

"I changed my mind."

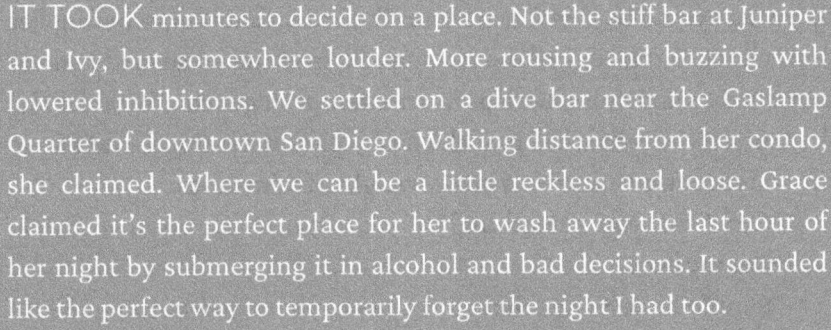

CHAPTER TWO
Andrew

IT TOOK minutes to decide on a place. Not the stiff bar at Juniper and Ivy, but somewhere louder. More rousing and buzzing with lowered inhibitions. We settled on a dive bar near the Gaslamp Quarter of downtown San Diego. Walking distance from her condo, she claimed. Where we can be a little reckless and loose. Grace claimed it's the perfect place for her to wash away the last hour of her night by submerging it in alcohol and bad decisions. It sounded like the perfect way to temporarily forget the night I had too.

"There's got to be a better way to meet someone," Grace grumbles, emptying her second Ketel soda. "I seriously can't believe men like this Harold guy exist."

She had her hair up in a loose bun, and as soon as we stepped into the bar, she took it out of the uncomfortable knot she had it in. She's running her fingers through her scalp, rumbling a low hum through the ease of literally—and figuratively—letting her hair down. The dark waves tumble down her back, and I can't decide if I like it better up where I can see the smooth slope of her neck or down like she has it now, framing her round face and making her look a little unruly and wild.

I only know Grace as an extension of my sister. I never thought much of her, merely meeting her a handful of times in passing. At graduation, the occasional birthday parties, all with a swift "hello" or "how are you" that always felt informal and stiff. And then Teeny got married, started a family, and those special occasions grew twofold. Baby showers, weekend barbecues, birthday parties with blow-up houses and elaborate princess cakes. I saw more of Grace. And while I assumed that most people plateaued once they hit thirty —an asinine assumption on my part—she proved me absolutely and unquestionably wrong.

I watch her flag down the bartender, leaning far over the bar top. Her body twists at her waist, forcing her to reposition herself on her seat. I get a glimpse of the back of her dress where the sliver of skin displays the blemish-free ridges of her spine. It's a different kind of skin exposure. Not the typical short skirt or low neckline, and I never knew less could be this much more. She orders another, scooting her butt closer to the edge of the stool to talk over the noise, and I watch her uncross and cross her legs in an attempt to get comfortable. The hem of her dress brushes past the fleshy part of her thigh, and I force myself to look away. With a heavy weight of reluctance.

"Can I ask you something?" I ask, tilting back my own drink, averting my eyes.

"Sure." She rests her chin on the heel of her hand, turning to face me with an adorable tilt of her head as she looks at me over the curve of her shoulder.

"Why did you even go on a blind date?"

She doesn't answer me. Instead, she starts playing with her glass, her eyes zoned in on the cold tumbler as she pokes at the loose ice cubes with a cocktail straw.

"It can't be that hard for you to snag a date," I add.

"You'd be surprised." She lifts the drink to her lips and tilts back what remains, just as a fresh one arrives in front of her. Her morose, sarcastically spoken tone, along with her defeated demeanor, says more than her words. Maybe I'm wrong. Maybe the dating pool isn't so much a small chlorinated body of water with a springboard and a lifeguard but more like an ocean. A dark vast one that's scary and ominous, and she's on a flimsy life raft, waving her arms at nothing.

I don't respond with generic words meant to be encouraging or a phony rebuttal filled with false hope. I wait, hoping my open posture and her second drink is enough for her to pour her heart out.

A deep, glum sigh leaves her pursed lips before she says, "It's not that I have trouble meeting men," she explains to me. "I guess I have trouble meeting the right man."

Her reasoning is like a hook, drawing more questions out of me. Making me want to know more about her and the confines of this so-called quest for the right man. "And what constitutes as the 'right man?'"

"What's with the twenty questions?" she responds, answering my question with a question. Deflection, I see.

"Call it a keen interest in a friend," I say, staying on neutral ground to coax out her answer. That hook tugs and digs deeper, reminding me not to pry too hard, or she might close right up.

"That's what we are? Friends?"

"Are we not?" I try not to sound offended.

She shrugs. "I guess."

"So?"

Another heavy sigh. She taps her manicured nail on the bar top. A pause while considering her answer. "Someone who has some ambition. And wants the same things I do." She smiles to herself before pointedly adding, "And *not* a twenty-something fuckboy."

I pull my drink away just short of a spit take. "'Not a fuckboy.' That's pretty specific."

"I've familiarized myself with the kind," she tells me, her palm pressed against the bar top. Another deflection technique to deviate her unwarranted shame through sarcasm. "The year after my divorce was...interesting."

Her divorce. I met her, albeit very quickly and in passing, when she just started dating the guy. She would fill my sister in on all her dating woes, and those stories would make it to my ears. By the time she'd gotten engaged, they moved, bringing the gossip and drama closer to home. And those moments we spent around each other became less fleeting and more purposeful. We'd chat beyond a simple "Hello, how are you," and I got to know a bit more about my sister's best friend. I found it odd that I never met the guy. She never brought him with her to those gatherings that inadvertently brought us into the same social space. And I may have heard through the grapevine—the long twisty telephone-like string being my sister—that he never wanted to join her. He preferred the company of liter-ally anyone else but her, and it made me wonder why he even both-ered marrying her in the first place. When I heard she was getting divorced a few years ago—another tidbit from a sororal little birdie —I thought, "Finally," ignoring the way my ears perked up when Grace's name and the word "divorce" came hand in hand.

"So, you're looking for Mr. Right. Not Mr. Right Now."

She nods. "I'm not getting any younger. Can't be wasting the last of my childbearing years on meaningless hookups and—"

"Twenty-something fuckboys?" I eye at her over the rim of my glass, my brow dancing with a cheeky taunt.

She throws a finger gun at me. Bingo.

"Probably for the best," I tell her. "Guys in their twenties aren't that great."

She peers up at me from her drink, and her eyes narrow, a curi-ous, inquisitive perusal that has her eyes roaming over my face. Something tells me that between the drinks we've shared, the condensation rings drawing whimsical patterns where our elbows are bumping, this is the first time she's actually seeing me tonight. I'm no longer Teeny's younger brother but just Andrew. "Are you not a guy in your twenties?"

"No, I am. I'm twenty-nine."

She nearly chokes on her drink.

"I'll be thirty in a few weeks."

"You know, I forget how young you were when I first met you."

"I wasn't that young."

"I believe you weren't old enough to drink yet."

"I was plenty old enough to drink."

"Legally."

"Yeah, okay. Technicalities. What's your point?"

Her teeth clamp on her bottom lip, and I see the haze of alcohol sweep across her glassy eyes. That, along with the vodka-laced flush making her cheeks pink. She reaches up to pinch my cheeks, and I flinch. "You were such a baby. And you're all grown up now."

The contents of my drink trickle down my throat with an icy burn. Like a bed of coals being doused with cold water. A piqued sting starts to gnaw at my insides, and I have a feeling it has something to do with the way Grace just wrote me off as immature and juvenile, much like those fuckboys she swore off, even as we share our third drink of the night. "Yeah, well. I'm not a baby anymore," I mutter under my breath. My jaw tics, and my tie suddenly feels stifling.

"Hey." She offers a consoling touch to my forearm at the same time her brow pinches together, regret plaited in the single-syllable word. Her fingers graze over the thin material of my shirt, exposing all the stress and wrinkles, an attempt to smooth her rough words that weren't meant to be rough at all. They were meant to fit the mood, an honest and hasty backdrop surrounded by loud noise and impulsive decisions. "I didn't mean anything by that. It's just that... seeing how grown up, you've gotten makes me realize how old I am, and—"

My jaw tics again. A Pavlovian reaction, it seems, when age—a sequence of irrelevant numbers we use to gauge just about anything worth quantifying—is the topic at hand. "News flash, Grace. You aren't old."

She rolls her eyes. "I'm almost forty, Andrew."

"Again, you. Are. Not. Old." I lean forward, letting her hand pull me closer, though I'm not sure if it's her tugging at me, or if it's the gravitational pull of what lies between us bringing me inches from her face.

I watch her breaths leave her in sharp staccato-like gasps. Her chest rises and falls, and her lips part, causing my eyes to flit to them. The sweet smell of vodka lingers on her tongue, as does something else that's characteristically her. Something soft yet noteworthy.

"We should order another drink."

I don't argue that maybe I've met my limit. That the third drink I just tossed back is the harsh line I've drawn for myself before I cross over from buzzed to shitfaced. But like a twig dragged across a bed of fine sand, lines can be erased. Swiped away with a determined hand and a precarious compulsion for something more daring. So, I nod. And I opt for something bolder.

I flag the bartender down, and order our drinks, aware of Grace's wary yet intrigued gaze.

"Tequila?" she asks, her voice taut with doubt. "I was just going to order another round of cocktails."

"Come on, Grace. Live a little."

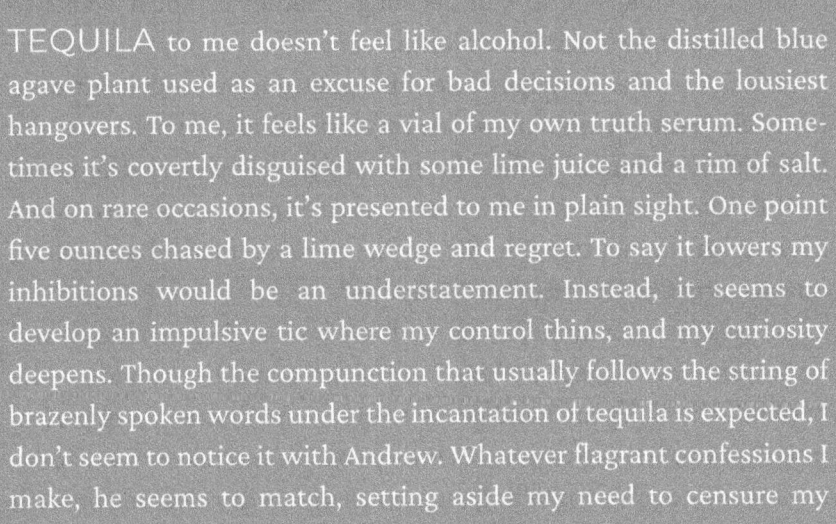

CHAPTER THREE

Grace

TEQUILA to me doesn't feel like alcohol. Not the distilled blue agave plant used as an excuse for bad decisions and the lousiest hangovers. To me, it feels like a vial of my own truth serum. Sometimes it's covertly disguised with some lime juice and a rim of salt. And on rare occasions, it's presented to me in plain sight. One point five ounces chased by a lime wedge and regret. To say it lowers my inhibitions would be an understatement. Instead, it seems to develop an impulsive tic where my control thins, and my curiosity deepens. Though the compunction that usually follows the string of brazenly spoken words under the incantation of tequila is expected, I don't seem to notice it with Andrew. Whatever flagrant confessions I make, he seems to match, setting aside my need to censure my thoughts.

A second round, and I may have him help diagnose the questionable mole on my thigh. And he may become a very willing novice pathologist.

"So, was there a reason you asked me to join you for a drink?" I ask, diving in headfirst.

"Yeah," he answers with a sincere smile. "To make up for your shitty date." His eyes glisten, and I've been noticing the flush creeping up his neck to his cheeks. What was a mere blush is transitioning into a light crimson, and it makes him look surprisingly fallible yet oddly charming.

"I poured my entire heart out for you, right down to the fact that I've dated fuckboys, and you're not even going to be honest with me?" The words spill out of me like my lips have been squished and folded into a neat little spout. The tequila is doing its job efficiently.

I watch him toy with his empty shot glass. "I just had a rough night."

"Don't tell me you had a horrible blind date too."

"It was a work thing," he reminds me. "I wasn't lying to you about that." I see his tongue press against his cheek, like a confession is tumbling alongside it, still deciding whether or not it wants to leave the safer confines of his mouth.

It's my turn to stay quiet. Let him pour out his own heart onto the sticky bar top to join my woes. I start to wonder if tequila has the same effect on him as it does for me. Maybe a few extra drops, and he'll tell me if and where he keeps his private stash of porn. Most likely in an unmentionable file on his desktop marked something unassuming like "Pictures" or "Solitaire."

"I was just at a dinner thing with my boss and some clients, and he is just...the biggest asshole." He signals another round to the bartender, making the hand gestures quick and discreet. A blip of an interruption. "He sees me as his little peon. He has his own assistant, but he has no problem telling me to pick up his dry cleaning or fetch him a cup of coffee. I think it's his life mission to make my life as miserable as possible. And tonight, he was so belittling. I know it's his way of trying to impress the clients we had dinner with, but fuck, it's so demeaning."

"You can't just quit?" I ask cautiously, keeping in mind that some problems don't have such easy solutions.

As expected, he shakes his head. "I've been at it for a few years, and I know I just need to do my grunt work until I'm promoted. Or until I can get enough experience to find a job with a different company, but I just have to take it for now."

I nod. "Can I give you some of my old-lady wisdom?" He rolls his eyes, and I give him a light punch to his arm. A request—or maybe a demand—to humor my self-deprecating comment. "If this job brings you this much misery, don't wait it out so long for a promotion. Life's too short to spend it doing something you hate."

He looks at me, a contest of opposition and accession swirling in his eyes through a wrinkled brow and a stark realization as the truth washes over him. He finally nods, words too absolute to take back should he change his mind.

We've been spending so much of our night in a flippant repartee. This sudden change in topic makes the air around us murky, filled with silent questions and the realization that just a few hours ago, Andrew and his sharp jawline and protruding Adam's apple that slides over his throat with every swallow and laugh was exceedingly far from my mind. And now he's everywhere. A pair of blinders has been slapped onto my face, and Andrew is all I see.

Our drinks arrive, and I eye them warily. More truth serum. "I think I've hit my limit on tequila for the night."

"You had one shot," Andrew argues.

"Yeah, and I was already pushing my limit when I tossed that one back."

"Come on, Grace. Live a little." He clinks his drink to mine, causing some of it to slosh over the rim, and holds it up in front of him, urging me to do the same.

I give. Through the thick, distorted composition of alcohol and glass obscuring more than just my view as I hold up my drink in my hand, I have a moment of fallacious hope. A deceptive thought that I need to loosen up, take more chances, and drink more alcohol. What a damn fool.

"Fine," I say. "But only if you talk some more shit about this horrible boss of yours."

"No arms need to be twisted for a deal like that."

When I drink, my laughs tend to come more loosely. A joke that isn't really funny is usually followed by an uncontrolled giggle. And when someone says something categorically clever, I find myself a snorting, guffawing mess. That's what's happening right now with Andrew. Over some complimentary roasted peanuts and ridged potato chips the bartender presented like a magic trick, a pleasant surprise we found particularly funny for absolutely no reason at all, we've found ourselves in a heap of stomach cramps and watery eyes.

Another factor adding levity to our night: Andrew's hatred toward his boss. And I mean *hate*. From what he's been telling me, it seems to be reciprocated by this asshole whose life goal really is to make Andrew's life a living hell.

"So you just let the security guard take the hit for it?"

He lifts his shoulders in mock innocence. "What was I supposed to do?"

"I don't know," I tease. "Maybe don't let some stranger take the hit for your slipup?"

"I mean, it's way more believable that a diligent security guard making his nightly rounds knocked over his decanter of scotch than me," he states, defending himself. "And besides, I didn't say it was the security guard. I just didn't deny it when he came to that conclusion."

"What were you even doing in his office that late at night?"

"He forgot his wallet, and he was on a date with his girlfriend, so he asked me to bring it to him." He starts to tilt back his third tequila shot but stops, adding, "No, asking is the wrong word. He *ordered* me to bring it to him."

"What does he do? Threaten your job?" I lift my own glass, my refusal for more thrown clear out the window in exchange for the best night I've had in a long time. I genuinely can't remember the last time I've had this much fun. And there are no ties behind it. It doesn't feel transactional where he's giving up his valuable time to be here. When I hang out with Teeny or Jade, it always feels like our minutes are measured. While my time with them is appreciated, I always feel like they have a laundry list of responsibilities that keep them distracted. With Andrew, I'm just enjoying his company. Just as much as he's enjoying mine.

"At first, he did. But now, it's a given. He's said it enough times for me to know to keep my mouth shut and do what he says." Those stories about his boss started out with a tinge of bitterness and spite, but now they're lubricated with a more matter-of-fact tone, slipping out of him with an added flair of jokes and sarcasm. I have a feeling it has to do with the informality this night has bled into, which I'm taking note of as I reluctantly realize is going to have to end at some point.

We both empty our shot glasses. And I say through a lime wedge pressed to my teeth, "He's a fucking piece of shit."

His tongue rolls over his bottom lip, and a smile curves his mouth into a Cheshire cat-like grin. "I appreciate your support, Grace."

"What is it that you do, anyway? Just so I know never to make a career change to the same path."

"I work for an investment company," he explains.

"Like, finance?" I ask through a disappointed grimace. My personal experience with men in finance has left a bitter taste in my mouth. A lingering acidity I'd rather not dive into right now, so I shove away my reaction and replace it with an impassive one.

But Andrew notices anyway. "Yes, is there a problem with that?"

I shrug, brushing off my discontent with indifference. "No."

He inches closer to me, his warm breath brushing against my cheek. "I think you're lying," he comments in a low, drawn-out voice. From here, I can see a ring around his irises. A darker shade of brown that frames his lighter-color eyes. They roam over my face, somehow changing the accusation he threw at me, making it sound darker and less playful.

Those keen, curious eyes flit to my mouth as I ask, "Why would I lie?"

He reaches past my shoulder, bracing his hand against the back of my chair. It shifts him closer to me, and his forearm brushes against my shoulder with a jolt of electricity I almost recoil from before I realize it isn't a threat. Yet, it isn't innocent or an accidental slip of hand-eye coordination. It's deliberate and calculated. "Maybe you don't want to admit that a man who's good with his money is attractive?"

"Okay," I say through a sarcastic tone, a scoff rattling my throat. When the heat of his gaze makes my already flushed face feel hotter, I sidestep it by rolling my teeth over my lower lip.

I watch as he studies the way my mouth twists under the pressure of my teeth. How my tongue follows, leaving behind a glistening sheen in its wake. That Adam's apple of his bobs, and it does something to my insides I'm familiar with. An impulsive tumble that raises a hiccup at the back of my tongue. I suddenly feel hot. Really hot.

"Want another drink?" Andrew's voice is dark, authoritative, determined.

I nod, feeling helpless under his steely eyes. But he doesn't do the usual methodical steps to order a drink. He doesn't flag someone down, he doesn't order another round of tequila, he doesn't tell the bartender to just add it to our tab. At least, not yet. He takes his time, not wanting to break whatever daze or spell has us wrapped up in each other. Where his arm continues to bump against mine. And where my eyes flit to his lips this time, throwing my own gesture of a goading challenge.

"Did you want me to order the drinks?" I offer.

"No." A single two-letter word that suddenly feels like it weighs a ton. He sets it down between us, landing with a dull thud, waiting for my next move.

"Then—"

He lifts a hand, catching a bartender just as she's passing by. "Two more tequilas please," he orders, keeping his eyes on me.

I guess one more round can't hurt.

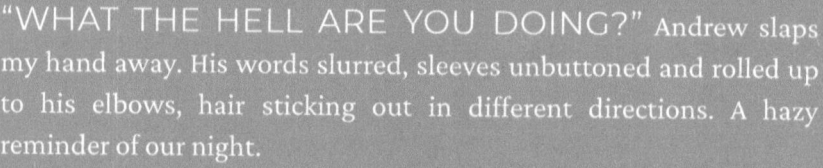

CHAPTER FOUR

Grace

"WHAT THE HELL ARE YOU DOING?" Andrew slaps my hand away. His words slurred, sleeves unbuttoned and rolled up to his elbows, hair sticking out in different directions. A hazy reminder of our night.

"Paying the tab?" I lift my hand, my credit card wedged between the tips of my middle and index fingers. His own card is gripped between his fingers, and we start a duel of plastic and magnetic strips.

He slaps at my hand again, shooing it away and making him the winner. My card lands on the wooden surface with a clatter. A whimsical giggle bubbles up my throat, and I don't know if it's from Andrew's sloppily moving hands as he slides his card to the bartender, or if it's because I'm buzzed.

I vaguely remember the additional round of tequila shots we ordered. It was followed by a heated debate over the correct use of the plural form of the word moose. If it's mooses or meese. Which segued into whether or not the luxury car brand Lexuses are in fact Lexi.

I remember having the best time with Andrew. My date with Gerald? Or was it Henry? Harold! It was Harold. I'd forgotten all about him—apparently—and my sudden wave of memory loss isn't attributed to the amount of tequila I consumed but to the company by my side.

"It's this way," I tell Andrew, shuffling my steps toward my condo. We settled the check after I lost a lazy battle, and we're heading back to my condo where our cars are parked in the parking garage. Andrew has his suit jacket looped over his arm, and he follows my steps while we leisurely end the night. "You can't drive like this," I say, knowing damn well he's in no condition to get behind the wheel.

"I'm fine. I'll just sleep it off in my car for a few hours," he tells me. He lightly punches my arm, his arms swaying as if that minor control of his arms and equilibrium is too much for his drunken state.

"No way," I argue. "Just crash on my couch for a few hours."

"Nah," he assures. "I don't want to intrude."

"Don't flatter yourself. Your presence isn't as imposing as you might think."

He does a gesturing motion. His hand cups the back of his neck, craning his head up toward the sky. We both peer in the general direction of my building a block away. His feet shuffle underneath him, dithering between the path that'll either provide a soft, warm couch or a cold, uncomfortable seat and a neck cramp.

"Are you sure?"

I nod. "Come on."

It never dawned on me that I have no reference as to what thirty-five hundred pounds is. Is it the weight of an average-sized sedan? Or maybe a teenage elephant? My lack of density awareness is probably because I've never stood in my elevator, pondering over the words "CAPACITY 3500 POUNDS" on a metal placard while Googling

"Things that weigh almost two tons." My attention is usually on other things like my phone screen or my purse while fishing for my keys. But not tonight. Tonight, the center of my attention is on a safety code regulation.

Or at least, I'm *trying* to make it the center of my attention if not to hold on to my restraint and willpower, then at least to prove to Andrew there are zero subtexts to my invitation to free use of my couch. It's exactly what it's meant to be—a friend considering the safety and well-being of another friend. But with the alcohol still buzzing in my veins and Andrew's close proximity making the tequila run at a low simmer below my skin, I'm struggling. Desperately.

I'm trying to shove away the image of an unruly Andrew. His rumpled hair and loosely untucked dress shirt. Even the way his heavy-lidded eyes look more playful than lethargic. All of it needs to leave the deep recesses of my mind. Maybe swerved off the road by an adolescent elephant driving recklessly in a sage-colored Toyota Camry.

"What's so funny?"

"Hmm?"

Andrew looks at me with a crooked brow and a smug simper. "What's so funny?" he repeats.

I quickly shake off the image of a teenage elephant trying to talk its way out of a speeding ticket using words like "Bruh" and "No cap" and "This is high key sus" and slide on my poker face. "Nothing."

"Oh, so now you don't want to share your jokes with me?"

"I don't have a joke," I say innocently. "I'm just...enjoying my buzz." It's not a complete lie. Imaginary elephants with a license to operate heavy machinery don't slip into my thoughts unless they are inebriated with a little liquid courage.

"Hmm," he hums with disapproval.

The elevator continues its ascent and whirs loudly on its way to the sixteenth floor. Just as we pass the fourth floor, I feel a warm brush tickle my back. It's slow and gentle. And acutely intentional.

28

"You have really soft skin."

I peer over my shoulder just in time to catch Andrew's eyes raking over my backside. More listless sweeps of what feels like rough knuckles roam over my spine, and I turn on my feet by reflex. But the axis my heels rotate on is more than my alcohol-infused brain can handle.

"Whoa," Andrew exclaims, catching my elbow in his strong grip just as my balance teeters in the other direction. "You okay?"

I look up at him and nod. "Just lost my footing."

His other hand is on my waist. To prevent a face plant, I assume. He squeezes my side and suddenly my hands are on his hard chest. To push him away, I suppose.

"Tree Hut had a sale on the watermelon shea scent."

"What?"

"My skin," I say. My paltry attempt at an explanation. "It's a watermelon-scented sugar scrub. It's supposed to exfoliate all the dead skin off me. And it leaves behind a...flavorful scent."

He leans closer, the confusion edging away into intrigue. "So does that mean you taste good too?"

I nod. A dangerous gesture. I'm dangling a juicy piece of meat between us while telling myself to swat it away and claim I'm a vegetarian. But I'm not. Not even close.

I don't know if I get the chance to ask him if he thinks swallowing watermelon seeds will result in growing one in the lining of my stomach. A myth I never debunked as a child. The silly question, as rhetorical as it is, is on the tip of my tongue. But it's swiped away the second he pushes me against the elevator wall and kisses me.

As muddled as my head feels through the murky fog of desperate sighs and hungry lips, I'm vividly aware of his hand slipping past the opening in my back, running boldly over my rib cage.

It feels amazing. His hands on me, my hands on him. My knees feel wobbly. They buckle under the heat of our make-out session. He's *such* a good kisser. It doesn't feel sloppy or inept. He knows what the fuck he's doing. Yet, there's a little flicker of light going off in the back of my mind. The minutest reminder that this is wrong. I shouldn't be kissing Andrew in an enclosed space. Like a hook annoyingly tugging at the knowledge that this man I'm kissing is my best friend's brother, my hands press against his chest, ready to push us apart.

Confident, assertive fingers grip my wrists and pin them behind me. "Don't," he commands.

I look at him, his dark eyes suddenly fierce and menacing. "Don't what?" I ask weakly.

"Don't act like you want me to stop."

"I-I don't—" I stutter. Fear clashes with curiosity in my stumped brain, and I'm scared to death the latter is going to be the victor. "We can't," I whisper.

I watch his eyes grow dark. It's unnerving, and it sends a chill up my spine. He lowers his face, his nose running along the length of my cheek. "No one has to know." His words are a claim, maybe even a promise. But with his raspy voice gently dusting them over the shell of my ear, it feels like a plea.

My eyes flutter at the same time my stomach tumbles. Before I can argue, the elevator doors spring open. And curiosity wins in the end, holding up a gold trophy for all to admire with my reawakened libido and Andrew's claim to keep this between us.

I don't say anything as I reach for his hand and step off the elevator. I stay quiet as we round the corners, our steps moving at an urgent and resolute pace. The silence stretches across the threshold of my doorway. Andrew watches me while I dig around in my purse for my keys. I feel his hands on me again, poking and prodding within the confines of what my dress is allowing to expose. And the door opens, cautiously welcoming us into another closed space shut off from the rest of the world. Here, in my two-bedroom condo, it's just me and him.

Clunky taps of rough claws and a loud, jangly collar charge after Andrew, pushing him against the closed door.

"Whoa," he exclaims as Buster jumps to greet him.

"Oh, sorry," I say, looping my finger under Buster's collar and guiding him to the bathroom. He follows obediently, the standard process for when we have guests while we wait for them to acclimate before letting Buster sniff test them. "He just wanted to say hi."

"It's fine," he tells me, throwing in an understanding smile.

The stirred-up dust that created a cloud of bad decisions has settled, and the aftereffects of the kiss in the elevator seems to be nothing but an awkward silence. I try to fill it with logistics.

"I don't think I have anything that fits you," I start, pointing a vague finger to the couch. "But you'll have the living room to yourself if you want to just..." Sleep in his underwear? No, that's not where this conversation should be heading. "I'll get you some sheets and a blanket."

"Grace," he calls.

"I should have an extra pillow too. It has pretty good neck support. Not all flat and lumpy. It's in my closet," I inform him, ignoring what sounds like a protest. "I'll go grab it." I turn to walk away, avoiding his eyes.

He stops me. His hand curls around my waist, turning me to face him with just enough force I don't feel coerced. The right amount of fingers and palm and wrist veering and guiding.

"Do you trust me?" His eyes scour my face, taking in my hesitance. He watches me pull my lips between my teeth, and I take in the way his gaze hardens, turning determined and steely. His other hand cups the nape of my neck, and I shiver under his confident touch. He's sure and hopeful, a complete contradiction to the divergent thoughts in my head. Like two sides of a road traveling in opposite directions. He inches closer when I don't answer him. "Grace?"

My nod is barely a nod, but it's there. In the way my chin tilts toward my chest and how my eyes turn eager and obedient. "I trust you," I finally whisper.

And he kisses me.

This kiss upstages the one he gave me in the elevator. By a mile. It ticks off every check mark he left behind. Ones I didn't think were

31

possible. Like how his hands slip into my hair or how he takes control, adjusting his hips and shoulders so I know when and how to follow his lead. He nudges me backward so my butt perches on the back of my couch, and I'm completely at his will. Me, pressed against a solid surface while Andrew steps between my legs, and my knee hooks over his hip. It's mind numbing how quickly I've relinquished every ounce of control to someone who knows exactly where to touch me. Like the dip in my collarbone or the back of my thighs. The knowledge that he knows what the fuck he's doing slithers down my spine, looping down to the pit of my stomach where it feels tingly.

Deft fingers tickle my nape, blindly searching for the single button holding my dress up. I feel it peel away from my back, the cornered edge curling toward my shoulder. Time stands still as he glides his thumb over my collarbone. Time that feels phantom.

"I don't think you realize how fucking beautiful you are," he whispers. And he does the most intimate thing a man has ever done to me. He leans down and kisses my shoulder. But he doesn't just kiss me. He reassures me. He calms me and comforts me into letting me trust him with my entire body.

My hands shake as they undo his buttons. Starting at the top, trembling more and more with each button I meet. He finds the last two, gripping my hands in a firm hold.

"You don't need to be nervous," he whispers, his lips pressed behind my ear.

"I can't help it," I whimper. A helpless, wretched whine squeezes through my lips.

He pulls away and takes my wrist in a gentle hold. He turns my palm over, holding it up and creating a safe distance of space between us. A small break from the heated moment. When he presses his lips to my palm, he calms my anxiety. When those lips travel to my pulse point, he replaces that anxiety with anticipation and thrill.

"Do you want me to stop?" he asks sincerely.

I shake my head. "No."

A flash of a smile, and he asks, "Where's your room?" He slips off his dress shirt, exposing his wide chest and broad shoulders. Metal glints off his neck under the low light from my kitchen. A silver chain. Vines of black ink peek past a stretched undershirt I want to tear off and pile on top of his tossed aside shirt on the floor.

I gesture a loose hand toward his bicep, attempting to hide my efforts to catch my breath. "Is that new?"

He looks down at his arm, examining the object of my evasion tactic. "Kind of. I got it about a year ago."

I nod. "Looks...interesting."

His pinky brushes my knuckles. "Are you stalling?"

"And what would I be stalling?" I ask, avoiding his question.

"Since you said you don't want me to stop, I'm really not too sure," he muses.

"Well, I'm not."

"Then tell me where your damn room is."

"Down the hallway," I finally answer, smiling like a horny fool. "Second door on the right."

With one strong sweep, he hoists me up, forcing my legs around his waist. The world seems to tilt and spin as his feet stumble toward the hallway leading to my room. It's my home, my hardwood floor and recessed lighting guiding us, but it doesn't feel like any part of this moment is mine. Andrew takes control in a way that I don't even need to remember my own name. He leans into the slightly open door with his back. And then there's my bed, cloaked in shadows, stashing away the neat, orderly state of my room and replacing it with the racy, wanton dungeon I've been dragged into. There might as well be a large billboard hanging above it that reads "SEX HERE." Because we're going to have sex. There's no question about it.

He still has me in his arms when he climbs on the cushy comforter covering my bed. Over the stark white duvet cover, one knee after the other. He lays me down gently, lowering me so I sink rather than plop. I watch him reach back behind his shoulders and slip his T-shirt over his head, the last of the layers separating us. I see more tattoos lining his ribcage and chest, and he sees me eye them. He gives me the time to study the lines and curves, the details I trace with my fingertips.

"You like them, huh?"

"Didn't think I would, but yeah. They look nice," I admit.

He smirks a devilish smile, and I have a sudden urge to taunt him. Meet his smug smirk with something just as haughty and arrogant. I don't get a chance to, of course, because when he hovers over me, I forget all about his cheeky grin. All I see are his hooded lids, zoning in on my lips as a soft sigh squeezes through them. But he's just a hairbreadth too far away for a kiss. It's a tease, to provoke or torment me, I don't know. So I tug his torso closer using his silver chain. And the resulting kiss leaves me breathless.

"I didn't think I liked jewelry on men either, but here we are," I whisper through small gasps, hoping I sound as light and airy as my words.

My hands fumble with his belt and the zipper. My legs part, my knees falling open, while I reach into his pants. It sounds crass, but the only way I can explain what I feel is ample and *packed*. "Jesus, you're going to have to spend some time getting me ready if you plan to shove that thing inside of me."

"You make it sound like that'd be a chore for me." His lips meet the hollow space below my ear, and I feel his fingers go low. Past my dress and nudging aside my panties. "But judging by how wet you already are, I don't think it's going to take much."

He strokes his fingers, moving like he's carefully learning every crease and ridge. He does it with an intensely rapt intellect. Like he's going to be tested later, and he'd have to pick out my pussy in a blind lineup. And I hope he aces it. With flying colors. With his free hand, his occupied one remaining diligent elsewhere, he peels off the rest of my dress. Again, with an intentional deliberation almost as if it's too overwhelming for him to rip it all off, and an inch at a time is all he can handle.

The impatience starts to claw at my chest. I want nothing

between me and him. I want bare skin against bare skin. My arms slip out of the sleeves with urgency, and I discard the low-back ligature that masqueraded as a bra, the only piece of undergarment that worked with this dress.

"Enthusiastic, are we?" he asks as my bra lands on the floor with a soft thunk. His words are playful, but his eyes flare with heat as he takes in my bare chest.

"Shut up," I shoot back.

His response, though as effective as a cocksure retort, is his studious finger pushed inside me. I might as well sign over my soul to him. I feel everything tense and seize when he trails his kisses down my bare chest. He pulls my nipple into his mouth, letting his tongue rouse me, and I don't remember ever feeling anything this satisfying in my entire life.

"Holy *shit.*"

"That's it, Grace," he coaxes, feeling my body respond to his touch. "Just relax, baby. Relax." His thumb against my clit has my eyes rolling to the back of my head, and my nails rake down his back. The fog in my mind creates a dreamy cloud of ecstasy, and I can't even shift my thoughts to worry if I've drawn blood.

"*Ohhh* my fucking god," I exclaim. "Ho–how are you so good at that?" My voice falls desperately, the sheer volume of it growing and amplifying within the walls that encase us in this moment. A moment we both know we can't revisit in the future.

He doesn't acknowledge my unintended flattery. He doesn't chuckle a pompous laugh with a smug smile or a victory pose. Instead, determination flares his nostrils, and I feel myself tensing. He smothers my lips with his, swallowing the sounds coming from me as if that was his whole purpose. He patiently lets my orgasm tear through me, and it spreads all the way to my fucking toes. *Jesus,* if he can make me come like this with his fingers, I can't imagine what his dick can do.

"Do you have a condom?" he suddenly asks.

"Yeah, yeah," I answer, a flash of clarity in my lust-filled mind. In the blur of our tryst, I'd forgotten to think about protection. I point to my nightstand. "Bottom drawer."

He stretches his body, leaning over the edge of my bed. I hear some rustling, things being shuffled around, until he finally finds one and holds it up proudly. He helps me take the rest of my dress off before pulling off his pants. Undergarments come off, and the condom slips on, all happening under the shadows that make me feel like maybe I don't need to worry about the aftereffects of tonight. It's just sex, right? No need to make it a big deal.

He settles over me, our bare, naked bodies finally flush against each other. He scoops his hand under one of my thighs and loops his forearm under my knee. I know at this angle, he'll hit spots that'll make me see stars. But he doesn't fuck me quite yet. Instead, he edges me. All the way to the brink. He runs his cock up and down the wet heat between my legs, continuing his tease and holding firm on his promise to make sure I'm as ready as possible.

I watch him continue this push and pull to the threshold of my sanity, and I realize how his own control is slipping right through his fingers. I hear a groan rumble in his chest, his head hanging between his shoulders, and the muscles chording his neck strain. And I start to become obsessed with throwing him right off the edge and going right alongside him.

I buck my hips into him, testing him. Wanting to know what his limits are. And to let him know I'm ready. I'm so fucking ready. He grunts, quickly hiding it with a peck to the inside of my knee. He trails wet, open-mouthed kisses up my thigh, stopping those intimate touches with a harsh bite like he's become an absolute animal.

"Ow."

He smiles. "I'm sorry. Did I hurt you?"

"You bit me."

He smiles again, laughing through my accusation. But my annoyance dies the second he pushes into me.

"Oh, *fuck*."

"Oh my god," I moan. I expect movement. More thrusts, more pressure, but he's still. "You okay?" I manage to ask.

I feel him nod. "I just need a minute."

"Okay." I lay still, giving him what he asked for. Though I don't know if I can even make it that long. I need friction. I need to be stretched and wrung dry. I need him to fuck me like his life depends on it.

A painful grunt rattles his throat, and I feel his heart beating violently against my own. "Jesus, you're so fucking tight."

He inches further in, and I hold back the moan climbing up my throat, trying to remain as patient as possible. But I start to throb around him, and it causes an involuntary contraction that makes his entire body jerk.

"*Fuck!* Grace, stop." He sounds so desperate, I wonder if I hurt him. Or if he's going to cry.

"Can't help it," I croak, feeling another quiver that makes him mewl.

He grips my neck, pressing me into the mattress. "You don't know how to listen, do you?" Another inch deeper, and the sob I was holding back squeezes through the tight hold he has on me.

"Please," I cry, ignoring what sounded like a threat. But the minute he asked for is up. I can't wait any longer. "Please just fuck me."

A low rumble rattles his throat. A growl. An animalistic noise that sends him into a frenzy. He starts moving, thrusting in and out of me, and I feel like I'm going to lose my mind. His silver chain starts to brush my nose, and he quickly tucks it between his teeth, and I can't believe how fucking sexy he is. He stretches my leg, so it pushes against his shoulder, and just like I predicted, spots fill my vision. Things start to grow foggy, and there's nothing filling my senses except all the addictive, consuming sensations Andrew is making me feel right now.

"You going to give me another one?" his gravelly voice asks, but it's a demand.

I nod because I definitely am. My body feels like it doesn't even belong to me. I don't recognize all the sensations coursing through me.

"Good," he answers. And, without even a pinch of warning, another orgasm tears through me.

"Andrew," I plead. "I—I'm—"

"*Fuuuuck!*" Andrew howls. A course of curses string out of him, my screams matching the desperation in his voice.

We ride out the high. The gasps and moans swirl with all the senses making our bodies ultra-sensitive. I've never felt this kind of pleasure before. I could become addicted to this. Completely and absolutely addicted. In fact, I already want more. I want to feel him thrusting in and out of me. I want him to make me come over and over again. I want to watch him come. In me, on me, wherever and however he wants. I want to sign up to be his sex slave, let him lock me up in a cave for him to use me as he pleases.

But, of course, this is the one and only time this will happen. Tonight. That's it.

We sag on top of each other, and I feel like my body's floating four inches above any solid surface. I want it to hover for a little while longer because I don't think I'm ready to come back down to earth.

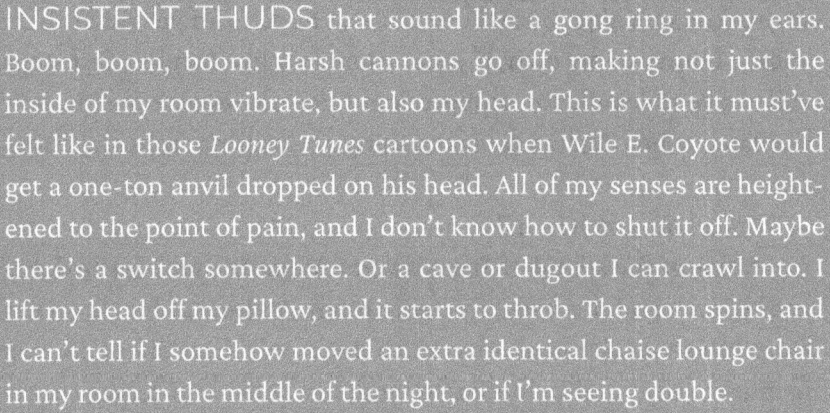

CHAPTER FIVE

Grace

INSISTENT THUDS that sound like a gong ring in my ears. Boom, boom, boom. Harsh cannons go off, making not just the inside of my room vibrate, but also my head. This is what it must've felt like in those *Looney Tunes* cartoons when Wile E. Coyote would get a one-ton anvil dropped on his head. All of my senses are heightened to the point of pain, and I don't know how to shut it off. Maybe there's a switch somewhere. Or a cave or dugout I can crawl into. I lift my head off my pillow, and it starts to throb. The room spins, and I can't tell if I somehow moved an extra identical chaise lounge chair in my room in the middle of the night, or if I'm seeing double.

"Holy shit," I croak through the frog lodged in my throat. The thuds continue, and they grow louder and more persistent. I feel so discombobulated. Everything feels fuzzy and faint. Like if I were to reach my hand out and try to clear out the murky smoke of my regretful hangover, it would only clear for a second before blurring right in front of me again. And then, just as quickly as another slice of pain cuts across my temples, I'm broken out of the fog of confusion by the sound of a completely foreign groan.

I turn to the other side of my bed to discover a bare back, lined with toned muscles and parts of it covered in tattoos, slowly rising and falling through heavy sighs.

"Holy shit," I repeat, only this time, there's more dread filling the two heavy words. Just as the events of last night come rushing back to me. I slept with Andrew. My best friend's brother. I had sex with him. More than once. And he's in my bed. Right inside the thick fumes of alcohol and sex radiating from our pores.

"Who is that?" Andrew's raspy voice demands.

I hear the thuds again, and my head jerks to face the urgent sounds. Someone's knocking on my door. I grab for the nearest item of clothing, Andrew's wrinkled Hanes T-shirt thrown haphazardly next to a used condom, and slip it on. I search for some pajama pants in my closet and reemerge while running my fingers through my hair. I don't know who could possibly be knocking at my door this early in the morning, but whoever it is, I hope I can get rid of them quickly. I hurry to my door, my feet stumbling like Bambi's first steps while I use the walls for support, and I become even more discombobulated when Buster comes rushing toward me from the living room.

"Grace! Are you home?"

I freeze at the sound of Teeny's voice. What the fuck is she doing here? Oh my god. I survey my living room. Andrew's shirt is on the floor with shoes that look very much like men's dress shoes. I scoop them up in my hands, stopping to grab his wallet and phone sitting on my coffee table, and grip them while Teeny's voice grows impatient.

"Grace!"

"Uh, yeah! I'll be there in a minute!" I rush to the nearest door—a small closet meant for coats and miscellaneous junk—and throw everything in there. Buster follows, holding a squeaky toy in his mouth like he mistook my excitement for playtime. Before I go to open the door, I remember one more final, and very important, detail. I run to my room and whisper shout, "Andrew! Teeny's here!"

His head bolts off my pillow. "What?"

"Stay in here. Don't make a sound," I instruct him. I try to ignore the way his triceps muscles, bulging as he presses the heels of his hands in my mattress, catch my attention. Instead, I don't bother waiting for a response and rush back to my front door. I take a moment to breathe a cleansing breath, reminding myself to not blurt out that her naked brother is in the next room, and open the door. The whoosh of reality slams into me, as does Teeny's relieved face.

"Hey, there you are," she huffs, brushing past me. "Were you sleeping?"

"Yeah," I muster while my heart feels like it's going to beat out of my chest.

"I could hear your phone ringing when I called it," she informs me, poking a finger at my phone sitting on the entryway table. "I thought something happened."

"No, yeah. I guess I was just really tired." I take my phone in my hands and scroll through the notifications. Sure enough, there are seven missed calls and four text messages from Teeny. And an odd email about an expiring car warranty for a Jeep. I drive a Volvo.

She eyes my current state. Hair in disarray, my attempts to tame it futile, while my puffy eyes show off a night not spent with cucumber slices placed over them. Her discerning gaze pauses over the shirt that obviously belongs to a man. I expect her to question me about it, but she chooses to focus on her early morning visit. "We were supposed to get our nails done," she reminds me.

"Oh my god. I'm so sorry, Teen. I totally forgot."

"I can wait if you want to get dressed." She plops herself on my couch and makes herself comfortable, her obvious intention to continue on with our plans. Buster joins her, and she ruffles up his head.

"Um, you think you can go without me?"

She gives me a sad look of disappointment. "Why?"

"I just...haven't been feeling too well," I say, flipping through all of the excuses I can give her. Sickness seems to be the most valid. And believable considering I look like I've been dragged through the mud. To add to the pretenses, I press my hand to my diaphragm, feigning an upset stomach. "I've been hugging the toilet all night." I cross my arms over my midsection and hunch my shoulders, adding a little theatrics as I slump onto my couch next to her. I feel like the worst friend in the entire world. Not only did I sleep with my best friend's brother behind her back, but now I'm masking my hangover with a coincidental stomach bug to get out of spending time with her.

She sits up. "Oh, no. Are you okay?"

I nod through a fake wince. "I just need to sleep it off. I should be fine."

"Did you want me to go get you something?" she offers. "I can pick up some Pepto."

I shake my head. "I'm good. Thanks though." I may not believe in hell, but if I did, I'd bet my Volvo I'd be going there in my afterlife.

I stride to the door, desperate to get her out, and thankfully, Teeny follows. I reach for the knob, letting up on my hastiness so I don't look as frantic as I feel. "Maybe we can reschedule for next weekend?" I ask, attempting to regain some of my composure.

She reaches for her keys. "Sure. Let me know if you need anything. And get some rest."

"Thanks." I watch her slip her shoes back on and walk out of my condo. I breathe a quick sigh of relief when I close the door behind her.

Shit! That was close. This is why I don't drink tequila. It's dangerous, risky, and apparently leads to a full-fledged fuckfest with my best friend's brother. Oh my god. I slept with my best friend's brother. The realization washes over me like being doused with a bucket of ice chips. It makes me feel like some charlatan who just deceived an innocent friend. It makes my stomach churn, suddenly turning a small fraction of my lie into a fact.

"Is she gone?"

My back is to my door with my face buried in my hands. My head perks up at the sound of Andrew's meek voice. I'm greeted by his still-undressed form. The only item of clothing on him is a pair of boxer briefs. His hair is as disheveled as mine, and the appearance of sleep is evident in his squinted eyes and raspy voice.

I hate that I still notice his arms, remembering those torturous triceps. Or those tattoos and silver chain that make me want to rush back into my room with him, peel off his underwear, and climb back under the covers.

I push aside those thoughts and nod. "She just left."

He runs a hand through his hair. "What was she doing here?"

I walk away from the door to the closet where I'd stored his things. "We had plans, but I told her I wasn't feeling well." He nods at the same time I shove his shirt and shoes into his bare stomach. "You need to leave."

His keys fall to the floor with a loud clack. My shaky hands pick them and nudge them into his hands, avoiding his insistent gaze.

"Grace."

I walk to my room, surveying the damage from last night. I'm welcomed by a complete disarray of what used to be my neat and organized room. There are multiple discarded condom wrappers on the floor from the subsequent number of times we had sex after our loose bodies acclimated to each other. The lamp that was sitting at the bedside is toppled over, the cream-colored shade accompanying it, and the comforter isn't even on the bed. It's tossed aside, pushed to the floor to give us more surface area on my bed.

I sense Andrew close behind me. I ignore him, picking up my room instead. "You should probably wait a few minutes to make sure Teeny's left the garage, but—"

"Grace." I ignore the sound of my name from his lips. A small protest. His hands are free after he sets everything on the floor. He walks toward me, still only in his underwear, and takes my chin between his index finger and thumb.

"Grace," he repeats.

"What?"

"It's fine," he tells me. A somber mask makes his eyes look

43

equally sad and afflicted, and I suddenly want to run my hand along his jaw. An act to soothe and reassure. "I'll get dressed and out of your way."

I almost tell him he's not in the way. That he's in no way intruding or impeding or anything in the category of inconvenient. I almost tell him to take his time. To stay for a cup of coffee or something as bold as some bacon and eggs. Or maybe even sit him down to go over what the hell happened last night and comb through our foggy memory to find ways to let it happen again without letting our guilt and shame ruin the best sex of my life. But I know we can't. The thrill of our night has passed. The heat has cooled and in its place is this slimy film over my skin that feels akin to regret. All I can offer him is a pat on the back, a handshake if I'm feeling brave, before he walks out the door. And I hate it.

I'm sitting with my butt perched at the edge of my couch after he's disappeared into the bathroom, the hard skin lining my right thumbnail wedged between my teeth. I hear some shuffling, a toilet flushing followed by the water running from the other side of the bathroom door. After about fifteen minutes, the door clicks open. I bolt from my spot, shuffling my feet nervously as he approaches me.

"I used some of your mouthwash in there," he informs me, jutting his thumb in the direction of the bathroom. "I hope that's okay."

I nod. He's dressed back in his dress shirt and slacks, his blazer slung over his arm and his shoes dangling from his fingers. I watch him walk to the door, bending down to slip his shoes on. He pats his pockets, making sure he has everything as he finally turns to face me with an easy smile. Much easier than the stress rolling through me.

"Are you okay?" he asks, a tip of a smile lifting the corners of his mouth. But not in the way that says he finds anything about this situation funny. He's attempting to appear amicable. Probably to assuage some of the guilt rolling through me, but it does the complete opposite.

"Yeah," I say, sounding anything but "fine." "Thank you, I guess."

His smile shifts into a grin. This time, he definitely finds something funny. "'Thank you?'"

"Um, yeah," I respond, avoiding his intense gaze as his eyes linger over my face. "I had fun, and...so, yeah. Thank you."

He chuckles. "You're welcome, I guess." He doesn't move to leave, and I don't rush his exit either. We both stand there, stretching out this goodbye for a few more minutes. Pulling it taut so we can hold on to it for as long as we can. I don't really know why. All I know is I'm not quite ready to watch him go. And maybe he's not ready to leave.

"Look, Andrew...I'm really sorry about—"

My words are cut off the second he leans down and kisses me. I don't push him away or stop the kiss or any of the things I know I should be doing to rush him out the door. Instead, I let the kiss linger. I don't stop myself when my hands grip his waist, tugging him closer, and I don't freeze when his own hands graze over my bare skin as he tucks his fingers under my shirt. I give myself this moment so I can hold on to last night. It's all I'll have.

He pulls away and leans his forehead against mine. I feel his hands move over my hips, his fingers pressing into my flesh possessively. I feel a dull ache spread across my chest, and I know our time is up. He needs to leave, or I may ask him to stay forever.

"Andrew," I tell him, unable to stand the quiet and his intrusive gaze a mere inch away. "Last night was nice, and I had fun, but you know it's a one-time thing, right?"

He drops his hands and takes a tentative step back. A single brow curves up toward his hairline, and his lips flatten into a straight line.

"Like, this cannot happen again," I add, feeling like the room is closing in on me.

He hesitates a moment, looking like he's searching for the right words to say. But what words are there when we've been thrown into this mess? And it feels like he's having as much trouble as I am figuring out the right way to place this moment in our timeline. Where we go from here. And instead of arguing with me or telling me something that dissipates the crushing guilt that seems to be pressing me into the ground, he nods.

"Thank you," I say softly, realizing I've already thanked him. But it's all that seems to come to mind right now. The only words that feel neutral and fitting. And maybe even inconclusive.

"You're welcome." His face has a sulky pout, and I feel horrible. He isn't some random blind date I never plan to see again. He's Andrew Cohen. I may only know him as an extension of my best friend, but I still do care about him. I've never had any ill feelings toward him, and I hate that this is where we are right now.

I place my palm on his jaw. A placating gesture, and he looks at me. His face softens at the same time a small smile loosens his scowl, and his eyes turn round and innocent. It makes him look young. Or *younger*. It places him on a map. Somewhere among people his age who don't complain about loud noises at bars and day drink in a crowded pool with a DJ playing house music. Somewhere I don't belong.

"Thank you for being so understanding."

"Don't worry about it," he tells me. He leans down, brushing his cheek against mine to offer one last small, reassuring kiss.

CHAPTER SIX

Grace

"I REALLY THOUGHT you two would hit it off."

The expression I give my mom varies from disbelief to confusion, though I wish I could throw in a dash of outrage in there. "What made you think that?"

My mom shrugs and takes a small sip of her hot jasmine tea, brushing off my blind date from hell as a small bout of miscommunication. "He seemed nice."

"How did you meet him?" my sister chimes in, spreading her attention between our conversation, lunch, and Avery perched on her lap. She feeds Avery a small spoonful of egg drop soup to keep her occupied and waits for my mom's reply.

"Remember Martin? Dad's coworker? It's his nephew." She pauses a minute, considering her answer. "Or it might have been his friend's nephew."

"You never met him in person?"

"No," my mom says, her unbothered composure the epitome of nonchalance. She snaps her chopsticks together, her mind clearly on the food in front of her rather than her daughter's cast aside relationship status.

"So, in other words, you had no way to vouch for him," Jade comments in my defense.

"Mom, I thought you met him," I accuse now that we're taking a deep dive into the blame game. Maybe with Jade by my side, I can explain to my mom how setting me up with random men is actually destructive to my dating life. Even refute her incessant need to find me a husband without feeling guilty for giving her an earful.

"I didn't have a chance to. You know how busy I am. I can't go around meeting every man I want to set you up with," she adds to her argument. "Plus, I know Martin. He's very nice. He wouldn't set you up with just anyone."

"Except he did," Trevor states matter-of-factly. Though Jade tosses her husband a look of muted surprise, most likely not wanting him to add to the fuel when it comes to the fire of his mother-in-law and her overbearing tendencies, I appreciate his intent. It feels a little more hopeful of a battle when it's three against one. Even if my mom's caustic shame game, her own pivot of finger-pointing to cynically blame herself, feels like an unfair battle.

My mom shrugs again. It's her go-to gesture when she's the one at fault, shifting the blame to innocence or ignorance. "Well, at least you got out there. And I won't get involved in setting you dates for you next time if you don't think I can vouch for them."

"Yes," I answer with a strain of desperation in my voice. "Please, Mom. No more setups." I played with the idea of not cutting off all potential dates set up by my mom, whether driven by guilt or hope of the one odd phenomenon I might actually meet a unicorn of a husband, I'm not too sure. But Jade jumps in, arguing the chances of that happening are slim to none and the more likely scenario would be more Harolds.

My mom sighs. A melodramatic sound that's meant to gain our attention while diverting the blame back to me. "I'm just worried about you," she says, a stab of genuine concern in her words. "After Frankie and the divorce, I think you're having a lot of trouble getting back into the game."

"'The game?'"

"You know, the single life. Or whatever it is you kids call it." Oh god. Has she been perusing Urban Dictionary again? I swear, if she asks me what a bukkake is one more time, I'm going to lose my shit.

"Mom, I assure you, there is no 'game' I want to be involved in. I will meet someone on my terms, and it will happen when it happens." Hopefully.

"You aren't getting any younger, Grace."

I look at my sister, my eyes flat and vacant. A reactive tic we both developed in our teen years when Mom said something completely inappropriate and out of left field. I roll my eyes in Jade's direction, out of my mom's line of sight, before sarcastically saying, "Thanks, Mom."

"I don't want to sugarcoat it," she adds. "You left Frankie because you suddenly wanted kids, and he didn't, and now, with you pushing forty, that may not even happen. What the hell was the point of the divorce then?"

"It was more than that," I weakly argue.

My words sound as watered down as they feel. Thankfully, Jade butts in. "Mom, Frankie was an asshole."

"But at least she was married," my mom adds. "And he had that nice condo she got in the divorce. He had a good job, and Grace had a very comfortable life." Great. Now they're talking about me like I'm not even here.

"She was married to someone who told her getting pregnant was going to make her fat and lazy."

I cringe at the memory at the same time my mom waves a dismissive hand in my sister's direction. A memory I had almost forgotten about. I knew Frankie didn't bode well for the idea of becoming a dad, but I thought maybe he'd change his mind once he imagined me with a round belly and a pregnancy glow. Or at the very least, appease my silly little dream of becoming a mother. But that was my mistake.

While there really was more that drove my ex-husband and I

apart, the ultimate deciding factor was the fact that I wanted kids, and he didn't. I thought we had crossed our t's and dotted our i's when we got married. We decided early on we didn't want kids. We both enjoyed the freedom of being childless. Weekend trips to Vegas, New York, if we were feeling especially bold, without having to figure out childcare arrangements. It made our relationship daring and exciting. But as our marriage outgrew the terrible twos, I felt like I was missing something. Something that tugged at my ovaries and caused them to skip a beat every time I saw a floral dress sized for chubby infants or miniature sneakers with disproportionately wide soles. But Frankie didn't seem to agree. He thought those frilly dresses were overpriced and unseemly. He didn't see the point of putting shoes on a baby who couldn't even stand on their own two feet. So I let the dream die, along with my marriage.

"Mom," Jade continues. "We'll let Grace find her own dates from now on. She's a grown woman, and she can handle this on her own."

Another shrug, this one filled with a downcast look of defeat.

"But thank you, Mom," I tell her, leaning into her in an attempt to soothe away any ill feelings she may think I'm expressing to her. The last thing I want is a two-week silent treatment followed by an unannounced visit with fresh fruit and pastries, her form of an olive branch. "I appreciate your help."

She finally drops the topic. The events from two nights ago now swiped off our table surrounded by bamboo steamers holding fresh xiao long bao and shao mai. The conversation veers into how Avery is adjusting to her new nanny now that Jade is going back to work after her extended maternity leave. Trevor fills us all in on Avery's new adorable habit of screaming bloody murder when either one of them leave the room, and my mom fills us in on my parents' plans for their anniversary party in two months. Reception-style dinner, dance floor, open bar. The whole nine.

My attention wavers in and out, glad to have gotten that conversation with my mom over with. I have no qualms about leaving my blind date in the dust. In fact, I'd be happy to erase it completely from my memory, but the rest of that night remains clear as day in my preoccupied mind.

I haven't talked to Andrew thanks to the inconveniently forgotten fact that I don't have his number. I don't know if he got home okay. Or if he noticed the hickey on his collarbone I got a peek of when he skulked out of my bedroom in his underwear. I tried to forget the whole night. Put it past me like I did my blind date. But every time I made some measly attempt to distract myself, I caught glimpses of Andrew. His hands on my bare skin, our bodies moving in tandem as if we've been doing this for years. The flashbacks are confusing the hell out of me. They feel good, really good. And I wish they only felt good, but then reality washes them clean of all the good and what's left behind is a hard, concrete slab of regret.

I just hope my curiosity will eventually die out, and I'll stop wondering if my night with him was a one-hit wonder.

Our weekly lunches involve a bit of catching each other up while we fill our cups. Jade uses Avery as a distraction often, shoving her in my mom's willing hands when the topic veers in an unfavorable direction. And, while I don't have a distraction strategy attached to my hip like my sister does, I have Jade. A comrade as we march through my mom's meandering parenting style. As taxing as an afternoon of listening to her nudging herself into my personal life as if I'm still living under her roof is, I still enjoy spending time with my family. Though, my dad seems to need a break from her. Probably why he opts for a day at home, always claiming something needs to be fixed or installed or mowed.

Most would think I can't stand my mom. Or at the very least, they'd understand it if I decided to one day cut off all ties with her. Especially after bamboozling me into dinner with a man with 1950s housewife expectations. The thing is, underneath all of the overbearing tendencies and reproving comments, her intentions are good. She just needs to work on her delivery. She's always cared about me and Jade. Our childhood was one you see as a montage at the end of a movie, highlighting a sweet life with glossy eight-by-ten images. Snapshots of us at birthday parties, amusement parks, swimming pools with oversized goggles and floaties. I remember always being happy.

But then the thought of me dying alone entered the deep recesses of my mom's brain, as did the realization that divorce had become a very real possibility for her daughters. She saw my future, and I think it started to consume her. She made it her mission to help me find a man. And I don't think it helped when I mistakenly agreed the one time she made an offhand statement about me and babies and ticking clocks while huddled around a very exhausted Jade post-birth in her delivery room. I held on to the dream of having a family of my own, and in her mind, she's helping facilitate this dream. All of that turned into this stubborn, staunch cycle. She'd set me up with someone. A male, age ranging from mid-thirties to late forties. Preferably with a well-paying job, being a homeowner a plus. Each setup wouldn't amount to anything beyond a polite parting and an empty promise to "do this again." Luckily, the worst of the bunch was Harold the Accountant. And after I'd voiced my strong desire to find my own dates, she'd reluctantly agree. Until the matchmaker bug bit her again, putting me right back on the hamster wheel.

It didn't take me too long to get back out there after my divorce. I never told my mom about those twenty-something fuckboys or meaningless hookups. She thought I was spending most nights on my couch eating ice cream straight from the carton, but it was a way for my heart to heal. My own rehabilitation, though not the healthiest choice, was easier to stomach. No pressure, just sex, and I enjoyed the thrill of the unknown. Nothing beyond a first name and whether or not they had protection. Sometimes, I didn't even know if the name they told me was really theirs. It was completely unlike me. Out of character, yet it felt right at the time. The validation that came with each tryst, especially after living so long under Frankie's disdainful thumb. I just wish I didn't feel so empty now.

An emptiness drags behind me as I leave lunch and go home. We say our goodbyes. Jade lets me hold on to Avery longer than a typical embrace. I'm greeted by Buster as soon as I walk through my door as he charges toward me with his leash in his mouth.

"Hey, Busty," I call, crouching down to him. "You need to go for a walk?"

He drops his leash at my feet and lets out a small yelp. With my shoes still on, I hook his leash to his collar and go right back outside. I let him take his time, marking random spots and sniffing away at bushes and poles that catch his attention. With my attention swaying, I peer down at my phone. My thumb swipes away at the screen, not too sure what I'm necessarily looking for. Maybe something to distract myself? Or, more likely, a way to reach Andrew? To ask him if he's okay? If he thinks Teeny caught on that something was afoot when she stopped by and he was hiding in my room? Maybe it's good I don't have his number. I'd probably just fill his inbox with a slew of embarrassing text messages. Or, at the very least, typed out paragraphs that never leave my phone with the ominous and definitive whoosh of an outgoing text. Our night was a one-time thing. It can't happen again, just like I stressed before he walked out of my condo with a downcast look of defeat. It wasn't a date. We didn't even share a meal. Just a drink. Plus a couple more we definitely should've said no to.

A date should be something more quiet and mellow. Like a dinner over candlelight with a bottle of wine and a shared slice of chocolate cake. Where he'd do the gentlemanly thing of pulling my chair out for me and picking up the tab. Except, he did pick up the tab. After a clumsy scuffle of sloppily held credit cards in our hands, he won. And I barely put up a fight. In fact, I believe I laughed it off with a drunken giggle he may have misconstrued as me being charmed by the very date-like act. Especially when my real date that night couldn't even reciprocate in the same manner.

No, it wasn't a date. I know that. And he has to know that. Right?

Intent on clearing any ambiguity that may still lie between us, I continue scrolling through my phone. I find the Cash App logo and search my contacts list. I find Teeny's from when we had dinner a few weeks ago and quickly find Andrew's. It's there under the amount of thirty-six dollars sent from him to Teeny with a very obscure fish emoji. With shaky, hesitant hands, I send him my very roughly calculated amount for half of the drinks from Friday night. Though since I lost count of how many we had, I could be off by a few twenty dollars.

If I pay for my half, then it definitely wasn't a date. It was just two acquaintances who happened to run into each other, and one did the polite thing of offering a kind ear and company. Absolutely not a date. And if it wasn't a date, then our night can be written off as a one-time thing. A one-night stand. Nothing more. I can forget it ever happened and move on.

If only it were that easy.

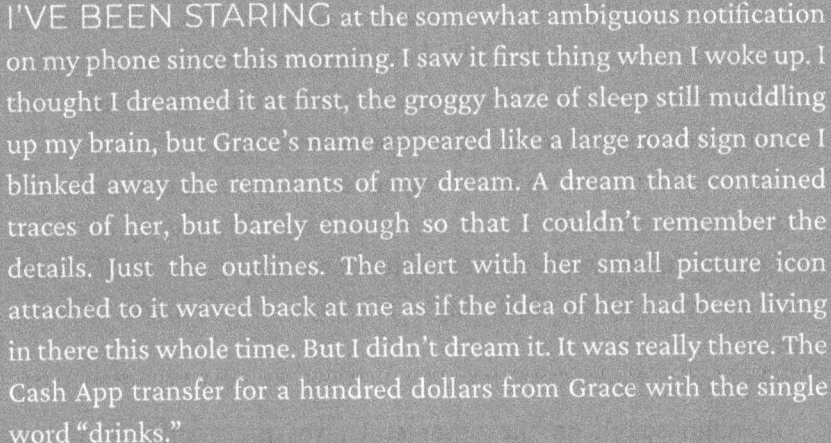

CHAPTER SEVEN
Andrew

I'VE BEEN STARING at the somewhat ambiguous notification on my phone since this morning. I saw it first thing when I woke up. I thought I dreamed it at first, the groggy haze of sleep still muddling up my brain, but Grace's name appeared like a large road sign once I blinked away the remnants of my dream. A dream that contained traces of her, but barely enough so that I couldn't remember the details. Just the outlines. The alert with her small picture icon attached to it waved back at me as if the idea of her had been living in there this whole time. But I didn't dream it. It was really there. The Cash App transfer for a hundred dollars from Grace with the single word "drinks."

It almost feels like a slap in the face. An insult that wasn't meant to be an insult but rather a simple transaction. Probably a form of closure she sought out. One I'm not sure if I'm ready to give. I know the gentlemanly thing to do is accept it and move on. Let her take the high road. I don't need to rub it in her face that I had already agreed to pay for drinks on Friday night. And I definitely don't need to remind her that she still has my T-shirt.

Before this little window of opportunity, I've been brewing over ways to reach out to her. Maybe through a handwritten letter sent by a messenger pigeon with all the reasons I'd like for us to hang out again, adding something especially daring to the mix like miniature golf or bowling. Or send her a fruit basket as a thank you for a wonderful night or ask her how she keeps her sheets so damn white and soft considering mine are always dull and coarse, no matter how many cycles they've been through the wash. Even just a simple passing question spoken in a low whisper, demanding to know if she blamed tequila for our night, or if she's had this hidden attraction for me all these years she never let slip because I happen to be her best friend's brother. Until three nights ago. There are so many things I want to say to her, but I can't. Except maybe I can? Maybe I can respond with something equally vexing and goading. Something to poke at the realization that maybe what happened the other night *can* happen again.

It feels like the smallest of openings. One I can manage to wedge through with a little extra elbow grease to pry open the barrier between us. No matter that it'll probably go against some unspoken rule she established as she reminded me that our night was a one-time thing then slowly closed the door behind me.

I attempt to come up with a response. Something cheeky and as equally insulting as the money she sent back. The money that'll be going right back into her account. Just as I reopen the notification, I'm interrupted by the shrill ring of my phone inside my small office cubicle.

"This is Andrew."

A rough cough on the other end gives me a split second to prepare for what's coming.

"I dropped off my car for an oil change." My boss's irate and impatient voice rings through the line. If I ever heard the term "being talked at" be explained, it would be this. The stony, impassive way he talks to all of his employees. "It'll be ready in an hour."

"Okay."

"Talk to Olive." The line dies before I'm able to offer even a hum or a grunt. The receiver balances in my hand, deciding between chucking it in the direction of his office or placing it back into the cradle. I see a new alert pop open on my monitor, hiding the company logo spelling out Sentry Investments—adroitly designed using a font like Helvetica or Avenir—behind my open tabs and emails. I click through the cumbersome tabs, minimizing some of them before reading his message. A curtailed version of our conversation with the adage of an address and the name Darren. The mechanic, I'm assuming. Or at least, I hope. Unless this turns out to be a drug deal—or some other illegal activity—and I'm just his pawn.

There aren't ever any formalities with my boss. Sometimes it's a Post-it Note left on my desk with some chicken scratches that I need his assistant's help translating. Sometimes it's an email, his demand in the subject line with a completely empty body. But every time he provides me a puddle of information, I feel like I'm dealing with The Riddler. Not only because a lot of his requests have nothing to do with my job, but also because they're so out of left field. There are so many blanks, and I have nothing to fill them with. This is the grunt work I've been subjected to. The insignificant details that weren't outlined in my job description when I got hired. The reason my night with Grace transitioned from scotch to tequila, hoping I could drown my woes right alongside hers.

I quickly return to my phone, looking over Grace's transfer. I sift through all the responses I thought of to send back to Grace and settle for something simple. Something with enough implication and undertone that it can be misconstrued by her for my benefit. Maybe even elicit a response. Hopefully.

I tap out the exact amount she sent me and add, "no thank you" to my own transfer. Keep it cool and mysterious. If she thinks she can send me money and write off the night as nothing more than a little release of steam, then two can definitely play this game. I'm about to shove my phone into my pocket when it vibrates. It's another Cash App notification with Grace's name in bold and the money I sent back. This time, no ominous one-word explanation attached to it. Just the money.

This distracting little game of hot potato gains all of my attention. My thumbs hover over my screen as I send the money back once again along with an added deterrent of an extra twenty dollars.

> Every time you send it back, I'm adding another twenty.

I hit send with a wide grin on my face, and I stare at my phone. Sure enough, another alert buzzes through. The money with an even higher sum lights up my screen with Grace's name and the Cash App logo.

> Fine. I'll do the same.

My brow shoots up to my hairline. I make good on my threat and tack on another twenty.

> I think you're underestimating just how stubborn I can be.

The money comes right back.

> And I think you're underestimating how determined I can be.

I chuckle. I don't know whether to be annoyed, entertained, or just flat out turned on. Maybe all three. I tap out my final coup de grâce as I send it right back.

> If you send this back, I'm bringing the cash to you in person.

I wait for a response. It never comes. I go back to my last transfer, hoping there's something there. An inscrutable emoji or punctuation mark I can dissect and overanalyze. But there's nothing. Just the same transactions and icy notes she sent over. I guess my final blow worked, but now I'm regretting it. My phone turns into a pot of luke-warm water on a stove as I sit and watch. And watch and watch. All while the thought of her burns a fiery hole in my head. Her thick wavy hair that she expressed an especially keen interest in having tugged, or rather pulled. Her smooth skin and the small oval mole over her ribs below her left breast. Even the sight of her toes, curling and flexing when I touched her exactly how she liked.

Jesus Christ, I can't stop thinking about her. I'm growing obses-sive. This compulsion I'm reminded of every time I see a silver Volvo or a whiff of something that resembles tequila—usually a dollop of hand sanitizer—or an overzealous dog begging for my attention. It feels almost Pavlovian. Except instead of a bell or some other indica-tive noise, it's literally anything that reminds me of Grace. Maybe I shouldn't have threatened her with an uninvited visit. Held on to this back and forth for a little longer, no matter how badly it drained my bank account.

"Hey!"

My thoughts on Grace's lips, how they seem to loosen and pucker when something feels good and how they look when her teeth are pressed against her lower pout, are interrupted by the sudden jump scare of Olive, Mr. Sheridan's assistant, leaning over the top of my cubicle wall.

"Hey, Olive."

"You're picking up Mr. Sheridan's car?"

"Looks like it."

Mr. Sheridan. Or sir. Either one to remind us of our place and his. Not his first name, Matthias. Or even his full name Matthias Francis Sheridan III. The ten syllables of his name sound superior and patronizing. Like nails on a stern chalkboard, slapping my work ethic into gear out of fear rather than ambition. Oddly enough, while I expect some level of vanity in maintaining his personal life as personal, it seems even someone with his level of arrogance lets small nuggets of gossip slip from time to time. The latest scandal is that his new girlfriend, a twenty-six-year-old beauty advisor at the

MAC makeup counter at Bloomingdale's, convinced him to buy her a brand new 3 Series in exchange for a certain "job" in his office. At least the ever-churning rumor mill keeps work interesting.

"I called you an Uber," Olive tells me. "It'll be downstairs in about seven minutes."

I exhale a deep, frustrated sigh, craning my neck back as if it'll somehow snap the tension at its breaking point. This is what Cinderella must've felt like.

"You want me to go get it? I am his assistant after all." Olive adds a look of apology perched on the back of her offer. It's tempting, but the potential consequences aren't worth it. I could probably bet a hefty amount of money, like the frivolous funds sent back and forth between me and Grace, that this task has little to do with convenience for my boss but is more of an expression of his power trip. A power trip that if I somehow sidestep, I'd never hear the end of.

I shake my head. "You know he'll be pissed if he finds out I somehow managed to avoid being his little gopher for the day."

"Sorry." She does that thing when I've become the subject of Mr. Sheridan's browbeating ruses. A small, placating frown turns her lips upside down, and she says, "You want to go out for drinks after work? My treat?"

"Nah," I tell her, waving off her offer. "If you bought me a drink every time he treated me like shit, I'd be a drunk, and you'd be broke."

She giggles, though anything more than a smile or a nod seems out of place. "Well, let me know if you change your mind."

"Will do."

She looks down at her phone in her hand. "Four minutes," she reminds me, waggling the screen in my direction. "And it's an Uber Lux."

"Thank you," I tell her, lightly pounding my fist on my desk to signal my exit.

I take one last look at my phone, my figurative still simmering pot, and see there's still no response from Grace. I wish it was

60

tipping over, boiling and bubbling and hot to touch with Grace's name filling the screen. But it remains in my palm like an annoying cold brick offering me nothing but a heavy weight and a distraction. Maybe my threat, as empty as it was, worked. But now I'm rethinking my steps that led to this self-inflicted silent treatment. I should've played it in her favor for a few more transfers. Kept the ball volleying back and forth to hold on to her attention. Or just showed up at her front door, a wad of cash in my offering hand, without a single warning.

I walk past Olive's desk as I leave the office. She waves, the smile on her face wavering between a simple farewell and pity. I consider her offer. Much like my offer to Grace and what led me to this conundrum. And while Olive's offer does sound tempting, if not to loosen the tightening knot coiling behind my temples, then at least to remind myself that I can spend a night without obsessing over Grace and her lack of response because I have plans.

CHAPTER EIGHT

Grace

CHICKEN LINGUINE OR LASAGNA.

I tap the two frozen boxes of Healthy Choice together, letting a sprinkle of shimmering freezer burn frost to fall on top of Buster's head. He whimpers as if whatever selection I make is going to affect his own dinner of dried kibble and wet dog food.

"Sorry, buddy," I tell him, ducking my head to face him. A set of round puppy-dog eyes joins another chorus of whimpers. "It's one of these or popcorn."

His paws tap on the floor, the clicks of his nails expressing his preference for popcorn over anything else. Preferably while sitting on the couch cuddled up in my lap while we watch a movie and I hand feed him. He nuzzles his snout into my tattered pajama pants, my business casual attire tossed into my hamper after I got home from work, a day filled with the occasional diversion in the form of multiple unwarranted remittances.

Maybe I should've picked up some takeout on the way home. Or planned some elaborate meal, shopped for ingredients like saffron or a wedge of pecorino Romano at the specialty market. Carbonara sounds really good right about now. But it's just me tonight. Just like most nights. And it feels a little inane to spend my hard-earned money just to feed myself when a meal cooked in the microwave for three to four minutes, taken out, stirred and re-covered, then cooked another two to three minutes would do just the trick.

I lay to rest the possibility of anything besides a dinner that was once frozen and settle for the chicken linguine. I'm chucking the lasagna back into the freezer when I'm interrupted by a knock. I immediately look at Buster, the both of us silently asking if the other is expecting company through confused looks. I walk to the door after realizing I'm expecting an actual answer from my dog. I'm still deciding if I should play it off like I'm not home, when I hear another knock, this time more urgently.

"Grace?" I hear from the other side. It's a male voice, sounding insistent and pleading. And oddly familiar.

"Who is it?"

"It's Andrew."

The blood in my veins runs cold. "Andrew?"

All plans to play the "no one's home" game vanish when his name is spoken with suspicion and disbelief. I undo the locks, Buster letting out a low whimper for the wishful playmate on the other side. When I swing the door open, Andrew's standing there, just like he announced. His hair's a little disheveled, shirt slightly rumpled and askew, and his sleeves are rolled up to his elbows. I allow myself a second—just a second—to admire his forearms before meeting his eyes. And I suddenly realize that I don't know if I'm ready to face him.

"Hey," he calls. Though I expected something a little more playful and flirty, it doesn't necessarily surprise me when I'm greeted with a solemn grave expression. A part of me feels like I deserve it. Even asked for it.

"What are you doing here?"

It's then he procures a plastic bag from behind his back. From his index finger, he's dangling what looks like two square Styrofoam takeout containers, and the contents smell hopelessly delicious. Maybe it's the serious look on his face that doesn't transition into something lighter and hopeful, curling a painful ribbon of pity to knot in my chest, or the fact that he soothed away the aching woes that actually convinced me the frozen dinner sitting on my kitchen island is equivalent to a warm, home-cooked meal, but all I want to do is wrap my arms around his neck and let him hold me.

"I got dinner," he answers, "and I was wondering if you'd help me...eat it?"

I cover the tearful pout on my face with a pinched brow. A measly attempt to hide my curiosity and my genuine gratitude for such a simple act of consideration. "Whatcha got?"

"You in the mood for sushi?"

Dammit! My weak spot. I almost want to burst into a puddle of tears. No one's ever brought me sushi. Not even my ex-husband. No one. Ever.

I don't answer him, worried if I spoke, my emotions would be on full display by the raspy crack in my voice. Thankfully, Buster chooses that moment to interrupt us, nudging his snout through the door. The guilt of turning Andrew away when he's done something so sweet prevents me from telling him to go home, so I turn to walk back into my kitchen. With my back to him, I use the moment to get my shit together. The Grace who appeared cool and collected, even a little aloof, during those Cash App transactions needs to make an appearance immediately. Because if he sees the Grace I want to be—the Grace he saw the other night—this isn't going to end well. It's going to end with more complicated feelings and an itch we both know we can't scratch.

I hear the door close and lock behind him, and I continue, making sure to maintain the nonchalant energy by keeping my eyes ahead of me. When we reach my kitchen, I round the island and face him. With the slab of marble between us, I feel an inch safer. I need it. A buffer, a line of defense while we're in the same room. A room without a mediator to keep us from ripping each other's clothes off again.

He plops the bag between us, and his eyes land on the frozen dinner, still in the box.

"Dinner?" he asks, gesturing a hand toward my pathetic evening plans. The easy way he braces a hand on the edge of the counter and the calm, even way he asks his question—void of any judgment—makes the gratitude claw up my throat. As does the need to sink into his wide chest. A warm place where I can enjoy some sushi and easy conversation.

I look down, avoiding his eyes, and nod, swiping the Lean Cuisine out of sight and walking it back to the freezer. "I've had a long day," I tell him. "I just needed something quick and easy."

He nods, adding a gentle smile that quickly vanishes. He starts to undo the ties of the bag and opens everything up in front of me. He lays out a selection of rolls, steamed edamame, and a small side of ginger and wasabi. Buster whimpers at his side, giving Andrew a perfected set of puppy eyes, and Andrew acknowledges him with a playful scratch under his chin. He continues, undoing a pair of chopsticks, pulling apart the tough planks of wood, and rubs them in his palms to buff off any loose splinters before extending them in my direction. I don't miss the domestic touch of his movements. His shoulders hunched over this task he assigned himself, making sure everything is within arms-length for me. He does everything with a soft ease that doesn't make me feel like I'm an imposition. In fact, if I suddenly decide I want to take over—nudging the food closer to him and urging him to take the first bite—he'd probably refuse. Those chopsticks, still in its paper wrapper by his side, would remain unwrapped until I popped the first piece of sushi in my mouth.

I take the chopsticks from him—a peace offering, it seems—though not without a beat of hesitance, and poke at a fresh California roll. "So, you just thought to order some sushi and bring it over?" I ask as I stuff my face.

He shrugs, as if it was something less thought out than that. Like he just happened to visit a sushi joint close to my house, and he coincidentally decided to drive through my neighborhood on his way home, and he chanced an impromptu food delivery to my doorstep. But I know him better. I don't expect to, but I realize I do. He wouldn't do this on a whim. It was planned, probably while he was still at work, and he played a little gamble. A risky game I was completely unprepared for, and he was at a great advantage with his delicious sushi and his kind gesture.

"Something like that."

We eat in silence, the clicks of our chopsticks and the sharp rubbing of Styrofoam creating filler noises so it doesn't feel like our dirty little secrets are being screeched into all of space. The silence continues as I bring him a cold bottle of water, omitting the opportunity to ask him if he has a preference for something else.

"Thank you."

"You're welcome," I answer quietly. I keep my gaze on the food, too timid to hear the truth, when I ask, "So are you going to tell me why you're really here?"

He tilts the bottle back, taking a healthy guzzle, and I look at him, still too nervous to hear his answer. My eyes flit to the way his throat bobs, inwardly smacking myself on the side of my head for finding it hot as hell. Right alongside those forearms.

"I can't randomly bring a friend some sushi?" His question is the epitome of innocence. So much so that I almost believe him. Almost.

I smother my smile while I skeptically eye him over the lip of my own bottle of water, tilting it back for a quick sip. "So, we're friends now?"

"Unless you can think of something else more fitting," he casually answers with a shrug.

I find his nonchalance, and the truth hiding behind his easygoing apathy, frustrating. Boldness radiates through my body, and it causes a firm question to bubble in my throat when I ask, "What. Like fuck buddies?"

His lips pucker forward. An attempt to hold back a smile. He forces down what's in his mouth and says, "Hey, if the shoe fits."

I huff, finding his daring candidness too annoying and galling to let slide. "No, it doesn't."

He doesn't offer another cheeky retort or something more courteous or refined like putting a stop to this confusing repertoire that feels too much like flirting. He just watches me remain flustered and stumped.

"Andrew—" I say his name with the intention of saying something meaningful. Something constructive and discouraging, but I come up empty handed.

"Yes?"

There's a pause, letting this ambiguous atmosphere simmer between us. It isn't quite boiling, becoming untouchable. We can still run our hands through it, test it out to see if it's worth a quick feel. Sift through it until it soothes into something comforting and easy. Or let it continue to heat, combust into an explosion we can never come back from.

"Look," I finally say, searching for my words while trying to reason with him. I can do this. I can talk to him without letting all the opacity fog up my brain. We're adults. I can have an adult conversation with him and lay out all the reasons he shouldn't be here under the guise of visiting a friend, using sushi as an excuse for what can only look like a late-night booty call. "I think what happened between us was a...moment of weakness."

"Weakness?"

I nod, firmly stamping my point. "We were lonely, and quite possibly horny—like *really* horny—and fate just happened to bring us together at the moment we were feeling those two very unreliable emotions. And now it's passed, I think it's smart if we give each other some distance so we can move on from this, and it won't be weird between us."

He does a little head tilt that burrows into my weakness, tugging it out of hiding. "Why would it be weird between us?"

We've stopped eating, our chopsticks lying over shiny foam edges of to-go boxes in different formations of X's. He rounds the two corners separating us, moving cautiously with his gaze firmly on me. He closes the only line of defense I had from him, and I feel completely exposed.

I huff, trying to ignore the way the air around me has been syphoned out of the room. "Because you're Teeny's baby brother. Because you're a practical child. Because I'm me, and you're you. And..."

He crowds the space around me, and I start to feel small. All the conviction I tried to hold on to so strongly is withering away. But I stand my ground. Only it doesn't feel firm beneath my feet. It feels soft and malleable, so easily swayed.

"Andrew, please," I plead. My words come out thin and weak, and I know they lack the conviction I wish they had.

"Please, what?" He braces his hands against the counter at my sides, and I watch his throat bob, pushing down the words he knows he shouldn't say. His forehead presses against mine, and my hands find the collar of his shirt. They fist the fabric, unsure if it's to push him away or pull him closer.

My heart starts to play a jagged game of tug of war. How easy would it be to give in to this. To guide his hands around my waist and circle me in a casing of safety and comfort. If only it didn't feel so wrong.

"Please," I repeat, my voice sounding the complete opposite of opposition but more of an actual plea. "Don't make this harder than it needs to be."

He doesn't argue, knowing I'd just argue right back, leading us into a pointless bickering standoff. We just stand there, an inch of space sitting between our torsos with this static charge that seems to be buzzing inside that hollow space, taunting and provoking. His eyes roam over my body, pausing over the rumpled state of my shirt. My chest rises and falls, my breathing growing desperate and erratic.

"I like my shirt on you a lot better than on me," he finally says in an intimate whisper, dissolving some of the ache that settled in my chest. I'd changed into it earlier, picking it over my usual DOG MOM sleep shirt.

I snicker a loose chuckle, my watered-down version of a laugh. I lift the collar to my cheek and take in a small whiff. "It's soft," I comment. I don't add the small detail that it smells like him too.

His eyes avert to my other hand. I'd inadvertently pressed my fingers to his stomach. An attempt to create some space between us. It feels safer there than bunching his collar again where I can easily twist and tug.

"I'm sorry, Andrew."

He offers a smile, though the slight scowl on his face remains intact. "Don't worry about it." He says it earnestly, accepting his defeat.

I step out of the tiny cage of his arms, wishing I could linger there a little longer. I walk to my purse and shuffle through my wallet. His eyes stay on me the whole time, and when I reach his side again, I can't ignore the completely expectant way he looks at me.

"Here," I say, jutting out a stack of twenties in his direction.

"No," he immediately says, stepping away from me and my offer.

"Please," I say, poking my hand at him. "Like you said, we're friends. And friends go dutch. The only way you'd have paid for me is if it was like, a date or something, so..."

"Was that why you were sending me the money?" he asks, the hurt misting his eyes. "To make sure that I knew it wasn't a date?"

I nod. "I sent it because that's what friends do."

"So, we *are* friends." His words sound sad in the way they lack hope, filled with resignation instead.

"Yeah," I finally say, realizing that if anything can come from this, it should at the very least be a friend. Someone who I feel safe and comfortable around. "Of course we are."

"Grace," he pleads. "You can let me pay for some drinks without...it's fine," he adds after a hesitating pause. He gestures a hand toward the money. "I get it, but you don't have to do that."

I hesitate for a second and nod, placing the money on the counter where it sits under a figurative spotlight, showing how the word 'friends' still doesn't seem like the accurate word to describe what's brewing between me and Andrew.

He exhales a defeated sigh. His frustration weaves into my heart, and my determination starts to waver. Guilt starts to spread its way to my bones, and it blurs all the lines I decided to draw between us. I lift a hand to his cheek, wanting to smooth away any resentment that may lie between us. It's risky, but I can't let him go like this.

"I really am sorry," I whisper.

He turns his face, planting a wet, gentle kiss into my palm. And I give, just a little. Just enough to put to bed what was never meant to be. I lift up onto my toes, brushing my cheek against his. When I pull away, I see how the mask Andrew was wearing has fallen to the ground. Gone is the cocky, flirty man I had one drunken night with. In its place is someone I somehow don't recognize yet understand completely.

He takes my hand in his, letting my fingers rest over his palm. He looks at it like he's committing it to memory. Every line, every crease.

"I'm sorry too," he finally says.

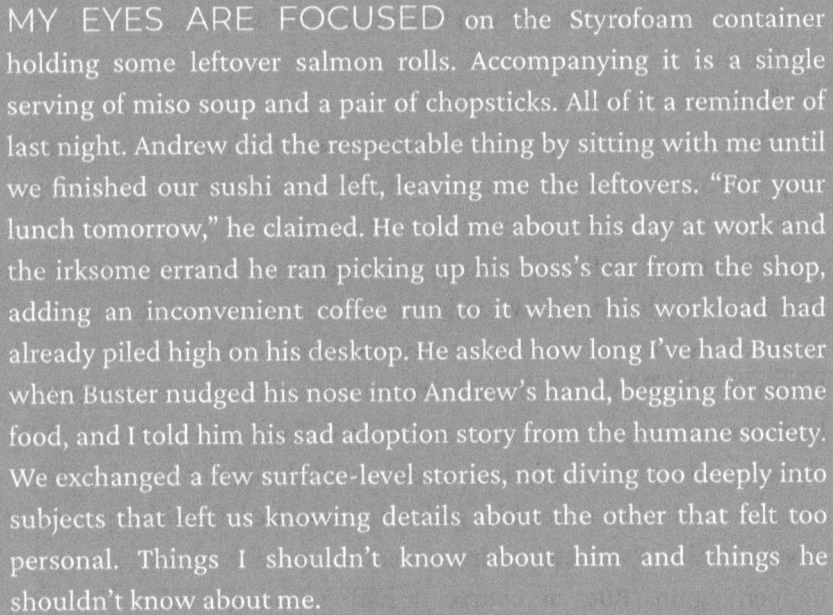

CHAPTER NINE
Grace

MY EYES ARE FOCUSED on the Styrofoam container holding some leftover salmon rolls. Accompanying it is a single serving of miso soup and a pair of chopsticks. All of it a reminder of last night. Andrew did the respectable thing by sitting with me until we finished our sushi and left, leaving me the leftovers. "For your lunch tomorrow," he claimed. He told me about his day at work and the irksome errand he ran picking up his boss's car from the shop, adding an inconvenient coffee run to it when his workload had already piled high on his desktop. He asked how long I've had Buster when Buster nudged his nose into Andrew's hand, begging for some food, and I told him his sad adoption story from the humane society. We exchanged a few surface-level stories, not diving too deeply into subjects that left us knowing details about the other that felt too personal. Things I shouldn't know about him and things he shouldn't know about me.

During the brief moment when we forgot—or rather set aside—our confusing tryst, it felt nice to have company. I enjoyed having someone to wind down and share a meal with instead of the frigid silence and Buster's insistent eyes. It made my night feel light and fun rather than the usual morose tone it carried until I went to bed, alone.

When I finally walked him to the door, he bent down and placed a small kiss on my cheek. It didn't feel underhanded or misleading. It felt like I was saying good night to someone I cared about. Someone I considered a friend. I went to bed with a hollow divot in my heart. Like Andrew scooped out a small chunk and took it with him, making me want to know if he got home safe.

"Hey!"

My head perks up at the sound of my coworker entering the breakroom. I instinctively sit up straighter, as if I've just been caught red-handed with the thoughts of Andrew brewing in my head.

"Hey, Jayne."

Jayne, the other social worker in our ER, plops herself in the seat across from me. "What are you having today?" she asks, peering over my lunch.

"Just some leftover sushi. You?"

She procures a large glass Tupperware container from her lunch bag. "Matty made some alfredo," she tells me, showcasing the appetizing pasta her husband made. "Want some?"

"I'm good," I tell her, shaking my head. I start poking away at the sushi, remembering how delicious it all tasted. Surrounded by Andrew's warm laugh and easy conversation, I didn't feel ambushed. His presence didn't feel like an imposition and waves of regret kept hitting me unexpectedly. He was sitting in front of me, thoughtfully chewing on a piece of edamame, and I kept thinking about him leaving. How sad I'd be to see him go home. Since he left, with a painfully wistful smile, I've been trying to come up with ways to make it happen again. But, of course, I hadn't thought of exchanging numbers with him. With my confusing refusal to entertain another night with him, having a more concrete form of contact felt risky and almost immoral.

I look at the clock on the wall to see my lunch hour is up. I start collecting my trash, leaving Jayne with her double serving of alfredo.

"I'll see you on the floor?"

"Dr. Noah wanted to talk to one of us," she informs me as I'm stepping back out. "I told him we'd check in with him when either one of us are back."

"Dr. Noah..." I repeat, trying to place a face to the name. "Why don't I remember who that is?"

"The new one from Vegas?"

"Oh!" I respond. The sharp jaw and light stubble dressed in navy scrubs suddenly comes flooding back to my memory. His badge actually reads Dr. Santos, but he prefers everyone to call him by his first name, Noah. I guess Dr. Noah is what everyone settled on. "Okay, yeah. I remember. Did he say why?"

"Something about placement for a patient? I think he was sent in by the nursing home he was at, and now they aren't taking him back."

"Okay."

I leave the break room and head out onto the ER floor in search of Dr. Noah. He's exiting treatment room four, ripping off a pair of gloves, when I catch him.

"Dr. Noah," I say, familiarizing myself with calling him anything else besides just Noah. "I'm Grace Han, one of the social workers. Jayne mentioned you needed one of us?"

"Yes, hi." He extends his right hand, and I immediately take it. His warm smile is all charm, making me wonder how likable and effective his bedside manners are. "Nice to finally meet you."

I smile a polite smile, keeping with my professional demeanor, instead of asking what he means by "finally." "Was there a patient you needed to discuss?"

He walks to the nurses' station, keeping his head ducked low, and I follow. A considerate sign of discretion. "I have an eighty-six-year-old male sent in by his nursing home. He had a fall which led to a large gash on his forehead I just stitched up, but when I looked into sending him back to the facility, they're giving me the runaround."

"Has the nurse attempted to reach out?"

He nods. "But they're giving her the runaround as well." He reaches across the nurses' station and grabs a stack of papers. "These are the records from the facility. Maybe you'll have more luck talking to them."

I scan them over briefly, and my shoulders sag at the name of the facility. "They've done this before," I inform Dr. Noah. "I'll reach out to his next of kin, and we can go from there."

"Great. Thanks."

I offer a smile, gratitude for going the extra mile when this kind of undertaking is usually left for the nurses or social workers. We've had a revolving-door effect when it comes to ER doctors. I'm not sure if it's a hostile work environment I'm not exactly privy to or if the last two ER doctors just have had other reasons that caused them to leave our ER within three months of becoming employed, but I hope Dr. Noah doesn't follow their path. "How are you settling in?"

He chuckles, cupping the back of his neck. I notice a small dip hollow in his left cheek, a subtle start to a dimple forming. "Do I have that fish out of water look?"

"No," I immediately dispute, worried I may have offended the new physician. "I heard that you moved here from Vegas, and I was just wondering how they're treating you."

"Well, no initiation hazing from the nurses just yet." He lifts both his hands and crosses his index fingers over his middle fingers. The witty, flippant gesture makes me laugh.

"Let me know if they do," I tell him, returning his playfulness in equal measure. "I'll make sure to put them in their place."

He laughs, reminding me that I'm at work, and this conversation has somehow veered into flirting territory. "Thank you."

"I'll let you know if I get anywhere with...Mr. Davis," I say with the patient's face sheets in my hand, my professional guise slipping back on as I take a quick glance at the demographics.

He nods, dipping his chin with the absence of a double—or triple —chin. A noticeable contrast to Harold the Accountant, but not unlike Andrew. "I appreciate it."

I walk back to the office Jayne and I share to be welcomed by my phone ringing and immediate attempt to erase the unsolicited thoughts of Andrew. The thoughts I have trouble shaking from my head, though Harold the Accountant and his wife list seem to have leisurely walked away without a single look back. I answer the phone, leading to more calls on the ER floor. The hours following my lunch turn busy. Though it should be a nice distraction from botched setups from my mom and illicit one-night stands, I feel it isn't as effective as I hoped it would be. By the time the day is over, after an emotionally draining meeting with a woman dealing with her dementia-ridden mother and discussing options for respite care, Andrew remains at the forefront of my brain, settling into the comfy grooves as if he lives there. In particular, this thing he does with his fingers when he traces irregular shapes over my pulse point and trails up to my shoulder and around my neck, making every muscle in my body turn to Jello.

By the time my day is over, I dump an imaginary bucket of cold water over my head. A pathetic attempt to wash away those tempting thoughts of Andrew and his hands. I hook my tote bag over my shoulder and head back to the ER floor in search of Dr. Noah.

"Hey, Betty," I say, trying to get the attention of the charge nurse. "Is Dr. Noah around?"

"He just left. Why? What's up?"

I hand her the face sheet Dr. Noah gave me earlier with a sticky note taped to it. "For Mr. Davis," I tell her. "I got a hold of his son out in Montana. He reached out to the facility with a very scary lawsuit threat, and they are ready to take him back as soon as he's cleared with you guys."

She breathes a sigh of relief. "Thank goodness. He's been crying about where his kids are, and I'm this close to sharing a pack of tissues with him," she says, holding her pinched index finger and thumb up in front of me.

"We need to figure out what's going on with that facility," I tell her, remembering that this isn't going to be the last time we hear from them in this manner. "We can't keep trying to find placement with this much short notice, and they need to get familiar with the term 'patient dumping.'"

"I know. I've already emailed the director."

I nod. "I'm heading out."

"Hey," Betty calls, stopping me in my tracks.

"Hmm?"

She smiles, clasping her hands in front of her. "Dr. Noah asked about you."

My brow furrows. "What about me?"

"Just...how long you've been working here, where you're from," she answers offhandedly. "If you were single."

"He asked if I was single?" I ask with skepticism, knowing Betty tends to occasionally stretch the truth.

"No," she admits. "But I could tell that he wanted to, so I told him you were."

I roll my eyes. "Betty, let's leave the bad matchmaking to my mom."

She ignores my bitter comment and asks, "Why? You don't think he's cute?"

"I don't know," I answer honestly. "I haven't thought of him that way."

"Well, we have," she admits. "We're taking bets on how long it'll take Natasha to make a move on him."

"Natasha from radiology?"

She nods eagerly. "You know she has a thing for hot, young doctors."

I roll my eyes, shaking my head as I turn to walk away. "I'll see you in the morning, Betty."

"Bye, Grace!"

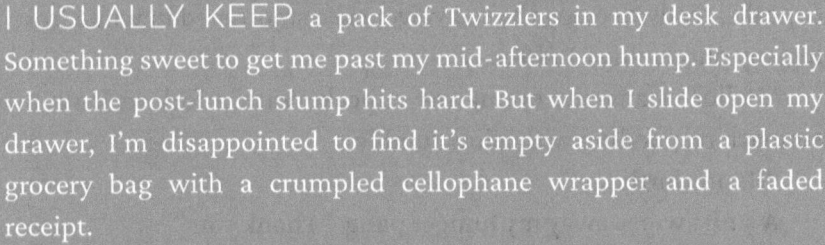

CHAPTER TEN

Andrew

I USUALLY KEEP a pack of Twizzlers in my desk drawer. Something sweet to get me past my mid-afternoon hump. Especially when the post-lunch slump hits hard. But when I slide open my drawer, I'm disappointed to find it's empty aside from a plastic grocery bag with a crumpled cellophane wrapper and a faded receipt.

The spreadsheets I've been staring at since this morning are hazy at this point, hence the need for an afternoon pick-me-up. The numbers and words start to double while nothing seems to compute in my brain besides a list of incongruent data with little sequence. It all starts to look like a weird jigsaw puzzle, and that's when I realize I need a break. Like a real break, not just a handful of snacks while the shallow imprint on my chair continues to deepen and abrade from my deeply seated ass. The financial models I've been working on, calculating expenses and revenue growth, can wait a little longer while I go on a search for some sweets, as long as I don't get any interruptions from Mr. Sheridan with more servile tasks. Though I'm not completely out of the woods quite yet with another two hours until I'm off work.

I'm about to go raid the snack drawer in the breakroom, hoping it's stocked with the usual array of cookies and candy bars, when a lone cupcake in a plastic container lands in front of my keyboard.

"Happy birthday."

Olive hovers over me, her elbows perched on the ledge of my cubicle, and she's looking down at me with an expectant smile. I smell something sweet, like vanilla and buttercream, seep through the cracks of her surprise.

"How'd you know it's my birthday?"

She shrugs, a modest smile on her face. "Company calendar."

I take the cupcake in my hands, noticing a small round "happy birthday" adornment atop the frosting and sprinkles. "Thank you."

"That little happy birthday topper's also a ring," she informs me.

Olive walks away, looking over her shoulder with a small departure salute, and I dig in. Just as I've peeled back the paper liner of the cupcake, ready to enjoy the red velvet cake smothered in white frosting, my phone rings. It's Teeny.

"Hello?" I answer, eyeing my cupcake with a forlorn look, my stomach responding with a low rumble.

"Happy birthday!"

A smile wipes away my hunger pang. "Thank you."

"Any plans?"

"Well, I was about to dig into this company-issued birthday cupcake, but you called."

"I meant for dinner, smartass," she reiterates, her tone flat yet playful.

"I have some plans with my friends, but that's about it." I haven't seen my friends in a few months, since they live over an hour away from me, so we decided to meet up for dinner to celebrate my birthday. While I insisted it wasn't something worth a big fanfare, it's an excuse for us to catch up.

"You aren't going to Mom's?"

"I'll see her this weekend at your party," I answer.

"It's *your* party, not mine," she corrects. And she's semi-correct. It's a weekend bash at her place. An over-the-top celebration with cake, music, and probably something else extravagant considering Teeny and her husband, Everett, are organizing it.

"Okay, fine. Mine *and* Sadie's." Another excuse for Teeny to go all out in the party planning sector of her entertaining needs. It's her daughter, Sadie's, birthday too. With the convenience of our birthdays being just a few days apart, celebrations are usually combined. As was the birthday I celebrated over a decade ago at a trampoline park complete with balloon animals and pepperoni pizza. Fun times.

"But call Mom," she firmly instructs. "You know she'll be upset if you don't call her on your birthday."

"I already did," I tell her smugly, remembering my call with her as I drove into work. It ended with her tearful voice telling me the last of her babies is now officially in their thirties, making me feel like I'm a toddler again.

"Good," she answers proudly. "So, I called for another reason."

"Okay, shoot."

"This weekend, any special requests?"

"Whatever Sadie wants, I'm okay with." One of the best parts of having a birthday a mere two days before the first grandchild of the family is that a lot of the attention tends to shift to Sadie. I can fall into the shadows and let a lot of the decisions surround Sadie's needs while having the luxury of avoiding any unwanted attention, an added plus after the first birthday debacle where I was left wearing a pink party hat, and the magician made a dove appear from my shirt pocket. It also didn't help when a fat blob of bird poop landed on my knee.

"So, you're okay with a DJ, a photobooth, and karaoke?"

"That's what Sadie wants?" This sounds even more over-the-top than any birthday before. But I guess it's not every year Teeny's daughter turns sixteen. It could also be the added benefit of Teeny's more recent living quarters and, even more likely, her attentive new husband. To say that he spoils Teeny and Sadie would be an understatement. While Teeny has him wrapped around her tiny finger, Sadie has her stepdad wrapped around her own. Two persistent strings he responds to with the smallest of tugs.

"Well, your niece is tenacious."

"Open bar?" I guess if Sadie's making demands, I can tack on one of mine.

"Everett's taking care of that," she answers. Of course he is.

"That's about it then. As long as there's food, I'm happy."

"Done!" she exclaims. "So, I'll see you Saturday?"

I pause, tempting myself into bringing up a topic that I've never brought up to my sister. "Hey, uh..."

"What's up? You think of something else?"

"No, it's not that," I answer before tentatively asking, "How's Grace?" I ask her against my better judgment after the curiosity began gnawing at my insides, scratching away at any wall or barricade to remind me I shouldn't be wondering a single thing about her. She should be in the deep recesses of my mind, not right at the edge, teasing me with little threats to jump right into the more gratifying fabric of my dreams.

"Grace? Like *my* Grace?"

I roll my eyes. *Her* Grace. "Yeah."

"She's fine. Why?"

"I ran into her a few weeks ago," I answer. I can tell her that, right? I don't need to dive into what that chance run-in led to. "I was just...curious, I guess."

"Oh, okay." Her voice trails off, confusion weaving into her dubiously spoken words. "She's going to be there on Saturday."

"She is?"

"Of course," she says, shocked at the thought that her best friend would miss my—er, Sadie's—birthday. "Seriously, why are you asking?"

She's catching onto my bluff. I need to cool it. Stop sounding so eager. "I told you, just curious."

"All right," she says, not sounding the least bit "all right."

"Cool." I guess I do have something to look forward to at my party. "I'll see you Saturday then."

The rest of my birthday passed without much of a hitch. Olive informed me of Mr. Sheridan's early afternoon departure. Something about hot yoga and his girlfriend in tight leggings. Whatever his plans were, it felt like a fortuitous birthday present for me. I left the office at a reasonable hour for once and prepared for the evening traffic on the I-5 to Orange County.

I told my friends to keep dinner light. Nothing fancy or extravagant. The last thing I needed was to treat today as if it's some celebratory event. It's just another Wednesday night with the added deed of maneuvering through the late afternoon traffic to see my friends. Though sitting in bumper-to-bumper congestion wasn't my ideal after-work activity, I was looking forward to seeing them. We decided on a quaint hamburger joint, and my friends insisted they be allowed to bring me a birthday cake. Mainly to satisfy their own sweet tooth cravings, but also so they could spend thirty-two seconds singing Happy Birthday while simultaneously embarrassing me.

"Happy birthday!" Hayley throws her arms around me, Rohan following in her path.

I met Ro in college my sophomore year taking a geography course. A class that I thought I would ace but ended up struggling through. That was when Rohan stepped in. He helped me understand the concept of erosion and plate tectonics with an invitation into a local study group. Our friendship lasted beyond the knowledge of the earth's atmosphere, all the way to graduation. I met Hayley a few years ago when she and Ro started dating, and since then, she seems to have joined our little friend group with ease.

"Happy birthday," Ro adds, sans the over-extended enthusiasm. Just a firm pat on my back and a broad smile.

By their side stands another UCI alumni holding a cake slathered in thick chocolate frosting under a clear plastic dome lid. Jake, Ro's old roommate from his freshman year, motions a loose salute in my direction, his bold facial hair joining him as if it has a whole personality of its own.

"Those whiskers are growing in pretty well, Jakey," I comment, gesturing a finger at the sharp ends of his handlebar mustache. "Soon you're going to look like the Pringles guy."

"Ha!" he exclaims, the mocking tone in his flat laugh bouncing off the walls. "The birthday boy has jokes." He lightly punches my gut, making me bow, and we laugh it off as he adds another birthday greeting to the many I've received today.

After Olive let the word spread that I am officially over this proverbial hump everyone reaching the grand age of thirty seems to fear, I got a few more greetings throughout the day. Add to that a few text messages from my brothers and the random acquaintances who send me emails or texts only on special occasions, it's been a pretty steady flow of birthday wishes. Except I haven't gotten one from a specific someone.

There's no way Grace would know it's my birthday. Not unless my sister happened to bring it up. Or if she'd done some stalker-status digging and happened to come upon the sliver of information. So, I shouldn't keep holding on to the expectation that she'll call me or text me to wish me a happy birthday. But I can surely hope. I can keep wondering what it would feel like to discover her waiting at my door, never mind that she'd have to really lay into that stalker persona to find out my home address. Maybe a more realistic Cash App transaction alert is what I should be hoping for. A light shove to get the momentum going. Like a Newton's Cradle, the metal balls hitting each other with a loud clack. That's what it feels like when Grace's name fills my phone screen. A pulsating snap that makes me want to push back with something just as stirring and playful.

I guess there's one plus to having my friends embarrass me with an open display of my birthday celebration. I can always wish for Grace to make an appearance—physical or digital— when I blow out the candles.

Once we're shown to our table and we've ordered the first round of drinks, Jake fills us in on a recent Hinge date. It turns out his date was roommates with a girl he hooked up with and never called back over a year ago. He ran into the realization when she invited him over, and low and behold, that ghosted date was sitting right on the living room couch.

We're laughing, watching Jake grow uncomfortable with chagrin, when the attention suddenly turns on me.

"How about you, Andrew?" Ro asks, using the segue to his advantage as if he's had this burning question held at the tip of his tongue all night.

The sudden shift has me rearing back my head. "What about me?"

"Have you met anyone recently? Been on any dates?"

"We were talking about Jake," I point out, not wanting to dive into my dating life or lack thereof.

"Yes," Ro answers. "But you're the one with the commitment issues. If we're going to worry about anyone dying an old maid, I think it's you."

"What the hell are you talking about? As if Jake doesn't go on a date with a different girl every week. At this rate, he'll never settle down."

"No, no," Hayley rebuttals. "The thing with Jake isn't commitment issues. He has an issue with limerence."

It's Jake's turn to look offended. "What's 'limerence?'"

"It's intense infatuation that's occasionally characterized by obsessive behaviors," Hayley explains, her tone taking on a Merriam-Webster's Dictionary-like graveness. "The way you plan the honeymoon after the third date or how you call and text ten times a day—"

"That's limerence?" I ask, curious about her offhand psychology lecture.

Hayley nods and tells Jake, "You tend to fall fast and hard, and I've noticed that the women you date are usually turned off by it."

"And I have commitment issues?" I ask.

She nods again. "You tend to find anything and everything wrong with the women you date."

"No, I don't," I argue.

"Yes, you do," Ro says, adding his two cents. "Remember Candice? The girl you met in your marketing class? You didn't want to have coffee with her because of the way she curled the edges of her textbook."

"That was in college," I point out. "And it lowered the value when it came time to sell them."

"No, he's right," Jake butts in. "You never called back Hayley's friend a few years ago because you thought the way she texted with her index fingers was weird."

"The one we ran into when we were in Vegas," Ro explains when the confused look on my face translates into a lapse in my memory.

"Who texts with their index fingers when their thumbs work perfectly fine?" I throw back, placing the night when Hayley's friend slyly asked if she could set her up with me, before turning to Hayley, saying, "No offense."

"I barely knew her," Hayley answers, shaking her head and saying, "But see? Commitment issues."

"You also swore off Hinge after the nut mishap," Ro adds. Hayley giggles by his side, no doubt remembering my own dating app fiasco when my date forgot to mention having a very serious nut allergy and ordered a walnut crunch salad, not realizing it had nuts when it very clearly lists them in the ingredients on the menu. Not to mention the word "walnut" in the actual name of the dish. I spent the evening in the emergency room before taking her home.

"I think that was an actual valid reason," I tell them. I feel like I'm being ganged up on. Have they always had this opinion of me? A guy freshly in his thirties, wasting his prime dating years blowing off women for something as absurdly trivial as how they unwrap a straw wrapper or the fact that they don't know the difference between "there," "their," and "they're." Although, just like the nut incident, I think that last one is completely valid.

And it dawns on me, like a bucket of cold water dumped over my head. I can't think of a single thing about Grace I find offensive. Nothing. In fact, it's the complete opposite. I find the way she dangles her drink from her thumb and middle finger when she's growing a little loose and tipsy charming. I like that she holds her chopsticks at the far end, showing how it's a skill she's obviously had her whole life. And I'm actually obsessed with how, when she's standing in one spot, her feet tilt to one side, avoiding her soles from fully touching the ground.

"So," Ro reiterates. "Any prospects? Or did you meet someone who licks all their fingers when eating wings?"

A round of cackles surrounds me.

"Wait a minute," Jake adds, cutting into the laughter. "When's the last time you've been on a date period?"

I do some mental math, not really having thought about this question recently. Though if I count my night with Grace last week, I believe the number in days would dwindle down to single digits.

"It's been, what? Two years since the nut allergy incident? Was that your last date? Has it been that long since you've gotten laid?" Ro's questions layer on top of each other.

Jake whistles. "That's one hell of a dry spell."

"I bet that right arm of yours is extra strong." Ro guffaws, slapping a hand on the table.

"It hasn't been two years," I argue boldly. All eyes face me, waiting for me to clarify. Has it been longer? Maybe more like three years? Or has it been something much shorter? Like a mere week? "I... had some drinks with a friend last week—"

"So, was it a date?"

"You hooked up with a friend?"

85

"What's wrong with her?"

More questions spill out of my friends in a symphony of curiosity and a pursuit for more answers. A part of me regrets saying anything. Not only because their persistence is near relentless, but also because this was meant to be a secret. A night between me and Grace. And now it's spilling into my friends' very nosy ears. Though I wouldn't say I have some high ethical standard and believe the act of kissing and telling is for philandering womanizers, I want to keep that night to myself. It's become this sacred keepsake I've been clutching onto, wanting to place it under a protective glass dome and display it somewhere in my apartment. And if someone were to ask why it's so special to me, I'd tell them with a far-off voice, "It reminds me of someone."

"You don't know her," I explain, knowing it'll do nothing to smother their interest.

"And?" Ro asks. "What does she do?"

"Like, for work?"

"No. A habit that you find repulsive."

I pause, thinking about those adorable feet flexing and curling as if the ground beneath her was sizzling hot. And it slips out of me before I can even think about it. "Nothing."

I feel their eyes moving, shifting across the table with silence and shock until Hayley gently asks, "Are you seeing her again?"

"No." My answer is firm, leaving little room for possibility. I watch the hopeful smile on her face drop.

The surly, brusque tone of my voice must ring out louder than I intended because when I look at my friends, a mixture of confusion and pity look back at me. I brush off their concerned looks with a caustic smile, poking at a dollop of ketchup with a lone fry. Just as a swarm of servers gingerly walk a brightly lit chocolate cake in our direction.

CHAPTER ELEVEN
Andrew

COMMITMENT ISSUES. That's bullshit.

I have no problem with commitment. If anything, I have a problem with holding on to things way past their expiration date. Like my car for example. I love my Mazda3. It's reliable, or at least it *was* for the first five years I had it, roomy with its hatchback trunk, and I got it used for a steal eight years ago. I love that car, despite the rising maintenance costs as it's starting to wear and tear past a hundred forty thousand miles on the odometer. And if I really want to dive into the many ways my supposed "vacillating nature" is a completely erroneous accusation, I can whip out my Keurig. I've had that baby for almost a decade. How can I have commitment issues when I've been brewing my coffee the same way for ten years?

I realize I'm comparing human companionship to inanimate objects. At the risk of slapping some weirdly specific sentient qualities onto my coffee maker, I'm really not helping my argument. Especially when my friends have a point. I can't remember the last time I refused to go beyond a third date for an actual reason. I guess poor fashion choices like mixing brown and black leather or wearing Yeezys because it's trendy isn't really an actual reason. Though I'd like to argue that Yeezys should absolutely be a deal breaker.

But Grace probably wouldn't mix brown and black leather. She'd stick to one, adding rings and bracelets accordingly. Or if she did, she'd do it so flawlessly, I wouldn't even notice. Just like she's somehow managed to make a caftan look sexy while sitting poolside in my sister's backyard. Maybe it's the low-cut neckline that shows the small glimpses of her green bikini underneath it or the way the silky material seems to flow around her like an elegant train, outlining the shape of her body, but all I want to do is slip my hand under it to see what's underneath all that fabric.

The weather forecast showed low nineties when I checked it early in the week, and it delivered. Sweat starts to gather in every crease my body has. Under my arms, behind my knees, along my neck. Luckily, Teeny and Everett's infinity edge pool is the perfect remedy for the heat. I came to Teeny's place early to help set up, but Teeny insisted that the guest of honor should relax so I made myself useful by keeping Everett company outside. It was easy to focus on the smoky meat as Everett slathered sauce between poking at the hot coals to make sure his smoker remained the perfect temperature. But as soon as Grace walked into the backyard, all bets were off. Everett could've been talking about the Louisiana Purchase, and I would've probably just nodded along, all while gawking at Grace from across the pool.

She's finally slipped off the concealing smock, whipping it over her head and revealing her skin inch by inch. Her sunglasses get knocked askew and the knot her hair is pulled up in sits lopsided at the top of her head. It isn't a sultry, seductive act, but when she tugs at the elastic holding her hair together and shakes her head to let her silky waves run loose down her back, everything moves in slow motion. With her back slightly arched and her neck craned back, the ends nearly touch the top of her round ass. An ass half exposed in a green bikini bottom. And the way one knee is bent, adding to the curvature to the small of her back, makes me want to run my hand over her skin, following those dips and bends like they're a guide to an interactive map showing me the pathways to her own erogenous zones.

"You want medium or medium-well?"

"What?"

Everett looks at me as he lifts a burger patty with his spatula for inspection. The juices drip onto the grate, causing it to sizzle over the hot grill. "Your burger. Medium or medium-well?"

"I—uh, I guess I'll take medium." I tilt my drink back, taking a long refreshing guzzle to douse the searing thoughts of Grace a few yards away.

But, of course, my eyes slip over to Grace again, now in the water, swimming around Sadie and Teeny. I do the thing where I stretch out an arm, hoping I look natural with each glance over the curve of my bicep. My eyes pause on Everett's new flat screen mounted under the outdoor cabana, another attempt to watch Grace from my periphery. She laughs at something Teeny says, and it reminds me of how loose she becomes when she's a little tipsy. Or how giddy she gets when her stomach is full. I can see how when she's around people she enjoys spending time with, everything lights up around her. Teeny laughs like no one is watching, and even Sadie squeals louder, clinging onto her Aunt Grace like she's her favorite person in the world. And a sudden pang hits my chest. I miss her. I want to be the one laughing at something she said. I wish I could ask her to join me for a drink after this. Or see if she'd want to raid a nearby gas station for all its chips and chocolate bars. Just so I can lure out a laugh like the one she's giving Teeny right now. I probably wouldn't even mind if she talked with a mouth full of potato chips and gummy bears.

"Grab a plate," Everett instructs. He looks like a meat master. He has a grill-slash-hibachi blazing in front of him with the smoker a few feet away and the tools he uses are lined evenly up on a small folding table set up just for his precious grilling accessories.

I do as he instructs, adding a fresh bun to my plate, and wait patiently as he gives the meat one last flip. "So how do you know if they're medium or well done?"

He presses his spatula into the charbroiled patty, emitting a low hiss from the fire. "By how firm the patty is," he explains with his focus zoned in on the grill.

"Impressive."

Everett's laser focus on the grill doesn't waver as he adds a few more fresh patties, so he doesn't notice when my dad steps up behind him. He peers over Everett's shoulder, watching Everett work through a layer of smoke with pride. "Do you need me to take over?"

Everett shakes his head. "Nope. I'm good here."

My dad pats Everett's shoulder with a pleased smile on his face, a clear sign of approval for all his grilling efforts. While the grilling bug bit my dad when I was a kid, it seems he's passed on the inherent talent of perfecting meat temperatures and marinades to his son-in-law instead of myself or my brothers.

I watch as Everett beams at my dad like he's brought him a report card with straight A's, and my dad responds with equal delight and satisfaction. I hold back an eye roll, wondering how much cheesier the pair would look if they had matching "Kiss the Chef" aprons and chef's hats.

A squeal from Sadie turns a few heads, and when I look at the water, I notice Sadie and her friends splashing water at each other while managing to toss a beach ball back and forth. Teeny and Grace watch the group of girls with smiles, and Grace's eyes catch mine for a split second. She quickly looks away, turning her back to me with some measly attempt to avoid me by reaching for a pool floaty. But I keep watching her. The water glistens over the curve of her spine while thick strands of loose hairs stick between her shoulder blades. The knot of her bikini sits just at the nape of her neck where I know if I gave it even the gentlest of tugs, it would unravel. Her fingers skim over the ripples of the water, enjoying the cooler temperatures of the pool while I stand in the baking heat.

"How's work going?" Everett suddenly asks just as I'm pulling my attention away from Grace and the wet rivulets of water running down her neck. Just as well. With the way I've been tracking her movements, it almost feels predatory.

With my eyes no longer glued to the sparkling water and its most striking occupant, I answer, "You know, same ol' same ol'."

A flash burst of flames causes Everett to curse under his breath, but he doesn't miss a beat. The meat continues to sizzle, and his focus remains vigilant. "That boss of yours still treating you like shit?"

"Yup." My family is well aware of the so-called "quirks" that come with my career. Though, it doesn't seem that all that's lacking in my work is related to the career choice itself but more to do with who I work with.

He adds a fresh batch of patties while he continues our conversation. "I told you, you can quit and come work with me."

"What am I going to do in tech?"

"I'm sure I can find you something," he answers with a shrug as if he hasn't thought about the idea of whatever would allow me to leave my current job. I appreciate his offer. And considering the tech company he started barely a few years ago is doing particularly well, I'm sure if I choose to take him up on his offer I'd thrive under his wing. But starting at some entry-level position like a mailroom clerk or customer service isn't the direction I want to be heading.

"I like what I do. And I'm good at it," I tell him, shaking my head. "I just..."

"Don't like your boss," he finishes for me. He finally looks up from the smoky fog hovering under him and offers a look that matches the very matter-of-fact way he says, "Then find a different job. You know, you don't have to work for a big corporation."

"Like what?"

"Accounting for startup companies?" he muses. "Or a smaller bank branch? Anything to get you away from that asshole."

"What asshole?" Josh, my brother who also happens to be Everett's best friend, joins us with a veggie platter balanced in his hands. A loud crunch rattles the air as he bites into a fresh carrot.

"My boss," I answer.

Josh sets down the platter on a nearby table and pulls a fresh beer from one of the coolers by our feet. "I've been telling you, you need to quit."

"I know, I know," I reluctantly agree. "I guess I'll start fine-tuning my résumé." And get over the dread that comes along with interviews and rejections and more interviews.

"A friend of mine works for a nonprofit company," Josh tells me, a trail of hope following his tidbit of information. "I think he mentioned they offer community resources or something like that, and they have a finance department that's growing. I can set up a meeting with him if you want."

"Hmm," I hum with a nod. It's a tempting offer. And a change I don't know if I'm ready for. A burst of pros and cons list off in my brain. While quitting my job sounds like a dream at this point, I'm not sure if I'm ready to quit. I like the work I do, and I get along with my coworkers. Benefits are pretty decent, like a ten percent match with the company 401k and other retirement fund options that could set me up for my later years. But then I'd be stuck under the wing of a boss I hate. Unless he quits or happens to fall into some heavy machinery on the way to work. I don't know how to explain all of this to my brother or Everett, or if they'd even understand, so I simply say, "I've already put a lot into this company. I'm just paying my dues."

"Those dues seem a bit hefty," Everett says.

My brow shoots up in agreement, and I offer silence with a long pull of the cool beer in my hand. While both of their offers remain a fickle thought in my head, I don't respond with anything more than silence and my still-hesitant answer. So, when my form of a non-answer comes with my fingers picking at the label on my beer bottle, they both thankfully take it as an opportunity to change the subject.

"Well," Everett adds. "You're still young, and it's not like you have a family. I guess it's good to see where this goes while you can."

Josh scoffs. "You don't need to worry about that for a *long* time."

I turn to him, a little insulted by his sarcasm. "What does that mean?"

"Why are you offended? It's not like you plan on settling down anytime soon," he argues.

"You don't know that." Actually it seems he does. Right on the nose in fact. The dubious look on his face matches the lack of conviction in my voice.

"Are you seeing someone?" Not really an inquiry of my personal life but rather a question to prove his point.

My eyes immediately scan the pool, catching a passing glimpse of emerald flitting in the water. "No."

He pokes his hand in my direction, a silent gesture saying "I told ya so" while adding, "Like I've said before. Never settling down."

What was it? Gang up on Andrew week? Was my birthday week a universal reminder to poke fun of the fact that I'm single, and I'm destined to die alone as well? And when did every person I know form this opinion of me? I never thought I gave off this picky, commitment-phobe energy when it came to my dating life. I thought I was more easygoing than that. While those thoughts ruminate in my head, it shows on my face. A twist and turn of confusion and uncertainty.

"Come on," my brother argues, obviously catching on to my unsettled discomfort. "What was it that you said about the last girl you dated? That her preference for chicken strips and french fries over actual adult food is why you broke it off?"

"Dated" wasn't really accurate. It was actually an acquaintance —friend being too strong of a word—I knew from my part-time job at Yogurtland when I was seventeen. I ran into her in line at the grocery store checkout and thought it would be fun to catch up. I guess it was a date? Or chatting it up with a hometown friend? Something to ease the sting of realizing I really didn't stray too far from home after graduating high school. But after a second dinner when I realized she ordered chicken strips for the second time in a row, and she boldly stated that she never thought she'd date a guy she knew when she was a teenager, contemplating all the time wasted finding someone when I was here all along, I stopped talking to her.

"What grown adult or anyone over the age of twelve doesn't even try shrimp tacos?" I ask in my defense. Though it feels out of place when I didn't categorize the interaction as a date to begin with.

"Or scallops," Josh adds with a smirk.

"Exactly." I pause, finishing the rest of my beer before adding, "Plus, that was over a year ago. What's your point?"

"Just that you have to be a little open-minded to meet someone. That's what a relationship is. Compromise and be a little vulnerable."

The thought of it nearly raises the hairs on my neck. I've never been open and vulnerable with anyone. Compromise is easy, practical. Letting someone in, that's scary. Maybe the commitment issues everyone has branded on me are a little accurate. I've been using my deviant standards as a shield to avoid a real relationship based on actual feelings. And I don't know which scares me more—that or realizing how vulnerability and commitment go hand in hand.

The hot air suddenly feels unbearable. The beer in my hand was helping alleviate some of the stifling heat, but I need something stronger, more effective. I set my drink down and walk to the edge of the water, whipping my shirt over my head. I catch the attention of Grace while she wades in the shallow end, and I wonder how easy compromise would be with her. How simple and effortless it's already been so far. How whenever I push, all she's done is shove, and I let her win without a second thought because I never want to say no to her. And being vulnerable? Well, she's already peeled back the corners with barely any effort. Maybe it isn't as hard as I make it out to be. Especially when it comes to Grace.

CHAPTER TWELVE

Grace

UNDER THE SEPTEMBER heat of Southern California, I ask myself why my best friend chose one of the hottest days of the year to throw an outdoor party. Though, with her sparkling pool, I can hardly dispute a poolside barbecue. The second I walked into Teeny's backyard, it seemed to call my name. Longing whispers chanting, "Grace! The water feels amazing! Jump in!" But after surrendering to a quick dip that did little to satisfy the mid-afternoon heat, I was pulled out by Teeny and Sadie for the usual birthday festivities. A cake was cut and a birthday song was sung. Even a few poorly played pop songs performed through the amp of a karaoke machine next to the lavish photobooth setup. But alas, the itinerary has led to the more relaxed portion of the party. With Sadie huddled over the photobooth with all of her friends and the hot grill now merely keeping the glowing coals warm, Teeny and I have returned to the pool with little forcing us out. And after a day of overexposure to the sun, it seems to be the perfect remedy.

"Sadie had a lot of fun," I comment, sitting on the shallow part of the steps in the water.

"She's been looking forward to this for a month," she tells me. "And Everett has been planning every detail."

We both look over at Everett, diligently picking up some of the trash leftover by the giddy teenage girls now fiddling with the karaoke machine after giving it a short break. "He's taking that stepdad role seriously."

She nods, a peacefully radiant smile on her face. "He's been talking about getting her a car for Christmas."

"A car?" I exclaim. "That's a big deal."

"I know," she admits. She flicks at the water, the ripples distracting her as she muses over a topic she and Everett have seriously considered. "I told him to press the brakes on the extravagant gifts for now. Plus, I should talk to Leo about these things before jumping the gun on something like a car."

I nod, proud of her consideration for her ex-husband's involvement in navigating this new co-parenting role. Still, I can't help but notice how much she glows. She's been married barely a year. Yet, with how at ease she is in this big, beautiful house, it seems they've been at it their entire lives.

I remember when my life felt that hopeful. When I thought I had a future with someone I planned to spend the rest of my life with. The sudden pang I feel looking back at a fresh thirty-year-old Grace hits my chest like an arrow aimed right at my heart. All the nights I come home to my two-bedroom condo and a meal for one with hours of binge-watching reality television has an empty weight to it. While it's hollow, it's also heavy as it hangs over my head. At least Buster helps keep some of the loneliness at bay when I need someone to share a bowl of popcorn with.

Just then, I get a glimpse of Andrew wading through the pool. He's got his brother James's adorable four-year-old daughter, Sophia, in his arms. He's lifting her above the water, her feet kicking the water into his face, and the two giggle in delight. The sight makes me smile too. My grin turns into a full laugh when she asks for "more uppies" with a whine he can't seem to resist.

Andrew peers over at me at the sound of my animated laugh, and I realize I'm staring. He throws a little wink in my direction, and I feel like I've been caught doing something I wasn't supposed to be doing. It's been happening all afternoon. I'd look up while perusing the snack table for a slice of watermelon or some chips to go along with my ranch dip only to find Andrew observing me. Like he's guessing what I'm going to add to my plate. Or when we huddled around Sadie as the candles on her cake lit up her face. I'd meet Andrew's eyes as we both smiled and clapped, his smile aimed at me instead of the birthday girl. I want to say I wish he'd stop, but do I? Without his perceptive eyes and knowing smile that seems to hide so much between its curved corners, I wouldn't feel this heat simmering along my skin. A low, stirring fervor that has nothing to do with the weather.

I keep telling myself it's because I hadn't gotten laid in so long and that night with Andrew left behind a hunger pang that I don't know how to get rid of, but this gnawing feeling keeps telling me there's more. Even if I decide to have another raucous night—this time with someone inconsequential—it wouldn't matter. It wouldn't alleviate that pesky, maddening hunger. It would spur it. It's something about *him* that's making it hard to move on.

Andrew's laughter starts to tug at me. Like a hook looped over my ribcage, yanking me toward him in this provoking, insurgent way I have trouble saying no to. I need to get away from him. Far away from him.

"Hey," I call to Teeny, who has her sunglass-shielded face pointed toward the sky. "I'm going to grab a drink. You want anything?"

She shakes her head. "I'm good."

I turn to hurry out, already feeling a wave of relief from the added steps of space from Andrew, when Teeny calls for my attention.

"I have the grapefruit Perrier in the fridge inside," she informs me. "I got some for you, and I forgot to add them to the coolers."

"You know me so well," I call over my shoulder.

I pad out of the water, a rush of water following my exit. My emerald-green bikini clings to my sopping skin, and I reach for a towel quickly as goose bumps start to scatter over my arms and legs. I let some of the chlorinated water drip onto the concrete, watching it immediately disappear in the stifling heat. I tiptoe inside, the bottoms of my feet burning against the scalding ground. As soon as I close the large sliding doors, I'm surrounded by cool air and silence. I walk to the fridge and grab a Perrier, cracking it open, enjoying the AC while sipping on my drink. It's with my hip perched against one of the heavy wooden barstools pushed under the kitchen island that I notice a worn photo album sitting on her kitchen island. A few strips from the photo booth are tucked inside, adding to the collection already slipped inside the clear slots. I start flipping through it. I'm surprised and pleased to find the older pictures inside are all of Teeny when she was a kid. Family vacations, school recitals, birthday parties, summer trips to the beach. I see her at various stages of her childhood.

I come across a picture of her in high school, and when I see Everett in one of them, it throws me off for a second before I remember they first met when Teeny was a junior. It looks like it was taken on a driveway in front of her house with all of her brothers too. They'd met in high school before they grew apart due to circumstances that pulled Everett out of her life, and this glimpse of them feels like a window through a time machine that's giving me a perfect snapshot of twenty years ago. This is what it must mean to find a soulmate. To have destiny bring them together again.

I turn the page to find another picture that brings a smile to my face. It's Andrew. He has a toothy grin, a few gaps in his teeth that make his mouth look like an uneven bar chart, and his haircut looks awful. Like it was cut by someone who was holding a pair of scissors for the first time. He has a large LEGO set in his hands, and it looks freshly built as he presents his masterpiece proudly.

"Aren't you a cutie," I whisper through a giggle.

"Who's a cutie?"

I feel my stomach jolt up to my throat. I turn around, my towel slipping down my body, to find Andrew hovering over my back. "What are you doing here?"

His eyes narrow, though a crooked smile curves his lips into an adorable angle. "Enjoying my party?" He omits the clear "duh" at the end of his question, making me sound silly for even asking.

"I mean, when did you come inside?" I demand, fumbling through my words. My eyes snag on his damp chest and wet hair dripping in silent splats around him. "I didn't hear the door open." My towel slips off completely, exposing my bikini-clad body, and I clumsily attempt to secure it around me again. All while Andrew watches, keeping a calm composure that I don't know how to decipher.

"I came in through the side door," he explains. "By the garage."

"Okay. And why are you skulking around like some secret agent spy?" I turn away from him and reach for my drink. In a moment of complete embarrassment and frustration, I knock it over, spilling its contents a millimeter too close to the pictures I was just admiring. "Shit!"

Andrew beats me to the paper towel roll, ripping off a few sheets in haste and quickly mopping up my mess. Andrew shoves the photo album away from the wet zone, and I join him after reaching for the lone sponge sitting by the sink. The tense, awkward silence that was sitting between us is filled with purpose and resolve by hiding the evidence of my clumsiness and attempting to leave behind a spotless kitchen counter.

"Thank you," I whisper as I wring the sponge out in the sink.

Andrew nods, transferring the slop of wet paper towels to the trash. "No problem."

I'm washing my hands to rid them of the sticky residue when he sidles up next to me. His hip is pressed against the edge of the counter, and he has his arms crossed over his bare chest. I try to ignore him, feeling the heat of his sharp, perceptive gaze, until I'm flicking my fingers to rid myself of the excess water on my hands, and our eyes meet.

"What?"

"Nothing," he answers with an innocent shrug. "I'm just wondering why you haven't called. Or texted."

"Because I don't have your number," I say matter-of-factly.

"Didn't seem to stop you before."

The silver chain around his neck glints in a stream of light coming in through the kitchen window. The sight of it sends a shiver down my spine, just as I remember the feel of it looped around my index finger. The power I wielded using it to drag him closer to me. The slickness of it caught between Andrew's teeth while he flicked at it with his tongue.

"Well, you wouldn't take my money the last time I saw you, so there's really no need to press on the issue, right?"

"Still."

"We already talked about this." I take a step backward, moving away from him and leaving behind my need for a drink to head back outside where it feels safer. My need to get away from Andrew, and this dangerous territory of a night that can't be repeated seems to trump the need for a drink at this moment.

"Yeah, that we're friends."

I shoot him a pointed glare. "And?"

"And friends hang out," he informs me. "They say hi, meet up for dinner, make plans—"

"We aren't that kind of friends," I interrupt.

His arm stretches, and he takes a step closer to me. The palm of his hand presses into the hard surface of the counter where my waist is resting, and it brings him closer to me. His face is inches from mine, and the fiery heat in his eyes followed by the slight tic in his jaw brings his voice down several octaves. "Then what kind of friends are we?"

My neck stretches backward, a pitiful attempt to create some space between us. "Come on, Andrew," I argue weakly. "I thought we agreed that—that it was a mistake."

He nods. The up and down motion of his head is purposeful, full of resolve while driven by something that he's holding back. "I changed my mind."

A scoff I don't mean to huff comes out of nowhere. "What do you mean you changed your mind? You don't want to be friends?"

"Or maybe I want to redefine what the word 'friends' means to us."

"We aren't doing a 'friends with benefits' kind of thing if that's what you're suggesting," I emphasize with a sizable weight of determination.

His face softens, and a sweet smile spreads across his face. I see a little bit of his hardness unthaw, and I appreciate that it didn't take more fight from him. "I know," he says gently. "I just like hanging out with you."

"You like hanging out with me?" Curiosity threads its way into my heart, and I suddenly feel so bad for spending the entire day either ignoring him or shooting him flat looks of indifference.

He nods. "Look, I heard what you said. It was a mistake, and it won't happen again. I had fun at the bar, and when we had dinner the other night."

"Okay?" I ask, not really understanding where this is going.

"And...I kind of want to do it again. Just as friends."

"Really?"

"Really," he answers sincerely.

"So sex is off the table?" I ask, needing that validation.

"Well, it isn't *completely* off the table, but—"

I cut him off with my hands thrown exasperatedly in the air. "You can't take anything seriously," I mutter under my breath.

"No, no," he protests. His hands instinctively move to grip my arms, and when I look at them, he immediately holds his palms up in the air. A silent truce. "Fine. Sex is off the table. And...Teeny doesn't have to know."

His sweet words crack through my chest. They make me realize how maybe a part of me needs to unthaw too. Let Andrew in a little.

A friend to help make the days less lonely, no matter that I can't fill other voids with him.

"So, like...secret friends?"

"Sure," he says, a single shoulder held up in agreement. "Secret friends."

"Yeah," I finally say. "Okay."

His face lights up. "Yeah?"

I nod. "A friend isn't bad to have. And...like you said, you like hanging out with me. And maybe I like it too."

"Friends." He juts his right hand in front of him.

I accept his peace offering. "Friends."

CHAPTER THIRTEEN
Andrew

THE SHRILL SCREAMS of children chasing each other feel like nails on a chalkboard. I try to dull it by sticking my finger in my ear when I catch a very apologetic mother getting multiple judgy glances from around her, which is when I transition my improvised earmuff into a feigned itch. It's chaotic and loud and overwhelming inside the LEGO® Store in La Jolla. I've only been inside for three minutes, but I'm on a mission. One that involves a new friend of mine.

When I don't find what I'm looking for, I find the nearest employee with a yellow apron and a LEGO badge, a little cowboy figurine perched above the name Patrick in all caps and block letters.

"Excuse me," I say, calling for his attention. I point my phone screen at him and ask, "I didn't see this set out here. Do you know if you have any in the back?"

He squints at my phone and says, "Sure, let me check."

I nod, standing off to the side where there's a display of a Mona Lisa LEGO behind a glass case. Another loud squeal, this one less sulky, buzzes past me followed by the urgent pitter-patter of light-up sneakers.

This isn't how I expected to be spending my Saturday morning. I figured I'd have a lazy start, enjoy a protein shake followed by a few hours at the gym. Or a trip to Ikea to replace my broken nightstand. But the unexpected turn the day is leading me through has a giddy trill rolling through my body.

My initial plan was to stay away from Grace. I had every intention of respecting her wishes. To maintain a more acquaintance-style friendship, even after our tryst. But then she walked into my party and stripped down to her bikini, as if she was asking for an invitation, and all bets were off. I tried to stay away from her. Even when I watched her walk into the house and followed her, knowing everyone would be distracted outside with the karaoke machine, all I was going to do was say a quick and simple hello. Greet a friend.

I felt like I was boring daggers into her body. Into the valley between her shoulders and the bumpy ridges of her spine. At the small mole under her collarbone, the exact spot I nipped at her skin, most likely leaving a mark. Up until the party, I was ready to erase her from my mind. Use distance as a method to move on. Out of sight, out of mind. Except she appeared right in my sight. All bare skin and flustered hands and blushed cheeks.

That's when I threw out the friend barter. A covert tit for tat she wasn't even aware of. But it seems I haven't quite discovered the lengths I'd go to spend a minute more time with her. The thing is, while I'm alarmingly attracted to her, I'll take this friend situation if that's all I'll get. Things seem to shift when I'm around her. My temples relax and my jaw loosens, and I actually have a good time. When I talk to her, I feel so engrossed, and it's like she actually listens when I talk. She doesn't just nod her head along, throwing out an occasional "yeah" or "mmh-hmm." I forget about Mr. Sheridan and corporate ladders and gopher duties. Even the sudden —and unsolicited—realization of my commitment issues slip my mind. She creates this amnesiac. An escape bubble where all the bad and terrible sit outside and I can simply enjoy her company.

So, if a friendship is all she's going to give me, I'm going to friendship the fuck out of her.

"Here you go," Cowboy Patrick says, extending the coveted set in my direction. "You're in luck. It was the last one."

I grin at him. "Thanks."

"Who is it?"

I clear my throat. All the confidence I had parking my car in a guest spot in Grace's garage and while walking up to her condo has dissolved, leaving me this helpless, nervous mess. "It's Andrew."

The locks click from the other side, and when the door swings open, Grace's wary face greets me. She's wearing my shirt again, but instead of a pair of soft pajama pants, she's wearing leggings. While she doesn't necessarily look like she's been lying in bed all day, she doesn't seem to have any plans to step outside today.

"Hi," I offer when she doesn't greet me with anything more than a skeptical look.

"What are you doing here?"

I ignore the flatness of her tone and pull the LEGO set from behind my back. Though I don't do a big fanfare of a cheesy "ta-da," my grin does enough to pull a small smile from her.

She takes the set in her hands, and she pulls her lower lip between her teeth as she taps her index finger along the side of the shiny cardboard box. "LEGOs?"

"Not just any LEGO," I correct, the both of us peering down at the picture on the box. "But roses."

When she looks up at me, her shoulder leans against the door-frame, and the sweet way she tilts her head makes me think that maybe it's working. This random ruse I thought up of to kick start our "faux"-ship into an actual friendship. She smiles an honest, genuine smile when she asks, "Is this your idea of being friends? Bringing me flowers?"

"Ah, but they don't count because they're LEGOs." I tap at the box, accentuating my point.

"And you just thought you'd drop off some LEGOs for me?"

I scoff a fake frown. "Hell no. We're building them together."

"What?" The laugh that rattles her confused voice is the wave of confidence I need to brush past her and walk into her condo. She follows me, closing and locking the door behind her. I slip off my shoes and step into her living room to see a small cozy nest of blankets, popcorn, and Buster. "I wasn't expecting company," she defends, setting the LEGO set down and folding a blanket that looks like it'd be as soft as a cloud.

"Leave it," I tell her. And I mean it. The thought of spending the day nestled in her soft, fuzzy couch with blankets to serve as extra nesting material sounds like the perfect way to spend time with a friend.

"It's fine," she assures, moving onto the popcorn bowl. It's half empty, salty crumbs lining the edges. Proof I interrupted a very lazy and relaxing Saturday morning.

I reach for it, taking it from her and placing it on her coffee table. "Just leave it. I'm not here to be impressed by your hospitality skills. I just want to build a LEGO set with my friend."

"There's that word again," she mutters under her breath, rolling her eyes and shaking her head. But she doesn't fight me on it anymore. She leaves the popcorn, and the other two blankets she had in a rumpled mess on her couch.

"So, are we going to build this baby?" I ask, picking up the LEGO set and waggling it in front of her. She opens her mouth and closes it, followed by what I can only translate as a wince or a grimace. I can't really tell because it's fleeting. But it's there. A flash moment of vacillation.

"You want a drink before we get started?" she asks, tucking away her hesitance and hiding it with a thumb pointed to her kitchen.

I pretend not to notice and answer, "Sure. I'll just have whatever you're having."

She walks away, her steps retreating to the fridge. I swoop down to one knee and greet Buster. He hadn't gotten off the couch and rushed me like last time. It seems a bit of a food coma, or rather a popcorn coma with the scattered crumbs around him, has left him a little listless.

"Hey, bud," I whisper, patting his head. His tail thumps loudly on the couch cushion at the same time he laps a warm lick to my cheek. I've always wanted a dog. I think all of my siblings did when we were growing up, but we've all yet to take the plunge and get one. James and Teeny are busy with their kids. I think Josh is busy making one (eww, gross). Maybe I can be the first one to get a dog of my own.

"He likes you." Grace reappears, two Coke cans balanced in one hand. She sets them down on the coffee table and nudges one in my direction.

"I like him too." I settle onto the ground leaning my back against the couch. Buster takes the opportunity to rest his chin on my shoulder, and I feel a soft sigh leave his lips. "I actually think he likes me a lot. Maybe more than you."

Grace laughs. "Don't flatter yourself. He likes everyone." She stoops down onto the carpet, on her knees with her butt resting on the heels of her feet.

I reach over and pat Buster's head. "Yeah but come on. He likes me the most." It's then I notice she's had her hand behind her. She moves her other hand back there, now free of the two frosty soda cans, and I see her arms slightly jostle like she's moving something around at the small of her back. "Whatchu got back there?"

A sweet head tilt is her answer. An attempt to hide her secret a little longer. Until she gives in, plopping a beaming stuffed capybara wearing a bib with the words "Get well soon" on it. She grins at me, and I pull together everything I have in me to stop myself from squeezing her into a giant bear hug.

So instead, I feign a quizzical head scratch and mockingly ask, "Wow, you shouldn't have?"

She leans forward, landing a playful slap to my shoulder. "You don't have to be an asshole."

"I'm not even sick," I argue back.

"I didn't get you anything for your birthday," she informs me, a smile slipping through her pout. "So, I got this at the hospital gift shop."

I take the grinning stuffed toy in my hands, ruminating over this gesture of hers. I've gotten various gifts throughout my life. A bottle of vodka for my twenty-first from Teeny. A refrigerator magnet from Peru from Ro and Hayley. A two-year membership to the meat of the month club from my dad just last week for my birthday. But of all the gifts I've received, this little stuffed animal more appropriate for someone recovering from an appendectomy is the best gift I've ever gotten in my entire life. "Thank you," I finally say, masking the delight in my voice with a wave of nonchalance.

"You're welcome," she responds. "And happy belated birthday."

"Thank you."

She grabs the LEGO set and jiggles it. It rattles with mischief and a peaked interest in spending the next few hours putting the roses together. "So, should we crack this bad boy open?"

CHAPTER FOURTEEN

Grace

"YOU KNOW, I've never built a LEGO set?"

Andrew's head jerks up from his freshly put-together rose stem. "Never?"

I shake my head just as I snap a petal in place, smiling proudly at my work. "Nope," I answer, holding the rose by the stem and twirling it between my index finger and thumb. That proud smile widens into a grin.

"And it looks like you're a natural."

We've been building the LEGO set for the last hour. We have a few more roses to go, and I think I'm slowing us down a bit because I'm still getting the hang of the Ikea-style of instructions, but I don't even mind. I ordered a pizza when my stomach started rumbling. I popped another bag of popcorn in the microwave, which Buster whined in front of the second I set it on the coffee table.

Andrew flips the page of the instructional booklet, a look of confusion mixed with determination on his face, and I suddenly realize I've spent the entire day at home. I woke up, changed my pajama bottoms into a pair of black leggings—my sad attempt at telling myself it means I've been a productive member of society—

took Buster out for a walk, and plopped myself on the couch as I started a *New Girl* marathon. It's my usual weekend itinerary so it shouldn't surprise me. Sometimes I choose something more enrapturing like *Law and Order: Special Victims Unit* or the *Twilight* movies. And if I'm feeling especially adventurous, I'll do some grocery shopping or take Buster to the park or the beach instead of just outside my building. But right now, with Andrew by my side as we sip on our sodas and munch on the ends of our pizza crusts, it feels like a small ray of sunshine peeking through a narrow slit in the clouds.

It feels nice to have company. A friend to spend the day with without feeling like our time is flowing through the narrow neck of an hourglass, the sand dissolving right in front of us as if to constantly tell us the day will eventually end. None of that seems to matter with Andrew. Time seems infinite.

We finally finish the last rose, and they're laid out in front of us. We both smile, appreciating our handiwork along with the few straggler pieces—"extras" as Andrew claims—and I turn to him.

"I had no idea LEGOs were this fun."

He nods in agreement. "You're talking to a LEGO master here. I made a Millennium Falcon when I was eight."

"A what?"

"Han Solo's starship?" he asks in surprise.

"Who?"

"You don't know who Han Solo is? Harrison Ford?"

"I know who Harrison Ford is," I admit. "Is that like, a nickname of his?" I can see him growing a little flustered, and I don't know whether to laugh or beg for forgiveness.

"N–no," he stutters. "It's a character he plays."

"Oh."

"But you know Princess Leia, right? Carrie Fisher with the space buns?" He does a gesture, holding his cupped hands to his ears. I want to laugh at the way his voice turns nervous and uneasy, but I refrain from causing any more distress when my lack of Han Solo knowledge already has him a little shaken.

"Oh, is that *Star Trek?*"

He winces, pinching the bridge of his nose. "Grace," he says hoarsely. "I didn't know you were this uncultured."

"I am not uncultured!" I exclaim defensively. "I'm just not a nerd."

His eyes pop open. "And I am?"

My palms face the ceiling. "I mean, yeah."

His gaze narrows, a silent stretch of a warning before he lunges for me. I squeal, jolting in the opposite direction away from him, but I'm not quick enough. He's able to grasp my hips, and his fingers pinch at my sides, eliciting another loud squeal from me.

"Andrew!" I screech. "Stop!"

"Say I'm not a nerd then," he bargains, shifting his weight so he presses me to the ground.

"No!"

Another hard pinch that has me bucking underneath him. "Say I'm not a nerd," he repeats, adding a more authoritative tone to his voice.

"Okay! Okay! I give!" I plead. "You're not a nerd."

"Now was that so hard?" He has his arms braced at my sides, and he's hovering over me. His hair hangs off his forehead, a little mussed and tousled from catching me mid-getaway. My chest heaves in deep breaths and his eyes flit down my body for a fleeting second. "You really like my shirt, huh?"

"I told you, it's soft."

His fingers move, soft and gentle strokes swiping back and forth over the soft material I can't seem to get enough of. I feel his chest expand against mine along with the rapid thumps of his heart beating. It crescendos, going wild while matching the fast beats of my own banging against my ribcage. I press my hand into his chest, pushing him off me so I can get away from the heat drifting between us. We don't need to be in this position right now. In fact, there should be a good amount of distance between us at all times. Preferably the size of a large mammal. Like a dolphin or a pony.

I push off the floor, stepping out of his grasp, and walk toward my kitchen. I get a quick glimpse of Andrew sitting on my living room floor. One knee bent where his forearm rests, a contemplative look on his face as if rewinding the last two minutes that led us to a horizontal position right where he's sitting. An uncomfortable flux of guilt and shame trickles down to my heart, making me wonder what the fuck I'm doing. Why I'm letting Andrew spend the day with me, building LEGO and eating pizza and wrestling each other to the ground. Doing shit that people in relationships do. It's so reckless. Not to mention risky while leading to this, a strong undercurrent of regret making me want to rush back and wrap my arms around him. But of course, I don't do anything of the sort. Instead, I ignore his rapt gaze narrowed at the floor and reach for my cupboards above the stove.

"What are you doing?" Andrew asks. I hear him shuffle followed by his sock cover feet padding closer to me. He's right next to me when I swipe my fingertips at the edge of the cabinet. The object I'm looking for is beyond my reach, and when Andrew looks up at the top shelf, I decide it's okay to push aside the thought of his hands on my waist and his weight pressed on top of me and ask him for help.

"Can you get that please?" I point my finger at the glass vase. It's hourglass shaped with a thick base and trumpet-style opening.

"This?" he asks, peering down at me.

I nod, and he grabs it with ease. Not while on the tips of his toes like I did but with barely any strain on his arms or legs. He hands it to me, and I walk it over to the LEGO roses on my coffee table. I'm on my knees, plucking each one by the stem and gently placing them in the vase as if they're real roses instead of made of plastic. I might as well walk the vase over to the sink when I'm done and fill it with water.

"You have to display them," I tell Andrew as he settles back down next to me. "Otherwise, they're just going to sit somewhere in a closet and collect dust."

"You are so right," he says, not bothering to hide the mocking tone in his voice. I nudge at him with my elbow, and he smirks at the same time I let out a soft, contented scoff. A little quiet banter to match the teasing we've been doing all day.

He watches me with rapt attention, a chuffed grin on his face, and he reaches for the last rose stem lying alongside a few sprigs of plastic baby's breath. He brings the vase closer to him and arranges the pieces so they look nice. The whole act, me providing the vase and him adding the finishing touches, feels so domestic and homey.

"Thank you," I say to him. With our recent history, a kiss feels expected. But we both know that's too dangerous. A hug feels more appropriate, but even that feels risky. So, I settle for a light punch to his shoulder, to which he responds with his own soft punch aimed at my arm. We both laugh. A soft, afflicted laugh filled with a gentle reminder. "I really enjoyed myself."

He reaches into his pocket, wiggling out his phone. He unlocks the screen and places the lit screen in front of me.

"Put in your number," he instructs. "So I don't have to show up unannounced next time."

I do as he says, though a part of me wants to fight him. Have a little sparring action of bickering and taunting. But I don't. Because I actually want him to have my number. Maybe next time, I can choose the activity. Put together a puzzle or play a game of Scrabble. Or have a *Twilight* marathon or do some crafts like learning how to crochet. Maybe even cook or bake something I've been wanting to try from the long list of YouTube cooking videos I've flagged. As friends, of course.

He takes his phone back. I expect him to shove it back into his pocket, but before he does, he taps away at it and opens up his camera app. He angles his phone at the bouquet of plastic roses and takes a snapshot. He takes a few, making sure to get it at the right angle and not have a single petal or stem out of focus. I watch him document our day in the form of more than our memory while shooing away that wave of guilt that starts to swell inside of me.

He smiles at me once he's satisfied with his photography work.

He looks at me with a poignant afterthought that leans just the smallest angle toward grief. I can see it hidden behind his pursed lips and the twinkle in his eyes as he says, "I really enjoyed myself too."

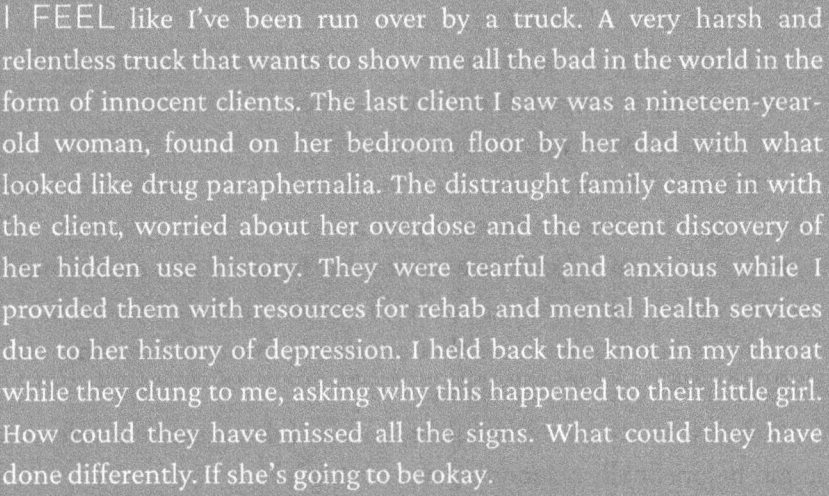

CHAPTER FIFTEEN

Grace

I FEEL like I've been run over by a truck. A very harsh and relentless truck that wants to show me all the bad in the world in the form of innocent clients. The last client I saw was a nineteen-year-old woman, found on her bedroom floor by her dad with what looked like drug paraphernalia. The distraught family came in with the client, worried about her overdose and the recent discovery of her hidden use history. They were tearful and anxious while I provided them with resources for rehab and mental health services due to her history of depression. I held back the knot in my throat while they clung to me, asking why this happened to their little girl. How could they have missed all the signs. What could they have done differently. If she's going to be okay.

I'm doing my job. Trying to keep a professional front while being as compassionate and sympathetic as possible. But sometimes, that compassion bleeds into my own heart. The images of the daughter crying in her mother's arms when she realizes she's met with concern and fear instead of reprimand causes me to imagine a child finding comfort in the one person who would move mountains for her. I left the small room to give them some privacy while knowing their journey has just begun. I tried to focus on the good. The fact that this incident didn't take her life. That both the mother and daughter understood they needed help and were willing to seek it, but I couldn't help the constant twinge in my chest thinking about this hurdle they'd have to overcome before either one sees any semblance of normalcy.

I'm sitting in the nurses' station, cradling a cup of vending machine Earl Grey tea while reviewing a chart for a patient ready to be discharged with a durable medical equipment order for a walker and shower chair. I have a few minutes before my lunch, and I'm using it to unwind and disassociate. Move on from one client to another in the hopes that I can help another person. Maybe even see a significant amount of good outweigh the bad so that the light at the end of the tunnel feels more feasible rather than this obstacle course that continues to lengthen and grow more arduous.

After a regretful sip of my tea that left my tongue seared, I'm interrupted by a completely offhand question.

"Do you know anything about catnip?"

I look up from the computer I've been scanning over. I had my pen wedged between my teeth, a very unsanitary habit I've been told by many I need to stop, and I whip it away from my face the second I see Dr. Noah's distracted face peering down at his phone screen. He has a pair of glasses on, ones that are clearly meant for reading, and he looks at me over the black rim.

I almost look over my shoulder, unsure if the question is directed at me, before finally responding with, "Catnip?"

He nods. "I just got a cat, or two cats actually, and they seem a little...overactive. I'm thinking some catnip may subdue them."

"So, you want to get them high?"

He chuckles. "Yeah, I guess so."

"Well, I'm sorry to tell you, but I am a dog person," I confess. "I believe that makes us incompatible."

An offended look crosses his face, and he removes his glasses, tucking them into the breast pocket of his scrub top. "There are plenty of people who have cats *and* dogs. In fact, my neighbor has two golden retrievers and a calico cat."

"Hmm," I hum with intrigue. The conversation suddenly feels like a metaphor about suitability and congruence. And not of the coworker dynamic but something that suddenly makes me a little uncomfortable that it's just me and him at the nurses' station.

I'm glad to see Dr. Noah adjusting well to the unit. These random questions that deviate from our regular day to day in the ER have been a welcome reprieve when I feel the day start to weigh on me. Usually, he has a bigger audience with the steady flow of nurses coming and going through the station, but it just so happens they're occupied with other matters at the moment.

"So, are these new cats, or..."

"My sister's cat just had babies, and I took two of them in." He swivels his phone screen, showing me two baby kittens with an assortment of black and white patches. "All they've done is rip up the socks in my hamper and cry all night."

I know I said I'm a dog person, but the two sets of yellowish-green eyes looking back at me makes a squeaky "aww" squeeze through my lips. Maybe I'm not as much of a dog person as I thought. Maybe, with the right feline, I can shift into a cat person and make myself and Dr. Noah less unsuited.

"And you want to medicate these poor innocent babies? Shame on you, Dr. Noah."

He smirks, taking his phone back and tucking it away in his pocket. "Don't let those sweet faces fool you. I'm down to my last pair of socks."

I laugh, and Dr. Noah does too. The two of us are caught in an innocent exchange when Betty slumps into the empty seat next to mine.

"What's so funny?" she asks, her focus on the chart she's urgently flipping through.

"Dr. Noah is dabbling in veterinary medicine."

Betty's brow shoots up, her eyes still on the chart. "I think that takes an entirely different field of study, but you know, whatever career choice you go with, we all support you, Dr. Noah."

I giggle at the same time Betty finally lifts her gaze from the chart. Her deep blue eyes dart from me to Dr. Noah who has his elbows braced on the counter. She tucks a loose strand of blonde hair behind her ear and gives me a look meant to convey a question, but I ignore it.

"Well, good luck, Dr. Noah." I stand from my seat and turn to Betty. "I'm on lunch in case you need me."

She nods, and I round the corner to leave the station. Once in the breakroom, with my freshly heated frozen dinner, I settle in for the next half hour. I'm mindlessly scrolling through my phone when it buzzes with a new message. A light snort rattles my throat when I see a new text message. From Andrew.

ANDREW

> Did we decide whether or not multiple moose are called meese?

I abandon the plastic fork in my hand that was jabbing at a sauce-covered piece of penne pasta and tap out a response.

GRACE

> I think the third round of tequila shots arrived before we came to a conclusion.

ANDREW

> But meese sounds pretty accurate, right?

GRACE

> Have you Googled it?

ANDREW

> You can't cheat!

I laugh, wondering where this sudden intrusion is coming from. But, with how entertaining my lunch break is turning out to be, it hardly feels like an intrusion at all.

GRACE

Is there a reason for this midday text interruption? Aren't you at work?

ANDREW

That's exactly why I'm texting. I need a break from my day.

GRACE

Ah, so I'm a distraction now.

ANDREW

But the best kind. The Cadillacs of distractions. A GOAT, if you will.

GRACE

Why are you talking me up? What do you want?

ANDREW

So I have to want something to compliment you?

GRACE

That's usually how it works. You want something, you talk me up. And vice versa.

ANDREW

How about just a friend needing a friend. Is that enough?

GRACE

I guess.

So, what are you up to?

My lunch grows cold in front of me, but I don't even bother to care. I've found something much more fulfilling to take up the remaining twenty-two minutes left of my lunch break.

ANDREW

I just sorted through my third bag of Sour Patch Kids.

> Did you know there are approximately sixty-
> four blue raspberry-flavored ones in
> each bag?

My face contorts with confusion.

> GRACE
>
> Why on earth are you doing that?

ANDREW

Boss's orders.

The simple two-word explanation is all I need to know how his day is pretty much going. And the knowledge that someone would task their employee with something so demeaning and belittling makes the anger and frustration inside me simmer. What grown man asks—no, demands—someone else to divvy up their candy according to color and flavor? What kind of childish person is he?

> GRACE
>
> Jeez, you weren't kidding. I'm sorry.

ANDREW

I'm sorry too.

That my boss is an eight-year-old boy.

> GRACE
>
> Anything I can do to help?

ANDREW

This? Talking to you helps.

He adds a half-smile, half-sad face emoji, and a small part of me cracks under the guilt of him having a rough day.

> GRACE
>
> How about an after-work pick-me-up?

I think about my message before adding,

GRACE

As friends, of course.

ANDREW

What did you have in mind?

GRACE

There's this new ramen bar near my house that I've been wanting to try out.

How about I order some to-go, and you can talk more shit about this juvenile boss of yours while we eat at my place.

I consider my offer. We *did* agree on this friendship thing. I'm definitely not breaking any rules by inviting him over. We'd just be having ramen while having a small venting session. And after the day I've had, I'm sure I need it just as much as he does. Suddenly, the idea of carrying everything I've been bearing during my workday home doesn't feel as daunting as it normally does. Because I'd be offloading it to someone who would sit there and listen while slurping away at his warm, savory noodles. I've finished convincing myself to stick with my invitation. To not go back on it and look forward to a night with a friend when I receive a response.

ANDREW

You've got a date.

A FRIEND date.

Just as expected, my half-eaten lunch remains unfinished by the time my break is over. I toss its remains into the trash, suddenly looking forward to dinner. A dinner *not* eating another frozen dinner like I planned.

I plan to spend the remainder of my day catching up on charting and discharge follow-ups. When I return to my desk, I find a small chocolate cake in a plastic disposable container. It's from the cafeteria, made obvious by the addition of a few coarse brown napkins, but there's the addition of a little yellow sticky note on it. I pluck up the note and read it with curiosity.

> *Your guilt trip worked. I'll try a motorized cat toy to*
> *wear them down instead. Thanks for the tip.*
> *— Noah*

Not Dr. Santos or Dr. Noah. Just Noah.

Even though I find myself rolling my eyes and shaking my head, the smile on my lips shows a far cry from vexed.

CHAPTER SIXTEEN

Andrew

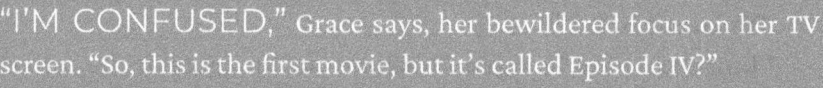

"I'M CONFUSED," Grace says, her bewildered focus on her TV screen. "So, this is the first movie, but it's called Episode IV?"

"Yes."

"And there's an Episode III, but it came out *after* this one?"

"Yes." I watch her. The way her question feels like it should be followed by a comical head scratch. Or how, no matter how stumped she seems, she can't seem to peel her eyes away from the movie.

She does this thing where she tugs at the corner of her shirt collar and hooks her chin into it before letting it fall against her chest. She's the opposite of the casual business attire that greeted me when I met her at her car. She's now a loose, more relaxed version of herself in her sweatpants and sleep shirt. Or rather, *my* shirt that she's taken full ownership of.

I noticed a small pep in her step as we walked to her door. The plastic bag containing our dinner dangled from her fingertips with a slight swinging motion, making me worry that the contents might spill over, but Grace didn't seem to care. She just grinned at me while she told me about the ice cream sandwiches she bought over the weekend. Dessert, she claimed. And now, I wish we could somehow delay it. Because after dessert, it means the night is over, and that's the last thing I want. I wish there could be some way I could freeze time. Let us live in this moment as if it were infinite.

She pokes her chopsticks at the screen. "So, you're supposed to watch it backward?"

"It wasn't on purpose," I explain. "George Lucas started the story in the middle to create an immersive experience to make it seem as if viewers were joining the story at a pivotal moment."

"You should hold a local *Star Wars* seminar," Grace jokes. She rests her chopsticks on the edge of her bowl. A bundle of noodles pools at the end, but she pauses her meal to peer sideways with a teasing upturned smirk before adding, "Why do you know so much about this?"

I shrug, poking at my own bowl of noodles. "I just liked them as a kid. The movies and figurines and all."

"You mean 'toys?'"

"Um, excuse me," I argue. "I believe 'action figure' is the correct term."

"You know, it's pretty good," she confesses. "I've never really watched these movie things, and it's pretty interesting."

I never realized how sexy it would be to find someone who would actually nerd out with me. And not even half-ass it. I mean fully nerd out without the dismissive comments or deprecatory words, writing me off as some nut job with some weird science fiction obsession. Her eyes haven't glazed over with boredom, and she hasn't requested to change it to something more fitting to her taste. And suddenly, I want to nerd out with her just the same. I want to know all the things she loves. The things she obsesses about.

"What kind of movies do you like?"

She's stirring at her noodles, and she scoops up a mouthful, chews thoughtfully, and considers my question. "I don't think I have a favorite kind of movie. I watch pretty much anything."

"But still. You should have a genre or a specific movie that you tend to gravitate to."

"I guess I used to watch a lot of rom-coms when I was younger," she explains, still a little unsure of her answer.

I nod, slurping away at my dinner.

"You know," she continues. "Like the early 2000s movies they don't make anymore."

"Like *Bridget Jones* or *Princess Diaries*?"

She drops her chopsticks and scoots her butt to face me. "What do you know about *Bridget Jones*?"

"I have a sister. Remember?" A glitch cuts into our moment. A nudge to remind us what we are on the surface. My sister's best friend. My older sister who would absolutely lose her shit if she found out about us. Her friend who happens to also be a divorcée and almost a decade older than me. Not that any of that matters to me, but I know it matters to Grace. All that superficial outer appearance shit.

She nods, letting the small snag in our dinner settle between us. "Right."

"We should watch one," I say, attempting to put us back on track, glitch and all.

"What? Like now?"

I shake my head. "No, maybe...another night."

She tilts her head, an inquisitive look of interest and curiosity on her face. The corners of her lips tilt upward. A silent demand for my intentions, no matter how innocent I make them out to be.

"What?" I ask when her eyes start to narrow.

"Do you plan on making this a frequent occurrence?"

I shrug. "I mean, we have five more movies to get through," I say, gesturing to the screen. "Plus a few more sequels and TV shows, etcetera."

"Do you not have any friends?" she asks, taking a jab at the fact that, after a long day at work, she seems to be the only friend I'm venting to. "Girlfriends?"

I ignore the intentional plural adage to the word "girlfriend" and say, "Uh, no girlfriends, but I have friends."

"Okay, then why are you here with me and not with them?"

I hesitate before answering. I don't really know why. Why I'm not planning another weekend dinner with the few friends I have so I can vent a little, maybe even ask for some advice to work through the commitment issues I've suddenly become privy to. Or even call up my brothers to see if they'd be up for a few beers. Anything for the company I'm obviously in dire need of. But when I realize the truth, I don't really want to hide it. So, I tell her. "I guess...you're just a little easier to talk to."

"How so?"

"To be honest, the friends I have live kind of far," I explain. "It takes some pre-planning for us to have dinner. And when we do, it's never anything like—"

"An impromptu *Star Wars* marathon?"

I smirk. "Yeah."

"What about James and Josh?"

"I mean, yeah, I hang out with them, but I don't really talk to them..."

"You mean they don't get a special *Star Wars* course curriculum like I do? I feel so special."

"Shut up," I tease. It's a brief reprieve, making a topic that's normally heavy a little lighter. A little easier to bear. So I continue. "But they know how much stress my work has been causing me."

"And?"

"They don't get why I'm still there after four years, taking my boss's bullshit every day," I tell her. Her smile falls, and I can feel her give me her full attention. Her presence is so extant and heedful, I know whatever I tell her, it'll be lasered into her memory. That's what she's doing right now. Making herself the focal point of my woes, letting me tumble them out so she can hold them with me. "They also tell me I'm still young. That I have a long life ahead of me and I shouldn't worry so much when I don't even have a family to worry about."

"So, they sort of brush you off."

I nod.

She rolls her tongue over her bottom lip before clamping her teeth over it. I can see her mull over the words, making sure to get out the right ones. "Look, I don't want to add fuel to the fire, but why don't you quit?"

"I—"

"And I know you said you're paying your dues or whatever, but is it really worth it? And let's say you move on up and get promoted or whatever it is your goals are. Is this really what you want to be doing?"

I stay quiet, contemplating her words. They don't sound disparaging or condescending. They sound like they come from a place of true concern. She isn't trying to brush me off, trying to move on from a conversation she has no interest in. She really wants to know.

"Do you like your job?" I ask, segueing into what drives her to get out of bed every morning. I know I'm answering her question with a question, but maybe this way I can find some answers for myself.

"I do," she admits somewhat apologetically. "It's not an easy job, but it's incredibly rewarding. I've seen the compassion drain out of a lot of the people around me, and it gets really hard sometimes. Just today, I saw this college kid almost die from an accidental overdose, and her mom was so scared and worried. It's not easy being exposed to all the trauma we see in the ER, but I'm hoping I'm making somewhat of a difference."

I never knew work could bleed into your soul like it does for Grace. I don't go to work to change the world or even make a difference. I go to work to make a living. Working to live. But not Grace. She's out here trying to do something with her life. Make an impact.

"That's very admirable of you," I comment earnestly.

She smiles. "I'm just doing my job."

"Yet, compared to mine, your job makes you look like a superhero."

A shy flush blooms across her cheeks, and she averts her gaze to her food, now just the soupy, oily remains of our dinner. The movie plays in the background as I catch flashing images of blasters shooting red, fiery beams through gusts of smoke. We watch as I answer the sporadic bouts of questions that slip through Grace's lips. I watch as her keen focus on the movie turns into near reverie. All while the conversation about life and work and meaning falls into the shadows, letting it sit there until we can pick it up later. Maybe in small doses to make it easier to reconcile. Hopefully on another night sitting on her living room floor in front of takeout and some movie we can obsess over just the same.

As the night wears on , Grace stifles a yawn and sinks into the soft cushions of her couch, sweetly patting her hand in the empty spot next to her. Though it's a weeknight, and we both have work the next day, she doesn't seem to be in any hurry to kick me out, even as the credits start to roll on the TV and her eyes blink heavily, a reminder that it's probably time to call it a night. Luckily, we still have dessert to get to.

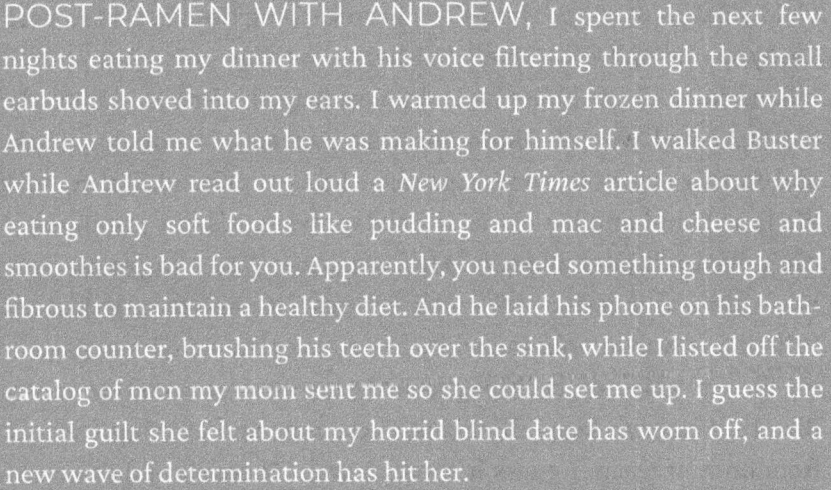

CHAPTER SEVENTEEN
Grace

POST-RAMEN WITH ANDREW, I spent the next few nights eating my dinner with his voice filtering through the small earbuds shoved into my ears. I warmed up my frozen dinner while Andrew told me what he was making for himself. I walked Buster while Andrew read out loud a *New York Times* article about why eating only soft foods like pudding and mac and cheese and smoothies is bad for you. Apparently, you need something tough and fibrous to maintain a healthy diet. And he laid his phone on his bathroom counter, brushing his teeth over the sink, while I listed off the catalog of men my mom sent me so she could set me up. I guess the initial guilt she felt about my horrid blind date has worn off, and a new wave of determination has hit her.

I'd be lying if I said Andrew's reaction didn't provide a moment of entertainment. It started off with baffled and toothpaste foam-filled *"what?"* which transitioned into some uncontrolled stuttering and a cough I imagine was expelled into a fist. Then the follow-up questions came. If I was going to meet these suitors and whether or not I thought Raymond, who my mom met in the checkout line at Trader Joe's, would have a wife list similar to the one Harold had. I laughed it off while secretly noting the discomfort I could feel through the speaker.

As my weeknights became consumed with Andrew, I realized by the time I received a text message from Teeny on Friday night, I had gone the whole week without talking to her. No meme or Instagram reel referencing an inside joke only she and I would get. No random pictures of a vanilla latte with a request for a mid-week coffee date. Not even a link to a cute dress or purse I found online with a plea crying, "Please tell me I can't afford this," knowing she'd only respond with, "You deserve it."

So, when the purpose of her message is to ask me if I'm free for brunch Saturday morning, I couldn't say no. Not that I don't want to see her, but as soon as I read her message—a sweet and simple "brunch?" followed by a grinning-smiley face emoji—I became vividly aware of all the things I've been keeping from her. I can't tell Teeny about Andrew. I can't tell her about this guy I just started talking to or all the hours he and I have logged over the phone. The old-fashioned way of communicating instead of through a back-and-forth game of text message tag. I have to pretend like my love life is as bland and listless as it's always been. It's not just Teeny. I can't even tell Jade about it. My own sister. The two people who have always invested so much interest in my dating history. Whether it was to hold me while I cried over my failed marriage or to clink a glass of champagne over my first rebound after my divorce. I have to keep all of this, these new and exciting feelings, from both of them. I guess it's just as well. There shouldn't be any new, exciting feelings to tell anyway. Andrew and I are friends. *Secret* friends. There's nothing to tell, and it should stay that way. Spreading gossip over these confusing thoughts would definitely complicate things.

I feel like a damn metronome, swaying back and forth with this annoying synchronous rhythm. I'm caught up in these wishy-washy feelings, going back and forth from feeling giddy and excited every time my phone buzzes with a new message from Andrew and quickly smothering it the second I remember he's just a friend. I'm giving myself whiplash.

But right now, I have to smother whatever waffling thoughts keep popping up in my head. I'm meeting Teeny in five minutes at a quaint mom-and-pop diner called Marie's in Del Mar Heights. Teeny brought me here for the first time about a year ago. I ordered a plate of hazelnut waffles, and I haven't been able to stay away since. I walk in, and just as I tell the hostess it'll be a table for two and step aside to wait for Teeny, my phone buzzes in my hand.

"Hey," I say, answering Teeny's call. "I just got here. It's just a few minutes for a table.

"Grace, I'm so sorry, but it's going to be a while until I make it there," she says. She sounds distracted and worried.

"What happened?"

"I don't know," she answers. "Sadie just called me and said her ankle rolled during morning practice, and now she can't walk."

"Oh, poor baby."

She sighs through the slight drum of traffic while talking through the speaker system in her car. "I told her not to join track. That girl is so clumsy. Organized sports is not her thing."

I laugh at her small attempt at a joke at Sadie's expense, knowing she's doing it to snuff the worry rattling her nerves. "Is she okay?"

"Yeah, I think so, but she wants me to come get her," she explains. "And I called Everett. He was playing pickleball with Josh. He's meeting me at her school."

"Pickleball?"

"Yeah, it's their new thing," she explains. "I told him it's probably nothing, but he wouldn't hear it."

"Okay, do you want me to wait for you then?"

"If you don't mind. If anything, I'll just pick her up and bring her with me. If that's okay."

"Of course," I answer. "I'm sure she's fine. You know, kids injure themselves like this all the time."

"Yeah. I'm so sorry."

"No, it's fine. Don't worry about it."

I hang up, a little disappointed while hoping this scare turns out to be nothing.

"I'll show you to your table."

The kind hostess smiles at me, a small stack of menus held to her chest, while the expectant look on her face urges me to follow her. I follow her despite the change in plans and once I'm at the small booth, I turn to her and apologetically say, "It'll be a few more minutes for my friend can get here."

"Okay," she answers with a nod. "I'll let your server know."

I open one of the menus, though I already know what I'm going to order. I consider adding a side of bacon or breakfast potatoes at the same time a server breezes by, placing two identical glasses of water in front of me. I order a cup of coffee, still waiting for the other half of my party, and continue my perusal of the menu.

It's when I'm adding two packets of sugar to my coffee that I look up only to be greeted by the last person I thought I'd run into here.

"Hey." Andrew smiles down at me, his arms out in the open for all of humanity to see in his cutoff sleeves. And of course, those tattoos licking down his strained biceps. He's wearing gym shorts and sneakers, the epitome of a lazy Saturday morning and someone who most likely spends his free time working out.

"Hi," I respond. "What are you doing here?"

"Just ordering some waffles to go."

"Waffles?" My brow shoots up, and I purse my lips into an approving smile.

"Yeah, why?" he asks. He slips into the seat across from me, settling into the cushioned seat with a pleased smile as if he plans to stay. His eyes gleam in the light streaming in from the window right next to us. They look even more caramel-colored than usual, swirling in pools of brown with small flecks of bronze and copper. They curve when he smiles, the brown turning warmer under the shadows now cast from his brow.

"What?" I respond, feigning innocence. Our eyes lock in a flickering pause filled with silent smiles. I can feel the taunt in the playful bounce of his brows and the slick way he rolls the tip of his tongue across his perfect teeth.

"What do you mean 'what?'" he goads. "What's that smile?"

"I just find it funny that you like the waffles here too," I tell him honestly.

"You like them?"

I nod. "Of course."

"And you just thought to come here all alone to enjoy a plate."

The reminder that Teeny is going to be here soon makes my smile drop. I look around, suddenly worried she's watching us from an obscure corner like some lurker or spy. Maybe she's even recording us to use as some video evidence to confront me later. "Um, actually, no. I'm meeting Teeny."

His smile drops too. "Oh."

"Yeah," I say, unable to hide the disappointment in my voice. "She's just running a little late. I guess Sadie hurt herself at track practice, so..." A stretch of silence sits between us while the happy chatter of diners surrounds us, along with the clatter of silverware against ceramic plates. I see Andrew hesitate, obviously deciding if he should leave or stay, when I tell him, "But you can stay until she gets here. You know, we aren't breaking any rules by running into each other."

"Yeah."

While I didn't expect some celebratory-level excitement, I also didn't expect the indifferent way he responds in a glum voice. It seems we've reached an impasse. No matter what, it's not an ideal situation. While we're sitting here, pretending there's nothing going on, it doesn't make it any better that we're hiding all of this from Teeny. As soon as she walks into this diner, I have to act as if I don't know his favorite ice cream flavor is cookies and cream and that he knows how much I hate having my bare feet touch hard flooring.

"Did you want to order a coffee or something?" Just as I ask my question, my phone buzzes on the table. We both look at it with an air of anticipation while the question hangs above us. Is it Teeny?

Sure enough, when I flip my phone over, I see a new message from Teeny.

TEENY

> I have to take Sadie to the emergency room. Looks like she may have sprained it, but I want to make sure she didn't break anything. Sorry but looks like I'm going to have to take a rain check on brunch. I promise I'll make it up to you!

I should be worried. I should feel awful that my best friend will be spending all morning, and most likely a portion of her afternoon, in a packed emergency room. And I do. If I had some magical powers to telepathically heal Sadie's ankle, I'd do it in a heartbeat. But then I see the man in front of me, looking at me from the edge of his seat with his gaze flitting from the phone in my hand to me.

"Is that Teeny? She almost here?"

I shake my head. "She's actually heading to the emergency room with Sadie. I guess she hurt herself pretty badly." I look at Andrew just in time to catch one of his eyebrows tilting upward in amusement. "She's not coming."

"Oh?"

I narrow my eyes at his piqued interest. A silent rebuke. "You're not worried about your niece?"

"I'm sure she's in good hands," he answers calmly. A little too calmly. "My sister knows what she's doing."

I shake my head, doing a horrible job of hiding the smile creeping up my face. "You're horrible."

"Sure," he agrees, adding a small, uninterested shrug. "But aside from being horrible, there's a small silver lining to it."

"Yeah? And what's that?"

"I don't have to leave."

I lean back in my seat, crossing my arms, and shoot him with a flat look. It's not fair how he plays this game, using a moment of misfortune to two people we both care deeply for and this chance meeting to spend some so-called innocent time together. He's playing dirty, using his rooks and bishops while I'm barely learning how to use my pawns. "You aren't playing fair, Andrew."

He leans back too, his posture mirroring mine. "I'm taking what I can get," he corrects. "You know, beggars can't be choosers."

"And you're the beggar in this situation?"

"Feels like it sometimes."

"You're being dramatic."

"Am I?" he asks, goading. "Or am I realizing the cost of a secret friendship?"

"Are you saying it's not worth it?"

"It's worth every penny I don't have," he clarifies. "So I have to be...frugal."

I don't know how our conversation veered left, completely off track and onto a complicated path full of metaphors and nuances. I'm sitting on my side of the booth, deciphering his words, and I suddenly realize the ways our friendship has cost me. My sanity, my morals, quite possibly my friendship with Teeny. I start to wonder what it's cost him.

"Andr—"

"So, are we going to order some waffles?" His pushy interruption is sudden but welcomed. A moment for us to both disregard the gregarious expenditure we've suddenly become so vividly aware of and enjoy what I came for.

CHAPTER EIGHTEEN
Andrew

SHE'S RIGHT. I'm not playing fair. I'm using every advantage, every cheap shot, I have in my back pocket. But look at where it's led us. This is the first time we're admitting even the slightest murmurings of what lies under this friendship. Giving it a moment to breathe and be noticed before we continue to pretend this is the extent of whatever *this* is.

I've been getting so good at snuffing away the impulse to stroke her cheek or reach for her hand, this feels completely foreign. It's not like I *want* to think about these things, wondering what it would feel like if I ran my thumb down her side, how she would react to such a sensitive touch. It goes against our agreement. One I have every intention of upholding. Like a damn scout leader. But every time I see Grace's smile or hear her voice or even get an impromptu text message from her lighting up my phone, my restraint withers. It chips away, bit by bit.

For now, breakfast seems like a good distraction. An effective way to focus on our friendship so what we've managed to forge doesn't crumble due to impulsive mistakes. Like a plate of warm hazelnut waffles drizzled in syrup with a side of potatoes to fill our stomachs while I pretend I don't know what she feels like under me.

Or on top of me. Waffles and a frosty round of Coke floats. To be safe, I ordered two. I didn't suggest sharing one, two straws dunked into the same vat of soda and cream, making it that much more intimate and date-like. Kind of like that cartoon with the two dogs sharing a plate of spaghetti while an Italian chef with a thick mustache serenades them.

"So?"

Grace's tongue darts out, swiping away at a small bit of foam that made it to the corner of her mouth. "Oh my god."

My mouth splits into a grin. "What did I tell you?"

"Why haven't I tried these before?" She looks up at me, a look bordering indignance and betrayal on her face. "I've been coming here for over a year, and this is the first time I've ever had one."

"Aren't you glad you ran into me today?"

"Mh-hmm," she manages to hum in between sips.

We continue to eat, sawing away at the waffle sitting between us. That one we decided to share. It's actually the most practical choice considering an order is enough to feed a small family. One with two small children who most likely prefers mushed peas and not particularly in a famished state, but still. Grace chomps on a sliver of crispy bacon in between bites, enjoying a little bit of the indulgence I encouraged her to order when she couldn't decide between that and a side of breakfast potatoes. We have a decent spread between us. Enough to keep us busy for a while, which was the secret Machiavellian plan I concocted as the server took our order. Something to occupy the next few hours if by some chance she throws an excuse to leave.

"Do you know about this place because of Teeny? Or..."

She nods, chewing through her food. She does that thing most people do to be polite, covering her mouth with her hand and answering me with a small bulge to one cheek. "She brought me here about a year ago. I think right around the time she and Everett got married."

"We've actually been coming here since I was a kid," I tell her.

"Really?" She gives me the sweetest smile, the straw from her Coke float dangling from the corner of her mouth. Her head tilts to the side as if she's attempting to picture me with my awful bowl haircut and gap-toothed smile, making a mess of my meal.

"Is it hard to imagine?"

"A little," she admits. She taps her finger against her fork and adds, "You sitting here with these utensils too big for your small mouth and some crayons for your paper menu."

I chuckle, ducking my head. "It was surely a sight I'm willing to forget."

"No," she disputes, dragging out the single-syllable word. "It must've been adorable."

"My mom would probably be the only one who would agree with you."

"Maybe," she teasingly agrees. "But still. It sounds nice."

"What about you and your parents? Any fond memories?"

"Nothing that sticks out," she answers. "Just the usual. Like weekend trips to the beach or the zoo."

"Are they close by?"

"My sister lives kind of close by," she tells me. "Up near San Clemente. And my parents too."

"So, no stories your mom loves embarrassing you with?"

She shakes her head through a giggle. "I don't think so..."

"Come on," I protest. "They don't have *any* stories? Like you being chased by a chicken or some awkward school performance where you made a complete fool of yourself."

Her eyes round with intrigue. "A chicken?"

"We have family in Montana," I explain. "Apparently I don't do well on farms. Or with poultry."

She cackles a laugh. Her entire face lights up, and I genuinely can't remember the last time I enjoyed someone's company this much. I cross my arms in front of me, resting my elbows on the table, and observe her in what seems like a new light. She's not in her pajamas, hair a bundled mess on the top of her head wearing my oversized shirt. She's not in her tight work clothes, all wound up in wool or linen. She's wearing a large hoodie despite the fact that it's the middle of summer. It's a light sand color with long sleeves she has bunched up to her forearms. Not a hint of makeup touches her face, and her hair is braided along the back with the end slung over her shoulder. She looks sweet and uncomplicated. Like she's just here to enjoy my company while we spend the next few hours pouring our hearts to each other. Just like last time. Only this time it'll be over sweet diner food and not tequila.

"More coffee?"

"Sure," Grace tells our server as she brings the carafe to Grace's mug. When she moves to my mug, silently asking if I'd like to be topped off, I nod and thank her.

Grace lifts her coffee mug to her lips, ditching her Coke float, and takes a careful sip. When she sets it down, she looks at me with a sideways tilt of her head and an inquisitive nibble on her lower lip.

"Can I ask you something personal?"

I set down my fork, linking my fingers in front of me. A silent gesture of my undivided attention. "Sure."

"Why no girlfriends?"

"What?"

She looks away, seeming suddenly shy after asking such a bold question. But I want to know what she means. What the intention of her question is and why such details of my personal life matter to her.

"Never mind," she responds, shrugging a shoulder as if she didn't really mean to ask the question in the first place.

"No," I press. "Why did you ask me that?"

"Because...you're my friend," she finally answers, her eyes focused on a perfectly cut triangular piece of waffle doused in a puddle of syrup. "And, as your friend, I guess I want to know."

"Friend," I mutter under my breath.

"Huh?"

"Nothing." If it weren't for the figurative elephant that seems to come and go as it pleases, I'd probably believe her. I'd take her answer at face value and ignore the swirl of assumptions making my brain murky.

She drops the fork in her hand and looks at me. She gives me her full attention, a soft amicable look of unreserved interest in her eyes. "So, are you going to answer my question?"

"I guess..." I huff a sigh. The difficulty finding the right words clog up my throat. Talking about *Star Wars* or my hatred for my boss or even a detailed, step-by-step LEGO set instructional feels easy. But discussing in fine detail what my fears and doubts are? That's going to require a more gracious approach. And Grace's gentle, affectionate smile seems to do the trick. "It's a little scary."

"What is?"

"Being that vulnerable with someone," I tell her. "Letting someone into my life. It's a big deal."

She nods in agreement.

"When you make a commitment to someone and create a life they're naturally a part of, it isn't something that should be taken lightly," I continue. "And I don't think I'll ever find anyone who I can fully let in that way. To be completely myself without hiding a single part of me. Who can I do that with?"

More silence from her, and I can see how my words are making the gears churn in her head.

"You know, my friends recently told me about my commitment issues, and I'm beginning to see what they mean."

"I mean, it is a big deal," she says in agreement. "Committing to someone and being open and vulnerable. And if it doesn't work out, you end up feeling like such a failure." The look in her eyes is vacant. This failure we're talking about set her down in a place she's familiar with. Somewhere she once walked away from and has no plans to walk back to.

"Have you ever...felt that vulnerable with anyone?" I ask carefully.

"Yeah," she answers with a sad smile. "My husband."

A stretch of silence settles between us, and it feels like a small moment of grief. A paused in memoriam for a slice of her life that was all happiness and hope, now only reminding her of what could have been and what never will be.

"Can I ask you something personal?" I say, throwing back the same question she asked me. "Since we're friends and all."

She smirks. "Sure."

"What happened?"

She pauses again, this time, the quiet feeling heavy and burdensome. "You know," she starts. "In the beginning, it was really good. We were young and still figuring ourselves out, but we were doing it together. The thought of growing old with him made me happy. It was good until..."

"It wasn't?"

She nods. "He gradually turned into someone entirely different. Our needs and wants started to change, and it was like I married a complete stranger, not the Frankie I fell in love with."

I nod. "So, you decided to end things?"

"It was a little more complicated than that," she says. Her shoulders slump, searching through the right words to tell me her story. "I convinced him to move to California after we were in Phoenix for so long. We stayed there because of his work and to be close to his family, but I wanted to be close to my own family. And Teeny was here too. For a while, I thought it was just a phase because he was settling into his work and getting used to the change. I thought we'd get through it, I just needed to be patient, and he'd go back to being my Frankie. And then he didn't. I realized we wanted different things. I wanted to have a family, while he wanted to live this lavish life filled with expensive cars and designer clothes. Kids weren't part of that plan. It was my fault."

"How?" I ask with a furrowed brow.

"When we got engaged, we decided that we didn't want kids," she explains. "We just felt kids weren't for us, and we were happy with our freedom. And then I got this itch. He was working a lot, and

I got a case of baby fever. My sister was talking about having kids, I saw Teeny with Sadie, and I couldn't help but wonder if I was missing out on something."

"He didn't?"

"No," she tells me with an added punch of certitude. "And after I brought it up, he started treating me differently. Going days without talking to me, and when he did, it was to rub in my face that I was backing out on our deal."

"What deal? Your marriage?"

"Wanting kids," she answers. "In the end, I just couldn't take it anymore. I hated being treated like an unwanted guest in my own home. Always walking around on eggshells, worried he'd lash out his anger at me. So I asked for a divorce."

"Wow."

She nods. "If you ask him now what happened, he'd probably blame it all on me. And I guess, he'd probably be right."

"That doesn't seem fair."

"Is it fair that I changed my mind after we already discussed it?"

"Grace, all you asked for was a future," I argue. "You were still his wife. You exchanged vows. I think that overshadows any promise like kids."

"So you think he should've just had a bunch of kids he didn't even want?"

"Who says he wouldn't want them once they're born?"

"And who says he *would* want them?" she rebuts. "Would it be better that he resents me?"

"I mean, no, but..."

"I wouldn't have won either way," she confesses, waving the white flag she already flung at her ex-husband. "I already lost the second he decided it was all an excuse to treat me like an enemy instead of a partner."

It's like she's had this discussion a thousand times. She has a comeback for every scenario, and they're all good, viable responses. Ones I can't argue with. As much as I think she was essentially placed between a rock and a hard place, she has a point. And that's the problem with letting someone in. There's no win-win situation. At the end of it all, everyone loses. Hearts are broken, lives are ruined, and souls are crushed.

"So, commitment and marriage and that jazz," I say. "It's as scary as it sounds?"

She smiles a downcast smile that looks sadder than a tear-ridden pout. "Even scarier."

"Then I shouldn't even try?" I ask. As lighthearted as I try to sound, I can't help the slight melancholy in my voice. I don't even know why. It's not like marriage or the ostentatious display of soul-mates is something I was striving for or even on the horizon for me. But to learn it may all be some kind of weird propaganda to uphold the sanctity of weddings and vows and all that "'til death do us part" bullshit feels a little heartbreaking. Like learning your favorite celebrity is actually an asshole in person.

"No," she argues with true sincerity.

"No?"

"As bad as the divorce was, I don't regret it," she continues. "I loved being with someone and knowing I was going to grow old with him. To have someone to come home to, eat dinner with, watch movies with.

"I was never really...alone."

"And now you are?"

"My ex-husband's grandpa passed away about two years after we got married," she says after a pause. It's an unexpected segue, but I listen. "He was devastated. He'd lost his grandma about eight months before, and he was still grieving her death.

"We got to the grave site, and I saw his grandfather was being buried right next to his wife. They were going to spend their afterlife together. And I thought how grateful I was that I would be buried next to Frankie. I'd have someone to spend my afterlife with. I wouldn't be stacked under a bunch of coffins in some single section of the cemetery. I'd be with my other half."

"But then you got divorced." I don't mean to say it out loud, don't mean to spotlight what she views as a flaw or vice of her character. Her plans didn't pan out the way she thought, and it changed more than her marital status. It changed her opinion of herself into some spinster destined for solitude.

"But then I got divorced," she repeats. "So, I guess it's either let my mom continue to set me up on these blind dates, or, you know, check out the single side of the cemetery for future prospects."

I laugh a soft, morose chuckle which Grace mirrors, and then she starts picking at the skin lining her thumbnail. "I don't know," she murmurs. "I'm starting to wonder if maybe it's me..."

Her voice trails at the same time she ducks her head. Whether in shame or because the conversation took a turn she wasn't expecting, I'm not sure. And it doesn't really matter. But when her gaze remains solemn with it zoned in on her lap, I no longer fight the urge to comfort her.

She notices me when I slide in next to her. She looks a little surprised—a little confused—but when I gently place my hand on top of hers, she doesn't pull away.

"There's nothing wrong with you, Grace."

She scoffs. Her weak protest falls short when her lips turn wobbly. "I wish it was that easy," she whispers. "Someone telling me there's nothing wrong with me and just accepting it and believing it. But thank you."

I realize then that, while she's clearly made it out of her divorce alive, the aftereffects of it have left her broken. She really believes it was her doing. She blames her hopes and dreams for the downfall of her marriage. And it's completely unfair.

I don't try to argue with her. Debating and discussing something she so strongly holds on to, no matter how incorrect she is, isn't what she needs right now. What she needs in this bubble of heartache and regret is for me to be her friend. What we've already established we are. But with her small hand hidden under mine, I wish I could do more. I wish I could show her all the ways she's completely enough. Sit her down for an hour-long PowerPoint presentation with a laser pointer in my hand, running down a long bullet list of things that make her the perfect partner. No, not just a perfect partner, but a perfect person. Someone who's kind and funny and considerate. Someone who sits through a two-hour-long movie she has zero interest in just because she wants to know about the things I love. Someone who guards her friendship with my sister because she's basically family at this point.

"You're welcome," I tell her. My head tilts a little toward her, but her temple sitting mere millimeters away from my ear doesn't meet. I hover over her, letting myself imagine what it would feel like to hold her. And before we know it, our coffee is refilled once again. We ignore the fact that what we have is starting to blur. Calling her a friend feels inaccurate. To the point I feel we need to create a brand new word to describe our natural affinity for each other. Something that aligns more closely to words like want and need and adore.

"Teeny said Sadie didn't break anything," she informs me, looking at the new message on her phone. "They're getting ready to be discharged."

"That's good."

"Yeah."

She'd just finished telling me about her trip to Japan last year, her mouth nearly overflowing with saliva as she talked about all the food. While the interruption from Teeny comes with good news, I know what's next. It's a reminder. A little alarm chirping in the form of a text. Time's up. And just as predicted, Grace sets her phone down and searches the restaurant, looking to flag down our server. I can see how her eyes have already changed, returning back to a place where our friendship will always have a curtain pulled in front of it.

We settle the check—a swift battle that I win with wits and speed—and walk out in silence. I press my hand to her lower back, an impulse I don't mean to act on but can't help.

"Thanks for breakfast. And the company. And conversation."

We're standing in front of her car, each holding a Styrofoam box of leftovers. It's finally time to say goodbye, and I don't want to.

"Yeah, well if you ever want a...friend, you know who to call."

"Yeah," she says softly.

I watch as she gets in her car and drives off, leaving behind a small divot in my chest. It's barely noticeable now, but I can imagine how much bigger it will get with every goodbye.

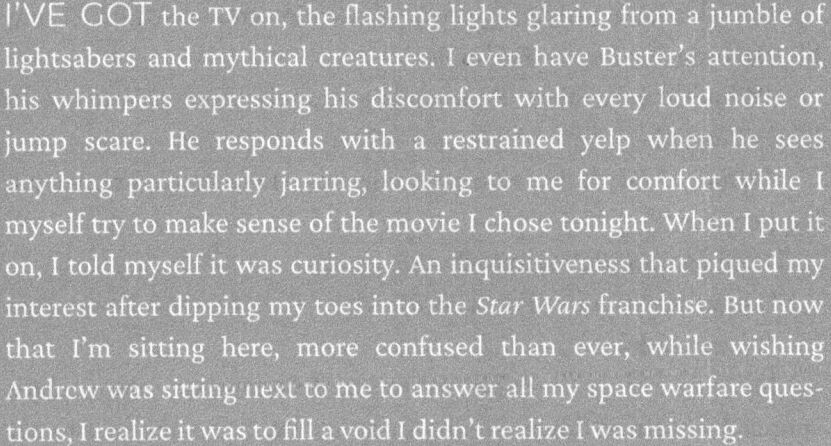

CHAPTER NINETEEN
Grace

I'VE GOT the TV on, the flashing lights glaring from a jumble of lightsabers and mythical creatures. I even have Buster's attention, his whimpers expressing his discomfort with every loud noise or jump scare. He responds with a restrained yelp when he sees anything particularly jarring, looking to me for comfort while I myself try to make sense of the movie I chose tonight. When I put it on, I told myself it was curiosity. An inquisitiveness that piqued my interest after dipping my toes into the *Star Wars* franchise. But now that I'm sitting here, more confused than ever, while wishing Andrew was sitting next to me to answer all my space warfare questions, I realize it was to fill a void I didn't realize I was missing.

After our diner run-in, we've been texting here and there. Random messages throughout the day. Sometimes things like what my theories are as my interest for the *Star Wars* saga grows. But mainly more trivial topics, like what toppings I like on my pizza or if I prefer Pepsi or Coke. When he asked if I've been watering my LEGO roses and giving them enough sunlight, I responded with a sassy "duh" and a picture of a perfectly thriving bouquet of plastic red roses.

My brow furrows as I continue to watch the movie, the scenes unfolding while the questions grow and brew in my head. I start to wonder if I made a mistake by watching it without Andrew's commentary. I don't have someone in my ear, explaining all the finer details that are invisible to the untrained eye. With the thought of Andrew fresh in my mind, I pry out my phone from between the couch cushions and prepare to tap out a new message.

> Is this thing between Leia and Han an enemies-to-lovers type of situation?

Instead of a response via text, my phone starts buzzing in my hand.

"Hello?"

"Why are you asking me about Leia and Han Solo?"

I smirk a laugh, resisting the urge to taunt and tease him. "I may be watching *The Empire Strikes Back*."

"What?" he exclaims. He sounds genuinely shocked, and even a little offended.

"What?" I ask flatly, feigning innocence. "I wanted to know what happens next."

"And you couldn't tell me?"

"I have to ask your permission?"

"I mean...yes?"

My giggle rings through my room, drowning out the galactic sounds I've turned down coming from my TV. "I'll make sure to ask you before watching the next one."

"I think the sound of your laugh just saved my day," he comments with an exhausted exhale that sounds pained and tense.

I ignore the pang hitting me straight in the chest. Like a weighted medicine ball thrown at me full force. I should feel pleased that my laugh alone lifted his spirits, but I can't let his morose mood go unnoticed. "What are you doing?"

"I'm at work."

I pull the phone away from my ear to check the time on the

screen. It's close to nine. "This late? I thought you'd be home by now."

"I thought so too, but my boss had bigger plans for me."

"I'm sorry this is how you're spending your Friday night."

"Eh," he says, brushing off my sympathy. "I'll live." After a short pause, one that dismisses the stress I can almost see resting on his shoulders, he adds, "What part are you at?"

"Leia and Han just got handed over to Vader by Lando."

"*Ooohh*," he comments, maintaining a mysterious air to his response, but it only eggs on my curiosity.

"Why? What happens?"

"Just watch."

"No, tell me! Is it bad?"

"Let's just say it's one of the greatest cinematic plot twists of all time."

"Really? Bigger than *The Sixth Sense*?"

"What happens in *The Sixth Sense*?"

"You've never seen it?"

"No."

"Well, I'm not going to spoil it for you," I tell him with playful defiance. "I don't like this Lando guy, by the way," I add. "I don't trust him."

He laughs. "Just keep watching. You might change your mind."

"I shall prepare some popcorn then." I press pause on the TV and walk over the kitchen with my phone still pressed to my ear. "Do you need to get back to your work?"

"I'm good," he answers. "I'm really not doing anything productive right now. Although I did make a hanger out of a paperclip."

"To...hang some Barbie clothes on?"

"Huh, that's actually not a bad idea. I wonder if Mattel will want a patent. I bet I could make millions off something like that."

"A little ambitious of you, don't you think?" I toss a flat bag of unpopped popcorn into the microwave and press some buttons before it buzzes to life.

"I'm just thinking of ways to make my first million without putting all my eggs into the lotto ticket in my wallet," he explains with an exhausted rasp to his voice. "Maybe a game-changing idea like Barbie hangers could be my ticket out."

"And you say you're not doing anything productive." The popcorn finishes popping, and I still have my phone pressed to my ear.

I take the bag at the edges, pinching the corners as the steam slowly filters through the narrow slit. I curl my feet under my thighs, settling into a comfortable nest of throw blankets and Buster's warmth. I'm wearing Andrew's shirt again. It's run through a few cycles in the laundry, so his scent has washed off, but it's still soft and warm whenever I slip it on. For some reason, it still seems to have a small part of him. As if his smile and playfulness has been stitched into the fibers.

"Okay," I finally say, adjusting the popcorn so it's out of Buster's reach. "I've got my popcorn. I'm ready to continue." I hear creaking, some movement like he's settling in, and a groan that usually comes with a long stretch.

"And I've got a cup of coffee and a half-eaten Snickers bar."

I press play on the TV and sit back with Andrew's voice pressed to my ear. We share moments of silence, relishing in the fact that we're enjoying each other's company without really being in each other's company. I blurt out questions and comments—or rather, outbursts—of protest as the movie plays out. And when the moment he so covertly brought up happens, I gasp.

"Oh my god."

"Right?"

"Oh my god," I repeat, my voice a quiet whisper. "So what happens next?"

"I don't know," he tells me, the sound of his voice full of pride. "You have to watch the next one to find out."

CHAPTER TWENTY

Grace

"WHEN DID YOU START BUILDING LEGO?"

Jade's index finger pokes at the hard plastic petals, shifting the bouquet sitting on my kitchen counter with an inquisitive brow turned squiggly and twisted.

"Just recently," I tell her innocently. "I thought it would be a fun hobby."

"They look cute." Avery juts her chubby fist where her mom's hand is still curiously examining my new hobby when she adds a little oomph to her touch, knocking a petal off one of the roses. "Oh, no, Avery," Jade warns. "Let's be gentle with Auntie Gracie's flowers."

I hide the concern in my face with a fond smile while wondering whether or not I kept the instructional manual for the LEGO set. Luckily, Jade is able to snap the broken piece back on with expertise. No harm, no foul. But to be safe, I tug the vase closer to tuck it further onto the counter out of reach of probing hands.

I slide the coffee I brewed in my Keurig over to her, scooting the sugar bowl and the Coffee-mate creamer closer to her reach as well. She does the smart thing by handing me Avery while she prepares her coffee, making sure Avery's active fingers don't hook over the lip and make a mess.

"So, did you get the list of suitors Mom sent you?" Her question is joined by an enticing bounce in her brow with her focus on stirring in just the right number of sugar scoops.

"How do you know about that?"

"She sent them to me too." She lifts her mug to her lips, taking a loud sip.

"Why?"

"I think she wants me to help vet them," she answers with a shrug. "Especially after the last one."

"I guess she really does feel bad."

"Honestly, she felt horrible," Jade admits.

"Really?"

She nods. "She called me every night for a week, asking me if I thought you were mad at her—"

"I wasn't mad at her."

"I know. And I told her that, but she was also worried that she might end up shoving the wrong men onto you."

"I mean, she kind of did."

"She's trying not to make the same mistake."

"Yeah." I stare down at my own cup of coffee while Avery grows squirmy in my arms. Who knew my love life would be such a hot topic among my family? I thought I was past all that drama. If not temporarily while I was married, then at least now I've grown way past the age of becoming a matchmaking spectacle.

Avery makes grabby hands toward a lone banana sitting on my counter, and Jade reaches for it. Avery demands to return to her mom, who also happens to be holding her appetizing snack, and I hand her over. The banana starts to slowly turn into mush in Avery's hands but at least it keeps her out of reach of the hot coffee. Or the LEGO. Maybe I need to be more mindful about making my condo more childproof.

"Don't worry too much about it," Jade says, consoling my sudden downcast mood while doing the motherly multitasking act of wiping banana remains off Avery's fingers. "The guilt is obviously going away, or she wouldn't be sending you all those prospects."

I chuckle. "Did you see Rick?"

"The guy with the soul patch?"

I cackle a hard belly laugh. "Oh my god, Jade. Why would she think I'd find him attractive?"

"I told her not him," she adds, her face turning a bright shade of pink with her own breathless laughter. "But she said he's a dog person, and he would love Buster."

"Aw," I croon. "That's actually really sweet."

"I know."

"See? She's trying," Jade says, her tone lighter with more genuine reassurance creeping into her rosy cheeks. "And who knows? Maybe she'll help you find the right man, and you can give Avery here a little cousin to play with."

I roll my eyes. "Oh, please."

"What? I thought that's what you wanted?" She walks over to the small playpen she set up for Avery and plops her in the middle with a rattly toy.

"Yeah, I do. But..."

"But what?"

"I don't know, Jade," I say, my defeated, dejected voice sounding like I'm on the edge of giving up. "Maybe I'm just not meant for that life."

"What are you talking about?"

"Come on. I'm not getting any younger, and I don't think I should be thinking about having kids at this age or—"

"Grace." Her interruption cuts into the self-deprecating rant I've practically memorized at this point. "There's nothing wrong with you. You're going to meet someone and have a family like you've always wanted. You're going to get your happily ever after."

Andrew said the same words to me. An unexpected protest, proving he's on my side. He's the one standing behind me with a large poster board sign, the words "This woman is perfect" etched in bold block letters. It's such a new feeling. Having someone root for me instead of pointing out my flaws, cheering me on in spite of my shortcomings. To Andrew, I have no shortcomings. I'm just me, and I'm perfect the way I am to him.

"So are you going to give Rick a call?"

My middle finger runs a mindless path along the handle of my mug. Up and down, up and down while I consider Jade's question. "I don't know. Maybe?"

"Maybe?"

I shrug, adding a little gusto to my answer. "I...don't think I need Mom to find my dates for me."

"Really?" Confusion and curiosity dance on Jade's face until the moment I can see a thought cross her mind. "Are you finding your own dates?"

Though no words leave my lips, the room rattles with a loud slurp. I look at Jade over the lip of my tipped coffee mug.

"Are you dating someone?"

"No!" My response is like a knee jerk. Like drawing my hand back with a hiss and shaking the sting from the hot end of my curling iron. I mean, it's absurd. Why would she even ask that? "Why would you ask that?"

"Because you're acting all mysterious and purposefully vague," she answers. "You can't say Mom doesn't need to find you dates and not explain why. I mean, besides the obvious meddling and helicopter mom behavior."

I consider all the reasons for my sudden inscrutable confession. It could possibly be I've met my wits end, and the barrage of dating profiles my mom has curated is getting to be too much. Or maybe—more likely—because the constant text messaging, the back-and-forth banter, between myself and Andrew has led into the same hazy territory as my answer.

I'd forgotten our friendship has been the whole point of it all. Every text message, every phone call, every shared meal and movie. It's become all blurred, leaving me disoriented like I've got on a pair of Coke-bottle glasses. But he can't be the reason my mom can finally give up her efforts. He can't. We're all wrong for each other. We want completely different things. His commitment issues and my hunt for monogamy go together as well as oil and water. Or mixing bleach and ammonia, a somewhat disastrous—and deadly, some might say—combination.

"It's because of her meddling," I finally answer Jade. I draw out the nasal "-ing" ending to stamp my point. But it comes out a little whiny, and Jade nods with a frown that isn't a frown at all but more of a statement. An obviously sarcastic "sure, whatever you say" frown.

"All right," she says. A lazily thrown white towel as she accepts my answer for what it is: a cover. Good thing she doesn't know for what. "But if...you know, there was something going on, you'd tell me, right?"

"Of course." It's amazing how easily the lie slips from my lips. No, it's not a lie. It's a...fib. I've taken the lie and stretched it out a little bit. Just until I can mold it back into the truth, whatever that may be.

And I know just the way to do it.

"But you know, maybe as long as you're there to vet for me, it really can't hurt."

"Yeah?"

I nod. "Yeah. Only if you—"

"I will take my job as the official date vetter-er very, very serious-ly." She has her palm facing me next to her solemn face with the three middle fingers held up.

"What is that?"

"It's the Girl Scout symbol of honor and duty. Oh, and sisterhood."

The straight faces we attempt to hold start to twist into loud snorts and cackles. Our sudden outburst startles Avery in her playpen, and she lets out a tearful wail.

"Oh, Mommy and Auntie Gracie are sorry. We didn't mean to scare you."

Jade rushes to an upset Avery's side, and I'm left with a fresh, new moxie. A hearty determination to clear all the murky, confusing things that make my friendship with Andrew questionable territory. He's my friend. That's all. Clear as day. There's nothing confusing about that.

Maybe I will give Rick a call.

CHAPTER TWENTY-ONE
Andrew

MY EYES BURN as the glare from the computer screen seems to singe my retinas. I've been staring at the same reports for the past two hours, and the numbers and letters are starting to turn into a columned sequence of ones and zeros like I'm in the Matrix or something. I lean back in my chair, letting the squeaky hinges from the springs below me echo off the walls of the empty office. The empty office even I shouldn't be occupying on a quiet weekend afternoon. But I am. Surrounded by the occasional whirring of the vacuum being pushed around by the weekend cleaning crew and the coming and going of Olive as she brings me binders from Mr. Sheridan's office.

"You really don't have to be here," I tell Olive as she dumps a stack of papers on my desk.

"And leave you here all alone on a Saturday? What kind of friend would that make me?" She turns to perch her hip on the edge of my cubicle and adds, "Plus, after what happened last time, I think it's best you at least have a partner in crime if you're going to get yourself into trouble."

"What trouble?"

"Mr. Sheridan's scotch? You spilling it in his office?"

My eyes round into large saucers. "You knew it was me?"

"Of course I did! Who do you think covered for you?"

"How did you cover for me?"

She shrugs innocently. "I may have planted the seed that the security guard was checking on some suspicious noise that came from his office," she explains. "And maybe that he was doing his nightly rounds."

"Oh my god," I exclaim with quiet realization. "You saved my ass. I mean, I'm sorry the security guard—"

"Scott," Olive interrupts, a smug smile adding a little salt to my long-healed injury, making it soften with guilt.

"Uh, yeah, Scott. Hopefully he didn't get into too much trouble."

"He didn't," she assures me. "Just a small slap on the wrist. Nothing to keep you up at night."

"Yeah, well, you know...thanks."

She taps my shoulder, proving her point that I may drown in this office without her or even cause another accident. This time with no scapegoat. "Don't mention it. Just maybe grab me a Coke from the vending machine."

"Consider it done." I smirk, but my smile fades quickly as soon as Olive steps away, and I see how thick the stack she set down is. A deep, disgruntled groan is all I can manage to greet it with. "Fuck," I mutter under my breath. "I need a break."

"Go get some air," Olive calls, tapping away at her phone from an unoccupied desk two cubicles down. She has her own makeshift workstation going, and I notice how she settles in the same way I've cocooned myself in my own cubicle, surrounded by loosely strewn trash and a few pens and highlighters. I guess we're going to be here for a while.

"Yeah," I tell her, scooting my chair back. "I'll go grab you that Coke."

"Okay," she answers, her voice sounding far-off with her shoulders hunched and her head hanging between her shoulders.

I reach for my phone as I wait for the elevator, waiting patiently as the numbers ascend to the twenty-seventh floor while I look through my messages. The last one in there is a back-and-forth thread between myself and Grace. She ended up watching *Return of the Jedi* last night with either her phone on speaker or pressed to her ear. Either way, it felt as if I was watching it with her. Me with my memory and her with it playing live in front of her. My last message to her—sent this morning as I was sitting at a red light—was an inquisitive one, asking when she was going to continue her apparent *Star Wars* marathon now that she's invested so much of her time. She responded with a vague "wouldn't you like to know." A complete non-answer that left room for some flirting and maybe an invitation. But of course, I sent back an unenthused like-button option which turned into the disappointing demise of our back and forth. Not the outcome I hoped for.

Is there a way to sound nonchalant over text without seeming rude or cold? I was going for chill and easygoing, hoping to smother some of the overzealous enthusiasm rattling my insides. Hopefully without adding an unconvincing "or whatever" to the end of each message. But how the hell am I supposed to play it cool? She's watching *Star Wars*. The damn movies that were the centerpiece of my childhood. I had to snuff out every single urge to leave my office last night to dash over to her place and slump right into her couch cushions to watch them with her. And that's just the tip of the iceberg. I can't even begin to address the other less savory thoughts swimming through my head. Like ones that involve me and her and her couch with us in a more horizontal position. Hopefully with fewer clothes and me on top—No! Jesus fucking Christ.

Look, I know what we agreed on. I get it. A friendship. That's what we're meant to be. That's what we established. *Friends*. The thought makes a scoff and an intolerant eye roll tumble out of me. It doesn't matter if I think it's a harebrained approach to salvaging a post-hookup relationship. Slapping such a cursory title between us when it feels like something the complete opposite. At least, it didn't *feel* cursory until Grace started showing me this completely enrapturing side of her. The Grace who builds LEGO and watches my favorite movies and willingly tries foods I like. The Grace who's so easy to be around, who can hold a conversation, who can make me fucking laugh like I've never laughed before.

We just seem to constantly jibe. And the way all the parts of our likes and dislikes seem to click into place feels significant. How the little details that individually don't really mean anything, but when thrown together, it's heavy and monumental. It's a chemistry that can't be forged or developed. It's natural. In the way soft moss likes shady, moist conditions. Things have to adapt and orient for moss to thrive, and that's exactly how it is with me and Grace. Things just... align. And as they align, everything feels perfect. But it's the defects that are hard to ignore. The ones we tend to pick at and focus on. Defects lead to obstacles, which in turn lead to drawbacks. Dilemmas. Headaches. Ones we can't take back and ignore, turning into something even more consequential like resentment and broken hearts.

For now, I push aside those defects. I ignore them and cover them up with the more aesthetically pleasing attributes keeping us glued to our phones. For the next text message or emoji or GIF or even the occasional phone call. I'm channeling my attention to Grace and me and the fascia of a friendship that's grown stronger over the weeks. Friends. Since that's what we decided to call each other, I'm going to friend the fuck out of her.

"Hello?" Grace answers on the first ring. I step into the elevator with my chin ducked toward my chest, a hand in my pocket, and a smirk answering Grace's easy voice, ready to head down to the sixth floor where the breakroom and the vending machines are.

"Hi." My voice comes out loose and relaxed, the complete opposite of the tension pulling my shoulders taut just minutes ago.

"I was just going to call you."

I grin. "You were?"

"Yeah," she answers. But then she stays silent, and I take it as my cue to pry. To dig deeper and see if there was a purpose to her planned yet thwarted call.

"Just because, or..."

"I was going to watch another movie tonight, and I thought maybe you'd want to join me. I can order a pizza?"

"Oh..." I do a mental calculation along with a rundown of how long I'd be able to survive off boxed macaroni and cheese and canned soup if I quit my job now. Maybe I can sell my car—and a kidney—to pay my rent for a few months. Anything as long as I get to leave work right this second. My plans to slam my resignation on my boss's desk and have him walk into it first thing Monday morning are interrupted by the harsh reminder of what it would feel like to get around via bicycle. The man I'd be in Grace's eyes locking a chain to a bike rack when I go to the store or to get coffee or to Grace's condo. Add the imagery of me in a helmet and the insult-to-injury effect would probably maim me for good.

The lack of enthusiasm and my non-answer translate as hesitation, and Grace catches on.

"Or, not," she quickly retracts, making me want to kick myself in the ass. "If you have plans, it's fine—"

"No, Grace. It's not that," I try to explain. How perfect would it be if I could sustain off thin air and grass and the biggest worry holding me hostage would be how I like my grass, straight from the source or plated with a glass of lemonade? "I'm working all day."

"Oh." There's a wave of relief plaited in the single-syllable word, and I don't know how to fully interpret that. "That's fine. I guess another time then."

"Yeah."

"So, are you at work right now?" she casually asks.

"Yup," I answer bitterly. "And most likely tomorrow."

"So the whole damn weekend. Is that even legal?"

"I don't think the law stands in the way of my boss's demands."

"I'm sorry."

"Yeah, well," I answer, brushing off her sincerity with nothing more than dejection. "Are you still going to watch the movie without me?" I make it to the breakroom and beeline for the vending machines. I wedge my phone between my shoulder and ear and reach for my wallet.

"Of course!" she exclaims. Her voice shifts into indignation, though it's dripping with playful sarcasm, and it manages to put a smile on my face. "You can't expect me to put it on hold just because of you."

"And here I thought you actually cared about me."

"I'm sorry, Andrew. You thought wrong." The loud clunk of the Coke can hitting the bottom rings through the phone, and Grace asks, "What's that noise?"

"I made a trip to the vending machines, and I'm deciding if I should get a bag of Doritos or a small can of Pringles for lunch."

"That's your lunch?"

"Yup."

"No way."

"Unfortunately, yes way."

"You have to have real food," she comments. "Let me bring you something."

"Here?"

"Yeah," she answers assertively. "What are you in the mood for?"

"Grace, you don't have to do that," I start to argue, though seeing her on a random Saturday when I'm having one of the worst weekends of my life might significantly lift my spirits. "I can just get something when I get off."

"No, you need real food. Not some vending machine crap," she argues. "I'm leaving right now, so unless you're going to make me do some light stalking, just send me the address."

I sigh. "Okay."

"And you have two minutes while I put on my shoes to decide what you want. Or else I'm making the final call and bringing you ramen."

CHAPTER TWENTY-TWO
Andrew

GRACE

My nerves start jumping into overdrive. The scatter of crumbs and trash on my desk catches my attention, and I swipe it away. Mainly on the floor with the exception of the few bigger scraps being haphazardly shoved into the small waste bin under my desk. I attempt to straighten the mess on my desk but give up immediately when I realize how hopeless that is.

The second Grace said ramen, my mouth started to pool with saliva. The argument, though it was gratuitous, died on the tip of my tongue. Not only did the craving for ramen start to thicken, but my insides started to churn with hunger and excitement. The second I hung up with her, I laid out a plan. We'll have lunch, shoot the shit while we eat—pillow-talk style—and then maybe she can just sit next to me while I get some more work done. Nothing romantic or suggestive, just company. Specifically, Grace's company.

I hear the elevator ding followed by soft footsteps hitting the carpeted floor. I stand from my desk and do one of those half-jogging, half-speed walking motions, attempting to reel in my overzealous energy but doing a terrible job of it. The rampant beating in my heart picks up as I watch her round the corner. She's wearing leggings paired with tennis shoes, topped with a chunky open cardigan that looks cozy and warm over some kind of athletic top that stops high above her midsection. She has a plastic bag dangling from her fingers, and the scent of something savory and appetizing hits the air around me.

"Hi."

"Hey." I grin at her, unable to smother my foolishly wide grin. Gone is the glum mood that hovered above me when I had to turn down her invitation. In its place is this cheerful ray of sunshine that could power me through the rest of my workday without a peep of a complaint from my lips.

I take the food from her and lead the way to my cubicle. There's a lone chip bag sitting on the corner of my desk, I missed along with a paper cup with about half of my coffee still in it. Her eyes scan over the remnants of my very quick snack break and her lips twist to one side.

"What did I say about a proper lunch?" she asks, pinching the Doritos bag between her index finger and thumb. She rattles it and the remaining crumbs rattle inside, reminding me about her concern over my lunch habits.

"I got hungry," I answer with an innocent shrug.

She eyes me with judgment, though a coltish tilt at the corners of her lips shows how little threat lies behind her steely demeanor. She turns to open the plastic bag and gingerly removes two plastic bowls. "Ramen," she announces, opening the lids and letting out the appetizing scent of miso, pork belly, and green onions. "Just like I promised." My stomach chooses that moment to embarrass the shit out of me and grumble loudly.

Grace looks at me with wide eyes, and I can almost see the muscles in her jaw fight the laugh creeping up her face.

"I guess those chips weren't as satisfying as I hoped," I sheepishly confess.

She gives in, giving me a full giggle. She reaches out and squeezes my forearm. A reassuring touch that dissipates the embarrassment from my very vocal stomach. She grabs a pair of chopsticks and hands them to me. "Eat. Before it gets cold."

I walk over to the cubicle next to mine. Craig's cubicle is a lot neater than mine. Sticky notes sit at the corner of his metal mesh desk organizer—each stack the canary yellow kind—with exactly four retractable gel pens, all black ink. A stapler and tape dispenser are lined up along the far edge as if he measured the number of millimeters between his office supplies and the rounded corner of his desk. And, of course, there's a chair that's just as impeccable as his space with a cushioned bottom and back support. Rumor has it, Craig threatened a workers' comp claim if he didn't get the chair he asked for. I wheel it over to my cubicle, reminding myself to tuck it back under his desk exactly the way I found it, and pat the seat, gesturing for Grace to sit.

"I get the fancy chair?" she comments, a little taken aback by my gentlemanly deed.

"Of course," I answer. "What kind of host would I be if I didn't consider your comfort?"

She leans back, rocking back and forth while testing out her seat's quality and comfort. After one more squeaky lean backward and an approving nod, she picks up her own set of chopsticks.

I settle into my chair. The one with minimal back support and about an inch too low for my comfort due to a broken lever. I perch my ankle over my knee as she faces me, and we both start poking away at our ramen bowls. We eat mostly in silence with the mix of our slurping and quiet chewing until Grace's curiosity has her roaming over the work on my desk.

"So, what do all these numbers mean?" She pokes her finger at a colorful pie chart, Sentry Investments written in its old, outdated font across the top. It's smudged with a few coffee stains and what looks like ketchup or marinara, and I know the few pages underneath it in the binder are probably just as equally grubby.

"Well, if you look past the dried sauce and questionable liquids, it's all just a jumble of statistical data from two years ago," I explain. "My boss is having us go over it. We're adding more recent data and creating new charts. It's a lot of tedious work and time-consuming."

"Hmm," she responds, her eyes still searching over the jumble of colors and numbers. "Sounds a little..."

"Boring?"

"Intimidating."

I smirk, twirling my chopsticks around my noodles. A diversion tactic at the mention that what I do can be intimidating in the least. "I don't know about intimidating," I say to the steam rising above my food.

"Well, it's intimidating to me."

We sit in silence for a moment longer. The noodles in our bowls dwindle down, leaving behind the appetizing oily broth I'm ready to slurp down. Grace seems to be enjoying her food just as much. I walk over to Olive's desk at the reception area where I know she stores a few bottles of water and take two before returning to Grace's side. I extend a bottle to her.

"Thirsty?"

"Thank you."

We both move in synchrony as we uncap our respective drinks, and the soft guzzle is followed by thirst quenching gulps as we peer at each other over the plastic edges of the bottles.

"So," I say, cutting into our silence with an airy curiosity. "What did you think about the movie?"

She slams her bottle onto the desk, a splash of water sloshing onto the same paper that's already stained with other various food items. "Oh, shit," she exclaims. She reaches for a napkin and starts dabbing at her little mess. "Sorry."

"It's fine," I assure her. "I'm sure a little water isn't going to ruin it." I gesture at the other spills and splatters made by my boss to prove my point. "But you were saying?"

"Oh my god," she states with zeal. "You got me hooked."

"Yeah?" I ask through a thoroughly tickled laugh. "So you're going to continue your little movie marathon?"

"Yup," she answers with a smug nod. "I already got some candles laid out in my living room and a bottle of Riesling chilling in my fridge. I may even whip up a batch of brownies."

My brow shoots up to my hairline. "Wow, wine and dessert. Who are you trying to get to put out?"

"Hayden Christensen." Her eyes take on a far-off look, and her chest rises and falls with a soft sigh.

A tug of jealousy turns my insides a shade of green, and I start to wonder if it'll seep through my pores, and I'll end up looking like Kermit the Frog or Gumby. But I keep my emotions in check and take another sip of my water, nodding in agreement.

"But aside from hot villains with a six-pack and daddy issues, I really didn't think I'd enjoy it so much," she adds. "You know, my brother-in-law loves all those science fiction movies and whatnot, and he's the one always telling my sister to watch the movies with him. She just always brushed it off as his weird nerdy obsession. I think I may have to tell her she's wrong."

"I like this brother-in-law of yours."

"You'd like him," she points out with a sweet smile. "Jade and Trevor have been married for eight years, and they're actual soul-mates. He's a great dad too. Just amazing with Avery. You know, you two would actually get along really well."

When Grace talks about the things she loves, her eyes twinkle. There's a shift that rolls through her whole body easing the tension in her shoulders. And it's contagious. It's enough to make the daunting pile of work look like a small speck, enough for me to ignore it completely as if it were all some small menial task, like taking out the trash or checking the mail. I want to sit here and listen to her talk about everything. About her sister's baby and the rest of her family. About all the little details she loved most about the movie, aside from Hayden Christensen and his physique. About all the things that have been occupying her brain as of late. Like her favorite song or album she's been listening to. Or what she plans on watching next after she's done with the other *Star Wars* movies. If she wants me to watch whatever is on her queue next with her like she asked me to, or if she prefers to watch them on her own and fill me in like she is now. Though I'd prefer the former, I want to know all the little musings and thoughts in her head in any way I can.

"How old is their baby?" I ask, letting our conversation trickle in small drips so it can last longer.

"Avery's almost nine months." She pauses to tap away at her phone and angles the screen in my direction. "They're at the children's museum today," she explains, showing off an adorable video of little Avery slapping her chubby hands at a puddle of water in a plastic plaything meant for innocent water play. She lets out a happy squeal, and we both smile.

"Ah, so she's at that really cute age where she can't walk yet so she stays out of trouble and doesn't talk back to you."

"Yeah," she answers with a laugh. "How do you know so much about the cute baby stage?"

"I have two nieces, remember?"

She nods. "I remember." She smiles a smile that's all covert yet wholesome.

"What?"

"What," she responds.

"What's that smile?"

She shakes her head. "Just that...you and Sophia. You two looked really cute playing in the pool at Teeny's house."

I try to stir up something playful, even a little risqué. But then I choose not to. I'm enjoying this warm, mellow tone we've set. It feels like a set of open arms, and I want to wrap the both of us inside a tight hold where we don't have to think of all the things working against us. Like the fact that Grace coming here to my place of work pushes the boundaries of this friendship we've forged. Or that I want to hold on to her a little longer. Take up more of her time and keep asking her questions and demanding more deep, relevant answers.

I'm about to ask her another question. A vaster inquiry that requires thought and debate, when we're interrupted by Olive.

"Hey," she huffs, perching herself over the wall of my cubicle. "Did you—oh, I'm sorry. I didn't know you had company." Her gaze shifts to Grace, the cheerful affection on her face dropping as soon as she sees the scattered mess of our lunch in front of us.

"Olive, this is Grace," I tell her, gesturing a hand in Grace's direction. "Grace, this is Olive. Another Sentry Investments inmate being held hostage on a Saturday. Except she's here voluntarily so I'm not here all by my lonesome."

Olive chuckles a laugh that sounds overdone with a sloppy slap to my shoulder. "I'm glad you're enjoying my company."

My brow furrows wondering where in that small introduction it sounded like I've been particularly enjoying her company before peering over at Grace. The air between us suddenly feels taut and tension filled. She looks uneasy and embarrassed. Like she's been caught doing something she isn't supposed to, and it's making her look a little nervous.

"Are those my waters?" Olive asks, an accusing finger directed at the half-empty water bottles.

"Yeah," I answer uncomfortably, reminding myself she's told me many times the stash is there for whenever I need it. "We got a little thirsty. But I'll pay you for the bottles I took."

"Oh," she responds. "That's fine." Her answer doesn't sound fine at all.

Olive brusquely moves around the wall separating us, forcing Grace to scoot her chair back a few inches. It's like a harsh metal cleave cut into this moment that felt precarious and vulnerable to begin with. Olive reaches over my lap to sift through a stack of binders, looking for a specific one. The way she moves about, it looks as if she's done this a hundred times. Like this is just as much her workspace as it is mine. And I guess it kind of is considering the number of times she stops by my cubicle to vent or offer me a mid-workday treat, but right now, the last thing I want is for her to emanate a "my cubicle is your cubicle" vibe when I just want it to be me and Grace.

"Uh, is there something you're looking for?"

"Yeah," she says, her shoulder invasively nudging into mine. "I thought I left the reports from last September in here. It's the binder with the orange and red tabs."

"It's right here," I announce, reaching under my desk for the binder she's looking for.

"You're a lifesaver," she informs me, her fingers playfully rustling up my hair. A gesture that's completely foreign between us. I almost ask her why she did that when Grace places the lid back on her plastic to-go bowl that's barely halfway done. I settle for an awkwardly flustered laugh in the hopes that I can find a way to get Olive to leave and give us our fragile privacy back.

"I think I'm going to get going," Grace announces. She stands from her seat, swiping away at my desk to erase all evidence of her visit. Paper wrappers are tossed in my waste bin, spilled soup is wiped away, and her little tote bag she brought with her is already hooked over her shoulder.

"You didn't even finish your ramen."

A tight smile that doesn't quite reach her eyes causes her jaw to set, and I can't help but notice how unbearable this goodbye feels. Like it's ambiguous and I don't know when I'll see her again, if ever.

"It's fine," she tells me, her voice subdued and void of all the playfulness it carried a minute ago. "I wasn't that hungry anyway."

Before I can convince her to stay a few more minutes, she turns and walks away.

"Is she your friend?"

I look at Olive. The innocence in her face could get her out of a traffic violation. "Yeah," I tell her. "Something like that."

CHAPTER TWENTY-THREE

Grace

I'M SO FUCKING STUPID. I don't even know what possessed me to offer to bring Andrew lunch. Like I'm some kept woman fetching her man his next meal and waiting at his beck and call. We're just friends. Friends don't ditch their entire day at the drop of a hat to bring lunch like they were summoned only as a thoughtless ruse to spend time with them. And they definitely don't cancel plans with their sister in hopes to, what? Get laid? Because that wasn't what was going to happen today. Then why did I do that? Why did I call Jade the second I decided I was going to bring Andrew some ramen to let her know I was going to have to take a rain check on our trip to the children's museum with Avery.

I reach my car, my hands fumbling with my keys, and my phone buzzes in my bag. A short single buzz indicating a text message. I can bet the pack of unopened gum and the twenty-dollar bill I have roaming around in there it's Andrew. I should just ignore it. Maybe covertly silence it and put it on Do Not Disturb mode for the rest of the day without sneaking a glance at what is most likely to be a clueless text message.

I, of course, do nothing of the sort because curiosity is my biggest weakness. So is hope. Hope he'll tell me to come back, maybe even beg. Hope he'll ask me why I left so suddenly. Hope he'll tell me the cute office friend who sabotaged our lunch is just a coworker and not someone who seems to be showing him a keen interest in more things than just being his colleague.

I huff a sigh and reach for my phone. Just as suspected, it's Andrew. Some of that irritation—with a wavering scrap of anger—melts, and I wonder if I'm being too harsh.

ANDREW
Thanks for lunch.

There goes that hope, flitting away as the regret settles in my gut, and the irritation returns tenfold. It sits right alongside all the coulda-shoulda-woulda moments replaying in my head. I should be eating an overpriced hot dog at the children's museum and buying Avery a bubble gun or a stuffed bear from the gift shop. Not riddled with embarrassment and shame.

Too frustrated to go home and simmer, I set about running some errands. More things I put off because I planned to bring Andrew lunch. I'm about to pull out of my parking spot and head to the grocery store to pick up some apples and yogurt when my phone rings through the speaker in my car. Teeny's name lights up the screen on my panel, a welcome reprieve from a particular someone I'd prefer not to hear from for the rest of the day.

"Hey, Teeny," I call as I exit the lot. I try to snuff away my dejected tone, not wanting to bring up the cause of my current sulky mood. Especially since it's because of her baby brother.

"What are you up to?"

"I was just going to the store to stock up on a few things. What's up?"

"Nothing," she answers. "I was just wondering if you wanted to hang out. Everett's out of town for some work thing, and Sadie's with Leo for the weekend. So, it's just me for the night."

"Sure," I say, considering her offer for barely a second. A night with Teeny to distract me from what I practically ran away from sounds like just the thing I need. As long as I don't have to even *think* about Andrew.

"You want to have dinner at my place? We can do takeout."

More takeout. I just hope this has a completely different outcome from my last takeout run. Something more amicable and gratifying. "Sure. I'll see you in a few hours."

No matter how many times I walk into Teeny's mansion, I'll never get used to the sheer size of it. We're sitting at her dining table, the chandelier hanging above us creating a kaleidoscopic effect with the light reflecting off it. It's dark, but I know just outside the large glass wall sits a stunning infinity-edge swimming pool. The same pool I ogled Andrew in with his short swim trunks and glistening skin dripping with chlorinated water. What a fool I was.

"You want another bottle of the white or something else?"

"I'll take a Perrier if you have any."

She nods, scooting out of her chair to walk into her kitchen to her fridge. We've been picking at the sushi rolls I brought over for dinner while she supplied the wine. The litter of trash along with two wine-glasses and a finished bottle of Riesling has collected over the last hour we've gabbed and laughed. I've forgotten, or at least temporarily dismissed, my afternoon with Andrew. The reminder of his bubbly office girlfriend and the staggering realization that Andrew and I would make as much sense as trying to mix two immiscible liquids has been dulled by a full stomach and a low humming buzz. My head feels clear and free from all the muddled thoughts Andrew put there with his tattoos and beckoning silver chain. I'm ready to move on from all of it. I want to wash it all away with a can of refreshing mineral water and resume my life. My dull, boring life full of awkward blind dates and frozen dinners.

Teeny disappears into the large pantry in her kitchen. While I'm waiting for her to come back, I hear my phone buzz a few times in my purse. It's out of my reach, which is an intentional choice. A diversionary tactic so I'm not bothered or distracted—or quite possibly tempted—but when the incessant buzzing becomes urgent, I huff a sigh and walk over to my purse. It could be my parents or Jade, and the thought that my family might be trying to reach me causes me to give in. When I dig out my phone and find that it's the exact person who I'd been planning on avoiding, my mood immediately sours. Four text messages and two missed calls. All from Andrew.

> **ANDREW**
>
> Hey, you left so suddenly. Did you make it home okay?
>
> I'm about to have another bag of chips for dinner. Kinda miss you.
>
> Can you at least let me know you made it home okay?
>
> Did I do something to piss you off?

I'm about to chuck my phone back in my bag when another text message comes through. The tone of it is darker, more insistent and intense.

> **ANDREW**
>
> Grace. Seriously. Text me back. Let me know you're alive.

As much as I'd like to continue this one-sided conversation and make him suffer a little longer, a small niggling part of me feels bad for making Andrew worry. One more message can't hurt. Just to let him know I'm still in one piece. And then I can wash my hands of him. No more jumbled, messy friendships and confusing lunch dates.

> I'm alive. Don't bother yourself with worrying about me.

It's curt and dismissive, and I'm sure confusing as hell. But a petty part of me doesn't even care. I want him to feel bad. I want him to feel just a pinch of the irritation and regret I feel. I hate that I feel so damn stupid and embarrassed, and I want him to feel just as upset.

ANDREW

Grace. Come on. What's going on? Are you mad at me?

> No. I don't even know why you're texting me. I thought you had to work.

What the hell am I doing? I'm egging him on, that's what I'm doing. Showing him how deeply he's crawled under my skin when that was probably never his intention. I need to chuck my phone into Teeny's fancy pool.

ANDREW

I do. But when you never texted me back, I got worried.

> Like I said, I'm fine. So just worry about your work and your friend.

I regret it the second I sent it. I sound jealous and bitter, which I'm absolutely not. And I don't even know what possessed me to say something like that. Forget Teeny's pool, her garbage disposal sounds like the more appropriate place for the ticking time bomb in my hand.

ANDREW

Are you talking about Olive?

> I don't care what her name is. Just leave me be and concern yourself with what you have going on at work.

ANDREW

> Grace. I'm coming over right now.

> I'm not even at home.

ANDREW

> Where are you?

> I'm having dinner with Teeny.

I purposefully leave out the minor details of my exact whereabouts. All he needs to know is I'm busy, and he's interrupting a completely relaxing night with my best friend.

I'm about to tap out another message to him. Something equally flippant yet purposeful so we can end this conversation, but I stop short when Teeny's phone buzzes on the dining room table. Teeny rushes out of the pantry, places a cold Perrier on the counter from the small drink fridge she has in there, and answers her phone.

I return my attention to my phone, trying to figure out how to stop this redundant back and forth when Teeny's words catch my attention.

"I'm at home. Why?" I look up at her. She has a confused furrow cutting between her brows and one hand is braced to her hip. "I'm just having dinner with Grace." Another pause as her puzzled scowl deepens. "Okay. I'll have to look for it."

She hangs up, and instead of sitting back down, she heads to her stairs while calling over her shoulder, "Hold on. I'll be right back."

I've forgotten all about my message to Andrew, and by the looks of it, so has he. I don't bother sending him anything else. It seems I've made my point, and he's leaving me alone for the night. Good.

A sudden pang hits my chest. It's unexpected, and it feels a little like disappointment. Was it so easy for him to give up? Was this Olive woman so much more important that he's waving a white flag and throwing in the towel just so he can go and spend more time with her? How low do I sit on his totem pole of priorities? Probably right around the bottom below slutty swim trunks and LEGO. And several notches below his "work wife."

Whatever. I shouldn't be concerning myself with stupid shit like this. I'm a grown woman. I'm getting myself tangled up in something I have zero business getting gnarled in. I'm relieved I've gotten out of it before things got messy. I don't do messy. I've done messy my whole life. I'm done with messy.

I open my can of Perrier and continue eating my sushi with Teeny occupied upstairs. I wait it out a few more minutes until I start to grow curious. Who could have called with such a demanding request that it interrupted our dinner? I stand from my seat and follow the sounds of rustling. I finally find her in one of the four upstairs rooms. It's Everett's office with a large mahogany desk and an expansive computer setup that scares me just looking at it. There's a picture of Teeny in a silver rectangular frame sitting on the desk, all bright and shiny, and she's hunched over one of the drawers, rifling through a stack of papers.

"What are you looking for?"

She huffs. "Andrew said he left his credit card here and that it should be in Everett's desk."

My body freezes at the sound of Andrew's name. "Oh," I manage to squeeze through my lips.

"I tried calling Everett, but the hotel he's staying at has really spotty service. His phone goes straight to voicemail." She stands upright and huffs, her eyes roaming over the room in the hopes that it might be somewhere else. "I'm just going to have to tell him to ask Everett about it when he gets back." She pulls out her phone from the back pocket of her jeans and starts tapping away at her phone. When she's done, she smiles at me. "Sorry about that."

I shrug, trying to brush off the ominous presence of Andrew with nonchalance. "It's fine."

We both start walking down the stairs and back into the dining room. We pick up where we left off, finishing the last of the tuna roll and edamame. Teeny takes another look at her phone and frowns.

"Is everything okay?"

"Yeah," she answers, her voice a little distracted. "I was telling Andrew not to come over because I can't find his card, but it looks like he's already on his way. He's not answering my texts."

My throat dries. "Here? He's coming here?"

She nods at her phone screen. "Whatever, it's his fault for leaving his card just lying around everywhere."

I set down my chopsticks with shaky hands, and one of them flings across the table, splattering splotches of soy sauce along the rich oak table. "Oh my god," I gasp. "I'm so sorry." I rush to wipe away the dark stains, my hands remaining fidgety.

Teeny stands and helps me. "It's okay," she assures.

"You know," I start, reaching for my purse. "I just realized I have to—" My measly excuse to leave is interrupted by a sharp knock at her door. I feel my ears start to grow hot, and my heart rate kicks up several notches.

Teeny huffs a frustrated sigh, completely oblivious to the panic coursing through me. "That's probably Andrew."

I watch her get up from the seat, realizing it's too late to make a sneaky exit. I have to face the music. Andrew's here, most likely to seek me out, and I have to continue the avoidant, aloof façade I carried through our text conversation. I slip on the mask of someone who doesn't even have two shits to give and act as if my dinner is the center of my attention.

"I told you," Teeny says as I hear two sets of footsteps enter the dining area. "I couldn't find it. You can go look if you want, but I think Everett might have put it somewhere safe. He'll probably be able to tell you where it is."

Against my better judgment, I look up, only to be met by Andrew's stern glare. He looks at me like he wants to challenge me to something. And I can bet my still-full can of Perrier it isn't to a thumb war or fencing duel.

"Grace," he calls, his voice flat and steady.

I tilt my head to the side, attempting to show as much apathy as possible. "Hi, Andrew."

"Do you mind if I stay and wait for Everett to call back?" His question is directed at Teeny, but his fiery gaze is pointed at me.

"Sure," Teeny answers. "Did you already eat?"

"Yeah. The vending machine at work had a pretty good selection of chips." The spiteful sarcasm in his voice is just subtle enough for me to pick up.

"You were working? On a Saturday?"

He finally tears his eyes away from me and looks at his sister. "Yeah, I left when I realized I couldn't find my card. My boss is probably going to be pissed."

His lie sounds so believable, I wonder if it's a lie at all. Maybe he did leave his credit card here, and all of this is just a silly coincidence.

"I'll grab another plate," Teeny offers.

Teeny stands up from her chair and walks off to the kitchen leaving me and Andrew alone. He stalks toward me and sits in the seat next to mine, his glower making me squirm.

"Why are you mad at me?"

"I'm not mad at you," I say meekly. I sound frightened, but everything inside me is growing hot and heady. I swipe my finger at a spot of soy sauce I missed, trying to avoid his gaze but it's pointless. His eyes feel like laser beams and the heat from it is almost unbearable.

"Really? Is that why you're telling me to leave you be?"

"Andrew," I plead, feeling too flustered. "I don't want to talk about it here. Teeny might hear us."

"Fine. Let's go to your place so we can talk."

"I don't want to talk to you."

"Too. Fucking. Bad," he argues. He waits a beat for me to respond, but I try my best to ignore him, failing when I catch his eyes boring daggers into me. "Grace, did I do something wrong? Was it something I did at lunch?"

"I don't know," I say, trying to sound as flippant as possible. I return my attention back to my dinner. "Maybe you should ask your *friend* if you did something at lunch that might have upset me." I say friend with a little more disdain than I intended to, but I don't care anymore. There's no point in hiding things anymore.

"So, you're mad about Olive."

I stay quiet. It's hard to fight back and deny it when the air around us is growing thick and taut. I feel like my breaths are going in and out of me in short gasps rather than at a steady pace. I feel like he's hovering over me, piercing me with his sharp eyes to force the truth out of me.

Teeny returns with the extra plate and a bright smile, completely oblivious to the tension coiling around us.

"Here," she announces, placing a ceramic plate in front of Andrew. "We have a few rolls left, and an extra cup of miso soup. You want a beer?"

"Sure." He looks uncomfortable as he takes the plate from Teeny. I can see his arm flex when his hand fists on the table. His jaw tics as he takes one last glance at me. A warning, it seems. Or a promise that we're going to have this conversation whether I like it or not.

I need to leave. This is getting too weird and uncomfortable. I can't sit through the rest of our dinner like this. With Andrew's harsh demeanor and the heat between us I can barely ignore.

"Hey, I'm going to head out," I abruptly announce.

"Already?" Teeny asks with a pout.

"Yeah. I have to feed Buster." I collect some of my trash, piling it in the plastic bag in haste.

"Just leave it," she assures. "I'll clean it up when I'm done."

My lips pull tight into an uncomfortable smile, and I catch Andrew watching me as I continue to tidy up despite Teeny's instruction to leave it be. I hook my purse over my shoulder and manage to avoid looking at Andrew before walking out of the dining room. I beeline for the exit with Teeny at my tail, leaving dust in my wake as I leave the room where I felt like I'd been holding my breath.

"Get home safe," she instructs. "I'll see you later."

"Bye."

A rush of fresh air fills my lungs, replacing the burn from when I felt like the presence of Andrew was going to suffocate me. I shake off the feeling that what happened inside was more than my words coming to bite me in the ass.

Whatever it was, it's over. Andrew and I aren't friends. And he needs to know that sooner rather than later.

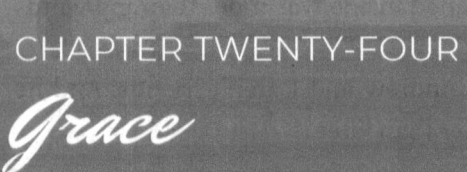

CHAPTER TWENTY-FOUR

Grace

I MAKE it to my condo with a slight sag in my step. My feet drag like they're being pulled through cement, making the walk from my car to my doorstep sluggish and dejected. I have a weighty moment of regret and guilt. It hits me in the gut like a sucker punch, and I try my best to ignore it. It's my weak heart in play, wanting to make sure I didn't hurt Andrew's feelings or anything just as damaging to our friendship. If there even is one left to damage.

I start to wonder if I was too harsh on him. So what if he has a girlfriend at work, or whatever she's supposed to be. It shouldn't change our dynamic. We can still have lunch and watch movies and build LEGO together. I can be an amenable, supportive friend. Or I can choose to be angry at him. Throw a fit, slash his tires, and cause a scene at his place of work. It feels like the more adjacent emotion to the current situation on hand. A situationship masquerading as a friendship with all the complicated components like jealousy and lust and hormones. And now, all of those cumbersome, confusing parts had a moment to sit over a low simmering fire only to stew into indignation and hurt.

I hold my phone in my hands, wondering if I should text Andrew.

Or even call him. Let him know I'm not even the slightest bit mad at him. That I don't care about Olive or whoever he meets in his free time. That there's nothing we need to talk about unless it's something arbitrary like noun declension or pop culture facts in reference to science fiction movies. Instead of tapping out a text message—my own digital olive branch—I chuck my phone onto the counter right next to my keys. I don't even know what the right words are right now. Letting things just cool down for a few beats might be best.

Buster greets me, lazily walking toward me as he works through a yawn. He settles for a light pat on his head and turns back to his sleeping area in the living room. I move in a monotonous haze as I reach for his can of dog food from the fridge and mix some kibble with it before setting it down next to his water bowl in the kitchen. He greets his food with more gusto as he comes out of his sleepy daze.

Just as I'm slipping off the heavy cardigan I've been wearing all day, letting the cool air-conditioned air hit my exposed skin from the sports bra-style top I'm wearing, I hear a knock at my door. I hold my bundled-up sweater against my chest in an attempt to cover up and answer the door.

"Who is it?" I ask.

"Grace," I hear from the other side, recognizing the voice immediately. "It's me."

There's a barrier between us. A solid door. And between the door and my heart there are more layers. My clothes, my skin and muscles, my ribcage, all of it a layer of protection to safeguard the weak beating thing in my chest. But it feels as if Andrew has his bare hand wrapped around it, holding all the power if I let him, and it scares the fuck out of me.

"Andrew, just go home." I wince through my words, laying my forehead on the cool surface.

"Please, Grace. Can we talk?"

"Why? What do you have to talk to me about?"

"I—I don't know," he stammers. "But I ju—I need to talk to you."

My hand lays over the doorknob, still unsure if I can face him. A shaky sigh squeezes through my lips, and Andrew's voice presses against the one solid barrier I thought I could count on, turning it frail and brittle.

"Please."

I give, unable to bear the sound of his desperate, quivering plea. I unlock my door, the deadbolt hitting the latch with a heavy thunk. Andrew's wounded face, all downcast and urgent, looks at me with one hand braced on the door frame and his head ducked in a way that shows he's knocking at my door in the middle of the night with an air of caution. He's tossed aside the inflated one-man show of someone confident and provoked like he was back at Teeny's. He looks hesitant and scared.

And I don't have it in me to taunt him like I did earlier. To egg him on with rhetorical questions or spiteful comments. I don't even ask him why he's here. Because I think I already know. And it seems he doesn't even care to tell me with the way he charges toward me. He crosses the threshold with so much intent, I feel as if it's going to physically push me back. His hand cups the nape of my neck at the same time his lips crash into mine. This time, I'm not drunk or buzzed. I don't have the excuse of alcohol to explain why I don't push him away. And he doesn't have the opportunity to use the same reasoning to explain why he showed up on my doorstep with all the actions to speak the words we can't seem to say out loud.

He closes the door behind him and nudges me backward to the closest wall. His hands thread into my hair, gripping the roots at my nape. I drop my sweater, and my own hands grapple at his waist, grabbing fistfuls of his shirt.

"I'm sorry," I whisper between kisses. "I swear I'm not mad at you."

"It's okay," he whispers back, speaking the words against my hot skin. "Be mad at me. I don't care."

His tongue sweeps inside my mouth, and my legs grow wobbly at the taste of him. It's so specific and unique to him, and I want to taste other parts of him. Lewd, indecent thoughts swirl in my head, wondering how I can smother those curiosities, and it seems he has the same thoughts because his tongue starts to travel elsewhere. From my neck to my collarbone to the valley between my breasts, trailing to where he leaves a path of wet kisses over my cleavage. It's like my skin, all the dips and curves, have become his own little smorgasbord, curated just for his palate.

"You have no idea how long I've been wanting to do this," he murmurs. "I thought I was going to lose my fucking mind."

All words have left my brain. I can only respond with my hands. My extremely greedy hands. I cup his jaw, pulling him closer to me. Trying to get more of that taste I'm growing obsessed with. I kiss him, feeling his teeth grate against my swollen lower lip.

Suddenly, it feels like the sports bra I chose to wear was a very intentional choice. It has a zipper down the middle at my front. It wasn't a conscious choice when I bought it. Probably something more to do with price and quite possibly a buy one, get one free kind of sale. But now, I'm thanking the athletic wear gods for creating something this resourceful and efficacious.

His fingers move like he's dismantling a live bomb. Like the zipper sitting between us might break and shatter. And all the noises around us have gone mute. Our heady breaths, our urgent kisses, even the low hum of the fridge and Buster's tongue lapping away at his food have dwindled down to complete silence. I only feel the vibrations as he tugs at the zipper pull, peeling back the one layer keeping me covered. When it finally gets past the last tooth, springing open, his eyes focus on the crease lining down my center. Like he's been hypnotized, his eyelids grow heavy. They flutter as if they've grown weak and helpless.

"You are so goddamn sexy," he rasps, a painful scrape scratching against his throat. His warm hands peel back the rest of the sports bra, leaving my chest completely bare. The cool air that hits me is smothered when his mouth finds my nipple. He lets it unfurl on his eager tongue, causing my back to arch and my head to hit the wall behind me. I moan, holding nothing back, and he pulls me closer to him with his strong hands pressed to my hot skin. He picks me up, his arms wrapping around my waist, and takes me to my room. He doesn't need my guidance this time. He knows where to go.

As soon as we walk into my room, I flip the lights on, and he kicks the door shut behind him. He reaches over his shoulder and rips his shirt off by the collar in one swift move. He steps out of his pants, urgently toeing off his shoes into a messy pile on my bedroom floor and nudges me back toward my bed. And I follow his lead like he has a complete spell over me.

He has me sitting at the edge of the bed, and he kneels in front of me. He keeps his eyes on mine, watching my every reaction. Like he's wanting to know how fast or how slow he should move. His fingers tuck into the waistband of my leggings, and I lift my hips up, letting them slip over my butt and down my thighs. When they reach my calves, Andrew dips his head, kissing the fleshy part of my leg, just below my hip.

I'm left in a thong while he nuzzles his cheek against the parts he kissed, taking a moment to relish the quiet before we dive headfirst into this. My hands run through his thick hair, and my nails scrape over the back of his neck, encouraging him to continue.

"This isn't like last time, is it?" I ask. My question sounds more like a thought spoken out loud, but it's a thought we're both sharing.

He looks up at me, his hands hooking under my knees. His fingers graze over my skin in soft strokes, and he shakes his head. "No, it isn't."

We can't deny this anymore. We can't act like being friends is what makes the most sense for us. I can't just be his friend. I don't *want* to just be his friend. I want to do more intimate things like this with him. Learn what it's like to feel his heart beating against mine. I want to lie naked with him, our legs tangled with the sheets as we talk and laugh and kiss. I want to wake up in the morning with him. Without the hangover and regret.

"I don't want it to be like last time," he adds. "Grace, I want you." He tilts up, kissing me lightly. A slight tickle just to feel my lips. As if the time spent getting from my entryway to my room was too long, and he needs to make sure the kiss we had mere minutes ago was real. All real. "I want you so fucking bad. And I don't mean just tonight. I want you so much more beyond that."

"I think...I want you too," I tell him, a tremble in my voice showing how scared and nervous I am. "I want you tonight. I want you tomorrow. I want—"

He lunges for my lips, finally closing the distance between us. His body lays flush against mine as he presses me into the mattress. I slip off his boxer briefs, the last stitch of clothing on him, and my palms slide over his round ass as I take them completely off. His erection prods against my soft stomach, as if probing around and looking for its depraved counterpart hiding between my legs. I grip him in my hands, and my fingers grow slick as his rampant precum trickles out of him, like desperation dripping from him with each slow deliberate stroke, waiting to burst at any given moment.

He shudders over me as his own curious hands tuck into my thong and his fingers feel me. His hands don't move with purpose but rather with interest. Like testing the waters, starting with a cautious toe before plunging all the way in and discovering how ready and wet I am. How needy I am. He starts with light strokes, watching what makes me squirm and what makes me turn into a big pile of mush. He knows exactly what to do and how to touch me, turning me into his own little puppet, moaning and shaking and writhing, all at his will.

"I'm going to fuck you," he informs me. A matter of fact, not opinion or something to be discussed or swayed. "I'm going to fuck you hard, and then I'm going to take my time."

I nod. "Yeah. Okay, whatever you want." A breathy laugh or an amused giggle might fit perfectly in this moment considering how little protest I give, but I mean it with my whole heart. Whatever he says right now, goes. I don't care what it is. He can treat me like his own personal fuck toy or wring the pleasure out of me until there's nothing left. I'll say please and thank you before begging for more.

I buck underneath him, my hips moving back and forth on their own as if miming what my body wants. "Now," I plead. "Can you fuck me now?"

He thrusts forward too, mimicking my motions with a silent answer. Yet he falls just short of his promise, leaving me wanton and needy. As determined as he is to fuck the shit out of me, I can tell he's trying to let my body adjust to the moment. But foreplay is the least of my worries.

"Really," I moan. "We can skip the foreplay. Please, just—" My words are cut off when I feel the head of his cock nudge against the slick mess between my legs. A preview of what I've been craving for too long. I want to tell him to stop teasing me when he continues those slow, torturous thrusts. It's the act of fucking but not quite. Like settling for the nonfat, dairy-free, sugar-free soft serve when all I want is some real fucking chocolate fudge ice cream.

"*Jesus*," he grunts. "How do you feel this good, and I'm not even inside you?"

I love the sound of his voice. The way he sounds so confused and desperate. It scrapes against my skin, leaving behind tracks I hope will never go away. My knees fall back, giving him room to settle in, get comfortable, and stay between my legs for however long he wants.

Being the responsible one, Andrew stretches his body over mine to reach for the condoms he knows are already in my nightstand. All while sense and reason left my brain, and I was ready to let him fuck me bare. I watch him lean back on his heels, and in the distracted haze of me gawking as his fingers expertly move over his length, I forget I still have my underwear on. But Andrew's over me before I can slip them off, and instead of giving me a moment to remove them, he pulls the measly strip of fabric aside and pushes inside of me in one swift, slippery go.

"Holy shit," I gasp. "That feels so *good*."

"*Oh, fuuuck me,*" he groans. He only spends a second adjusting, giving me a moment to adapt to his sheer size, and he starts pounding into me. He pistons in and out of me, and everything inside me starts to grow tight. The live wire coiling in my gut twists and tightens, and it intensifies everything. I can feel him down to the tips of my toes.

"Harder," I urge, an aching moan stamping the end of my demand. "I want you to make it hurt."

A low growl rumbles across his chest. A sign of approval and zeal rattling between us while we both process what I just said. I want it rough and hard and fast. I want to feel him tomorrow every time I move or walk or even sit. I've never wanted it like this, and it scares me just as much as it excites me.

He pulls out of me, leaving me bereft. He scoops his hand under my back and flips me over with such ease, I feel like I've been spun on a Tilt-A-Whirl. Suddenly, I'm on all fours, and his hard erection brushes against the backs of my thighs. He quickly shoves back into me, pushing me forward. He hooks his hand around my neck and pulls me flush against him. I feel his firm chest against my back, his heartbeat drumming against my spine. He continues to fuck me, hard like I asked, and he promised.

From past sexual experiences, I've needed a bit more to get to the finish line. A little clitoral stimulation or an interminable time spent on foreplay. Something most men aren't willing to undertake. So, it renders me nearly speechless when I find myself already there with neither.

"I'm going to come," I tell Andrew, surprising myself more than him. "*Holy shit,* I—I'm going to fucking come."

"Yeah," he says with a strained voice. "Me too."

And it hits me. Like a Mack truck. I shriek, unable to hold back the keening sob ripping through my throat. He grunts just as loudly, groaning through his own orgasm as he continues to fuck me from behind.

He wraps his arms around my front, holding on to me like I

might disappear. His ragged breaths filter through the air, and my own rapid gasps follow. He kisses my shoulder, a stark contrast to the harsh and dizzying sex we're having. I reach behind me, ruffling up the hair at the back of his head. My own gesture of soothing comfort. To let him know he didn't go too hard. It was exactly what I wanted. What I needed.

CHAPTER TWENTY-FIVE

Andrew

WE'VE BEEN LYING in Grace's bed. My hands have been roaming over her naked body in leisurely strokes. Touching her where I want and as much as I want. After our first intense round, I took my time with her. Just like I promised. I kissed her in places I hadn't yet. Places where I wondered how she felt. The dip in her hips, the hollow behind her knees, the arch of her feet. I tasted her, drawing her orgasm out of her in every which way I could. She turned into a sex-starved seductress as she took me in her mouth, bobbing up and down as I fell at her mercy. She wanted it all as much as I did.

The minutes ticked away on her clock, and we watched the night grow quiet with the occasional siren passing by on the streets or a shout or a holler echoes against the tall buildings. With how late it is, I know we're probably going to watch the night grow lighter. The sun will probably peek over the horizon, letting us know our time together is measured, and we'll have to soon step back out into the real world. But for now, we remain in our own private bubble. We didn't have to think about all the things outside of Grace's bedroom. We didn't have to think about my sister and what she would say if she were to find out Grace and I are becoming something more than just a rash one-night stand. We even set aside my work and the angry email I was sure to come back to on Monday considering I left without so much as a warning thrown over my shoulder to Olive to track down Grace.

We glazed over all the little details we've kept from each other over the past few weeks. How I was doing my best to respect her space and her wishes. How I almost gave it all up when I saw her in her green bikini at Teeny's house. How every minute I spent with her under the guise of a friend hanging out with a friend only made me want her more. I told her everything, wanting it out in the open so she knew this wasn't some empty tryst I was going to walk away from unscathed. In fact, no part of me would walk away from this unscathed. I was all in.

"We were really stupid, weren't we?"

I nuzzle my cheek into her temple, listening to her speak her playful words against my chest. "So fucking stupid."

"I really thought we could be friends," she continues.

"I didn't."

She looks up at me. "You didn't?"

"Nope."

"Then why did you agree to it?"

I shrug, making her head bob against me. "Because it's what you wanted."

She rolls her eyes, shoving her hands against my stomach. She starts pulling away, but I wrap my arm around her, bringing her flush against me. "Come on," I argue. "What was I supposed to say?"

"I don't know. Tell the truth?"

"And then what would've happened?"

"I probably would've told you..."

"That you and I could never happen?" I ask, stating what seems to be the obvious.

Her silence proves my point. "Still," she weakly claims.

"It's fine," I assure her. "I did what I had to do to keep seeing you."

She pinches my side. A reproval for my little white lie and something she's obviously willing to overlook as she wraps her arm around my midsection and nudges her knee between my legs.

"There's nothing going on with me and Olive," I tell her, speaking the honest truth into the crown of her head. I know it's a little out of left field, but I want to clear the air. There's no one else but her. No Olive or some other random girl filling my thoughts. Just her.

She nods. "I know."

"Okay," I whisper. "I just want to make sure you know."

"I'm sorry."

"No," I protest with a fleeting shake of my head. "Don't be. I should've said something or done something. I just didn't think...I didn't think."

She lifts herself up, straddling my lap. "No, you didn't," she says with hooded eyes and a coy smirk. I feel her rocking herself against me, and I'm already growing hard again. We've already done it twice, and a third time seems to be on the horizon.

I sit up, wanting her closer to me. "I'm a little offended."

Her head rears back in confusion. "Why?"

"It's like you just want me for my body."

"Ah," she responds, a smile teasing her lips. "I'm so sorry. I didn't mean to make you feel...used."

"You're just going to have to make it up to me," I respond, "so I don't feel so cheap."

She kisses me, her rolling hips driving me crazy. My dick twitches, and she hums as it brushes against her. "I just thought... you know, we should be making up for lost time."

I give her ass a firm squeeze. "You are so right."

"To think we've been depriving ourselves of this. All this time."

"I told you," I respond, my voice weak. "So. Fucking. Stupid. And for what?"

Her movements stop. As if my off-handed question caused a

sudden realization to dawn on her. She grips my head, cupping my jaw and tilting my face to force my eyes to hers.

"What?" I ask, watching her eyes search mine.

She sucks in a deep breath, letting out a regretful sigh. "Should we talk about this?"

"About what?"

"Like...where do we go from here?"

I don't know the answer to that question. As much as I wish I knew and hope our hearts are in the same place, I don't know what's okay. I don't know what's allowed between us. So, with the uncertainty weighing heavy on my chest, I ask, "Where do you want us to go from here?"

"I don't know."

I respond with silence, a small twinge of disappointment twisting in my gut.

"But I know I want to keep seeing you," she adds. "I want to keep spending my nights with you, and maybe my mornings with you."

"I want that too," I say honestly. But I know that's not all. There's a clause. A stipulation stapled to the back of it, and I need to flip the page and read the fine print before celebrating.

"I just don't know if I'm ready for everyone else to know about us."

"So, we keep things a secret." It's not what I want, but it's what I'll take. Grace isn't ready for the world to know about us. She's worried they won't accept us for what we are. Two adults who have fallen for each other. Two people who were never meant to fall for each other. So, until she is ready for that, she can keep me as her little secret. And when she is ready, I'll be the first person to shout to the world what she means to me.

CHAPTER TWENTY-SIX
Andrew

I NEVER REALIZED how many defects my studio apartment has. It's homey and cozy, perfect for a single man who mainly uses it as a place to eat and sleep and occasionally lounge around while eating leftover pizza. But the second I decide to have company over —and not just any company, but a woman—I realize how much it's lacking. I don't have a large French door fridge with an ice dispenser or a balcony overlooking sixteen stories with a view that includes a small section of the ocean and the Port of San Diego. My view is unremarkable with the tops of other two-story apartment buildings and a freeway overpass. In fact, my apartment doesn't even have a wall separating the bedroom from the kitchen. It's all one small open space where the only area with privacy is the bathroom.

I've spent the last hour cleaning. Picking up trash, wiping down surfaces, going around all the hidden outlets to see where I can covertly plug in a few scent diffusers. I even made sure to switch out the towels to newer, fluffier ones and laid out some toiletries I bought when I shopped for some flavored Perrier.

Grace is coming over to my apartment. She's heading straight over for dinner after work. We've been spending the past few nights at her place and when she casually mentioned she's never seen my apartment, I invited her over. I, of course, immediately regretted it. I've become so comfortable in her condo, I didn't know how she was going to adjust to my much smaller dwelling. Not that she seems to be the type of person who cares. Her digs aren't something that defines her. It's almost as if her home is just her home. Something that happened by chance and luck, and she's just enjoying the amenities. Still, I want to impress her. I want her to see that this place, as much as it's not grand or swanky, is very much me.

I'm cleaning up some leftovers in my fridge that turned out to be a container of chow mein from two weeks ago when I hear a knock at my door. I abandon the stinky noodles, shoving them deep in my trash can while hoping it'll be enough to mask the smell.

When I open the door, nothing could've prepared me for what's on the other side. It's not that Grace looks any different. She's wearing a pair of wide, flowy slacks that touch the floor with a V-neck sweater-shirt. Resting just at the dip of her neckline sits a small diamond stud hanging from a gold chain. Her hair is swept up in a sleek bun with wispy strands framing her face and neck, and gold earrings that look like teardrops dangle from her earlobes. She has a leather tote bag slung over her shoulder, along with a look of frazzled weariness. But aside from how stunning yet unimposing she looks, it's the sudden sight of her that has a physical effect on me. I'd been so busy cleaning I didn't have a moment to realize how much I missed her. I hadn't seen her in over twenty-four hours since I had to work late last night, and it seems that short period of time allowed my heart to grow fonder. I forgot how much I love being near her, running my hands over whatever exposed skin she lets me touch or even just spewing random things to each other. Questions that run on a tangent with no purpose or thought. Just things that pop into our minds we don't find the need to filter or hold back. Even the moments when we stay quiet and bask in the silence, not needing to fill it with superfluous words.

"Hi."

"Hey," I answer. I open the door wider, and as she walks through the threshold, I slip off her bag and place it on the chair tucked under my drop-leaf dining table. A set made for only two.

We skip past a formal greeting, and I swoop her into my arms. I nuzzle my nose into the dip in her neck, and I feel her fingers rake into my scalp. The tension in my shoulders melts off my bones and muscles. I hadn't brought up anything work-related to her, but today wasn't different than any other stressful workday. I've been looking forward to seeing her all day, and it seems it's more than just a simple date night in. I feel okay around her. I don't feel wound up or anxious or irritable. I feel calm and just...okay.

"I missed you," I whisper into her hair.

"I missed you too." She pulls away, brushing her lips to mine.

"You don't want a tour?"

I feel her shoulders shrug while her lips continue to seek out mine. "Sure. If you want." Her hands tuck under my shirt, fingers looping over my belt. "Or we can keep doing this."

"That's good too." I guide her to my bed a few steps away where we fall in a heap on top of my covers. And I realize, like how I missed our conversations and even the silent moments that fill our time together, I miss *this* just as much.

"I like your apartment."

"Yeah?"

"Hm," Grace hums against my skin. "It's nice and cozy."

We're lying in my bed, our bodies a little flushed and heated from the last hour we've spent over and under each other. I know I don't have much time before Grace has to leave and we should probably eat something soon, but the thought of ditching our warm nest doesn't sound the least bit appealing. I want to stay here until the moment she needs to get back home to Buster.

A part of me wishes she could stay the night. I could even offer to go and bring Buster back here. We could enjoy a leisurely dinner and shower together. Do things under the water until it runs cold and have her slip into one of my shirts before we go to bed. We could wake up together, possibly have a cup of coffee or a light breakfast before we head off to our respective jobs. I could maybe even pack her a lunch. The perfect way to continue the work week.

My thoughts of an imaginary sleepover are interrupted when I hear Grace's stomach grumble against mine. While I could stay in this spot forever, I know it's time for me to get up and feed her.

"All right," I announce, gently removing Grace's arm from across my stomach. "We have to get up."

"What? Why?" she objects. She tugs at my hand, attempting to force me back down on my bed.

"You need to eat," I tell her.

"No, I'm okay," she argues. "I just want to lie here with you." I watch as she settles back on the pillows, letting the comforter slip low so the rounded side cleavage of her perfect tits tempts me back to her.

But I don't give in. I shake my head and say, "Your stomach seems to disagree."

"That was your stomach."

I look back at her with a quizzically confused look. I could've sworn it was her. Just as I'm starting to question and reconsider her claim, she giggles, smothering her laugh with the comforter pulled up to her cheek. I fall into the temptation of letting the both of us go hungry and slip under the covers with her. "You're hilarious, you know that?"

"Of course," she answers. She runs her fingers through my already rumpled hair and tugs me closer to her.

I take another five minutes before finally slipping on a pair of sweatpants and sauntering into my kitchen. Grace trails behind me, throwing on one of my oversized shirts, and she keeps me company while I boil some water and pour it into two separate instant ramen cups.

"Sorry it's not much," I tell her apologetically. We're sitting at my cramped table, a stack of mail pushed to the side, with our dinner squished close together. Grace has one bare leg drawn up to her chin, and I'm growing infatuated with the smooth slope of her neck as the collar of my shirt falls to the side.

She stirs a pair of chopsticks in her noodles and swirls a heaping first serving. "What are you talking about? This is amazing."

I'd call her bluff, but it doesn't seem like a bluff at all. Either she really is enjoying it, or she was really that hungry.

"You want a drink?"

She nods with rounded cheeks that make her look like a chipmunk. I grab her a can of Perrier from the fridge, and I open a fresh bottle of beer for myself, and she looks at me with a look I can only describe as adoration.

"What?"

She shakes her head. "It's nothing."

"No, what is it?"

She pauses, contemplating her answer, and plucks at the cold can in her hand. "How'd you know these are my favorite?"

I look at the grapefruit-flavored sparkling water before saying, "I noticed you were drinking it at Teeny's, and you have a few cans stocked in your fridge, so..."

"And you thought to keep some in your fridge too?"

I nod, and she continues to eat, that look of awe settling over her smile.

Under the dim kitchen lighting, while we sit at what is probably the smallest dining table in the world, I feel like anything is possible. We can be this bare, completely vulnerable form of us without having to worry about consequences or an aftermath that may or may not come. I can hold on to this moment where the night seems to stand still, and morning never comes. I don't have to face my job, and she doesn't have to go home. And maybe in some alternate universe, we make complete sense. There's no one who would question the idea of us. She wouldn't be my sister's best friend, and I wouldn't be her best friend's younger brother.

CHAPTER TWENTY-SEVEN

Andrew

"I DON'T UNDERSTAND," I say, omitting an exaggerated head scratch to add to my confusion. "She's supposed to change his mind? Because he hates his life?"

A wayward piece of popcorn flits in my direction, Grace's objection to my criticism over her movie of choice for the night. Buster, sitting on the carpet just beyond the foot of the bed, does his due diligence by bolting it for it in the folds of Grace's comforter.

"He's a quadriplegic," she explains. "And he doesn't want to live the rest of his life unable to do the things he used to before his accident, so he wants to take the humane way out."

"And how is she supposed to change his mind? They hardly know each other."

"It's called a romance movie," Grace claims, her head tilted with a protective affectation in the way her eyes narrow at me. "You have to believe in the fictional narrative that love can conquer all."

"And does it? Does she change his mind?"

She shrugs an innocent shoulder. "You're just going to have to wait and see."

We've been lying in her bed, lounging over the cushy blankets with her laptop open to some romance movie she wanted me to see.

A retribution for making her sit through a few of my favorite movies, I assume. We have some take-out containers spread around us, and we haven't even bothered to get dressed properly. I'm in my boxers with an undershirt, and she's wearing one of the few shirts of mine that have been left behind in her condo and warm fuzzy socks. Her legs are bare, and when she adjusts her legs from a cross-legged position to having them outstretched with pointed toes, I get to see a sliver of the bright turquoise underwear covering her ass.

We've made several runs to the kitchen, adding to the snack pile on her bed. A few snickerdoodle cookies joined the Chinese food, and the popcorn was added when Grace wanted something salty to accompany the cookies.

It's Friday night, and I got off work at a surprisingly reasonable hour. I hooked my backpack over my shoulder as soon as I shut off my computer and beelined for the elevator. I have zero plans with the outside world for the next forty-eight hours. I'm staying within the confines of Grace's room. We may occasionally open the front door to bring in the DoorDash delivery and even venture outside to the actual sidewalk where people are to take Buster out to relieve himself, but I've gone on Do Not Disturb mode.

While our activities have been of the homebody variety the past few weeks, I don't mind. A regular cycle of sex and takeout and movies and more sex is an itinerary I can definitely get used to. And I think Grace prefers this too. She hasn't mentioned it, but I know it's daunting to step outside where we run the risk of running into someone we know. Or just being out in the public at all. It means this is actually *something*. It means we can't go back to just being friends or two people who know each other as an extension of another. We haven't had a hard-hitting conversation where we hash out some ground rules and dissect the reasons why neither one of us has suggested an outing in the real world. A part of me grows wary with the thought of having that kind of discussion. I've gotten this far with her, and I don't want to push her away with things that'll make her want to run.

But all the signs tell me she'll be fine. She'll be more open to taking things to the next level in the form of baby steps. She isn't just some woman I'm sleeping with. She's so much more than that. I realized it the moment she walked out of my bathroom completely naked one random weeknight she was at my place. The act wasn't anything seductive or a preliminary move to lure me back into bed. She'd just showered, and her hair was still dripping wet, and she didn't bother to cover up. She strutted around, looking for her pajamas and slipped them on as if I wasn't even in the room before asking me if I had a spare toothbrush because she'd forgotten hers. The realization hit me in the chest. I am absolutely and thoroughly falling for her. And it doesn't even scare me. In fact, it's the complete opposite. It thrills me. Like I'm willingly strapped to a rollercoaster, waiting for it to swoop up and down and go through a loop. All for the exhilaration of feeling alive.

There's also the fact that condoms have been thrown completely out the window. A clear sign of monogamy. Grace immediately went back on the pill after she confessed she's not a big fan of condoms. The feel of them. The clumsiness of interrupting a heated moment. It hadn't been a problem during her most recent celibacy period but now that sex was happening on a very regular basis, she tapped and swiped away at her phone before a prescription became available the next day. I've never done that with a woman. I've never developed a relationship stable and secure enough that the dilemma of protection was so easily solved. I've even inadvertently started keeping a few of her things in a drawer in my bathroom. A spare toothbrush to make sure she never had to remember to bring one again, more of her Perrier, an extra food bowl in the few instances she brought Buster with her when she spent the night. Even some of her preferred toiletries stashed in my shower. All things people do when in a committed relationship. And none of it scares me. I did all of it without really even considering why or how. I just did it.

The movie credits start rolling, and I notice Grace dozing off. She always sleeps with her mouth slightly agape and a small scowl that makes her look like she's doing long division in her sleep. She isn't quite there yet with a more relaxed look settled across her brow. I start to move everything off the bed, making a few trips from the kitchen and back to the bedroom. Buster follows me with every trip. Most likely hoping to catch a few scraps along the way. When I've taken the last of the leftovers, sealing them with Saran Wrap and placing them in the fridge, I attempt to move Grace under the covers.

"Hmm," she protests, stopping my hand when I scoot her to her side of the bed. "I don't want to go to sleep yet."

"I think you're already asleep."

She responds with a listless hum. Another protest, I assume. I continue to pull back the covers when she stops me again.

"I want to finish the movie."

I kiss her on her temple, and she smiles. "It's already over, baby."

She pouts, her eyes remaining closed. "I didn't get to see the ending with you."

"It was very sad," I assure. "I cried all the way till the end."

One eye pops open, and she smirks. "Liar."

I lay down next to her, hooking my arm around her waist and tugging her closer. "You want to get under the covers? You're gonna get cold."

"I have to take Buster out before I go to bed," she manages through droopy lips. Buster sits up from his spot, letting a low whine fill the room. He looks to me when Grace shows no signs of getting up.

"I'll take him out," I offer. "Just get under the covers."

She turns on her back and looks at me through heavy-lidded eyes. "You sure?"

"Yeah." I lean down to kiss her, stroking my hand over her stomach. I manage to peel myself away from her and get off the bed while Grace settles herself under the covers. Buster follows me to the door, and his paws start excitedly tapping on the floor when he sees me slipping on my shoes. He lets out a loud yap when I reach for his leash, and I bend down to shush him.

"Shh, Buster," I whisper. "Mommy's sleeping."

I pad out the door, closing the door carefully, and head toward the elevators to the ground floor. Buster doesn't shy away from me. He doesn't appear timid or annoyed that it's not his owner taking him out. Instead, he trots along with his tongue hanging out and his tail whipping happily behind him.

Grace usually takes him around the block, and by the time we've made a full circle, Buster's almost ready to go back inside. I let him lead the way, and as we round the final corner, he settles in for one last perfected leg lift to a tree. He's sniffing around the skinny trunk as my phone buzzes in my pocket.

I see my brother, Josh, is calling, and I balance the leash in one hand while sliding my thumb across my phone screen to answer.

"Hello?"

"Hey, are you busy?"

"No," I answer. "Just...out for a walk."

"Can you talk for a minute?"

"Sure. What's up?"

"I was talking to my friend," he informs me. "The one I was telling you about who works for the nonprofit."

"Oh, yeah."

"Anyway, they're hiring."

My interest piques. "Oh?"

"Do you want to meet with him? It doesn't have to be anything formal. Maybe you can pick his brain, see if nonprofit work is something you'd be interested in."

I consider his question. I'm not *not* interested. "What was the name of the company?"

"The company's called The Hope Foundation."

"Does a nonprofit have the budget for a finance person? I thought they'd outsource that or something."

"I'm not too sure," he answers. "But I think Thad mentioned he's putting some feelers out. I guess the organization is growing, and they need someone with experience to manage the budgeting and financing end."

Buster tugs at his leash as we reach the main entrance to Grace's building. "Thad?"

"Yeah, that's my friend's name," he explains. "I've known him a long time. Since college. He's good. Nothing like that boss of yours."

I cringe at the mention of Mr. Sheridan. A reminder of how badly I want out from under his reign. "Okay. Just text me his info, and I guess I'll give him a call."

"I'm going to send you his email," he informs me. "Send over your résumé. I'll give him a heads up."

"Okay, thanks."

CHAPTER TWENTY-EIGHT
Grace

I'VE BEEN TOLD I have a bleeding heart many times. At seven when I wanted to bring home the stranded cat lying half-dead at the end of our street. At nineteen when I wanted nothing more than to give some cash to the weary man sitting outside a McDonald's asking for some spare change. And now, after almost four decades of life, when I see three sisters huddled over their mother's gurney, wondering where they go from here as they're handed a terminal diagnosis. I can't help but watch as my heart oozes and trickles while they tell me they'll take the hospice referrals with a heavy heart. It comes with the job, and I shouldn't let it cut into my empathy with such a daunting burden, but sometimes I can't help it.

In an attempt to wash away the tearful thank you my client's daughter extended to me as I let the nurses take over, I'm having Jayne take the next referral and heading down to the cafeteria for some coffee. As I wait for my flimsy paper cup to fill, I reach for my phone from my back pocket and dial Andrew's number.

"Hey."

A smile replaces the heartbroken frown I've been wearing. "Hey," I respond quietly.

"You okay? What's wrong?"

I shake my head, brushing off his gentle concern. "It's nothing," I tell him. "Just a bad day at work. I'm fine."

"You don't sound fine."

"I know," I admit. "I will be."

"How about something to cheer you up?"

"What did you have in mind?" I ask, my mood effectively lifted just the tiniest bit.

"I'll pick up some of the hazelnut waffles and bring them over, and you can tell me all about your bad day. Or, if you don't feel like doing that, you can put on another movie you can fall asleep to."

"Okay, I don't do that with *every* movie."

"No, just the ones you choose." He laughs, and I feel like my heart is going to be okay. The tourniquet I tied around it to temporarily stop the bleeding can slowly come off with Andrew's reassuring words and distraction tactics. "So? Waffles for dinner?"

"Yeah. That sounds good."

"Okay, it's a date."

A date. We haven't had one of those. Unless we count the nights spent in my bed or his as a date. If that's the case, then we've had more than a dozen. But the kind of dates that usually involve candle-light over a pressed white tablecloth and a fork for the salad and another for the entrée? We haven't had one of those yet.

It's not necessarily intentional. Andrew hasn't asked if I'd like to venture outside of our comfortable homes, and I haven't asked him to do so either. The mere thought of leaving our bubble of refuge and heading into the great big scary world of reality feels...too real. It does seem as though Andrew's caught on. He doesn't pressure me, using things like fancy dinners or activities that require a larger outdoor space to lure me. Instead, he just lets me be.

I'm pleased to find that the rest of my day takes a more opti-mistic turn. I meet with a client and her husband who's recently become her primary caregiver after an accident left her temporarily confined to the limitations of her mobility. She isn't able to shower on her own or get from her room to the kitchen without her husband's help. Their faces turn rosy and hopeful when I provide them with a list of resources at their disposal. Watching them realize this new dynamic in their relationship doesn't have to negatively impact her quality of life, even if it's only until she's recovered, feels like I'm doing my job. I'm helping someone.

When it's finally quitting time, I'm looking forward to spending the rest of the night with Andrew and an order of fresh hazelnut waffles. When I walk up to my door, my tote bag nearly dragging along the floor, I'm surprised to find Andrew already waiting there. He has a plastic bag which most likely contains our dinner, and his face brightens when he sees me walking down the hallway. He meets me halfway, and I sink into him when he pulls me close.

"Hmm," I hum.

He chuckles into my hair. "Hello to you too." I notice the shirt he's wearing is a little rumpled around the collar area, right where my cheek is nuzzled against, and the bottom hem is untucked. I get the faint whiff of sweat mixed with his cologne still lingering on his clothes, showing how long his day has been. Just as long as mine.

"I think you should carry me to my door." It's a joke, obviously not meant to be taken seriously. But I don't even have a second to grasp the fact that my feet have been swept out from under me. "Andrew!" I squeal. "Put me down!"

"This was your idea," he says without budging. We both laugh, the happy sounds echoing off the walls. My bag and our dinner dangle from our fingers, making Andrew's steps clumsy and awkward. It's quick to our destination, about ten paces, and he plops me back on solid ground with a pleased grin. All the energy that was drained out of me has been replenished. I grin back at him, and we stand there. My back facing the door and his face hovering over me.

"Have you been waiting long?" I ask as his nose brushes along mine.

"Maybe ten, fifteen minutes."

I frown, jutting out my lower lip. "I'm sorry."

"It's fine," he says. He kisses me, pushing me back while using his

209

palm as guidance to make sure I don't bash the back of my head against the wall. My bag drops to the floor, as do the waffles, and our hands join our lips. The make-out session turns heated, and a loud moan thrums between us. From him or from me, I don't even know who.

Footsteps sound nearby, and they grow louder, following the crescendo thumps with a harsh cough. We pull apart with a jolt only to find a man with two grocery bags walking past us, his gaze intentionally pointed toward the ground. We wait until the man rounds the corner, and we dissolve into giggles.

"You are such a bad influence," I scold. I reach down for my bag and fish out my keys. With my back to him, my hands fumble with my keys. I feel a jittery high vibrate just beneath my skin, and it feels unnerving and rousing at the same time. "We need to get you a key or something. Maybe that'll keep you in check."

I set my bag on the floor as I walk inside and slip off my shoes. When I turn to face Andrew, I'm graced with a look of confusion and intrigue. "A what?"

"A key?" I just realized what I said. A key. That's a big deal. While it'll make things convenient for us, it denotes more than that. So much more. It means commitment. It means a more formal relationship status. It means more nights like this, but without the formalities of an invitation. And that sounds absolutely blissful.

But then I remember his commitment issues. His fear of being open and vulnerable. A key would infringe on every one of those boundaries I'm sure he's not willing to bend. I'm about to take it all back, claiming it was just a silly little joke, when he asks a follow-up question.

"You want to give me a key?"

"No! I mean...I don't have to." I pause, trying to find the right words. "I didn't mean to say it. I just thought it would be more convenient. You know, last week you got here like, twenty minutes before I did, and you had to wait outside. If you had a key, you wouldn't be waiting around for me. And what if you have to use the bathroom, or Buster needs to be let out or..." I'm blathering. Taking the long-winded way out of this by saying a bunch of words to mask my embarrassment.

He saunters toward me, carefully placing the takeout bag on the dining table. "It would make things pretty convenient," he agrees. He smiles at me, a crooked little smirk telling me he absolutely agrees.

"But, I mean, if you think that's weird, or...whatever, then I get it," I stutter.

I idly trace my fingers over the back of a chair tucked under my dining table, attempting to hide my shame. But that's quickly snuffed when Andrew reaches for my cheek. He cups my jaw, running his thumb over my skin with a touch that feels like reassurance and comfort. I look up at him with a slowly spreading smile that starts to match his.

"I'd very much like a key," he tells me confidently. "And I'll have one of mine made for you."

"You don't have to. It's not a tit for tat kind of situation."

"No," he argues. "I want to, Grace."

I wonder where those commitment issues he so openly confessed are now. Because they aren't here, sitting between us while we discuss exchanging keys or other private access ways to parts of our lives. He kisses me, offering reassurance when I respond with silence.

"Are you sure?" I finally ask.

"Yes, I'm sure."

"You don't think..."

"What?" He asks as if he's trying to lure the words out of me, coaxing them into safety while I'm not completely sure if it's okay to say.

"It's not too soon?"

He shakes his head with his eyes piercing mine. The confidence that ekes out of him shows fear is the last thing on his mind. With his upturned lips and dark eyes, all I see is determination.

CHAPTER TWENTY-NINE

Andrew

I DON'T KNOW MUCH about nonprofit organizations aside from the obvious "not for profit" implication from the wording. I've worked various jobs since I was seventeen, and most were usually in some way or form an extension of corporate America. Of course, there was the exception of a small family-owned pet store I worked at the summer after my freshman year of college.

Sitting in the simple waiting area of The Hope Foundation, I quickly glance over the email on my phone. It's from Olive with the subject line WHERE ARE YOU? I can practically hear her urgent voice through the screen.

Mr. Sheridan is looking for you. I told him you're stuck in traffic. Hurry back!

I sent an email to HR this morning saying I'd be taking a long lunch, and I'd like to use some of my personal hours to cover it, the usual policy when we need any time off, even if it's just a few hours during the day. I probably should've cc'd Mr. Sheridan, but I didn't want to add another reason for me to rescind my appointment with Thad at The Hope Foundation. I'd barely convinced myself to take the meeting.

I tap out a quick message, letting her know I'll be another hour or so. All while the heel of my foot bounces off the carpeted floor. Hopefully the vein on his neck won't burst through his skin by the time I get back.

My phone buzzes in my hand with another alert. This time, it's a message from Grace. In the message, there's a picture of her lunch. A lunch I packed for her. It's a grilled cheese sandwich, wrapped in parchment paper to minimize any sogginess with an individual serving of minestrone. Under the image, there's a quick message accompanying it.

GRACE
Thank you for lunch.

I never brought up this meeting to her. I knew she'd be excited for me, possibly jumping to all the outcomes where I can finally leave my current job and getting both of our hopes up. The thing is, I'm not expecting much from this. It isn't a job interview, per se. It's more of a meeting to learn the ins and outs of the nonprofit business. See if it's a good fit for something I can pursue in the future. It's nothing more than some delving and inquiry that'll all probably amount to nothing.

I respond with a hasty 'Y' and 'W' with a kissy face emoji, just as I notice a man with dark curly hair and thick-rimmed glasses walk up to the glass doors leading to the waiting area. I quickly tuck my phone away, and as soon as he opens the doors, he greets me with a smile.

"Andrew?"

I stand from my seat. "Yes, hi." I extend my hand, and he offers a firm handshake.

"I'm Thaddeus," he says, warmly introducing himself. "It's nice to meet you."

"You too. Thanks for taking the time to meet with me."

"It's no trouble at all," he assures. "We're going to meet in the conference room. My office is a mess right now, and I don't think there's a place to sit beside my chair and the floor."

I chuckle, followed by an unimposing, "No worries." I follow his lead, and we veer down a hallway. The office bustles with amicable chatter and the occasional outbursts of laughs inside a thicket of cubicles. It's a setup similar to Sentry Investments, but there's a milder, more carefree air to it. People aren't tense and bitter. They look happy to be at work.

We enter the conference room, and I settle into one of the many seats surrounding a large oblong table. Thad starts with his fingers linked in front of him. "So, did Josh go over what we do here?"

"A little bit," I answer. "But I did some of my own research. It looks like you connect people with higher medical needs with state resources so they can take advantage of those services. There were some things I'm not familiar with, but it looks like you connect a lot of your members to services they might not be aware of or have immediate access to."

Thad nods along, patiently waiting for me to finish. "Yeah, it's a little more complex than that when you get into the details, but you summed it up nicely. Do you have any questions?"

"Maybe just the financing needs on your end," I answer. "I guess I just want to know how finance personnel would fit into your day to day."

"Of course. So, we're still a fairly small organization, but we're growing fast. The vice president who oversees the care management team handled all the finances because he has a background in accounting. But it's getting to be a bit much, so we're looking to have a finance manager on board. We still have to get it approved by the board, which is why there's no official job posting, but a lot of the leadership staff is open to it. We need someone who knows what they're doing to step in and help us. We need to make sure we're using our resources efficiently. We want to be able to speak for all our costs and budget, and we feel having someone with a background in finance can help with that."

"I see," I say. I take in all the information he gives me. It's a lot, but very informative. A small glimpse into the world of nonprofit organizations.

"Can I ask, how extensive is your experience in finance?"

I sit up straighter, a force of habit when talking about myself. An unboastful attempt to sell myself. "I've been at Sentry Investments for about five years. I started right after grad school. I handle a lot of the budgeting and planning throughout the fiscal year. I haven't quite made the transition to the investment side with advising clients, but I'm hoping a promotion will help with that."

"You've been there five years? And they haven't promoted you?"

I smile, though all I want to do is exhale a frustrated sigh. "Things are a little complicated with my boss."

Thad hums thoughtfully. "Well, it sounds like you have a good amount of experience for what we're looking for. I know I said we aren't hiring yet, but I can hold on to your résumé for when the board comes to a decision."

"Sure." That sounds reasonable. I don't know if I'm ready to completely walk away from a job I put so much time into, and I guess this will give me some time to do my own due diligence. I can gradually prepare myself and take new work opportunities in stride.

"There was another reason I asked Josh to have you reach out to me," Thad adds. "We have volunteer opportunities as well as internships. We don't currently have one for a finance department, but if you're willing to take an internship-type of position, I may be able to swing that.

"It doesn't have to be full time, just a few hours a week. Whatever you're able to commit to. And if the board sees that someone with your experience can help smooth out some of the kinks we have, they may be more inclined to open up a position."

"And this internship. Is it..."

"It would be unpaid, unfortunately. So I understand if it's not for you."

"No, I think the experience in itself would be good," I admit. It's the truth. In turn, I may find that this is the kind of work I'm meant to be doing. "Is it okay if I think about it?"

"Absolutely," he assures earnestly. "I still have to run the internship position by the CEO and vice president, so I'll keep you updated, but I hope you really do consider joining us in some way or form. Josh spoke highly of you."

"Well, he is my brother, so..." I say matter-of-factly.

"Of course, but he spoke on your experience and the current place you're at. I'm sure we can provide a less hostile working environment."

I duck my head, letting a nervous chuckle dissolve some of the unease talking about my boss. "Thank you. I appreciate your consideration."

"We'll be in touch."

When I get back to work, I brace myself for the wrath of Mr. Sheridan. I know it's coming the second I'm welcomed by Olive's panic-stricken face.

"Where the hell were you?" she hisses as soon as she sees me walk in.

"I had an appointment," I answer, some of the urgency in her voice carrying into mine. "What did you—"

"Andrew!"

Both my head and Olive's whip in the direction of Mr. Sheridan's office. He's standing there, his fists braced against his hips with an irate scowl stamped on his face. He strides toward me, the purposeful steps of his loafers pounding on the carpeted floor as he comes within inches of my face.

"Where the hell have you been?"

"I had an appointment, sir."

"And was this approved? I didn't see it on the calendar." He glowers at me, though with his height standing at about six inches below mine, it doesn't look as commanding as I'm sure he hopes it does.

"HR approved it," I explain. "They may have not added it to your calendar, but I let Olive know on my way out."

He looks to Olive for confirmation, to which she offers a slow, tentative nod. "He told me this morning," she says meekly.

"I thought you didn't know where he was."

"I forgot."

"Was there something you needed from me?" I interject, pushing aside this unwarranted investigation. With how many hours I put into this place on a daily basis, working way beyond my required hours, I'm sure an hour away shouldn't warrant any reprimand.

"I wanted some coffee after lunch. I had to send Olive, but I have something I need you to take care of in my office."

"Of course."

It's a small price to pay for my little hiccup. A punishment as if I'd committed a crime. I follow his steps into his office and find a banker's box filled with a heap of receipts. Some of them are worn, the text rubbed off and barely decipherable, and some are torn in half, practically trash at this point.

"Go through these and sort them by date," he demands. "I have two more boxes in the conference room once you're through with those." Mr. Sheridan slumps onto his chair and types away at his laptop screen as if I'm not even there. I hear him answer his phone with an elated greeting—a grating guffaw—and he leans back with his feet kicked up on his desk. Whatever infuriated tone he aimed at me is swiped away now that things are as they should be. Me, his little lackey, and him, the corporate version of the evil stepmother.

I almost ask him if he has another bag of Sour Patch Kids he'd rather have me divvy up by flavor before picking up the box and trudging over to my cubicle. Maybe an unpaid internship wouldn't be so bad. Anything to get me out of this snake pit and the slithering scumbag I work for.

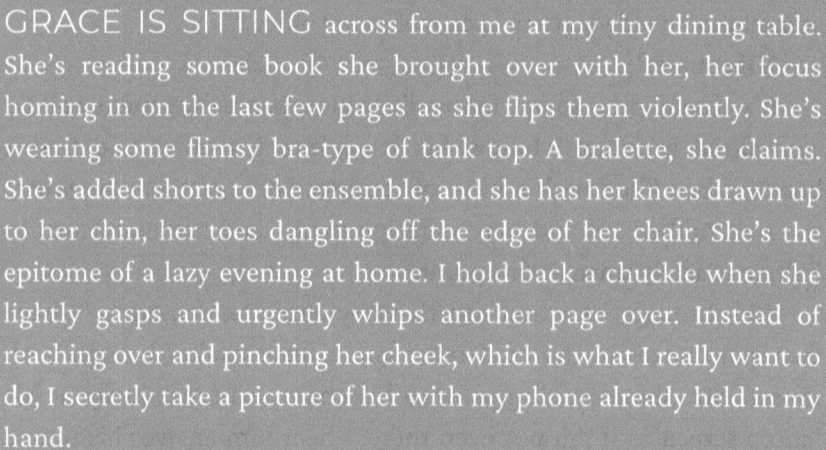

CHAPTER THIRTY

Andrew

GRACE IS SITTING across from me at my tiny dining table. She's reading some book she brought over with her, her focus homing in on the last few pages as she flips them violently. She's wearing some flimsy bra-type of tank top. A bralette, she claims. She's added shorts to the ensemble, and she has her knees drawn up to her chin, her toes dangling off the edge of her chair. She's the epitome of a lazy evening at home. I hold back a chuckle when she lightly gasps and urgently whips another page over. Instead of reaching over and pinching her cheek, which is what I really want to do, I secretly take a picture of her with my phone already held in my hand.

Satisfied with the candid moment I managed to capture, I return to the email I was reading from Thad. It's a standard follow-up email, though the level of sincerity makes the tone less formal and more personal. He added something new though. A generic job listing. Nothing official, but what was previously used for other internship positions. Just so I'm aware of what's expected as an unpaid intern. Still, it isn't so much the unpaid part that makes me hesitant. It's working more hours than I already am. There are days when I don't get home until after eight, and I don't know where I'd squeeze in a part-time internship. *Unless I quit my job altogether.*

"What are you looking at?"

I look up at Grace. Her book is closed and set aside next to her plate where a half-eaten slice of pizza rests. She picks up her can of Perrier and eyes me over the aluminum rim as she waits for me to answer.

"It's uh..." I pause to run a hand through my hair. "It's an email from this nonprofit organization."

"A nonprofit? Why are they emailing you?"

"I had a meeting with the president yesterday. Josh pulled some strings and got me an interview."

"What. Like a job interview?"

I shake my head. "Not really. It was more of a 'find out what they do' kind of meeting."

"So what are they emailing you about?"

"Just checking in, I guess."

She looks at me with doubtful eyes. "That's it?"

"He kind of mentioned an internship position. Something to get my foot through the door, and it can maybe transition into a full-time position...as the finance manager."

She leans forward, setting down her drink. "Andrew, that's a big deal."

"Eh," I answer, brushing her off. I don't know how to tell her I don't want to get my hopes up. What if it's not what I expect it to be? What if I'm stuck in the same place I am right now, just minus the shitty boss. With no room for growth or ladder to climb. I can't be some entry-level associate forever. So instead of telling Grace all of that, I simply say, "We'll see what happens."

Grace stands from her spot and walks the two steps to bring her right onto my lap, hooking her arms over my shoulders. "Hey," she whispers, placing a small peck at the corner of my mouth. "Talk to me. What's going on?"

I place my hands on her thighs, giving them a soft squeeze. I don't say anything, and she waits with patient eyes and an unwavering calmness that makes me feel like I can tell her anything. "I guess," I start. "I feel like I put so much into this company, and as much as I hate working for my boss, I don't hate the work. I'd like to move up there and finally get out from under him. I feel like I'm so close, but I don't know how much more I can take." I exhale a breath, my words jumbling together as they pour out of me. "And what if this nonprofit stuff just isn't for me? Then I'd have left my job for nothing, and then I'd be starting all over."

"But you'd have some experience under your belt, so you wouldn't be starting from scratch wherever you go. That experience has to speak for something."

"True," I admit, appreciating her honest and frank opinion. "It just feels like a lot for me to just try something out. I've held on for this long, maybe I need to suck it up. Just a little longer."

She cups my face with both her hands, squishing my cheeks together, and she kisses me. "Whatever you want to do, I'm here, okay? If you want to rot in this job with your asshole boss, I'll hold your hand and maybe pop his tires."

I lean my head back, looking up at her with a lopsided smile, and she scratches her nails between my shoulder blades, smothering any hint of vacillation I may feel as I stand in front of this self-imposed crossroad.

"And if you feel like you want to take this other job, I'll be here too. I'll even pack you a sack lunch on your first day," she says, grinning adorably.

I pinch at her sides, and she squeals. "Are you going to take a picture of me like it's the first day of school too?"

She nods, unable to answer through her giggly outburst.

"You're a little smart ass, you know that?"

"We can even get you a small chalkboard and write 'first day of work' on it," she manages to whimper out through her laughter.

We both fall into a laugh, the grim and somber conversation washed away with a playful round of teasing. Just as a happy sigh sags her body against mine, her eyes catch on my phone as it lights up with an incidental alert.

"What's this?" she asks, bringing up the screen closer to her. She studies it as her smile softens. "When did you take this?"

I look at her picture, her messy hair toppled over her head with her fist perched under her chin. "Right now," I answer. "While you were reading."

She smiles at me, her fingertips swiping away at my jawline like she's checking to make sure I'm real.

"What?" I ask when all she does is stare at me with shiny eyes.

She shakes her head. "Nothing."

CHAPTER THIRTY-ONE

Grace

MY FEET FUCKING HURT. I was going through my closet last night, and I found a pair of nude platform pumps. I completely forgot how badly I do in heels, and by the time I'd walked the ER floor twice, I was already regretting my decision. As soon as I walk into my condo, I kick them off and stuff them in the back—far back —corner of my closet.

I'm placing a small Band-Aid on my right pinky toe when I hear the front door open. The key I gave Andrew is being put to good use. He let himself in over the weekend when I babysat for Jade, and I needed him to feed Buster. Jade and Trevor's date night went a little late, into the wee hours of the night, and I was more than happy to spend the extra time with Avery. She babbled while I fed her dinner, and Jade and Trevor stumbled through their door past midnight, holding back their voices to hushed tones to make sure they didn't wake Avery. They looked happy and carefree after their first child-free outing in months.

"Grace?"

"I'm in my room," I call from the floor, patting down the Band-Aid to smooth out the creases.

He walks in and finds me, giving me a quizzical look as I examine my handiwork. "What happened?"

"I wore some stupid heels today, and they gave me the worst blisters."

He settles himself in front of me, taking my feet in his hands. He looks at the covered part of my toes and lifts my foot to get a better look. It tilts my balance backward, and I press the heels of my hands into the carpet.

"Here?" he asks, looking at my mediocre bandage work.

I nod. He leans down and puckers his lips before gently brushing them over my toes. His thumb rolls over the arch of my foot, and the pressure travels to my stomach. My head lolls back, and I sigh as the sensation spreads everywhere.

"Hmm, that feels good."

I catch him smile as he ducks lower and places another kiss where his thumb was, replacing the rapturous pleasure with soft, tender lips.

"That feel good too?"

I hum again, closing my eyes as he reapplies pressure, focusing on the achy balls of my feet. "I should wear heels more often."

He chuckles warmly, amused by my tactic to get more future foot massages. "I'd love to stay and do more of this," he announces, "but I'm afraid I have plans."

"Oh?" I respond, doing a horrible job hiding my disappointment. He catches on, and he leans forward to kiss me. When he does, my legs part, giving him easier access, and my suddenly sour mood lightens. I inhale a deep whiff of him, taking in the freshly sprayed cologne mixing with the scent of the long day settled in the fibers of his shirt. I fist a handful of his collar and tug him closer, whispering against his lips, "You're leaving me already?"

"I was actually thinking you could join me."

I pull away. "Where?"

"A few of my friends are meeting up for drinks at a bar in Ocean-side," he explains.

"What friends?"

"Hey," he protests, visibly offended. "I have friends."

I laugh, realizing how that sounded. I run my hand over his jaw, soothing away the unintentional barb. "What I meant was who are they? How are they your friends?"

He laughs too. No harm, no foul. "My college friends. They're the ones who live closer to Orange County. We're meeting in the middle."

"And do they know you're bringing a date?" I ask, avoiding his casual invitation.

"No," he admits, "but they know of you, so..."

"You talk about me to other people? You've never told me this."

"Because we don't really talk about things that go on outside of our little bubble here."

I frown. "What do you mean?"

He shrugs, looking a little uncomfortable with the shift in our conversation. "It's not a big deal. I just noticed you don't really seem to talk about things besides work, or maybe your family sometimes. You don't really talk about Teeny, and I feel like that's on purpose. I just thought you don't want me to talk about...certain things too."

"Like what?" A daze of confusion swirls in my head. How long has he felt like this?

"I don't know," he answers, his continued attempt to not turn this into anything more than an invitation for some drinks. "Like, I don't really talk about my family with you. Mainly because I don't want to remind you you're Teeny's friend, and that's the reason we keep this between us."

I don't mention there are other factors. Things like the fact that when I was entering middle school, he was still in diapers. Or that I'm pushing forty, and I'm reminded every single day my biological clock is ticking away while Andrew has no plans to settle down and start a family any time soon. It seems in the grander scheme of things, Teeny finding out about us sits at the bottom of the list.

"But I don't want you to keep things from me," I assure him.

Though, I know the assurance falls short because he's not wrong. I find myself not talking about Teeny either. I had dinner with her the other day when Andrew was working late, and I never brought it up. In fact, I was finding ways *not* to bring it up, intentionally keeping my plans from that night from him.

He ducks his head, averting his eyes from mine. "I just don't want to scare you away. You seem comfortable and yourself when we're just here. Or at my place. And...I don't want you to feel like I'm pressuring you into making this more than what you're comfortable with."

I grip his face and kiss him. The kiss turns deliberate, long and drawn out. He leans forward, forcing me further backward to the carpet.

"I'm sorry," I whisper. "I don't mean to keep this so private. I'm just..."

"It's okay," he whispers back. He brushes his nose against mine. "I get it."

I like him so much. All of the feelings tug at my heartstrings, and I realize how I never want him to feel like I'm hiding him away because I'm ashamed of him or us. I feel so seen when he tells me he gets it. I don't have to explain to him all my fears, and he just understands.

"Let's go," I tell him. "Tonight. I'll go with you."

His eyes light up, making a dull pang hit dead center in my chest. "Really?"

I pout a sad frown, my brow crinkling as I realize how much he's been holding back. "Really."

When we walk into the loud and cramped dive bar, it feels like we've walked through a small portal, not the stairs leading down into a

hunkered basement-style taphouse. Andrew has my hand enveloped in his, and when he looks down at me, he smiles.

"Thanks for coming with me," he says over the loud vibrations of music and chatter.

"You don't have to thank me."

He leans down and places a kiss on my bare shoulder. I opted for a floral dress. Flowy and light to get me through the summer air that remains stuffy even at night. It's held up by two thin strands, leaving behind enough bare skin that shimmers with the extra layer of moisturizer I used. Andrew hasn't been able to keep his eyes off me. At the back that dips low enough to expose the ridge of my spine. Every time he runs his thumb across my sensitive skin, I see his eyes flare with heat. He seems to have a thing for my backside.

We weave through the crowd, his hands at his side with the occasional stroke of his fingers against my waist. We reach a table where Andrew greets everyone with hearty hugs and keen handshakes.

"Hey, guys," Andrew announces. "This is Grace. Grace, this is everybody."

They go around the high table, following the pattern of the circle they're huddled around.

"Jake," says the first, a few inches taller than me with a mop of curly hair atop his head and a handlebar mustache.

"Ro."

Andrew interjects and says, "That's short for Rohan." Ro bares his pearly white teeth from behind a full beard.

There's a woman within the group, and she smiles warmly at me and extends her hand. "I'm Hayley."

"Hi," I respond, folding her hand in mine. I watch as Hayley leans into Ro, hooking her hand over his bicep.

"You want a drink?" Andrew says in a low voice close to my ear. He's hovering behind me, his chin less than an inch over my shoulder. Nearly skin to skin, just like the pads of his fingers still possessively running over my back, right between my shoulder blades. He's speaking at a volume barely over the noise, but I hear him over everything.

I look at him and nod.

"You good if I leave you here?"

Before I can answer, Hayley interjects.

"Come on, Andrew," she calls. Disbelief rings through the mockingly wounded look on her face. "We don't bite."

Andrew looks back at me with a grin at the same time I smile at him over my shoulder. "I think I'll manage."

Andrew leaves my side, sauntering away, and I catch his backside as he makes his way to the bar. I catch a few women's gazes shift to him, distracted as he walks by. Their eyes take in his height, then linger over his broad shoulders before landing on his face. Catching the sharp edge of his jawline and perpetually provoking eyes that seem to narrow when he's in pensive thought and candid when he's telling me something personal or intimate.

"So, how do you know Andy?"

"Andy?" I repeat. I look at Hayley, my lips downturn in amusement, and I nod, finding this new nickname intriguing.

"Are you his new girlfriend?"

I smile, ducking my head when I feel a flush spread to my cheeks. "Um, no. Nothing like that. We're...just friends."

She leans in close, and her elbow bumps against mine. "Sure," she appeases. She nudges her arm into me, a clear sign she's calling my bluff. "I won't tell anyone." She winks at me before tilting back the glass tumbler in her hand carrying something red-tinged.

"Have you known Andrew long?" I ask. My hands find a lone cocktail napkin, the edge damp from a ring of condensation. I start folding it, twisting the corners and tearing off a small piece. An apparent nervous tic making my hands fidgety with the mention of the foreign and somewhat inexact title.

"A few years," Hayley says. "Ever since Ro and I started dating. He's a good guy," she adds. "First time he's brought around a girl though."

227

That catches my attention. "Really?" The second I utter the question, I realize how desperate I sound. How eager I look to know more about Andrew's dating life.

Hayley opens her mouth to say more, but she's cut off when Andrew returns with two drinks in his hands. He has the usual Ketel and soda I drink and an amber-colored bottle for himself. Hayley returns to Ro's side, playing innocent with her eyes ping-ponging from Andrew to me then back to Andrew.

"Andrew," Hayley calls. "You should bring Grace to the Coldplay concert in November. She can have Jake's ticket since he can't make it."

Andrew turns to Jake. "You can't go to Coldplay?" he asks with disapproval.

"It's my niece's christening that weekend," Jake informs him, adding a resigned shrug. "I'll be in Michigan."

"Great! It'll be a double date." Hayley claps her hands together and grins at us.

Andrew flits his brow up and down. A taunt or some kind of tease, turning this innocent night out into something much more serious.

"So, how about a round of pool?" Jake asks as he slams his empty beer bottle down. "Girls against boys."

Andrew looks at me. "Ready to have your ass handed to you?"

I face him with narrowed eyes, welcoming his challenge. "Bring. It. On."

CHAPTER THIRTY-TWO

Andrew

GRACE HAS BEEN TAUNTING me all night. Gliding her hand up and down her pool cue while she waits her turn. Bending far over the edge of the pool table as she lines up her cue ball with the solid colors that seem to be dwindling down as the game goes on. Maybe boys versus girls was a bad idea. Who knew Grace and Hayley would be hustling us the whole time. Hayley went as far as asking how to use the pool chalk, feigning ignorance as she ran it over a wayward striped pool ball rolling her way. Before we know it, the girls are giggling over their impending victory.

"Is this why you didn't play?" Jake hollers at Ro. He's sitting in the corner, nursing a drink while watching me and Jake get our asses handed to us.

Ro nods. "I made a silent pledge to never play pool against Hayley," he admits.

"And you couldn't warn us?" I accuse as Hayley smacks the cue ball into the solid red, knocking it into a corner pocket.

"And miss this?" He gestures his hand to our smothered dignity, laughing at our diminished arrogance and how far we've fallen.

Hayley misses her next shot, not that it matters since the stripesto-solids ratio is laughable at this point. Jake lines up his next shot at Grace saunters up next to me.

"What's wrong, sport? Sad you're going to lose to *girls?*" Her lips carry a glistening shimmer, an effect from the lip gloss she applied between turns. They act as a homing device, her lips the target and my horniness a missile, the two ready to combust right here in this sticky bar with loud music and zero privacy.

My hand lands on her hip, and I give her a determined squeeze. "Easy there, slick," I warn. "You haven't won yet."

She points her index finger at the table, showing how inaccurate my statement is about to become. "I think it's safe to call it at this point."

I scoff. A faux jeer meant to brush off her competitive streak with indifference. But in all honesty, all I want to do is perch her ass at the edge of the pool table and make her spread her legs.

"Your turn, Grace." Grace turns around at Hayley's signal, ignoring the looks we're getting from my friends from every corner.

"Excuse me," Grace says, confidently pressing against my groin with her hip. "You're in my way." She bends at the waist right in front of me, the cue ball at the perfect angle from where she's standing. I take a step backward, enjoying the view. I take in how the soft muscles on her back move as her arms get into position. My eyes trail down to her thighs where the bottom hem of her dress has lifted, exposing the soft skin I know feels like silk.

A loud crack splits my thoughts, and when I look up, I see Ro eyeing me with a smirk. Grace whips around to face me, an arrogant grin splitting her mouth in two.

"I guess I should've bet something, huh?" She tilts her shoulder and clicks her tongue in smug triumph.

"Yeah? And what would you have bet?"

She taps her finger to her chin. "I don't know. I was thinking something like a drink but then realized how boring that is."

"Then something more daring?"

She nods. "Something risky."

"Hmm...something risky," I comment. "That would've made this game much more interesting."

She leans forward, and I run my fingertips up her arm, seeing a smattering of goose bumps follow in their wake. She gasps, her lips in that limbo stage between a smile and the round shape it makes when she moans.

"We can still make it interesting," she suggests, her mouth hovering over mine. "Pretend I didn't just wipe that pool table with you, and we can set the stakes a little high."

I squeeze her waist, and it elicits a sharp shudder. A tremble rattles just beneath her thin dress. The same dress I want to hike up just so I can get a good look at what's underneath. My other hand, the one just hanging at my side, slips across her thigh as soon as I lean forward to move another inch closer to her. I feel the smooth skin right where her knees touch. Where it feels fiery and feverish. Her thighs squeeze together, and I move higher, lifting the hem of her dress.

"Watch it," she warns. "Those hands are getting a little too curious there."

I smirk, forgetting our wager or how her pool skills surprised the shit out of me. I almost forget the fact that we're in public. That there are people who can see how Grace's face turns flushed from my wandering hands and how I'm getting just as turned on with my dick painfully pressing against the zipper of my jeans.

"Hey, Andy! You and your girlfriend want a shot?"

Grace covers her mouth to snuff a discreet giggle and ducks her face. I immediately cup my hand over the back of her head. To shade her from an embarrassing moment. To let her know that, as compromising as this moment has just become, the idea of her being referred to as my girlfriend makes me want to kick my feet in the air.

"Yeah, we'll take a round," I call to Ro over Grace's shoulder. I look back down at her, my hand now gripping her nape. My fingers tangle with the soft strands of her hair, and she smiles up at me. "That okay with you?"

I don't clarify if I'm asking about her new title or a second shot of tequila, but regardless she smiles up at me and answers, "Sure."

"That was fun."

I look at Grace over the curve of my arm. My wrist is draped over the steering wheel, and from this angle, she looks absolutely adorable. Her hair is a little disheveled with whips of it slashing across her face. She's slouched against the passenger seat, her bare feet propped up against the dash. I see the small Band-Aid she applied before we left still intact, and I want to reach for her toes. Rub my hands into them and lull her into a peaceful sleep.

"Yeah?"

She nods lazily. "We should hang out with your friends more often."

"They said to bring you around again. Looks like they like you more than they like me."

She laughs and her head lolls to the other side where she peers out the window with a dazed look of bliss on her face. "Looks like you've got some competition," she says, through a deep yawn as she sinks lower into her seat.

"Maybe I should meet your friends," I suggest. "Even the playing field."

"I don't have very many friends. The only one I have, you've known longer than I have."

"That's it?"

"I guess," she muses. "I have my sister."

"I can meet your sister."

She eyes me skeptically. "You want to meet Jade?"

"Yeah, why not?"

"I don't know. I just...didn't think you'd want to meet her."

"Of course I do. Maybe I can babysit your niece with you next time."

Grace laughs. A sleepy chuckle that makes her voice raspy and sexy. "Sure. If you like watching Blippi for three hours."

"What's Blippi?"

Her hand slides over my thigh, giving me a placating pat. "You don't want to know."

It's just after two in the morning. We still have about twenty miles to go to get to her condo. After that rousing round of pool, the excitement dwindled down to casual talk and nonalcoholic beverages. We sat around a table, ordered some onion rings and fries and caught each other up. I told Ro about my interview with Thad after Grace insisted it was more important than I made it out to be. Grace told my friends about what she does for a living and the hospital she works at. Jake told me about the cat he adopted. Though adopted doesn't seem like the appropriate word when the little guy just snuck into his apartment when he had the door propped open to bring in a new coffee table. We could've talked until the sun came up, but as soon as Hayley grew weary against Ro's side, and Grace started stifling the first of many yawns, I knew it was time to head home.

"You know, we never did decide on the bet."

I keep my eyes on the road, but I'm sure Grace gets a glimpse of my smirk even in the dark. "No, we did not."

The dashboard lights glint off her impish grin. "I was thinking the loser has to..." She pauses, clearly in thought, before she excitedly exclaims, "Get me hazelnut waffles."

"Right now?"

She nods. "Alcohol makes me hungry."

"Okay," I answer without putting up a fight. It's a good thing Marie's is open twenty-four hours.

I love seeing this side of her. She looks so loose and happy, and I wish I could always see her like this. I start to wonder if maybe this idea of us and keeping things a secret is what causes her to be wound up sometimes. Almost as if the constant reminder that no one is supposed to know about us is the cause of the tension sitting between her shoulders. After tonight, maybe she can see it doesn't have to always be this way. Sure, maybe we can keep things quiet for now. Ease our relationship out to the surface with time and care, but maybe that's the point. We can move slowly but keep moving. Get to a place where we don't have to hide things, and she can always be this way. Buoyant and carefree.

The car continues to whir in the quiet night, and I glance at her before adding, "I'm sorry if that was weird. You know, them calling you my girlfriend." I worried it might have caused a few warning bells to go off in her head, but I loved it. It made a beam of pride burst through my chest. *My girlfriend.* I imagined introducing her that way. To my friends or my family. To anyone.

"Don't be," she answers. "I...kind of liked it."

"You did?"

"Yeah."

It's quiet, and when I peek over at her, she's beaming at me with a sweet smile I just want to kiss. She reaches to hook her fingers over my bicep. She gives me a tight squeeze, and I take her hand in mine, kissing her knuckles gently.

"Does that mean you want to be my girlfriend?" I ask boldly with our fingers intertwined.

She shrugs. "I guess. I mean, if you have an opening." She leans forward, as far as her seat belt allows, and she kisses my cheek.

"Does that mean I'm your boyfriend?" I ask as her lips travel to my jaw. I shiver at the same time her hand grazes my chest. She deliberately hooks her thumb over and under my chain and gives it a quick tug.

"Yeah," she answers huskily. "I mean, that's the matching title. I'd hate to call you my friend if you're going around calling me your girlfriend. That's just embarrassing for you."

Her fingers play with my belt buckle, tickling my skin as her hand searches for more. "What are you doing?"

"Celebrating this new title of ours." Her cold hand goes all the way down my boxer briefs, and the touch sends a jolt right to the lower pit of my stomach. I grunt as she grips me, and it's a good thing my thinning focus manages to find a shoulder to pull into off the PCH. "What are you doing?" Grace asks as soon as the car comes to a halt.

"Celebrating this new title of ours," I mimic. I open the door and swing around to the back seat, slamming the door as I scoot to the middle. Grace watches me the whole time, her mouth slightly agape in pleasantly surprised shock. "You going to join me back here, or are you going to just stare at me from the front seat?"

She wedges herself over the center console, immediately settling over my lap as soon as she crosses over to the back of the car.

"Hi," she whispers, her arms wrapped around my neck.

"Hi." I kiss her. First at a sluggish pace. I take my time, wanting to drag the kisses from her lips, lick them off her tongue. But she has other plans. She threads her fingers into my hair, crashing her lips to mine. She rocks into me, my hips meeting hers as I feel her body build a rhythm I know she's chasing.

"Off. Now," she demands, tugging at my pants. I quickly undo my belt and slide my jeans down just past my knees. She looks down at my rock-hard erection, gliding her palm over the precum already building at the tip.

"*Ooh*, fuck," I groan, my head hitting the headrest and my eyes rolling back. Her hands are so determined, running along the sensitive ridges and even sweeping over my balls to make them tighten and pull. She could do so much with just her hands. As if there are a hundred different buttons or weak spots only she's aware of, and she uses them as she pleases. "That feels so fucking good, baby."

Calling her that spurs her on even more, and I nearly lose it when she runs her thumb over the tip, making everything slippery and wet. My hands fly to her wrist, a plea to make her stop, but she slaps it away, holding on to the control. The control I'm painfully letting slip away while she watches with hungry eyes.

"No," she commands. "I'll stop touching when I want." Another firm stroke, and I worry I might just come in her hands.

"Grace," I rasp. "Please."

"I kind of like this," she says, ignoring my plea. "You at my mercy, begging me to stop."

She uses her other hand to cup my balls, and she tugs at them, giving me a whole new sensation as she continues to stroke me in tandem. I slam my hands to her ass, hearing a dull slap as my fists grip her through her dress. Anything to hold on to the last of my will. I let out a loud moan, feeling dangerously close to the edge.

"Are you going to be a good boy and wait to come until you're inside me?"

My eyes focus on hers, and I notice how greedy they are. She wants me like this, all vulnerable and helpless. It turns her on to be in control. To have me be putty in her hands. "Let me fuck you then," I urge, my voice wavering as I'm pushed closer and closer to the edge. I bunch up her dress higher, hiking it up to her waist. It's then I'm surprised to find she's not wearing any underwear. "Have you been without any underwear the whole night?"

She bites her plump lower lip and drags it against her teeth. "Maybe."

"And you didn't bother to tell me?" I ask, disapproval coursing through the gravelly tone of my voice.

"It was a surprise."

I growl, jerking my hips toward her sweet pussy and thrust inside her. As soon as I do, her back arches.

"Holy *shiiit*," she gasps, her chest heaving with heavy breaths. She clings to my shoulder, something to ground her as she rolls her hips over me. "*Fuck*, Andrew."

I'm holding back my own sounds, trying to take back some of that control I let slip away. I watch her, my hands bracing her back as she trembles in my arms.

"What's wrong, baby? I thought you had it all under control."

"Shut *up*," she says through gritted teeth. Though her words hold very little weight.

"Aw, what happened to all that confidence?"

She scrapes her nails down my arms, leaving tracks, I'm sure. She moves, her body pulling away from me. Her feet, still strapped in sandals, hit the seat. They press into the cushioned area at my sides, and her bent knees part, spreading her thighs wide. This gives her the advantage, moving herself in and out at her own pace, and it drives me fucking wild. Her ass starts to bounce off my thighs and her moans grow louder, more dire and hungry. She slips one of the straps off her shoulder, sliding her arm out and letting her dress fall off one side of her chest.

"Jesus, Grace," I rasp, leaning forward. "You're driving me fucking crazy." I hook my fingers over the lace bra she's wearing, slipping it down to free her nipple. I become hungry, ravenous, looking at all the naked parts of her I want to run my tongue over. As soon as I pull her nipple over my tongue, she starts tensing.

"Fuck!" she cries. She slams back down, coming around me like a damn vise. I follow so quickly, it's pitiful. My grunts mix with her moans, the sounds filling the car like our own symphony. We cling to each other, desperate to catch our breaths. I feel her heart pound against mine. It's so frantic and fervent, I start to worry it's going to stop. But then the rapid beats start to steady, bringing us back into our bodies.

"Are you trying to kill me?" I ask, my face pressed against her bare chest.

She grips my face in her hands, our breaths still soft gasps. "Me, kill my brand-new boyfriend? Never."

I kiss her, cupping the back of her head to angle my lips to hers. "I could get used to you calling me that."

"Yeah, boyfriend?"

And I realize I don't think I'll ever get used to it because the butterflies fluttering in my gut feel everlasting.

CHAPTER THIRTY-THREE

Grace

"YOU LOOK DIFFERENT."

I look up from my chicken pesto panini. Oily crumbs rub along the pads of my fingers, and I reach for a napkin. "What do you mean?"

Teeny looks at me with narrowed eyes, setting down her own half of the panini we're sharing while on my lunch break. "I don't know. You have a little rosiness in your cheeks."

I scoff. "Okay."

"Are you pregnant?"

I almost spit out my food. "What!"

"Or you're getting laid," she continues her search for answers. "I don't know. You have this...glow."

"Um, no," I lie. In fact, it couldn't be further from the truth considering Andrew and I had a quickie in the shower this morning.

"That's it! You had sex."

"Shhh! Teeny, I work here. Can you keep it down?"

She rolls her eyes. "You work at the hospital across the street. *This* is a sandwich shop."

"Yes, but people I work with come here," I argue. "So don't say 'sex' so loudly."

She doesn't budge. She pokes her finger in my direction, a clear sign of determination. "I'm going to find out who you're screwing."

"Don't hold your breath."

A wave of guilt ripples through my gut. I'm lying to my best friend. The same best friend I called after having sex with Mikey Michael my sophomore year of college. I told her in gory detail how Mikey, who occasionally liked to be called Eminem, kept his socks on the whole time and asked how the best three minutes of my life was. We laughed until we turned red and drowned one of my worst sexual experiences with a pack of Seagram's.

I consider telling her for a second. Not that I've been screwing her brother, but that there's a man in my life. Not just a man, but a boyfriend. A whole ass boyfriend she doesn't even know about.

"You know, Teeny," I start to say, my voice shaky. "I actually have to tell you something."

"Yeah?"

"I guess, I wasn't being completely—"

"Grace." I look up from my half-eaten lunch at the sound of my name called by a deep voice. One that's equal parts surprised and pleased.

"Dr. Noah. Hi."

He approaches our table, a coffee in his hand. It looks like the same size as my own matcha I've been sipping on, but in his large grip, it looks child-size. A granola bar and a red apple are balanced on his other hand. He's wearing dark navy scrubs, a smattering of a five o'clock shadow along his jawline, and though it looks like he needs a haircut, the shaggy style he has looks charming and boyish.

"I think I've asked you to call me Noah more than once now." He has, the last time being just this morning when he showed me an updated picture of his cats. He named them PB and Jelly, and they were napping together, their paws linked together in their sleep.

I huff a nervous laugh. "Sorry, Noah." I pause, and I catch Teeny's eyes turn round with heightened interest. "This is my friend, Teeny. She's just visiting me for lunch."

Noah makes a charming gesture of smiling and offering a nod. Though his hands are full, and he can't extend a formal handshake, the sentiment is just as gentlemanly.

"Do you work with Grace?" Teeny eagerly asks.

"Sure," he answers. "If me always asking her for pet ownership advice is considered 'working together.'"

Teeny laughs, giggling behind her hand covering her mouth like a teenage girl talking to her crush. It's a little embellished, and I suppress an eye roll.

"Anyway, I'll let you ladies enjoy your lunch," Noah announces. He turns to me and adds, "I'll see you back on the floor, Grace." He does this little salute with his snack-occupied hand, and he does it with a suaveness that's all slick and natural. Teeny watches him walk away and whips her head to face me with a gaped mouth.

"Who is that?" she asks in a hushed voice. Her hands brace the table as if my workplace drama is going to physically hit her in the face with a satisfying blow.

"I just introduced you. It's Dr. Noah."

"No, that man told you to call him *Noah*. Not *Dr.* Noah. Just *No-uh*." She drags out his name, enunciating it in excess. "Is that who you've been boinking?"

"Don't say 'boinking.'"

"It's him though. Right?"

"No. I don't shit where I eat."

"Why not? You know forty-three percent of marriages are a result of work-related romances."

"Why do you know that? That is such a specific statistic."

"I just do," she answers before quickly adding, "So?"

"Teeny, I am not in any kind of work-related romance with Dr. Noah—"

"Noah," she interjects.

"With Noah," I correct myself. "It's just not happening."

"Why not? He's really handsome. And he's a doctor. He's a hot handsome doctor you work with. The rom-com is writing itself,

Grace. I can almost hear Nancy Meyers tapping out her screenplay at her Hampton Beach house."

"Your imagination is wild."

"You think Sam Claflin would be available to play Dr. Noah?"

Our laughter echoes off the walls of the small sandwich shop, and that wave of guilt rolls through me once again.

"I had lunch with Teeny today."

Some garbled sounds muffled by foamy toothpaste come out of Andrew's mouth. The end of his toothbrush dangles from the corner of his mouth, and he looks at me through the reflection off the medicine cabinet.

"What?"

He spits, rinsing his mouth. "How was it?" Water drips from his chin, and there's still a white dollop of toothpaste at the corner of his mouth.

"Good," I answer, handing him the towel I was using to dry my face. "She asked me if I was having sex."

He uses the unsettled blank look on his face to ask for more information. Probably what the context was that led to the topic of my sex life. He leans his palm against the bathroom sink counter and runs his tongue across his lower lip, a tell that he's worried this conversation may shift into a too-much-information territory that involves what we do behind closed doors and his sister.

"What?" he asks.

"Actually, she *told* me I'm having sex. And then she asked me who it was."

"She can tell you're having sex?"

"I guess so."

"Is that a skill most women have?"

"I don't know." I face him, my hand landing on the cool surface right next to his. I look at him with narrowed eyes, flicking my gaze up and down, and say, "Yup. You're definitely having sex."

He pinches my waist, and I squeal as he hoists me over his shoulder. He walks into my room with my legs kicking. He lands a hard slap to my ass, a loud smack bouncing off the walls with the lack of cushion on my pants-less bottom. He tosses me onto my bed before crawling over me, the sting on my skin suddenly the least of my worries as that chain I love dangling off his neck tickles my chin.

"I guess it *is* a skill women have," he says in a raspy voice. His hand braces my waist, gliding down to my hip.

This feels like a nighttime routine at this point. Andrew and I come home from work, sometimes his place, sometimes mine. We eat, fill each other in on our day, and make our way to bed. Sex is usually on the itinerary, just like a shower and brushing our teeth, and we fall asleep like we've been doing this for much longer than just a few months.

None of it's anything remarkable. In fact, it's almost mundane. But it's the mundane I'm finding a new level of comfort in. Not fancy gifts or expensive dinners. But spread out on the sofa or our beds, fighting our sleep with the TV playing the last bits of whatever we decided to put on. Or evening walks with Buster, where all we do is take a stroll around the block, holding hands and picking up some dessert. It was never like this with my ex-husband. Our lives were always in motion. Going to the next party or dinner or whatever event where I stood by his side dressed in something steamed and smoothed, always looking like I was a porcelain doll instead of his partner.

"So, do you think Teeny caught on?" he suddenly asks. His lips make their way to my neck, leaving behind a trail of wet kisses, and the words feel like I'm being doused by cold water.

"Are you worried about it?"

He pulls away and bumps his nose against mine, a playful nudge to warm the suddenly shifted mood. "No, just curious."

"I don't think so," I answer him. "But..."

"What?"

"I don't know," I say. "Maybe it's not the worst thing if she knows. I mean, if we keep this up, we can't keep it a secret forever."

"Really?" His sweet grin makes my heart melt, and then I realize how much he's been holding back this whole time. He wants Teeny to know, and he's been keeping his thoughts quiet for me.

I pause, walking past the point of no return. "I mean, Teeny's my best friend," I tell him. "I hate keeping this from her, and—"

He kisses me, and it's crushing, expressing all the excitement in his chest through his hands. Hands that move all over me, touching and caressing and squeezing.

"Hold on there, cowboy," I say, pressing a hand to this chest. "Let's take it slow." I don't want to smother his excitement, but I'm still trying to find that middle ground I'm comfortable with. I hate to have to put him in this situation, but the blow from my last relationship left me unsettled and, quite honestly, scathed. I guess I'm not as over my divorce as I thought I was.

He clears his throat, a serious furrow shading his eyes, though remnants of that grin still remain on his face. "Right. Take it slow."

"What I mean is we can talk about how we want to tell Teeny," I assure. "Make sure we have the right words, so we don't give her a stroke or something."

"Yeah." He nods, and I watch a little bit of that elation dim.

"Hey." I cup his jaw and force his eyes to mine. "It'll happen. I just have to...work up to it."

A smile that doesn't quite reach his eyes looks down at me. The small smirk looks more appeasing than expressing the honest emotion coursing through him. It feels consolatory. Placating. Letting me know whatever it is I want, he'll go along with it. For the sake of this. More kisses and hands and touches. No matter that it's behind closed doors.

"How about we go out on a date this weekend?"

"A date? Why?"

He nonchalantly tilts his head. "Just because."

"No reason?"

"I just feel like I've never taken you out," he answers. "And I want to take you somewhere nice."

"You want to wine and dine me?"

"Anything to get you to put out."

I smack him on his butt, a sharp rebuke displayed through my bottom lip pulled between my teeth. "You ass."

"An ass you're going to put out for when you see where I take you." He grabs my wrists and pins them above my head, pressing them into the mattress with his strong hand.

"Oh, yeah?" I taunt. "Where is this magic, aphrodisiacal restaurant?"

"It's a secret."

"Hmm, I'm intrigued." He leans down to kiss me, letting it linger for longer than a quick peck. Much longer.

"Oh," he says, his lips against my jawline. "Don't forget, we're going to the Coldplay concert next month. Hayley's been bugging me about it."

"This suddenly reminded you of Coldplay?"

He smirks. "I just didn't want to forget. I'm scared of Hayley."

"When is it?"

"The second weekend of November. On a Friday. I think the tenth or the eleventh."

I pull away as regret draws my brows together. "My parent's anniversary is that Saturday. I'll be busy with party prep and keeping my mom somewhat sane. She'd kill me if she knew I was going to spend the night before her big day at some concert."

"Oh," he softly exclaims with a furrow growing between his own brows. "I didn't know your parents were having a party."

"Yeah," I explain. "It's their fiftieth, so they're throwing this big thing up in Malibu."

He smooths his thumb over my cheek. "It's fine," he tells me.

"I'll make it up to you. I promise."

"Actually, I think you need to make it up to Hayley. She's the one who's been excited for this double date."

"I will," I promise. "We'll...play pool again."

"Hell no," he argues, shaking his head in urgent protest. "Once was humiliating enough."

I laugh, just as his hips press into me. "Fine then, I'll think of something."

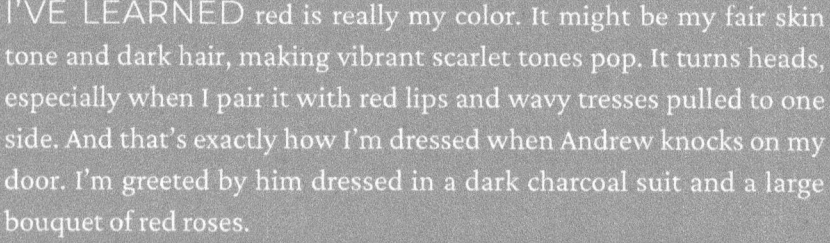

CHAPTER THIRTY-FOUR

Grace

I'VE LEARNED red is really my color. It might be my fair skin tone and dark hair, making vibrant scarlet tones pop. It turns heads, especially when I pair it with red lips and wavy tresses pulled to one side. And that's exactly how I'm dressed when Andrew knocks on my door. I'm greeted by him dressed in a dark charcoal suit and a large bouquet of red roses.

"I thought you might like the real ones this time."

"Thank you." I take them from him, the rich floral scent mixing with his spicy cologne. I notice his hair is slicked back, tamping down the wayward waves I love to run my fingers through. I turn toward the kitchen to set the beautiful arrangement on the counter, and when I turn to face Andrew, I see he's keeping a considerable amount of distance between us.

He eyes me, up and down, and I realize the purposeful space is so he can admire me. Take in all of me the way one would take in a painting, appreciating the array of details you'd miss at the edges out of your periphery if you were to be standing too close.

"You look amazing, Grace." I didn't expect him to react this way, seeing me in anything but my unremarkable work clothes or wrinkled pajama pants. He looks surprised. Almost speechless.

"You look shocked that I look good in a dress."

He closes the space between us, looping his hand around my waist. "I just can't believe you're my girlfriend. That's all."

I roll my eyes, though the compliment hooks all the way to my chest, tugging at my insides and stirring them awake. "Stop blowing smoke up my ass."

"What?" He sounds genuinely insulted. "Why would you think I don't think my girlfriend is beautiful?"

"You've seen me in a dress," I point out. "Don't act like this is something new."

He cups my cheek, running his thumb over my jaw. "Every time I see you, I feel like I'm seeing you for the first time."

This time, I don't shoo away his flattery. In fact, it doesn't feel like he's sweet-talking me at all. He sounds sincere.

"How come you didn't use your key?"

"I'm taking you out on our first date," he answers matter-of-factly. "First dates don't let themselves in."

"Oh, if that's the case, I'll make sure I do what *I* do on first dates."

"What's that?"

"Go home alone." I scrunch my nose and poke my finger into his chest, playing into our little game.

"Ho—hold on. Let's not make any rash decisions."

I offer a delighted giggle and a quick peck to the corner of his mouth. Assurance that of all the outcomes tonight may have, either one of us going home alone isn't going to be one of them.

"I just need to grab my purse, and I'm ready to go."

After I have my small clutch, I slip on a pair of nude pumps by the door, relieved my blisters have healed since I've opted for some footwear that's been properly broken in.

Andrew's picking some lint off his suit lapel, and he runs his hands over it to smooth out any wrinkles. I take over, gliding my palm over his shoulders, swiping away at any small specks he may have missed.

"You know, you don't look too bad yourself," I tell him. "Boyfriend."

He grins like a damn fool. "You think so?" He stands up straighter, plucking at the collar of his white dress shirt he wore sans tie. His chin is tilted upward with pride, and I want to just pinch his cheeks. Instead, I settle for buttoning his suit jacket and grabbing my keys.

Andrew makes a show of opening the passenger door for me to his freshly washed Mazda and closing it after I slide in. I watch him round the hood to the driver's side. I'm surrounded by a waft of new car smell, an air freshener that most likely came with the car wash he obviously paid for.

"So, you really aren't going to tell me where we're going?"

Andrew pulls out of the parking spot in my building's garage, taking the turns around stretches of packed parking spots. He holds an impassive look directed toward the barrier boom as we leave the garage. When he finally peers over at me, a smirk hides behind his cool look of composure.

"I told you, it's a surprise."

"But like...is it nearby? Or..."

"Can't handle the pressure of a surprise?"

"No, it's fine," I answer meekly with a dismissive shrug.

I really can't pinpoint it. My stomach feels a little jittery, and I don't know if this "first date" makes me nervous, or if I'm hungry. I can't help but feel that everything is perfect and as it should be when we're in our bubble. What if outside of it, he realizes we don't really fit? All the elements of the outside world will mix with what we have, making it muddled and tainted.

"If you're worried about running into someone we know, we're going out of San Diego," he tells me.

Is that why I'm nervous? Am I worried about running into someone we know? I consider it a possibility for my slightly rattled nerves as I jokingly ask, "What, like Tijuana?"

He laughs. "No, like Orange County. Specifically, Irvine."

"Irvine? What's in Irvine?"

"I know a place." He winks at me, holding tight to his ultra-secret itinerary.

Though the drive is a little longer than we're used to, we fill it with random pillow talk. The kind of conversation that comes naturally between us. He tells me about his work, if he's heard anything else from the interview with The Hope Foundation. He tells me about a recent CNN article he read about artificial intelligence and the misuse of it, commenting how creating reels of a hundred cats doing yoga isn't as productive as using it for something like cancer research. I add in my two cents, throwing in how AI is a detriment to the creative community. He also tells me about a new fish oil for dogs that can easily be added to Buster's food after he noticed he's been scratching behind his ears more frequently.

By the time I tell him about a new book I started about two estranged sisters who come together after one has been diagnosed with a terminal illness, we're exiting the highway. The conversation somehow segues into what song we'd want played at our funeral—"Shake It Off" by Taylor Swift for me, "Eye of the Tiger" by Survivor for him—when we're pulling into Warehouse 72.

The valet opens my door, and I step out with care. Andrew's already at my side, his hand extended in my direction to help me out of the car. He doesn't let go, linking our fingers as soon as the valet hands him his ticket.

"I feel like royalty," I whisper as he leads the way inside.

"Does that mean I should call you princess tonight?"

"Hmm, I kind of like that." He hooks my hand into the crook of his arm. With his elbow bent, securing my loose grip, and my boyfriend looking so handsome and suave, I really do feel like royalty. Maybe not the kind with a gold throne, but one a very doting subject.

Once we round the entryway to the hostess desk, I notice it's bustling. Saturday night at peak dinner rush time, and it looks like date night is on everyone's itinerary. I cling to Andrew closely, using my other hand to grip his bicep. He gives a gentle tug. A clear sign we won't get separated.

He tells the hostess his name and that we have a reservation, and we barely have a minute to ourselves before we're following a young man in a white dress shirt and pressed slacks holding large menus to a small, secluded table for two.

Large glass goblets and polished silverware are systematically placed on the table with a votive candle in the middle. The lights in the restaurant are low, creating a muted effect. It tints the room with secrets and intimate rendezvous, all behind dark shadows. I look across the table, and the engrossed scowl on Andrew's face is adorable as he looks over the menu. I reach across the table and hook my fingers over the top of his menu to lower it. He looks at me and the deep furrow between his brow vanishes, a sweet smile in its place.

"It's really nice here."

He grins, lighting up the dullness around us. "I wanted tonight to be special."

"And it is, but I just want to tell you," I add. "It would've been just as special at home. I like your home-cooked meals."

"You haven't gotten tired of my grilled cheese sandwiches?"

I shake my head vigorously, expressing how far from the truth his question could be. "I appreciate this too. I just don't want you to think I want this all the time."

"I know." He reaches for my hand, grazing his thumb over my knuckles, and a small part of me wishes we were home. Where we'd be in private and the darkness would be from watching movies with the lights out to create a theater effect, not overdone ambiance lighting.

"I'm going to go to the little girl's room," I announce. "Can you order me a—"

"Ketel vodka?"

I smile. "Yes please." I lay my napkin on the table next to my shiny forks and sashay away to the ladies' room, knowing Andrew is watching me. The bathroom looks like an extension of the restaurant with its shimmery white countertops and rich afterglow. It smells like plumerias inside instead of the usual stench of toilet water most bathrooms have. As I'm finishing up and washing my hands, a young woman who doesn't look a minute over the age of twenty-one stumbles out of a stall. Her dress, much like her obvious youth, is a direct contrast to mine. It's a metallic kind of color, one that looks like it should be draped around a ball and hung over the center of a dance floor. She smiles at me, giggling a little sloppily. Her alcohol consumption seems to make her as friendly as it makes her bold.

"Oh my god, that dress is gorgeous," she gushes at me as she's towel drying her freshly washed hands. Her hand trails my arm, and her friendliness oozes into my own pores.

"Thank you," I tell her with a smile. "Yours looks amazing too."

She glides her hands over her dress, running over the curves that are showcased with its sleek design. "Oh, this," she comments, brushing me off. "It cost a pretty penny too." She leans over the sink and touches up her makeup with a tube of glittery lip gloss. "The guy I'm here with tonight bought it for me. It's not usually my style, but when he whipped out his black AmEx, I thought, 'Why the hell not?'"

I laugh, appreciating her candor. We both face the mirror, touching up our makeup and fluffing our hair. I'm patting my lipstick on my puckered pout when she wiggles her index finger at me and comments, "I hope whoever brought you out tonight knows how lucky they are."

"He does," I tell her shyly.

"Good." She turns to leave but changes her mind and faces me. "I'm Kimmy by the way."

"Grace."

"It was nice to meet you, Grace."

"You too."

She dashes off, the clicks of her high heels clacking away as it fades in with the bustle outside the bathroom. I tuck my lipstick back in my clutch and head back out.

Kimmy's right. I do look amazing. And while my dress does much to complement me, it's more than that. It's the glow of someone falling for another. I haven't felt this in a long time. When I'm with Andrew, I feel completely myself. I don't worry about making a fool of myself. I don't feel insecure or self-conscious. I feel confident and sure. He considers me in so many aspects of his life. When he stocks his fridge, when he buys his usual bathroom toiletries. Even when he cooks dinner. He tries to brush off my preference for his homemade meals by saying all he can really prepare is grilled cheese sandwiches, but he's actually really good at other things too. I can tell it's all a first for him, but he takes the time to look through recipes. He doesn't just settle for takeout or air-fried food, he actually cooks. He even leaves out his old shirts for me to wear when I'm at his house. He knows what I like, and he doesn't try to pressure me to do things out of my comfort zone. If that's not love, then what is?

Is that what this is? Love? Has our relationship already steered that course into love? That's pretty serious. And yet, it doesn't scare me. It doesn't seem to scare Andrew either. He told me before that being vulnerable seems scary and daunting, yet he seems to be his barest form when he's around me. Maybe it's because this is stepping into love territory. We're taking it one step at a time, dipping our toes instead of fearlessly cannonballing in.

I'm smoothing out my dress as I turn the corner back to our table. I catch Kimmy take a healthy pull out of a glass tumbler, and when we make eye contact, she waves at me. I grin and quickly wave back, eager to get back to Andrew.

"Grace?"

My heart drops all the way down to my feet when I hear that voice. The voice that used to mock and tease me. That used to belittle me into thinking the things I wanted in life were too complicated and purposeless.

I look beyond Kimmy's confused face. Right to the seat across from her where Frankie, my ex-husband's, smug smirk greets me with discomforting keen interest.

"Wow," he exclaims through a disbelieving chuckle. "You look amazing."

I look at Kimmy, and she catches on to my uncomfortable posture. My tight shoulders and the dumbstruck look of shock on my face. I see a frown wipe away what seemed like her usual bubbly demeanor, and it's directed at Frankie with disapproval.

"Jesus, if you looked like this when we were married, I would have never left." His sarcasm leaks out of him, seeping into the suffocating air I want to bolt from.

"Baby, I want another drink," Kimmy pleads, an obvious attempt to distract him.

"Yeah, yeah. Give me a minute," he tells her. He stands from his seat, pressing a hard, unwelcome hand on my arm. "So, are you here by yourself, or..."

I straighten my back, squaring my shoulders. He's nothing. He's less than nothing. He's barely a speck of lint. Something I can pinch and flick off. I look at him, refusing to shy away from his depraved eyes as they travel down and back up. "I'm here with my boyfriend."

"Whoa, boyfriend," he comments. The taunt isn't in his words, but it's there in the way he talks to me. With cynicism and forced shock. He leans closer and says in a low, threatening voice, "You don't say. You going to chase this one away too?"

My ears feel like they're on fire. Like steam is leaking out of them. My head feels fuzzy, and the panic rattling me from the inside spreads to my toes.

Pleased with my reaction to his callously spoken words, he adds, "I should warn the poor schmuck, so he knows what he's getting himself into."

A rise of hot anger bubbles in my chest, and I do everything I can to smother it down. Count to ten, clench my fists, take a few deep breaths. He always did this. Find ways to make me feel two inches tall. It seems like our relationship, all the moments where words "soulmate" and "significant other" were the perfect descriptors for us, happened in some alternate universe. Because this can't be the same man I fell in love with in my twenties. That man was kind and funny. His work and social circle turned him into this arrogant scumbag I don't even recognize.

"Baby." Kimmy's high-pitched voice doesn't match the apologetic look on her face.

"I said give me a minute," Frankie snaps at her. I look at Kimmy, our faces frozen in discomfort as we share a silent mutual agreement that this run-in needs to end. I catch her mouth the word "sorry" at me, before I shake my head, dismissing her apology. No one should have to apologize for Frankie.

"You know, Frankie," I start to say, the need to leave clawing at my insides. "This was...interesting, but I have to go."

"To your boyfriend. Gotcha." His hand stays on me. It feels like a death grip, though it's barely his palm grazing over the bare skin on my forearm. I almost shake his hand off, but stop myself, not wanting to egg him on even more.

I smother the errant comment at the tip of my tongue and just nod, my lips pressed together to hide the scowl I'd prefer not to wear. I smile at Kimmy, offering her a kinder sentiment.

I turn on my feet to head back to my table when I catch Andrew walking in my direction. A concerned frown has his lips sitting in a straight line, and his steps are urgent. The way his face softens when he finds me shows I must've taken a little longer than anticipated. His eyes travel to where Frankie is by my side. To his grimy hand still on my arm, and he stops in his tracks.

"Mr. Sheridan."

Mr. Sheridan? How does he know Frankie? And why is he calling him Mr. Sheridan?

"Andrew? What the fuck are you doing here?"

I step away from Frankie, no longer caring to appease him. I don't care, I just want answers. "How do you know Andrew?"

Frankie's face starts to flush, a clear sign of indignation evident also by his hands now fisted by his side. His mouth is agape, his eyes looking between me and Andrew who now stands by me with a protective hand placed on my back.

"Are you okay?" Andrew's voice sounds dark, like it should come with a warning label. His eyes, just as threatening as his voice, leers at Frankie.

"How do you know Frankie?" I ask, my voice wavering. I'm so confused, it feels disorienting.

"This is my boss," he answers plainly.

What the fuck. My hand tightens around his arm. A plea and desperation in my death grip. "Andrew," I manage to squeeze through my dry throat.

"Did he hurt you?" He doesn't know. Of course he doesn't know. I haven't told him Frankie is my ex-husband. All he's seen is his smarmy boss with his hand on me, his girlfriend.

I squeeze harder, and he finally looks at me. When he sees the panic on my face, the tears brimming in my eyes, and the short gasps making my chest rise and fall, the worry returns.

"What's wrong? What happened?"

"Oh, this is hilarious." Frankie claps his hand, clear amusement in his wide grin. He bends over laughing, pressing a hand to his stomach and overdramatically slapping his knee with the other. "This is just fucking hilarious."

Andrew looks at him with a fierce glare, and he moves his feet to create a blockade between me and my ex-husband. I notice then that we're drawing a crowd. People have stopped eating and talking, and their curious eyes are on the three of us.

"What's so funny?" Andrew asks, still oblivious.

"This is your boyfriend, Grace?" I can feel Frankie looking at me. All while I wish the ground would crumble beneath me and swallow me whole. "He's a little young for you, no? Or is that what you're into now?"

"What did you say?"

I pull at Andrew's arm to get his attention, hopefully defusing the explosion before it bursts. "Can we just leave?" I plead.

"No, don't go," Frankie urges. He pokes his hand in our direction, taunting us, and I wish I was stronger than this shriveled-up version of myself under his scrutiny. "Tell him, Grace. Tell him who I am."

Instead of telling Andrew the truth, I look up at him. A single tear spills from the corner of my eye. "I'm so sorry," I whisper.

Before Andrew can process my apology, what it's for or why it's needed, Frankie cuts in. "I'm her husband."

"Ex-husband," I correct in my watery voice.

Andrew slips his arm from my grip. A step backward creates a space between us that feels like a large crater. "What?"

"I'm so sorry," I say again, the tears now streaming down my face. "I didn't know he was your boss. I didn't—"

Andrew grabs my face, cupping my cheeks between his palms. "Hey, it's okay. Let's go."

I nod. His touch is careful and gentle as he slips his jacket off and drapes it over my shoulders. I watch Frankie take us in with so much disdain, I worry he's going to cause an even bigger scene than the one we've already created.

Andrew moves quickly, leading me outside with his tender hands guiding me. And it's quiet. Like a flurry of snow, a blizzard of chaos with all the unsettling quiet making me want to scream into the void.

CHAPTER THIRTY-FIVE

Andrew

I DIDN'T REALIZE two such strong emotions could lay over each other. When I saw Mr. Sheridan lay his hand on Grace, I felt like my insides were going to boil over. I could feel the little bubbles scale the walls of my stomach, spilling over the edges through a barely contained fury I managed to tamp down. And then there's the worried side of me that aligned more with panic and sheer fear. Grace looked like she was having a nervous breakdown. An anxiety attack that rattled her from the inside. Her entire body shook, and her breathing spiked like she was trying to catch her next breath.

In that moment, I realized my concern for her trumped everything else.

I don't know what he said to her before I saw them, but whatever it was, it rattled Grace. She's been quiet the entire drive home, and when we finally make it into her condo, she slips off her heels and stands at the door. The blank look on her face tells me she's replaying the events of tonight. How it went south so quickly. In the blink of an eye.

Buster runs up to us, his wide smile with his tongue hanging out an obvious reminder that dogs really don't know how to read the room. Still, Grace pats his head, and he nudges his snout into her thigh, adding a soft whimper.

"Hey, buddy," I tell him, tugging at his collar. "Let's give mommy a minute." He obeys my command and turns back to his spot on the couch.

"Mommy?"

It came out without me even realizing, only going by what she calls herself when she's talking to Buster. "I don't know. It just came out," I respond hoarsely.

She cups her hand to my jaw. "It's cute." Her soft smile doesn't reach her eyes, and it cuts into my chest.

"Hey." I stoop so my eyes meet hers. She's trying to not let the whole night be ruined, but I can see her efforts being pulled thin. "Are you okay?"

She nods. "Sorry. I don't really know why I'm like this." She runs her hands through her hair and exhales a deep cleansing breath, though it does little to ease her nerves.

I pull her into an embrace, and I feel her fall into me. "It's fine, Grace." I pull away to look at her. She's not crying, she stopped as soon as we got in the car, but she doesn't look any better than when we walked out of the restaurant. "Go shower and change into something comfortable. I'll order a pizza or something."

"Actually," she says with her arms wrapped around my waist. "Can you just warm up some leftovers? There should be some of that pasta you made the other night in the fridge."

"You sure? I can get something else if you don't want pizza."

She nods. "I want something you made."

I lean down to kiss her. A small gentle peck on the tip of her nose. "Yeah."

"You know, I hardly recognized him."

Grace is loosely holding a glass Pyrex container of carbonara over her lap. She must've been hungry because as soon as I set down the steaming hot container fresh out of the microwave, she devoured half of it. She looks calmer, more relaxed, though the somber look on her face hasn't fully gone away.

"How long has it been since you last saw him?"

"About four years ago," she tells me, stirring her fork through a loop of noodles. "When he packed up his things and moved out."

"Here? He lived here?"

She nods. "Perks of having a good divorce attorney. I think he's still pissed about that one."

"Why do you call him Frankie? I thought his name was Matthias."

"Francis is his middle name. His whole family calls him Frankie, and I did too. Since we met. Though, I don't think anyone calls him that anymore. He grew out of that nickname. Kind of like he outgrew me." After a weighty pause, she adds, "Why do you call him Mr. Sheridan?"

"Because that's what he told me to call him."

She scoffs. "Of course he would." She takes a sip of her water. When she looks at me, I see a morose smile on her face. "I'm fine. Really. I think just...seeing him threw me off. And I think he thinks he won or got out of what he thinks was a trap of a marriage. He's probably right."

My head rears back in disbelief. "What? Why would you say that?"

"It's true," she argues. "If I hadn't changed my mind and wanted kids, he wouldn't have had to treat me the way he did, and we wouldn't have had to get divorced."

"Grace, you have it so wrong."

"What do you mean?"

"What he did...that's abuse. He made you feel like it was all your fault when all you did was tell him what you wanted. I mean, yeah, maybe you two wouldn't have worked out anyway since you ended

259

up wanting different things, but he didn't need to treat you the way he did. That was a choice he made."

She sets down her dinner, the remaining oily contents of it now grown cold. She doesn't necessarily agree with me, but she doesn't argue the facts I set down in front of her.

"Do you regret divorcing him?"

"No," she answers quickly. "I want what I want, and yeah, if we can't agree on something like having a family, then we shouldn't be together."

"Then that's it. Don't let him get into your head." She finally smiles a real smile. "And this place that's rightfully yours? Don't feel guilty about that either."

This time she laughs. "I don't."

"Good."

We continue to eat in silence, the clinks of silverware on glass creating a soft buffer we didn't know we needed. By the time I've washed the pile of dishes in the sink, and Grace is sitting on her couch with a few throw blankets draped over her legs, it's late. Buster has his head resting on her lap, and his eyes flit to me as if he's attempting to ask me if his owner's okay.

"I'm going to take Buster out," I announce. "I'll be back."

She stops me, pulling at my hand. I sit next to her, temporarily putting off the duty of walking Buster for his bathroom break. "Thank you."

"For what?"

She sighs, sinking her cheek into my chest. She doesn't look at me when she answers me. Instead, she wraps her arm over my stomach. "For taking care of me and not getting upset. And taking care of Buster." Buster lifts his head and licks Grace's chin at the sound of his name.

I want to tell her she doesn't have to thank me for taking care of her or Buster. Not because I don't appreciate her appreciation, but because I do it all because I want to. I want to take care of her. I want to take care of Buster, who I'm starting to feel like I share ownership of. I want to tell her she means more to me than any other woman has. I want to tell her tonight has made me realize how much I've fallen for her. Overlooking the resentment I have toward Mr. Sheridan, the sheer disdain I carry for him every time I walk into work, I pushed all that aside the second I realized Grace needed me more. She needed me more than I needed to be mad and resentful. But I don't know how to say all this without hooking on the memory of tonight to it. I don't want to tell her what she means to me only for it to have a bittersweet taste, knowing it came from a painful trip to her past. So instead, I kiss her temple. "You're welcome."

CHAPTER THIRTY-SIX

Andrew

GRACE and I spent the weekend in our own self-made nest. Grace's mood lifted over the course of forty-eight hours, and I learned what it's like to be a part of a relationship. Something beyond the titles we almost jokingly gave ourselves over a heated moment of car sex. I owned up to the responsibilities that come with being her boyfriend. It took a moment of her weakness to realize how serious this role is. I'm not just some guy she's sleeping with. I'm her partner in the most secure and devoted way possible. It didn't scare me to know that I didn't go back to my apartment the entire weekend, and it sure as hell didn't scare me when she didn't even bother to ask me to leave. I felt just as much at home in her condo as I would've in my own place.

But now it's Monday morning. I binged Grace all weekend like a man completely drunk on love. I drank her in, we saw each other in our most vulnerable, naked form, riding the high until I turned the page on what's waiting for me at the end of it. And I'm dealing with the hangover of it. The aftereffects that make me want to call her and tell her to meet me back at her place. To turn my car around and crawl back into bed with her.

We grazed over what might happen when I see Mr. Sheridan. We ran through a few possibilities, what words I might exchange with him or whether or not he'd treat me differently in the office, but we didn't really decide on what the most likely outcome would be. The truth is, Grace doesn't really know him. She told me if he's anything like how he was when she met him, he'd probably offer some kind words, congratulate us on our relationship, and step aside so we can go on with our lives. But something tells me this version of her ex-husband she isn't familiar with wouldn't think to be amicable or cordial. Something tells me he'll do everything in his power to make our lives hell.

I reluctantly park my car in the lot outside work and drag my feet to the elevator. When it dings, announcing my arrival to my floor, I walk onto the hard carpet with heavy steps.

"Mr. Sheridan wants to see you." Olive's emotionless face is focused on the computer screen in front of her, but I hear her message from Mr. Sheridan loud and clear.

"Yep." I was expecting it the second I woke up. Dreading it. And by Olive's cheerless face, I can almost sense what I'm going to walk into.

I knock on Mr. Sheridan's door. It's like I'm standing at the doorway to hell. I wish I could fast-forward this. Whatever uncomfortable encounter I'm about to face, I wish I could just remove myself from it and come back when it's all said and done. And then a thought dawns on me. Is he going to fire me? Surely he can't. I didn't break any company rules, and Grace isn't some commodity Mr. Sheridan can use to dangle my job in front of him.

"Come in."

I open the door, my steps reluctant and moving with obligation rather than inclination. "You wanted to see me, sir?"

He looks up from his phone wedged between his hands and when he sees who's at his door, an evil grin stretches across his face. "Andrew," he calls with derisive intent. "Have a seat." He sets down his phone and stands from his seat, rounding his large desk to welcome me into the span of his office.

I do as he offers, though if it were up to me, I'd rather stand where I don't have to look up at him. But something tells me that's his intention. To be able to hover over me while he says what he wants to say.

"Friday night was interesting." I don't know how to interpret his words. If he's trying to be friendly, make conversation as a way to break the awkward tension between us. Or if he's baiting me into something that's more contentious.

"It was," I answer, hoping I sound as neutral as possible.

"You and Grace," he adds, leaning against the edge of his desk. "That's pretty interesting too. How long has that been going on?"

"Not long," I tell him. "Few months."

He nods, and his lips do that downward, smug smile that makes me want to slap it right off his face. Like he's running through all the ways he outdoes me when it comes to Grace. Whether it's their past or that I don't hold a candle to what he might still mean to her.

"Oh, so it isn't serious. That makes sense." His words have an underlying meaning to them, and I can almost feel it coming.

"How so?" I ask, taking the bait I know better not to. Grace would want me to be the bigger person here. She'd want me to walk away and remember this is exactly what he wants.

"Well, you just don't seem to be her type," he tells me, as if he knows what Grace likes. "My wife—"

"Ex-wife." My interruption wipes off the arrogant smirk on his face, and his eyes narrow.

"Anyway, Grace prefers her men to be...established. More esteemed," he tells me. He looks at me, faux sympathy in the half-assed shrug moving his shoulders up and down, and adds, "Sorry." He doesn't sound sorry at all. In fact, he looks absolutely thrilled to be passing along this bit of false information to me.

"No need for an apology," I tell him, my voice carrying the same contempt he tried so hard to deliver with a metaphorical punch to my stomach. "And I know you haven't seen Grace for a while, but I don't think you know her as well as you think."

He crosses his arms. "Is that so?"

I stand from my seat, sick of having to crane my neck to look at him. He leans his head back as I say, "I think she might've outgrown you."

He gapes up at me, shock and insult apparent in the way he scowls and his nostrils flare.

"Now, if it's okay with you," I tell him when I'm met with more silence, "I'd like to get to work. Unless you have a bag of Skittles you want me to sort."

I turn to walk away, ready to leave this mess behind me and get to work. To do my fucking job and not let Mr. Sheridan—or Frankie —tarnish any more of my day.

I'm almost to the closed door when he adds, "You know, I don't think you're completely correct," he says. "because the way she used to let me fuck her isn't something she'd grow out of."

My vision turns red. Blood and fire edge their way to my murky brain, and I feel like my heart is going to beat out of my fucking chest. I turn on my feet, and I barrel toward him. I have one hand on his collar and the other reared back to land a heavy punch to his face. And another. I've gotten in three punches before he fights back, getting right at my side. I cower, and he manages to smack his palm into my ear, making it ring. I stumble back, the blow more than I was prepared for.

He pushes me back, making both of us fall to the ground. We take things down with us. Binders, office supplies, a chair along with its contents. Loud thumps and grunts fill the room. I manage to roll him over on his back and land more punches, just as Olive rushes into the room.

"Oh my god," I hear her gasp. More people enter the room, and I feel a set of hands pull my shoulders back. Another person grabs Mr. Sheridan, and with the much-needed space between us, I finally see the blood trickle out of his nose along with the fresh bruise blooming just above his cheek.

"Get the fuck out!" he roars. "You are so fucking done here! Get your shit and leave."

I shake the hand on my shoulder off. When I look over, I see that it's Craig. I offer him a look of apology, to which he nods grimly. I stand, wiping my mouth only to see my own trail of blood smeared across the back of my hand.

"I said get out!"

I sneer at him. "Gladly."

CHAPTER THIRTY-SEVEN
Grace

MY MONDAY DRAGS ON. All day, it feels like my ankles have anvils tied to them. It makes me want to sit at my desk and avoid everyone. There's an empty yogurt container on my desk when I walk into work in the morning. I left it there on Friday. I forgot to throw it away after I shut down my computer and clocked out. The person who scraped away at the bottom of the plastic container, happily eating the mid-afternoon snack her boyfriend packed in her lunch bag for her, seems like an entirely different person from who sits in front of it today.

It's as if an entire lifetime has passed over the weekend. I was so hopeful then. So ready to enjoy the weekend with Andrew, looking forward to this surprise date he planned. I was even considering telling Teeny about us. Take her out for a girl's day. Get a mani and pedi. Butter her up before delivering her a curveball while reassuring her that Andrew and I are adults who very much want this relation-ship. But now, I don't know if that's a good idea.

Maybe running into Frankie was a sign. A reminder of what I broke. A marriage, a life, a future. Maybe all those things just aren't in the cards for me. And like a bright red string tied around my pinky, I've been pulled back to my past and it's all the proof I need to realize

267

that Andrew and I aren't meant to be. We don't make sense in every way possible, and Friday night was evidence of that. If I was asking for a bigger sign than our ruined plans, I might as well be asking for an asteroid the size of Texas to hit me right on the head.

I try not to bother Andrew all day. I feel maybe a little bit of distance might be good for us at the moment. A night in our own beds where the high of our new relationship doesn't muck up our reasoning, and we can think rationally for a second. A clear mind will do us some good. And maybe it'll help Andrew reexamine a few things in our relationship. Even help him see how telling Teeny about us can't lead to anything good. We've been doing things at lightning speed, and this momentary lapse in judgment helped us realize we need to pump the brakes.

I finally make it home by six. Now that fall is approaching, dusk hits a little earlier than usual. A warm bath, filled with bubbles and some bath salts feels like the perfect remedy for an achy neck and muscles. I unlock my door and walk into a dark apartment. Buster greets me through the sparse lighting, finding me through scent and familiarity. I switch on the lights, and the sight before me makes my stomach jump up to my chest.

"Holy shit!" I gasp. My shock only settles an inch when I realize it's Andrew. He's slumped at my kitchen table, his head sagging between his shoulders and his hair hanging down his forehead. "What are you doing here?"

"I let myself in." His voice sounds strained. Like he's been yelling for a few hours before coming over. I barely hear him through the croaked-out words. "That's why you gave me a key, right?"

I ignore his sarcasm and slip off my shoes. Andrew doesn't stand to greet me. Instead, he slumps down further, his forehead hitting the table.

"Is everything okay?"

"Just fucking dandy."

This caustic bitterness is new to me, and I don't know if I should be worried or offended. "You don't look okay."

He finally lifts his face to look at me, and it's then I notice his lip. It's swollen and bruised. There's a gash cut across one side where it looks like it was bleeding pretty heavily at some point.

"You should see the other guy," he says with a scoff.

"What the hell happened?" I quickly set down my things on the floor and rush to get some ice from my fridge. I manage to haphazardly wrap it in a towel and pull out the seat in front of him. He winces when I grip his chin to get a better look, but he doesn't pull away when I press the ice to his lip.

"I think it's a little late for that," he tells me, speaking through pursed lips. "The swelling is already at its worst."

"Still," I protest, not budging. I sit there, holding the pack of ice to his face and study him. His eyes look sad while the rest of his face looks angry somehow. His jaw is tight, and his brows are pinched together, and his knuckles are white with frustration. "Are you going to tell me what happened?"

He takes the ice pack from my hands and sets it on the table. I'm about to tell him to put it back when he stops me. "Frankie called me into his office this morning."

"He did this?"

He nods. "He said some things that weren't really nice."

"What did he say?"

"I'd rather not repeat them," he tells me. After a pause, a moment of consideration where he decides what he wants to divulge and what he wants to hold back, he adds, "It was about you."

"Me?"

"And I might've thrown the first punch."

I don't know if he expects me to be upset or even choose to scold him, but I don't do either one. I don't have it in me. Instead, I cup my hand to his cheek, careful to avoid his injury. "I'm so sorry."

"It's fine," he whispers, ducking his head to show he's absolutely *not* fine.

"No, it's really not," I tell him. "You don't deserve this. To be treated this way. To be his punching bag."

"You don't deserve it either," he says in agreement.

I move closer, wanting to console him, but also needing him just the same. This has grown so much messier than either one of us could've imagined, and I fear it's slowly chipping away at what we managed to build. We were already brittle to begin with, forged off a secret that turned into something we never expected. And now, after seeing how quickly it could all be undone, I worry we may have bitten off more than we can chew.

"So..."

"So?"

I choose my words carefully, not wanting to add salt to his wound. "Your job..."

"HR called me into their office. They mentioned something about an investigation," he explains. "And since I hit him first, they've suspended me. Indefinitely."

"Andrew," I croak. I start to wrap my arms around him, but he winces, pulling away. "What is it?"

"Nothing," he answers, his voice strained. "My side is just..." He lifts his arm, and I look, uncovering his side to find a red bruise that's sure to turn purple by tomorrow.

"Andrew, what the hell. He did this?"

"I'm fine."

"We need to get you to the hospital. What if he broke something?"

"I'm sure it's just a really bad bruise."

"No, we—"

"Can we just go to bed?" he requests. "We don't have to go to sleep." His fingers wrap around my wrist, a soft plea to let him forget today by leaving it behind him while we slip under a layer of covers.

"Can I at least give you something? Maybe an Advil. For the pain?"

"Sure," he agrees. "And then bed?"

"Yeah, of course."

CHAPTER THIRTY-EIGHT
Andrew

IT'S ALMOST five a.m. when I wake from my sleep. I have another hour or so before Grace's alarm is going to go off, but something woke me. Not a loud noise or a jolting movement, but something that combed through my dreams, reminding me what happened in the last twenty-four hours.

I most likely don't have a job anymore. The one I've clung onto for the past five years has been basically stripped from me the second my boss decided to cross a line. A very deeply fixed line that anyone could've seen even from outer space. But he doesn't care. Of course he doesn't care. In fact, he did it with clear intention. Whether it was to anger me as his ex-wife's new boyfriend or to remind me that he will always have a leg up, at work or in my relationship with Grace, he seems to always be in a position where he holds something over me.

Grace stays asleep next to me. It's not quite light out though I can see the blunted silhouette of high rises surrounding us. Buster whines from his spot at the foot of the bed when I stir. When I sit up, he licks my shin where it's poking out from the covers.

"Hey buddy." His thick tail thumps loudly, and Grace turns over in her sleep. "Shh," I tell him, but that only excites him more. Not

271

wanting to wake Grace, I slowly climb out of bed, and Buster hops off and follows me out of the room. It's a little early for Buster's morning walk, but when he stands by the door with a perfected set of puppy-dog eyes, I give in.

By the time I get downstairs, I can see bright streaming lights peek through the skyline like the sun is hiding behind a stencil. This isn't how I expected my week to play out. I don't know what I'm going to do. Probably fine-tune my résumé and do some online job searches. Just in case. My job never really left any room for savings or emergency funds, so hopefully I can find something sooner rather than later.

I know I should be furious with everything going on, Grace's ex-husband throwing low blow after low blow in my direction, even all the shit he said about her in every derogatory way possible. But I'm not that upset. I mean, sure, my hatred for Mr. Sheridan isn't going anywhere, but knowing the reasons behind it, I don't regret it. He'll probably throw some assault charges in my direction, making the chances of me finding a new job that much harder by adding a possible misdemeanor to my record. But knowing it was all for Grace makes a thrill of excitement ripple through me. I love her, and the act of punching the daylights out her asshole ex-husband seems so insignificant in the grand scheme of things.

I'm in love with someone. With Grace. To the point that I'm willing to risk my job and my career for her. And all it does is make me wonder what lengths I would go to for her. It doesn't scare me. I've become this vulnerable man, oozing with all the things most would consider weak, but I feel the strongest I've ever felt.

I want to tell her I love her, even tell people about us. Do things couples do out in public without worrying about the wrong person finding out about us. Grace said she might be ready soon to tell Teeny about us. Maybe that can be now.

By the time Buster urges me to go back inside, the round border of the sun can be seen over the pearl of clouds hidden behind unlevel tops of buildings. And I'm ready to go back to Grace too.

When I get back into Grace's condo, I notice she's not in bed. The outline of her is there through the rumpled bed sheets and indented pillow. Her bathroom door opens, and she saunters back into the room just as I turn to pick her up in my arms. I kiss her, tasting the dewy traces of water mixed with her freshly brushed teeth.

"Whoa, you're in a good mood this morning."

"I am," I tell her, my nose buried in the crook of her neck.

"Where'd you go?"

"Buster wanted to go out."

"Figured." She kisses the tip of my nose and adds, "How's the lip? And your side?"

"It's fine." I'd taken another Advil during the night, and the effects of it haven't worn off quite yet. "What are you doing after work today?"

"Well," she says, thoughtfully tapping her finger to her chin. "My chess league meeting got canceled, so I guess I can call up my crochet club to see if they want to work on our community afghan."

"Really?"

She giggles, slapping her hand to my chest. "No! I'm all yours."

I poke at her side, tickling her sensitive spot to make her squirm. "Smart ass," I call her endearingly.

"Why? Did you have something planned?"

I think about how to tell her all the things that feel like they're bursting from my chest. That I love her. That I want us to be more serious and to tell people about us. Her family, my sister. Everyone. But right now, rushing with Grace having to leave for work in an hour, doesn't feel right. So, I tell her, "It's a surprise."

Her brows shoot up to her hairline. "A surprise?" she asks skeptically. "I think right now might be a good time to remind you what happened the last time you had a surprise for me."

I internally flinch at the memory. "Then think of this as a do-over. To make amends."

She bites her lip, uncertainty written all over her face through her silence.

273

"And we'll stay in," I add, hoping to ease some of her trepidation. "I'll cook."

Her face lights up. "Okay."

With Grace gone the whole day, I stay busy in her condo. I clean up and do some grocery shopping. I splurge on some lobster to take a stab at a pasta dish I found online. I leave Buster on his own after he's been following me around all morning so I can get a haircut and go home to get a few things. In particular, an outfit that's a little more appropriate for a date night, regardless of the fact that we won't be going out. It worked out since Grace's dog walker came by while I was out. I make a small mental note to tell Grace to give her dog walker a break while I'm temporarily unemployed. I manage to dig up some candlesticks and dinnerware that look to be set aside for special occasions with its platinum trim and porcelain feel. By the time Grace walks through the door, the scent of savory butter and cream fills the air.

"What's going on here?" she asks, a pleased look of approval on her face.

"Dinner," I tell her. What I don't tell her about are the acrobatics that were involved to prep and cook a lobster tail. I went in blind and ended up using a YouTube video after I realized how ill-prepared I was. The Pinterest recipe I used definitely kept that from me.

"Now this is the kind of surprise I like." She wraps her arms around my waist as I'm stirring in the last of the lemon zest. I turn down the heat and turn to greet her.

"Hi."

A contented, blissful smile looks up at me. "Hi."

"How was your day?"

"Okay," she answers. "Better now that I'm home. You?"

"Buster and I had a great day."

"You did?" She looks doubtful, but her support doesn't waver.

I nod. "Very productive."

She pulls away, studying me. Her eyes briefly skim over the cut on my lip. She moves over to the rest of my face like she's looking for any cracks, any slips where my positive pretense could merely be a mask I'm wearing over the glum attitude she's expecting me to wear.

"What?" I ask when her skeptical look doesn't waver.

She shrugs. "Just that...you seem pretty upbeat for someone whose job is up in the air." I know when she left this morning, my emotional well-being was a concern for her. She made sure I was comfortable in her apartment. Told me where she kept an extra box of Buster's treats, the different frozen dinners stacked in her freezer. I nearly shoved her out the door with the lunch I packed for her as I assured her I'm an adult and can take care of myself for eight hours. Even then, she left with an edge of caution. "Has...HR said anything?"

I nod. "They handed me my official termination via Zoom this morning."

She rubs a hand down my back. "I'm sorry, honey."

I lean down and kiss her cheek, smothering my misfortune with a little deviation. "I'm choosing to look on the bright side. I hated the job anyway, and some might consider this a sign. Plus, I have other things on my mind. More important things."

"Yeah? Like what?"

"I'll tell you over dinner." I wave a hand in the direction of her dining table for her to see I've set it with care. Gone are the usual plates and bowls she told me she bought from Ikea. I even whipped out some wine glasses and a fresh arrangement of flowers.

"What is all this?" she asks with a soft gasp.

"My do-over," I remind her. "Hopefully this will wipe away the first date from hell."

"Absolutely." She tilts up on her toes and kisses me, letting her lips linger over mine. I hold her in my arms while keeping in mind the food is ready to be served and running the risk of it getting cold.

A sudden wave of uncertainty and dread washes over me. My

plan tonight is to wine and dine her. To show her all the ways she means so much to me before telling her so. Maybe then she'll realize that whoever we tell, whether it's our family or the whole world, it'll all be welcomed with open arms. I understand her hesitation. We're involving the people in our lives who would be wholly invested. And if things went south, it wouldn't be a clean break. It would turn messy and complicated. Kind of like her divorce. But I'm going to go through with my plan. I'm going to get through dinner, and we can talk about our future. With that in mind, I pull out a chair for her.

"You know, maybe more of our dates should be disastrous," she comments, pouring the wine. "Especially if this is how you're going to fix it."

"I guess that's one way to look on the bright side." I serve the pasta and bring the plates over to the table, setting hers down in front of her. She takes in a big inhale and hums with a pleased smile.

"This smells amazing."

I sit down, suddenly famished with the scent of lobster and creamy sauce wafting into the air. We're quiet as I watch Grace dig in.

"How is it?"

"If you ever feel like a career change is an option, you can try your hand at the culinary arts," she comments, taking another heaping forkful.

I chuckle. "That good, huh?"

She silently nods. I let her eat without making conversation while enjoying the view. When I notice about half her dinner is gone and the speed at which she's been consuming her pasta slows to a more leisurely pace, I pour her more wine.

"So, I was thinking about...things."

The wineglass she had tilted back stops mid-sip. "What things?"

"About us."

"Okay." The single word trails with concern, making her sound scared and worried.

"It's not bad," I assure her. I reach out and swipe my thumb across the corner of her mouth, wiping off a smear of sauce. "I just had some time to think, and after this weekend, it would be irresponsible for us to not talk about things. Don't you?"

"Yeah," she answers, adding a nod to show no protest. Though the up and down motion of her head feels hesitant, and I wonder if the weekend we spent together left a different mark on her. One that allowed her to have second thoughts instead of a more assured frame of mind like mine. "I was actually wanting to talk to you too."

I sit up straighter, angling myself to face her. "Go ahead."

"I was just thinking that...what happened on Friday was a—"

"Shit show."

She chuckles a morose laugh. "Yeah. To say the least. And...I know I said we can tell Teeny soon, and maybe tell other people like my sister and the rest of your family too, but..."

I don't know if I like where this is going. It definitely isn't going in the direction I was hoping it would. But I don't poke or prod. I just listen. "But..."

"I think we should pump the brakes on that."

"You want things to stay between us?"

"Just for a little longer," she says with urgency. She reaches out to smooth her hand on top of mine. A placating gesture to ease the harsh brunt of her request. "I think running into Frankie and you losing your job can't be a good omen, and I don't know. Maybe it's a sign that we should slow down."

"Okay," I tell her, though all I want to do is say no. No, I don't want to keep us a secret for a second longer. No, I don't want to keep our bubble intact to protect what we have as if it's this fragile, delicate thing. We're so much more than that.

"Is that okay?" she asks cautiously.

I look at her, plastering on a fake smile along with a reassuring nod. "Of course. If that's what you want and if that's what makes you feel comfortable."

She leans forward, hovering over our unfinished dinner to kiss me. Her hand cups my cheek, and I feel the tension dissipate away from all the soft parts of her I love. How can I tell her otherwise? Especially if this is how relieved she is that we no longer have this daunting task of telling people about us. Only, it's not daunting to *me*.

"Thank you for understanding," she adds. "And, you know, this... is a good thing. Us officially being a couple means a big commitment for you too. I know that's a huge step, so...I—this is for both of us."

For us. I hadn't realized my now vanquished commitment issues bled into the fate of our relationship, but I guess I should've known. If all I've been presenting myself as was a commitment-phobe who thought the idea of a relationship meant vulnerability, I guess she would think I would be on the same page as her.

"Yeah, totally," I say, lying through the mask I've slid on.

"What did you need to tell me?"

"Huh?" I ask, suddenly thrown off.

"You said you needed to tell me something," she reminds me.

"Oh, just that...I think we should be sharing custody of Buster," I say, thinking on my toes, though I'm not opposed to the idea. A day with him on our own gave us a bonding moment.

She laughs. "Sharing custody?"

"Yup. I think you should be referring to me as 'daddy' from now on."

"Daddy?" she repeats. "I think that sounds way more obscene than you meant it to."

"You know, I think you're right. How about father?"

"Or papa," she jokingly suggests. "Sounds less formal."

The mood is somewhat lifted, hovering high above us instead of right over our heads. The strains of our relationship feel easier with sex or jokes (or sex jokes), much like a pair of training wheels strapped on to a two-wheeler, and it can stay that way a little longer until we're ready to rip them off and careen straight into the unknown.

"By the way," she adds. "Where did you find the plates?"

"In your linen closet," I tell her. "Why do you keep your plates in the linen closet?"

"Those are my wedding china."

"They are?"

She nods.

I suddenly want to hurl them off the balcony. "How about we find an empty alley to break them after dinner?"

She smiles slyly. "Yes, please."

CHAPTER THIRTY-NINE
Grace

AFTER WHAT WE like to call our "Date Night Debacle," we tried to settle into a routine. Andrew pretty much stayed in my place. Though I offered to spend the night at his apartment during the week, he said it wouldn't be fair since I was the one who had to go to work early in the morning. Some weekends, we'd stay at his place, schlepping Buster, our unofficial child, back and forth. He ran errands, job searched, kept Buster company until I came home in the afternoon, allowing me to give my dog walker a little break since she usually stops by around midday. A suggestion made by Andrew. Most of the time, he would have dinner ready, some variation of Pinterest recipes and other things he'd grown comfortable cooking without the need for a step-by-step instruction.

After two weeks, though, I saw his spirit start to fade. What used to be upbeat and optimistic, turned irritable and frustrated. He'd been doing his due diligence, sending his résumé to different companies, following up interviews with "It was a pleasure to meet you" emails. But the days passed, and he couldn't get past a first interview. So, with a lot of reluctance on his part, he decided to pick up some food delivery shifts. Uber Eats, DoorDash, anything to scrounge up a few bucks as his bills started to pile up. He hadn't even told his parents he lost his job. I know it's because if he did, then he'd have to explain what happened, which would in turn require an even longer story about how he and I are a thing now.

Our habitual pattern of dinner and sleep didn't change at first when he started this part-time gig, but once the alerts for delivery services peaked in the evening, I found myself alone more often. I started to miss him. Not just the physical presence of him, but my boyfriend. The man who would hold me when I came home from a long day at work while we exchanged stories like it was our form currency. And a part of me couldn't help but feel responsible for all of this. It's my fault he got into a fight with Frankie. If it weren't for me, he wouldn't be dealing with bringing random strangers their late-night snacks. He'd have a job, a future.

So today, I've decided to surprise him. He's taken the initiative to surprise me, and I feel like it's his turn today.

"Hello?"

"Hey," I call through the phone. "Are you working tonight?" Asking Andrew if he's going to be delivering today feels a little unfitting, so I stick with a vaguer term to ask about his plans.

"Probably," he says. The raspy, flat way he answers me puts me on edge, and I start to worry if he'll shut down my offer to provide him a much-needed distraction.

"Can you take a night off?" I ask.

"Why?"

My throat suddenly feels tight, and a nervous quiver snakes up my back. "I, um, just thought that maybe you'd want to do something."

"What did you have in mind?" His voice picks up. Maybe it's silly of me to be so nervous.

"It's a surprise."

"A surprise? Should I be scared?"

"Not unless you think waffles and the beach is a bad idea."

"You are horrible at surprises."

"Oops," I say, feigning remorse. "But now that you know, are you up for it?"

"Yeah, of course."

"Great, I'll see you after I get off?"

"Can't wait," he answers, his voice carrying the hint of a smile.

I hang up, relieved for this much-needed interlude. We both need it, especially Andrew. Something to remind us we're two people who very much care about each other. And as we keep things on the DL, it's a good way to remember we still matter. Secret relationships, skeletons and all, mean just as much as all the conventional ones. Especially ours.

I'm about to get back to my workday when my phone buzzes on my desk. I expect it to be Andrew but am proven wrong when Jade's name flashes on the screen.

"Hello?"

"Hey," Jade responds. "Are you busy?"

"Not really. Just at work, but I have a minute. What's up?"

"I was just wondering if you'd like to go trick-or-treating with us next Thursday."

"You're going trick-or-treating? Avery can't even eat candy."

"Yeah, I know. But we got her a costume. We're going to go to a few houses in our neighborhood and take a *lot* of pictures."

"What is she dressing up as?"

"A baby lion."

I laugh, imagining little Avery in a brownish-orange jumpsuit with a mane of polyester and felt. "That is adorable."

"Right? And Trevor is going to dress up as a zookeeper."

"I have to see this in person. What time are you guys going?"

"We'll wait for you to get off work. So maybe around six? Seven?"

"Yeah, okay. I'll be there."

"Great! I'll see you next week then."

"Okay."

Halloween seems to have crept up on me this year. Usually, the more minor holidays leading up to the bigger ones like Thanksgiving and Christmas are easy to forget, but I didn't even realize we've entered fall. Soon enough, I'll be sitting around a large dining table waiting for my dad to carve the big juicy turkey. All of it bookended with the shimmery ball drop on New Year's Eve.

Maybe this year, things could be different. With Andrew in my life, the tree I usually decorate by myself can serve more of a purpose than its usual nonfunctional—yet decorative—one. Me and Andrew and Buster can sit around it while sipping hot cocoa, unwrapping gifts, and taking cheesy holiday pictures. And we can go to our childhood homes, enjoy whatever festivities our respective families engage in. Of course, there's the matter of telling them about us first. A part of me almost wishes they already knew. Then Andrew could even join me on Halloween. We could wear some tacky couple costumes and watch Jade collect a mountain of candy under the guise of doing it for her baby.

I get through work with the thought of hazelnut waffles on my mind. Once I clock out, I head straight for the elevators. The doors are shutting in front of me when a hand slices through the narrowing opening. The sensors kick in, letting in the last-second passenger, and when the doors slide back open, Noah is standing on the other side.

"Grace."

"Noah," I respond. "Heading home?"

He shakes his head. "I have a couple more hours left in my shift. You?"

"Yup," I answer. My attention shifts to my phone screen lit up in my hand. A message from Jade flashes through, and when I open it, there's a picture of Avery in her fake bristly mane, the rest of her chubby body in a floral onesie.

"Big plans?" Noah asks.

"Something like that." The elevator arrives at the parking structure, and I step off. "Have a good night, Noah."

"You too, Grace."

I text Andrew to let him know I'm leaving along with the address to where to meet me. I drive straight to Marie's to pick up the order of waffles I called in, and head to our rendezvous point.

It's not late enough that the nighttime marine layer is starting to settle in. The sun is starting to angle closer west, making the sky hazy and orange. Shades of purple hide behind the clouds, creating the perfect backdrop for an impromptu date night by the shore.

When I park and exit my car, the ocean waves crashing into the sandy shoreline sound more menacing than they are. From the distance where a large stretch of sand and concrete still sits between myself and any splash of salt water, I'm able to enjoy the beach without getting sand in my shoes.

"Hey," Andrew calls, meeting me at the curb. He has a large blanket folded and tucked under his arm, and he's carrying an extra sweatshirt along with the one he's already wearing.

"Hi." I walk up to him, smothering the sudden skip in my step, and greet him with a kiss.

"How was your day?"

"Long," I answer. "Too long. You?"

He shrugs. "Whatever."

I nod my chin to all the things in his hands, including an extra pair of flip-flops. "You came prepared."

"I figured you might need a few things to brave the beach weather." He drops the flip-flops on the ground, the flimsy foam soles hitting the concrete with a loud smack. He offers his hand, and I take it, slipping out of my work shoes and wedging my toes between the separating strap. He bends down and picks up my shoes, plopping them in the back seat of my car, and takes my hand in his. "Shall we?"

I nod, following his lead. He takes a narrow path lined with bushes that turns steep as it guides us to the first patch of dry sand. We stop about half the distance to the water, and Andrew starts to lay out the blanket he brought.

"Thank you," I say once he's dusted off a few specks of lingering sand. I plop the waffles in the middle as we both settle in. Though we don't say much, the fragrant ocean breeze and occasional sounds of nearby chatter and laughter filter our way, filling the quiet with a lulling, comforting soundtrack.

"This is a nice surprise," Andrew comments as we're taking the first bites of our dinner.

"Not really a surprise if you came better prepared than I did." I slip on the sweatshirt he brought for me, one of his hoodies I've been wearing with the weather cooling down. He adjusts the hood so that any stray hairs covering my face are tucked inside.

"No, it's a surprise," he assures. "You just gave me a head start, that's all."

"I just thought...a break might be nice," I tell him, leaning my cheek against his shoulder. "I know you've been really worried about finding work, and I guess I wanted to say thank you."

"For what?"

"For taking care of me," I tell him. "Cooking me dinner, hanging out with my dog—"

"Our dog," he corrects.

"Our dog," I say, rolling my eyes. "And sometimes...I feel really bad you're in this situation. If it weren't for me—"

"Hey," he says gently, cutting off any chance for self-blame and guilt. "It wasn't your fault. We both know who's to blame."

"Yeah," I agree. "But still. Even if Frankie was the one who was egging you on, if we hadn't been...you know, then you wouldn't be in this mess."

"And if we hadn't been..." He waves his finger between us, a play-fully teasing gesture, pointing out how what we've been doing is something worth noting. "Then I wouldn't be here with you."

"That's what you want? To be here with me?"

He turns to face me, cupping my face in his large hands. The breeze blows between us, and it's a stark contrast to his warm touch, making me hyper aware of how cold it's suddenly become and how badly I want to wrap myself in his arms. "Grace, I honestly can't think of a place I want to be more than here with you." He kisses me, letting his words sink in. "You mean a lot to me, and if being with you means standing up for you and beating the shit out of someone who absolutely deserves it, then so be it."

"You mean a lot to me too," I tell him, my words squeezed through the lump lodged in my throat. "I don't think I've ever felt like this with anyone. You make me feel safe, and when I'm with you, I don't worry I'm doing the wrong thing or that you might find some fault in me that'll make you suddenly change your mind about being with me."

"Yeah," he rasps. "I've never felt this way about anyone either." A low rumble sounds somewhere in the distance, and the sky sits veiled behind a layer of dark clouds. "You know that—" His cautiously spoken words are cut off by a sudden downpour, and Andrew exclaims, "Oh shit!"

I scream, an excited squeal tacked on by a giddy laugh, and we both rush to collect our things. I shove the takeout container back in the bag it came in at the same time Andrew whips the blanket off the sand and holds it over us. I manage to toss the remains of our meal in a trash can on the way to our car, and as soon as we get to mine, we both pile into the back seat.

"I swear, that was not part of the surprise," I tell him. Our breaths are coming out in heaves, but the smiles on our faces are anything but strained.

"Are you sure getting all wet and breathless wasn't a part of your plan?"

I smack his chest, reacting to his bawdy words with a playful swat, but he grabs my wrist, pulling me to him. He kisses me, our damp skin creating a wave of heat filling the car.

"Honestly," he adds. "I wouldn't be mad if that was your intention."

"Then I guess now's the time to tell you I can control the weather."

A mock gasp has him pulling away. "And you are telling me this *now?*"

"Shut up," I demand. I hook my leg over his lap and straddle him. I'm thankful for the secluded street we parked on as well as the slowly fogging windows as his hands start to roam under my wet clothes.

CHAPTER FORTY

Grace

"BABY, you're going to miss the movie."

"I don't care!" I shout from behind my hands. When Andrew tugs at my wrist, trying to pry my fingers from covering my eyes, I bury my face into them harder.

"It's not even that scary."

"Yes, it is!" I argue. A shrill of loud, ominous music rattles through my apartment, and I duck my face behind Andrew's back.

"It just started," he reminds me. "Are you going to watch any of it?"

"Probably not," I answer meekly from my hiding spot. I have to admit, the scary movie was my suggestion. With Halloween just a few days away, I thought it would be fun. And even though my aversion to scary movies hasn't changed since middle school, when Andrew told me he enjoyed them, it seemed like the perfect way to get into the holiday mood.

The sounds stop, and Andrew's arms wrap around my back, guiding me upright.

"Why'd you turn it off?" I ask when I see the paused image of an unsettling demon on the TV screen.

"Because I'm not going to watch a whole movie while you're hiding behind me. We can watch one you can actually sit through."

"But it's Halloween week," I tell him. "I want to watch something festive."

"So we'll watch Casper or something," he suggests. "Or are you scared of cartoon ghosts too?"

"Depends. Do they look like bed sheets with googly eyes? Or something like that?" I point to the screen. Though my question is meant to be a joke, a small part of me hopes it's the first of the two choices.

He laughs, pinching my cheek. "You are so fucking cute." He nudges me backward as he climbs over me, settling himself between my legs.

"Hi," I whisper. I run my fingers through his hair, brushing some of it off his forehead.

"Hi," he whispers back. "You know, instead of watching a movie, we could do something else."

"Yeah? What'd you have in mind?"

He shrugs. "Something that probably requires less clothing." His hand snakes up my thigh, peeling back the shorts I'm wearing. A shiver travels up my spine when his palm cups the underside of my butt, giving me a firm, possessive squeeze. I moan against his lips, my index finger hooking his silver chain to tug him closer, when his phone vibrates on my coffee table. Andrew groans, the frustrated rumble quivering down my throat.

He pulls away, reaching across me for his phone. A scowl covers his face as he looks at his phone screen.

"Hey," I protest. "We were in the middle of something."

He kisses me. A quick, apologetic peck. "I know. I just got a delivery request."

"I thought you were taking the night off."

"I can't," he answers, shaking his head. "I need to do as many of these as I can if I want to make rent."

"Oh." My skin feels cold when he gets off the couch. I want to tell him to stay, to forget about making money and all the responsible things he should definitely be considering, but I know I shouldn't. This whole food delivery gig has already been wearing him thin. That, along with the dozens of résumés he's been sending out and the job applications he's completed. He even reached out to The Hope Foundation multiple times, trying to sound indifferent each time to hide his desperation. I think after the third email, he's given up hope.

I know it's weighing on him, this stretched-out period of unemployment. It's slowly chipping away at his spirit, no matter how much he tries to make it seem like it doesn't. Especially after having worked so hard to get to where he was at. And I wish there was something I could do. Something to let him know he's doing everything he can. But I'm slowly realizing this is something he needs to get through on his own. All I can do is hold his hand and let him know I'm here for him for whatever he needs.

I tug at his hand as soon as he sets his phone down. "Are you going to be out for most of the night?"

"Maybe," he answers, tucking his wallet into his pocket. "I'm not sure. I guess I'll see how the night goes."

"Okay." I reach for the remote, changing the TV to something lighter. My attention isn't fully focused on the TV though, and as Andrew moves about the living room, making sure he has everything before he leaves, I know I look bleaker than I should.

"You going to be okay?"

I nod, my eyes straight ahead like I'm focusing on what's on the screen. But if he were to ask me what I'm watching, I wouldn't be able to tell him. This feels like an interlude we never asked for. When everything about us was heading in a straight line, a gap disrupted our lives. A morose, daunting gap surrounded by barbed wire and a moat filled with piranhas. I wish we could go back, draw a bridge or something to help us easily maneuver over that gap so we can be happy.

"Yeah," I finally tell him, plastering a smile on my face to mask the guilt of being upset. Because I have no right to be. I should just keep my mouth shut and wait this out. Sit through the intermission by distracting myself. Maybe fill the time with some snacks at the concession stand or a trip to the ladies' room. "I'm fine. I'll wait up for you."

"You don't have to."

"I want to."

He bends down to kiss me on my forehead, making that guilt leak into the cracks in my heart where the need to be selfish reared its ugly face. "I'll be back as soon as I can."

"Okay."

CHAPTER FORTY-ONE
Grace

"WHAT ARE YOU SUPPOSED TO BE?"

Jayne looks down at her costume. The all-black attire with a long tail hanging from her lower back points toward some class of feline, including the whiskers painted on her cheeks with the black triangle drawn on the tip of her nose. "A cat."

"That's what I thought," I say, appreciating the details including a yellow choker with a bell. "Where are your ears?"

She picks up a set of ears sewn onto a headband resting on her desk and wiggles it in the air. "They were giving me a headache." After a pause, she takes in my attire and asks, "Where's your costume?"

"In my car," I tell her. "I'm changing into it when I go trick-or-treating."

"You're going trick-or-treating?"

"My niece is," I answer. "It's her first Halloween, and we're all dressing up."

"Aw, that's cute."

We've been seeing people in the ER and throughout the hospital celebrate all day. Passing out candy, dressed in their variety of costumes, setting out decorative pumpkins and friendly ghosts to set the mood.

"What about you? Are you taking the kids trick-or-treating?" I ask.

"Are you kidding?" She shoots me an eye roll, evidence she's had her fill even though the festivities don't start until the sun goes down. "It's all they've been talking about. 'Is it Halloween yet? How many days until Halloween? Can I wear my costume to bed?' They've been driving me up the wall."

I laugh at the image of Jayne wrangling her twin girls, seven and full of curiosity and sass, bombarding her with all the questions in the world. I'm sure the only break she'll get is after the new year, once Santa has come and gone.

It's almost quitting time, and I'm excited to see Avery in her costume. I already told Andrew I'd be out with my sister, and a part of me wishes he could come too. Partake in the Halloween fun and dress up in something to match my own witch costume. Like a wizard or a warlock. Or maybe we could even go all out and put together a whole couple's costume like Barbie and Ken or Fred and Wilma. Even though Andrew said he'd be busy with a night of deliveries, I know if I invited him to come along, he'd drop all of that in a heartbeat. But right now doesn't feel like the right time to be introducing him to Jade and Trevor.

I follow Jayne out, walking past another wall of Halloween decorations reminding us of our impending plans.

"I'll see you tomorrow!" Jayne calls out as she slips into her car.

"Bye!" I respond. She's out of the parking lot at record speed. Meanwhile, I'm tapping out a quick message to Andrew to let him know I'm heading to Jade's.

A response comes instantly with a picture of him and Buster. He'd gotten Buster the cutest bumble bee costume, and he managed to slip it on him. Buster has his tongue hanging out the side of his mouth and the floppy antennae are hanging on for dear life over his head. The little selfie with Andrew's own smile makes my heart melt into a puddle. Instead of texting him back with some cheesy emoji like a smiley face with heart eyes, I call him.

"Hello?"

"Hey," he answers, sounding delighted at the sound of my voice. "I thought you were heading over to Jade's."

"I am," I tell him. "I just wanted to tell you that the picture you just sent me is the most adorable thing I've ever seen."

A low chuckle rumbles through the line. "Yeah?"

"Yeah. In fact, I think I just found my new lock screen."

"Really? That cute, huh? You aren't worried people might see it? Ask you who that handsome man on your phone is?"

I gnaw on my lower lip, considering what sounds like a dare. A playful challenge I hope to win. "I know," I finally say, still sounding a bit unsure.

"And...you're okay with that?"

I shrug, pushing aside the fact that he can't see me. "Maybe?" I tell him.

"Okay. I like 'maybe.' I can work with 'maybe.'"

"I think so too," I admit. It feels like a whoosh of air expelled from my lungs.

"I guess I'll see you later?"

"Yeah," I answer, excitement rattling my insides. "I won't be too long."

"Make sure to save me some candy."

"I will."

We hang up, and all the words, the boldly spoken ones and the nervously held back ones, swim in my head. There might be a hundred things we need to hurdle over before our relationship looks anything like what a typical relationship should be, but we're headed there. And who's to say what we have isn't ideal? Sure, it may be somewhat of the atypical variety with so much of it left in limbo, but I've never felt more secure than I do when I'm with Andrew. It isn't our fault the circumstances of everything are working against us.

I get into my car, excited to see my sister and Avery but also excited to hurry home to Andrew at the end of the night. I jam my key into the ignition to turn it, but instead of the sure sound of the engine being brought to life, I'm met with a listless chug as my car fails to start.

"Shit," I mutter under my breath. I try again, only to be met with the same sound, confirming the sudden turn of events. I reach for my phone and consider calling Andrew back. But I stop myself, knowing he has a busy night ahead of him. I try Jade but am met with an unanswered string of ringing. Defeated, I step out of my car after pulling the latch for the trunk. Though it could be anything, with the pathetic, rhythmic clacks it made with an unsuccessful attempt to start, I'm assuming it's a dead battery. I push aside a few random things in my trunk, hoping to find some jumper cables, only to come up empty handed. I slam the trunk shut, and head back for the driver's seat for my phone, hoping Jade will answer this time.

"Hi, Grace." I look up to find Noah. He has his backpack hooked over his shoulder, his AirPods wedged into his ears, and the beginning of a smile starts to edge its way to his lips. But as soon as he sees the distracted state of my worried face, his smile falls. "Is everything okay?"

"Um, yeah," I start to say, only to catch myself in the lie. "Actually, not really. You wouldn't happen to have jumper cables, would you?"

He shakes his head apologetically. "No, I don't." He takes a few steps closer to me, examining my car like he would when treating a patient.

I sigh, my hand on my hip while a string of remedies go through my head. I guess I might have to call Andrew.

"But," Noah says, interrupting the problem-solving mode my brain is in. "I have a friend who lives about five minutes from here who I'm sure has some in his garage. I can call him to see if he can bring them over."

"Really?" I perk up, hopeful that my night hasn't been ruined. "You don't mind?"

He whips his phone out of his pocket. "Not at all."

It's quiet between us as he taps through his phone. I wait patiently while he talks, giving him some privacy by sitting in my car with the door left ajar.

"So, I have some good news and some bad news," he says once he's done on the phone.

"Oh?"

"He can bring us the cables."

"Great!"

"But it's going to be about half an hour until he can make it home," he adds, delivering the bad news portion of his call. "Is that okay?"

"Yeah," I tell him, my tone defeated. I leave out the part where I have to be somewhere, not wanting to sound ungrateful. I mean, thirty minutes isn't too bad. I guess I can just catch up with Jade. I smile at Noah and add, "Thank you. I really appreciate it."

We sit in a pause of uncomfortable silence. Me with one foot hanging out the car and him standing with his hand on his hip and an air of uncertainty.

"Did you want to go grab a coffee?" Noah suddenly asks.

"Oh."

"I mean, if you know—you don't want to, it's okay. It's fine," he stammers.

"No, it's not that," I assure. "I just can't drink coffee this late. I'll be running laps around my living room."

He huffs a nervous laugh. "I see."

"But, maybe something else? There's a smoothie shop nearby. My treat," I say, reaching for my purse.

"No," he protests. "I can't—"

"Please," I interrupt. "To say thank you for saving me."

He answers with a nod, ducking his head shyly. "Lead the way."

I shut my car door, making sure it's locked on the inside with the alarm system out of commission. I wonder if I need to replace the whole battery while trying to remember the last time it was done. Just as I'm scrolling through my mental catalog of recent auto repairs, Noah asks, "Did you have plans for Halloween?"

"I'm going to go trick-or-treating with my sister and my niece."

"That sounds like fun," he comments. "How old is she?"

"She'll be one in a few months."

"That's a cute age." When I look at him, wondering why he would know the six-to-twelve-month age of an infant would be the cutest stage. "I have a nephew."

I nod, unsure how to fill the somewhat awkward silence. We reach the smoothie shop, and when we enter, I'm fully aware I'm spending an unusual period of time with someone I work with outside of work.

We order our smoothies, Noah fights me on the tab even though I preemptively said it was my treat, and before I know it, we're sitting off to a corner in the quaint shop.

"So, I have a confession to make."

I look at Noah, the magenta pink straw of my strawberry-banana smoothie hanging off the corner of my mouth. "A confession?"

"I may have asked about you."

I maintain a quiet poker face and duck my head to conceal the smile creeping its way to my lips. "Did you?" I ask, omitting the fact that I already knew he did. "What did you ask?"

"Just...what your story is. Nothing specific."

"My story? That sounds pretty specific." I see a flush spread across his neck, not quite making it to his face where the outline of a five o'clock shadow is forming, making him look a little rugged against the crisp edges of his navy-blue scrub top. "So, what did you find out?"

He takes a long sip of his chocolate-peanut butter smoothie, a staccato-like noise rattling through his straw. "That you've worked at Haven General for about four years. And you were married."

I resist the urge to flinch, hiding any outward reaction to him knowing those details about my personal life. Especially knowing how much of a piece of shit my ex-husband turned out to be.

"I, um...I'm divorced too," he adds. I wonder if he meant to tell me that, or if he caught onto the little slip of my inability to hide my feelings, but he adds, "It was a year ago."

"So freshly single, I see."

"Sure," he agrees tentatively. "But it was amicable. We separated on good terms."

"Must be nice."

His brow pinches together, the wrinkles on his forehead deepening. A clear sign he's reading into my ambiguous words. "Was it..."

"Rough? To say the least, yes."

"Sorry."

I wave a hand, brushing off his apology. "It's in the past." A past that reared its ugly head just a few weeks ago. In an attempt to shift the topic away from my failed marriage, I ask, "Was your wife a doctor too?"

"No, she worked for an art gallery," he answers. "Curating, I think. And...other things I wasn't really privy to."

"Understanding the divorce a little more."

"What?" He laughs, though he sounds genuinely offended. "So, I should know all the details about her work life?"

"I mean, you should at least know what she does," I answer honestly.

"True," he agrees. "And I'd usually blame it on my own busy work schedule. Those long hours didn't help, but I should probably take some responsibility, right?"

"Now was that so hard?"

He laughs, an honest, delighted laugh that bounces off the walls. His warm hand lands on my wrist, something I don't think he intended on doing. "Thank you for setting me straight. God knows my ex-wife didn't have the patience for it."

His thumb brushes against my forearm, and it feels like sandpaper. I don't know how to shake him off without being rude, so I cross my arms and lean away, creating as much distance as I can.

"You know, relationships are hard," I admit. "And sometimes, no matter how hard you work at it, it just doesn't work out."

He follows my lead, crossing his own arms so his elbows rest on the table. "Are you...in a relationship?"

Yes. The answer is yes. I should be able to say the words: "I have a boyfriend." I've certainly been calling Andrew that to his face. On multiple occasions. So why are the words so hard to utter? My throat suddenly feels tight, fear creating a vise around it, snuffing the words as they're squeezed out. Because what if, once it's out in the universe, he realizes it was all a mistake? Frankie sure did. We were happy once, assigning very official titles to each other. Boyfriend. Girlfriend. Fiancé. Husband. Wife. And then the title heard around the world. Ex-wife. Ex-husband. What if at the end of it all, Andrew opts to add "ex" to the beginning of our own established titles?

"Um..."

"Is it complicated?"

I laugh at the same time Noah's face turns absorbed, hanging on to my next words. His eyes round and disappointment exposes itself through the creases between his brows.

"No, nothing like that," I start to tell him, trying to figure out the words that describe me and Andrew. "My—"

"Grace?"

I'm pulled away from a conversation that appears more intimate than it is. The small space between myself and Noah suddenly feels like millimeters, and the dread that comes with being caught doing something I wasn't supposed to settles deep in my stomach the second I see Andrew's wounded face take in the scene in front of him.

"Andrew!" I exclaim, caught completely off guard. "What are you doing here?" I stand from my seat, leaving a confused Noah behind. When I take a step closer to Andrew, he pulls back, looking as if he's repulsed by me.

"I had a delivery order to pick up." He has the soft cooler in one hand, the bag he usually uses for temperature-sensitive foods. The bold "DoorDash" reads like a neon sign, and I feel like the worst person in the world. "I thought you were at your sister's."

"I—I was, but I had some car trouble, so Dr. Santos was waiting with me while he got some jumper cables."

"Dr. Santos," Andrew repeats flatly. His eyes flit to Noah, a shimmer of irritation and betrayal detected through his narrowed eyes and clenched fists.

An unsuspecting Noah stands from his seat and mistakenly assumes the moment is an opportunity to introduce himself. "Nice to meet you," he says. He smiles broadly at me and adds, "What happened to Noah?"

"Yeah—um, sorry, Noah. Or Dr. Santos," I stammer. "I guess I'm still getting used to that."

"Yeah," Andrew answers, his voice cold and level. "I have to go." He heads for the door. No smoothies to deliver in hand. Just the tight tension resting between his shoulders and a gait that looks unapproachable.

I hurry out of the shop, following him to his car. I manage to catch up to him just as he whips his car door open.

"Andrew, wait!"

"I'm working, Grace." The icy way he says my name makes me want to cower, but I refuse.

"No, Andrew. Please. Just hear me out."

"What are you going to say? Are you going to lie to me?"

"No, Andrew, I wouldn't lie to you!"

He chucks his bag into the back seat and finally faces me. Though the harsh anger is hard to ignore, I see the sadness creep through his eyes. They seem to plead, asking me to make the last five minutes disappear. "Grace, look. Fine. You won't lie to me, but whoever that was in there—"

"He's no one. I promise."

"Does he know you have a boyfriend?"

"I—I, what—"

"I take that as a no."

"I was getting around to it," I argue, though it sounds so stupid and weak coming from my own lips.

"Right," he responds, dry sarcasm dripping from the single word. He turns around like he's going to get back into the car, but he hesitates. He fists his hands, groaning through his decision to say what he wants to say or just leave without hearing me out. "Look, I'll talk to you when you get home, okay? I don't think this is the place to be doing this."

"Andrew, I was going to tell him, I swear. I was about to tell him, but—"

"But what?"

"I—"

"It's always something. You're not ready to tell people, you don't think it's a good idea. Your ex-husband beat the shit out of me, and you think it's a sign to hide this longer. What is it going to be next?"

"That's not fair."

"And this is?"

I respond with stunned silence. How long has he been feeling like this?

"Grace, you can't keep me your little secret forever," he continues. "I can't be your boyfriend in private, and a nobody to you in public."

"What about you?"

He rears his head back. "What about me?"

I'm grasping at straws when I say, "You're the one who said you're scared to be vulnerable with someone. You're the one with your commitment issues."

He scoffs, and I realize how little I have backing my words. After everything we've been through, everything he's done for me, to say he's the one with commitment issues is practically laughable. "You think I have commitment issues?"

"You're the one who said it." I don't add the fact how so much has changed since he told me that. Something he told me in confidence and never thought I would use against him.

"How about this for commitment issues? I love you, Grace. I am so fucking in love with you it scares me. But not in the way I thought it would."

My silly little rebuttal turns into a hard knot in my throat, staying lodged there with no outlet. He loves me.

"And every time you want to keep this a secret from everyone, I want to do the opposite. I want to tell the whole goddamn world. I want to tell my sister and my family, and I don't give a shit what they say. But if all you want is to hide me from everyone, then I have news for you. I deserve better."

Everything I want to say to him, how much I love him too, how sorry I am, dies the second he tells me he deserves better. How could I have been so fucking stupid? All this time, those moments when I thought he wanted what I wanted or that he might change his mind about us at some point, I was wrong. He wants more. To hell with all the repercussions and aftermath. People are just going to have to accept us, no matter how much we don't make sense. And I'm going to have to come to terms with having a boyfriend who truly wants me. Not just for a little while, but for a long while. Maybe forever.

Leaving me speechless and stunned, Andrew gets into his car and drives off. When I finally hear his wheels screech against the pavement, I realize I never got to tell him that I love him too.

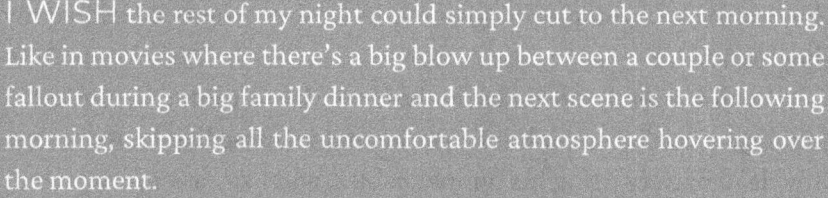

CHAPTER FORTY-TWO

Grace

I WISH the rest of my night could simply cut to the next morning. Like in movies where there's a big blow up between a couple or some fallout during a big family dinner and the next scene is the following morning, skipping all the uncomfortable atmosphere hovering over the moment.

But the thing with real life is there is no fast-forward button. There's no skip tab I can simply hover the cursor over and click on to move to the next episode. So instead of turning a blind eye and waking up the next morning with a clear head and a forgiving boyfriend, I'm standing in the parking lot of the strip mall with Noah guardedly approaching me.

"I take it that's..."

"My boyfriend," I say it with a level voice. The words I should've said the first time he asked. "Yeah."

I turn to face Noah and watch the apologetic look on his face spread to his slouched shoulders. "I'm sorry."

"Me too."

Noah announces that his friend will be in the hospital parking lot in five minutes. He suggests we head back with an air of caution. We walk to my car, me following a few steps behind Noah as I replay the last fifteen minutes. My phone is held between my two hands while I map out a text intended for Andrew. I consider calling him, but that feels scarier than whooshing a message out through the ominous cellular network. By the time we get to my car, I still haven't decided what to say.

What do I tell the man who just told me he loves me after he's seen me sitting at a cozy table for two with another man? Ask for his forgiveness? Start rashly arguing and tell him nothing was even going on? Which is technically true. But the truth doesn't even seem to matter at this point. I feel sick imagining the hurt and betrayal he must've felt as soon as he walked into the smoothie shop. Almost as sick as how I feel trying to understand why I couldn't just fucking tell Noah about Andrew. The thought comes with a sharp-edged knife sliced into my heart, mixing alongside the queasy feeling that my boyfriend isn't going to forgive me. If he even wants to still *be* my boyfriend.

Noah's friend meets us at my car. He introduces himself. I manage a cordial smile but forget his name immediately. He revives my dead battery using his jumper cables, and I say a weak, watered-down "thank you" to the both of them before they leave. Once inside the silence of my car, I slump my forehead against my steering wheel with a heavy exhale into the shiny metal Volvo logo. My phone rings in the cup holder at my side, and it echoes through my Bluetooth speaker. My head jolts up hoping it's Andrew, but my suddenly hopeful mood dissolves when I see it's Jade.

"Hello?"

"Hey, you called? Sorry, I left my phone in the other room."

"I had some car trouble, but I got some help."

"So, you're on your way?"

I don't know if I have the energy to face Jade and brave a fake smile through an evening of trick-or-treating. "You know, I think—"

A delighted squeal interrupts whatever half-assed excuse I was about to offer my sister, only for it to be outshined by my niece, the whole reason for tonight.

"Sorry. We put Avery's costume on, and she's giggling over her reflection," Jade tells me. She laughs, her joy blending with Avery's. "You're going to die when you see her."

"Yeah, I can't wait."

"So, I'll see you in a bit?"

"I'm on my way." I hang up, and my body feels like it's on autopilot. My thoughts are an entire step behind me as I get out of my car once I pull to a stop in front of Jade's house. My feet drag like a set of shackles are looped around my ankles. With my costume in a wrinkled Nordstrom's shopping bag, I knock on Jade's door.

"Hey!" Jade's bubbly greeting is like a ray of sunshine beaming down on the storm cloud hanging above my head, but I force a smile.

"Sorry I'm late."

"It's fine," she assures. I walk through the door, getting a quick glimpse of her mouse costume. "Just change into your costume in the bathroom."

"I'll be quick," I tell her.

I beeline for the bathroom through her kitchen. The mirror in her small one-and-a-half bath leaves me more disheartened than I already was. I'm looking at the culprit for my ruined relationship, and all I want to do is scold at my own reflection. My own self-destructive behavior led to me hurting someone I care about. And all I can do is call myself a coward instead of owning up to my mistake. I should be with Andrew. I should talk to him and tell him how I'm scared. How, in the biggest plot twist I didn't even expect, I'm realizing the possibility of another failed relationship is my biggest fear. I guess I should've been looking in this very mirror when I called him out on his supposed commitment issues.

I change, tucking away my self-wallowing for later. My effortless witch costume isn't anything show-stopping. Buster's bumblebee costume on the other hand, definitely show-stopping. The thought of Andrew and Buster's sweet picture in my phone makes me miss him to the point that it becomes painful. With a glum mood added to my otherwise fun little get-up, I walk out of the bathroom to find Jade, Trevor, and Avery waiting for me by the door.

"Ready?" Jade asks, her camera in her hand.

I nod with a tight-lipped smile, adjusting the antennae on my head. "Yep."

Jade leaves out a large bowl full of candy at the front door while Trevor snaps Avery into her stroller. Jade has a small orange jack-o'-lantern bucket swinging from her hands, and next thing I know, it's already halfway full. By the time we've made two left turns and a right into a part of her neighborhood I've never seen, our steps are moving at a more listless pace.

"Is everything okay?"

I keep my head ducked, my eyes aimlessly counting the cracks in the sidewalk. I've gotten up to thirty-eight. "I'm fine."

"You sure?"

Avery wails from her stroller. Her tight fists jut out to the sides, waving them in distress. Jade's concerned question fades into the background of little Avery's sudden outburst. It's a welcomed interruption. The perfect diversion to avoid Jade's probing inquiry.

"I think Avery's about finished," Jade tells Trevor. She unbuckles Avery and hoists her up in her arms. I take over stroller duty, and we veer back home. Thankfully—though Jade would probably disagree —Avery's fussing doesn't stop. Trevor attempts some distraction technique with a little tickling and raspberries blown into her bulbous cheek, but it only spurs her tantrum. The bucket of Halloween candy sits where Avery sat, and as soon as we walk through the front door, I help myself to a Snickers bar. And not a measly miniature size, but a full-sized candy bar. If only adult trick-or-treating wasn't frowned upon.

I'm almost done with my Snickers when Jade reappears from getting Avery settled.

"That was fast," I comment, the last bite pushed aside to one cheek.

"Trevor has her," she explains. She opens a pizza box sitting on the kitchen island and offers it to me. "You hungry?"

I shake my head. Candy looks a hundred times more appealing to me right now. "I think I'm going to head out," I announce.

"Already?"

"That car trouble just drained the energy out of me," I admit. It's not even a lie. Between the turn of events and Andrew storming off, all I want to do is climb under my covers and hide there for the rest of the weekend.

I reach for my purse and walk to the door before Jade can stop me and ask me once more if I'm okay. Because if she asks me again, I might fall into a puddle of tears.

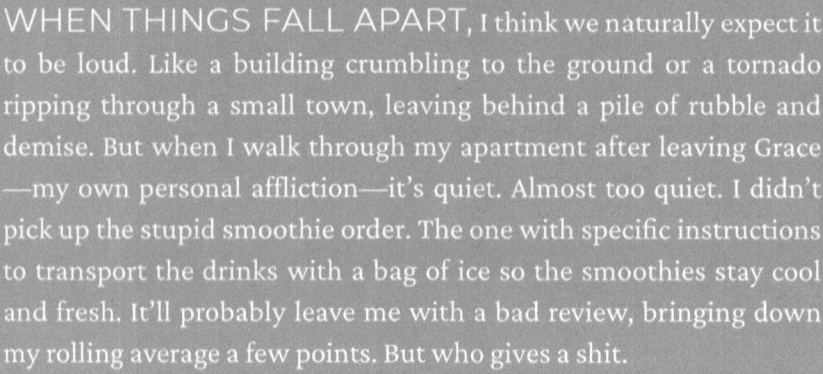

CHAPTER FORTY-THREE
Andrew

WHEN THINGS FALL APART, I think we naturally expect it to be loud. Like a building crumbling to the ground or a tornado ripping through a small town, leaving behind a pile of rubble and demise. But when I walk through my apartment after leaving Grace —my own personal affliction—it's quiet. Almost too quiet. I didn't pick up the stupid smoothie order. The one with specific instructions to transport the drinks with a bag of ice so the smoothies stay cool and fresh. It'll probably leave me with a bad review, bringing down my rolling average a few points. But who gives a shit.

I guess I expected a little more noise when I got home. Not necessarily calamity, but something. Maybe Grace waiting at my door, somehow beating me back to my place. But instead, I'm greeted by my quiet apartment. It's dark and still, showing no life. No girlfriend hiding in the corners, waiting to pop out and surprise me. Even tell me it was all some stupid prank. Her part of a variety show to earn herself a thousand-dollar prize or something equally petty. And as I walk through my apartment, slowly picking up the clutter from my day, a hopeful part of me anticipates more. A soft knock on my door with Grace on the other side. A cautious text message asking if we can talk. Even the quiet buzz of my phone with Grace's face lit up on the screen. That hope starts to feel like an itch. One I can't seem to smother no matter how many distractions I give myself.

Does she not care about us? Do I mean nothing to her? What if all of this was just a game for her? She's said herself she's looking for someone to settle down with. Someone to start a family with. And I was just someone to keep her distracted and happy until the right person came along. Because that right person can't be me. Unemployed, still trying to figure out what I want to do with my life, essentially about to be homeless with the last of my savings being spent on this month's rent. How can I be someone she views as a life partner? My mind spirals, jumping to odd conclusions and convincing myself that this is the end. Grace doesn't want people to know about us. That's the bottom line. Maybe she's ashamed of me, or some other relationship-related woe that makes her think people knowing about us would be the mistake of the century. Maybe this is the best for us. This fateful incident decided for us, and now there's no need to tell anyone about anything. Grace can move on, find someone worth introducing to her family and friends, and I can just slip out of the picture. It'll be like we never existed.

By the time the night turns dark, I've given up hope of hearing from Grace. Still, I change the setting on my phone from vibrate to a shrill ringing sound. Just in case. I guess hope is the real villain here, forcing me to hold on to the possibility of us. That there still *is* an us. It's two in the morning when my racing thoughts are put to a halt by a soft knock. A persistent rhythm of gentle urgency.

I get up from my bed and walk to my door, and just as the knocks shift into a pounding thud, I swing it open. Grace stands on the other side, her body wrapped in my hoodie and her hair thrown into a rumpled knot. Her eyes look round and red, like she's spent some time crying.

"Hi," she says.

I nod.

"I—I couldn't sleep."

"Me neither." It sounds like my throat is lined with sandpaper, and the words are grating against it, sounding choppy and coarse as they leave my lips.

"Can we talk?"

I open the door, letting her in. I get a whiff of her shampoo, a mix of roses and oranges. A strangely unique combination but one I've become slowly obsessed with. It makes me want to just pull her into me and hold her, somehow forget about what happened and lay in my bed so we can embrace the memory of everything away. The common practice we've accustomed ourselves to is to settle into whatever soft, cushy surface is closest to us. Right now, that spot is my unmade bed. But that feels a little risky. Throwing gasoline into the fire. Instead, I lead her to my small dining table. The same table where we sat and ate multiple meals of grilled cheese sandwiches or read a book or swiped through our phones.

"What did you want to talk about?" I ask her in a flat voice. My gaze feels just as leaden with all the things we want to hash out. While I may appear displeased, she looks almost inconsolable.

"Andrew," she starts, her voice breaking. "I'm so sorry about what happened. But there's nothing going on wi—"

My deep sigh cuts her off, and I don't know if it's from frustration or exhaustion. Or maybe a little bit of both. "Grace, I was never worried about..." I pause, searching for the right words. "Whoever that was. I trust you." I realize how true those words ring. As much as I hated the sight of him looking at her as if she were his to look at, I knew it was all one-sided. I could tell by her body language, the way she leaned away from him and had her arms crossed like an extra buffer in front of her.

I see her tense shoulders slump as if a wave of relief ripples through her, but it comes back when the moment of silence between us turns taut again.

"But Grace, you didn't even tell him you had a boyfriend."

She cowers. "I'm sorry."

Instead of telling her it's fine, that it was just a misunderstanding, and I forgive her, I ask, "Are you ashamed of me?"

"No!" She reaches for me, but I instinctively recoil. "Not even a little bit."

"Then why—"

"I don't know." Her mouth starts to tremble, and my will cracks. "I don't know if I'm worried it won't work out or—or...I don't know—"

"So, you don't think this is going to work out?"

"I don't know, Andrew," she says, her voice turning desperate. "I don't know. And that scares the shit out of me."

"Then maybe you don't want to be with me."

"That's not it," she tells me firmly. "I do. I want to be with you."

"But you just don't want people to know about us."

Her eyes search the space in front of us, looking for the right words so her plea comes out the way she wants it to. "I—I'll tell people. *We'll* tell people. We can tell Teeny first thing in the morning."

"Grace," I argue. I don't yell at her or even raise my voice, but it's enough to shut her down. She cowers, and all I want to do is console her. But I know I can't. We can't act as if nothing happened. "I don't want it to be like this. I don't want you to tell people about us only when you feel like our relationship is threatened. It's not fair to me."

"I know." Tears well in her eyes, and one rolls down her cheek. I look away, unable to bear the sight of her crying, mourning over the loss of something that was just beginning. "So where do we go from here?"

"I don't know," I tell her, answering her without even looking her straight in the face. "I think I just need some time to think. I've been trying to find work and make rent and think of a way to tell my parents I lost my job, and...I don't know, Grace."

"You're going to tell your parents?"

"Yeah," I answer. "I...might need to move back home."

She nods. "Okay."

With no more words left, Grace stands from her seat and walks toward the door. I stay in my spot, listening to the sluggish steps of her sneakers and the loud sniffle that rings through my small apartment. And the quiet returns.

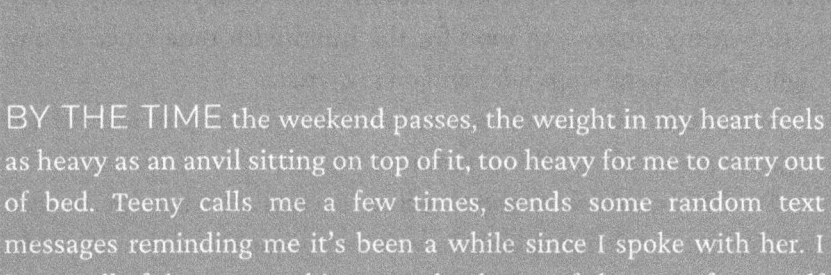

CHAPTER FORTY-FOUR
Grace

BY THE TIME the weekend passes, the weight in my heart feels as heavy as an anvil sitting on top of it, too heavy for me to carry out of bed. Teeny calls me a few times, sends some random text messages reminding me it's been a while since I spoke with her. I ignore all of them, something completely out of character for myself and our friendship, but I have too little energy to worry or care.

I call in sick from work on Monday. Just another day to help bring my mental state to presentable rather than nearly infirm. Though I have plenty of vacation hours for probably another week off, this isn't healthy for me. So, with the mindset to start tomorrow with a somewhat fresh start, I order myself a greasy burrito delivered right to my doorstep Monday night. I've been watching sappy romance movies—not the best remedy for a broken heart—and I'm a blubbering mess by the time the delivery person knocks on my door. But instead of the steamy hot burrito my mouth was salivating over through the picture in my online order, it's Teeny who greets me when I open the door.

"Teeny, what are you doing here?"

"Making sure you're still alive." She takes me in. Alive, but barely.

"By the looks of it, I'm thinking I did the right thing showing up unannounced."

With perfect timing, my burrito arrives, and I welcome the interruption by taking it from the delivery person with a forced smile. I turn to walk inside, leaving the door open for Teeny to follow, and slump back into a weekend's worth of used tissues and nonuniform food wrappers—from chocolate bars and chip bags and frozen popsicles—and throw blankets.

"Grace, what the hell happened?"

"Nothing," I tell her, the rustle of plastic drowning out the morose tone of my voice. I gingerly peel my burrito open and hold it in my hands like Simba presented to my tribe (or just Buster), ready to drown my sorrows in food for the hundredth time since Friday night, when Teeny slaps her hand on my wrist.

She points a stern look at me, her grip tightening in an attempt to gain my attention. "This is not nothing."

Too little of me cares about secrets. Secrets are what got me into this mess in the first place. It was never meant to be like this. Keeping Andrew and our impetuous hookup a secret should've been the extent of it all. Once I realized things were serious, I should've told people about us. I don't know if we can get past this. Whether or not he'll trust me when I tell him he means the world to me. I want to go back to how things were but with a few tweaks, so he knows how much he means to me. Maybe for now, I can start with the one person we've been keeping it all from.

I exhale a deep breath and set my burrito down. "I think you should sit down."

She does as I suggest, her worried eyes trained on how I seem to be preparing her for a slew of bad news. "Is it work? Did something happen? Did you get fired or something?"

"No," I tell her, shaking my head. "It's...about someone I've been seeing."

"Is it that Dr. Noah guy?" Her eyes widen, and the concern in her voice makes the guilt in my gut rumble to life.

"No."

"Then who?" Her brow furrows together as if she's making a mental calculation of all the potential men in my life who could've caused me this level of heartbreak.

I finally rip off the Band-Aid. "Andrew."

"Andrew?" she asks, more confused than ever. "Is that someone new your mom set you up with?"

"Andrew Cohen."

Her stumped expression turns to shock, and I swear I see a flash of anger pass through her glaring eyes. "My brother?"

I nod.

I watch her stand from her spot next to me. She paces my living room, her hands gripping the roots of her hair. She whips around to face me and repeats, "My brother?"

"Teeny, sit do—"

"I don't understand," she cuts in, pacing all over again. "You and Andrew? When did this happen? I didn't even—*holy shit*. How did you hide this from me?" She pauses, still attempting to grasp the situation, and she says, "Wait, so you guys are..."

"I don't know." It's the truth. I don't know what we are anymore. But regardless of official titles or statuses, there's something that is —or was—between us that Teeny needs to know about.

"What do you mean, 'You don't know?'" With the way she surveys me and my apparent downward spiral, she realizes something happened. Whatever was going on between her best friend and her little brother, it's not good. She sits back in her seat, bracing herself for the truth. And all of it. Not just parts of it, but the whole truth. From start to finish. "What happened?"

I tell her everything, leaving little out. How a botched blind date and Andrew's work woes led to an aimless hookup, and how it did little to snuff anything from just one night. Instead, it made our curiosity grow deeper. By the time I get to the ultimate bombshell, Frankie being Andrew's boss, I worry Teeny's head is going to pop with all the new information I just stuffed into her brain.

"Teeny?" She's been staring off into space, and the long pause of silence starts to worry me. "Are you okay?"

She clears her throat and blinks several times as her gaze focuses on me like she just remembered where she's at. "I think so," she says hoarsely.

"Okay." We remain hesitant, unsure of where to go from here. I wonder if I crossed a boundary so far beyond repair, and this is it for us. No more Teeny. No more Andrew. Just me and all the remains of my ruined relationships. "If you want to just go, I get it. I understand if you're mad and don't want to—"

"What? Grace, I'm not mad at you."

"You're not?" I ask dubiously.

"No," she assures. "It's a lot to take in. I mean, you and Andrew. And holy shit, *Frankie*, but...I'm not upset."

I don't know why this heap of emotions causes my throat to tighten, but I blink through a wave of tears and ask in a wavering voice, "Even though we were keeping it a secret from you this whole time?"

"I mean, I wish you would've told me sooner, but I get it. You were scared." She places a consoling hand on my arm, and I turn away just as a tear slips down my cheek.

"And I don't even understand why," I tell her honestly, quickly wiping at my face. "Every time I felt like I was ready for people to know about us, I'd get this impending doom kind of feeling. Like everything was going to come crashing down, and things just wouldn't work out."

"Kind of like how things ended with Frankie?"

"Yeah, something like that." The resemblance throws me a little off guard, yet I can't believe how right she is. As different as Andrew and Frankie are, the fears I had stepping into another committed relationship were the same. Only this time, I was bracing myself for the downfall with no actual cause for it.

"Do you think...that maybe you're not quite over it?"

"What are you talking about? You mean Frankie?"

"No, not Frankie, just the whole divorce. How he treated you, how badly it all played out." She pauses, like her next words might be too much to bear. "Do you think that's why you didn't want to tell me? Or anyone?"

I ruminate over her words, the possibility of them and how it still affects me now. It seems ridiculous to let something from my past dictate so much of my future. "But that sounds so silly. Me and Frankie were so long ago."

"It could be some kind of post-divorce trauma you never got over. You might be over Frankie, but you might not be over the actual divorce." She gives me a moment for this new revelation to sink in before adding, "He put you through a lot, Grace."

I consider everything Teeny says, wondering how after almost four years, all the ways Frankie tore apart my confidence only left me ashamed and vulnerable. As if no one could ever love me the way I am, and if I wanted the things I wanted in life, I'd have to settle. I'd have to settle for someone who never put me first. And I believed it was what I deserved with my entire being because Frankie engraved it into my brain every chance he got. But then Andrew came along, trying to prove to me how none of that's true. Yet, I couldn't find it in myself to believe him.

"I think he's...really mad at me," I confess. "I think he wants to end things."

"Just give him some time. He might just need a little space."

CHAPTER FORTY-FIVE
Andrew

THE MOST VIVID memory I have of growing up in my childhood home is watching my two older brothers share a room. While I had my own filled with bins of plastic toys and their hand-me-down electronics, they bonded over sleeping a few feet from each other. They'd connect through video games—ones I didn't quite have the hand-eye coordination for yet—and odd fashion choices like baggy jeans and puka shell necklaces. All while I played with my LEGO and action figures.

Now, looking at the dusty treadmill and elliptical machine from my door through theirs, I wish it was their two twin beds I was looking at. Thankfully, my parents didn't turn my own room into a home gym—if you call two exercise machines and a lone yoga mat a gym. Instead, my parents left my twin-size bed intact, swapping out the old navy bed sheets for pretty floral ones for guests. But the Star Wars decals my mom strategically placed on both sides of the window are still there. A nice little reminder of my childhood while I stay with them.

"Are you all settled in?" My mom is by the doorway, a stack of towels in her hands.

"Yep."

"Where are you keeping all your furniture?"

"It's in storage," I answer.

"So, it's just your clothes?"

I nod. "And a few other things," I say, loosely gesturing at the boxes I brought along with me.

She sighs, suppressing it with a placating smile. "Well, it's nice to have you back home."

I nod, the only response I have to offer that isn't ungrateful or dispirited. She and my dad are putting me up without charging me rent after all. But there is the narrowing margin of my freedom with the probing "Where are you going?" and "Are you going to stay out late?" I'm sure to expect in the coming weeks. Just last night, after coming home at one a.m. from the Coldplay concert I went to with my friends, I was hit with an impassive lecture in the morning about the hordes of drunk drivers on the road past midnight. It was my last hurrah before what feels like a sanction for falling for the wrong girl. I just hope this isn't a permanent situation.

"I'm just putting a few things away," I tell her. "I'll be down in a bit."

"Okay. Teeny's going to be here with Everett and Sadie for dinner." She turns to leave, and I shut the door behind her before slumping onto my bed.

Fuck. I can't believe the shit show of my life. With rent due next month and almost zero income, I had to let go of my apartment. Luckily, my lease was up—silver linings or whatever. And, of course, there was the awkward conversation with my parents. I explained to them I lost my job, claiming budget cuts and unforeseen layoffs, an easy cover for the truth. Now, I'm turning in my keys Monday morning and trading my independence for my childhood room, floral bedding and all.

Considering how quickly these changes are happening, it feels like my argument with Grace was ages ago. I miss her so much. I want to tell her it's all okay. That we can forget about everything and just go to my apartment, or hers, and go back to the way things were when we'd settle in for a quiet evening of television and home-cooked meals. But I don't even have an apartment to bring her back to anymore. How can we move on from this when I can't even give her anything beyond sneaking her into my parents' house in the middle of the night like I'm some delinquent teenager. Maybe once I have my shit together, I can talk to her. Unless she's found someone better. Like that doctor guy I saw her with who absolutely seems to have his shit together. No wonder she didn't want to tell anyone about us.

It's another hour before Teeny arrives at my parents' house. I hear them pull up into the driveway. The light slams of the car door and the carefree chatter from her, Everett, and Sadie can be heard from my room, and I know it'll be minutes before my mom comes back upstairs to get me. I trudge downstairs, and just as predicted, I run into her at the base of the stairs.

"There you are," my mom greets me. "Teeny's here."

I nod, walking past her to the kitchen to greet Teeny's brood. "Hey," I call morosely. Teeny and the rest of my siblings know about my big move back home. They haven't called me with a lecture about saving money for emergencies like this. Though Josh texted to ask about Thad and whether I've heard from him. I told him Thad has been courteous enough to respond to my emails but no news about a job opening. Just a kind "It's good to hear from you" followed by a regretful "I'll be in touch if we open up the finance position," adding a considerate "I hope it's sooner than later" before ending it with his sign off.

"Hey, Andrew," Teeny says with a sympathetic grimace on her face. It catches me off guard, but I guess it's expected. Thirty and moving back with your parents is enough to earn a look of pity.

I wave with a tight-lipped smile, passing the silent greeting to Everett and Sadie too. Sadie, dressed in what looks like her track uniform, waves back while Everett tips his chin up to acknowledge me.

"Andrew," my mom calls, walking into the kitchen. "Can you take out the trash?"

"Sure." I open the pull-out trash can from under the kitchen island. As I'm tying the plastic strings together, Teeny picks up the recycle bin in the corner near the back door.

"I'll help with the recyclables," she announces.

"I can get them," I tell her, gesturing my hand to the bin in her hands.

"No, no. I want to help."

My brow furrows in confusion, but I don't fight her. I walk out to the backyard in the direction of the trash bins when Teeny's urgent steps round to my front, stopping me in my path.

"Hey," she says, though not in a cheerful greeting sort of way, but as if she's asking me what's wrong with me in the single-syllable word.

"What?"

"You want to tell me what happened?"

"You mean moving back in with Mom and Dad?" I ask. "I thought they told you. I lost my job and had to give up my—"

"No," she interrupts. "With you and Grace."

My eyes round. "What?"

"What happened?" she asks again, this time not clarifying. She wants the details. Actually she might already know the details, and this inquisitive snooping for more may be her search for my side of the story.

"You talked to her?" She walks away from me, emptying the empty bottles and cans into the recycling bin a few feet away. I follow suit, heaving the trash bag into the regular trash bin. "Why did she tell you?"

"Because she's my best friend," she tells me matter-of-factly. "And she's going through a rough time, and she needs me. So, are you going to tell me what happened?"

"What do you mean she's going through a rough time? Is she okay?"

Teeny doesn't answer me. As if holding back the details I want like a hostage situation will force what she wants from me. I cross my arms, and when a weary sigh softens my lingering hurt and frustration, I give.

"I'm not who she should be with," I tell her.

"Why?"

"What do you mean 'why?' Do you *want* me to be with her?"

Her hands meet her sides as she considers my question. "That's not up to me," she says. "All I know is she's spending her time watching sappy romance movies and cries during all the sad parts. And she feels horrible about everything."

"She's the one who didn't want anyone to know about us," I say. "She's ashamed of me. I'm unemployed, I do food delivery to make a few bucks, I live with my parents. It's no wonder she didn't want anyone to know about us."

"Andrew." My sister places a warm hand on my arm and gives me a soft squeeze. "None of that matters to her."

"Of course it does. Why do you think she didn't tell you about us? Or her family?"

"Because she was scared."

"Yeah, she was scared people were going to freak out about us and—"

"No, she was scared that what happened with her ex-husband would happen again."

"What? What are you talking about?"

"She got freaked out, and all she could think about was how the divorce was her fault, and it was all because of her that her marriage turned out the way it did, and she was scared of it happening again."

"That's crazy. I would never treat her the way Frankie treated her."

"She thought that about Frankie at one point too."

My heart breaks for Grace. The shame and criticism her ex-husband treated her with left a mark after all these years, and I didn't even realize how badly it affected *our* relationship.

"Why didn't she just tell me this?"

"She didn't even realize that was why she couldn't tell people," Teeny explains. "All she knew was she kept feeling scared and nervous about people knowing, and—"

I bolt back toward the door, leaving Teeny talking to herself.

"Where are you going?" she calls after me.

"I need to talk to her."

"What are you going to tell her?"

"I don't know. I just need to talk to her."

"Do you even know where she's at?"

It didn't even dawn on me that she might not be home. "I'll go to her condo."

"She's in Malibu," Teeny informs me. "She's at her parents' anniversary party."

"Shit!" I mutter under my breath. I forgot about the party.

"But I have the invitation," she says, the optimism in her voice bringing back the urgency in my movements. She reaches for her phone in her pocket and starts scrolling through it. "I have it here somewhere. When I told her I couldn't make it because of Sadie's track meet, I let it get lost in my inbox." I grow impatient watching her, and she finally says, "She sent it such a long time a—here!"

She points it in my direction. A fancy Evite in calligraphy font for Elsie and Robert Han's fiftieth wedding anniversary. I take the phone from her, sending a screenshot of the invitation to myself and hurry to my room to grab my keys. Teeny follows at my heels.

"What are you going to tell her?"

"I don't know," I answer, shoving my wallet into my back pocket. "I just need...she needs to know I'm not Frankie. I'm not going to treat her the way he did, and if we need to keep things between us for her to understand that, then so be it."

I saw how he treated her. Like she was two inches tall. He ground into her brain this idea of herself. That she's not worthy of love and affection, and any bit of attention he gave her, it was given with spite and hatred. That's not me. I love her. And not only do I love her, but I

323

respect her and care about her too much to treat her like she doesn't mean anything to me. She needs to know this. Even if she doesn't want to be with me, she needs to know that she's worthy of love.

I come bounding down the stairs, and just as I round the newel post at the bottom, my mom stops us. "Where are you going?"

"I have to go do something," I vaguely tell her. "I'll be right back." A lie, considering Malibu is a good two and a half hours from here.

"But dinner—"

"Mom," I hear Teeny call. She offers some vague yet pertinent reason for my sudden disappearing act, but I don't hear it. I'm already halfway out the door.

CHAPTER FORTY-SIX

Grace

MY MOM really knows how to throw a party. Twinkling lights, delectable finger foods, an open bar, and a live band. If this is how my parents are celebrating a wedding anniversary, I can't imagine how over-the-top their wedding was. I get a brief glimpse into the festivities of their wedding night through the large blown-up picture of them dancing on a glossy floor, my mom in her shimmery ball-gown dress with puffy sleeves and my dad in his tux and bushy mustache. Tom Selleck was his style icon, and it shows.

"They look really happy, don't they?"

I turn to Jade, leaning into her arm. She wraps her hand around my waist, pulling me into an embrace while we both admire our parents' picture sitting on a large easel by the cake table. "They sure do."

"You okay?"

I sigh, and instead of answering her, I ask, "Do you think we'll ever have that?"

The side of her head brushes my temple. "I hope so."

"My money's riding on you."

The commiserating way she looks at me makes me almost regret telling her everything. Almost. Because as much as it was difficult to sit my family down to tell them about Andrew, it feels like a weight lifted off my shoulders. The first step to letting go of my past. I can't let my divorce be the rubric for my future. I love Andrew, and this is my chance for a fresh start. To embrace love instead of fearing it.

"Girls!"

Jade and I draw in a sharp intake of breath, preparing ourselves for the intensity of my mom. Especially when she's in center-stage mode.

"People are going to start arriving," she informs us. "We should go find your dad."

"I think he's with Trevor," Jade tells her.

"Is Andrew coming?" my mom asks. I can feel Jade's eyes on me. They swipe to my mom and back to me.

"Mom!" Jade hisses.

"What?" my mom asks, feigning innocence. "I want to meet her new boyfriend."

"They aren't even talking to each other right now," Jade reminds her.

"I'm sure they can patch it up. If they love each other, there's nothing they can't fix with a little chat." She turns to me and adds, "You just tell him how sorry you are."

When I told my family about Andrew, it wasn't to announce a happy union or the jovial end to my search for the perfect husband. It was so they understood where my apprehension came from. Why alarm bells ring when I hear words like "commitment" and "marriage" and "promise." Why I thought sacrifices needed to be made for a happy life instead of believing I deserved it all. A willing partner, someone who loves all the little bits and pieces of me that can become cumbersome. All the precarious, insecure, diffident parts of me I wish I could brush off my hands but are stuck. I don't think my mom got the memo.

"He's not coming," I inform my mom, set on answering her since it looks like it was a genuine question.

"Aw, I guess we'll have to meet him some other time."

"Sorry, Mom." I roll my eyes at Jade, glad I'm able to do it with my back to my mom.

We find my dad near the main entrance, greeting the first of the guests already arriving, and Trevor and Avery join us. It's a welcome shift as the music starts playing inside the great hall. Before we know it, dinner is served, people are loose from the free-flowing drinks and the cake cutting has commenced. Even the music has temporarily transitioned into slower tunes, allowing couples to cradle and sway.

I watch my parents dancing with a proud smile on their faces. Jade and Trevor are on the dance floor too, but a little off-center where the crowd isn't as thick. Trevor cradles Avery in the crook of his arm while his other is wrapped around Jade's waist. Jade rests her head on Trevor's shoulder, and he leans down to kiss her temple, and I have to look away.

What is it about me that I'm not meant for that? I'm so happy for Jade. I want this life for her, and I would always put her happiness ahead of mine. But watching her in her little trio of bliss makes it glaringly clear how far I am from having those things. A committed, loving partner, a family, a life where lonely graves aren't my biggest fears.

I got a taste of it with Andrew. Our domesticated life of sleep-overs and packed lunches. As much as I was a dedicated wife to Frankie, it was never like that. He didn't assume the role of a care-taker. He was just my husband. Someone who filled the spot to the empty grave to my right. But Andrew is so much more than that. He's someone who will walk the path of life with me before laying in our final resting place. And I let that wither away because I was scared. Because I believed I didn't deserve it.

Maybe it's how it's meant to be all along. Me alone for the rest of my life. At least there'll be plenty of room for more dogs.

The urge for some fresh air gets me on my feet, and as I turn to the exit, I see the person I least expect standing at the doorway. His gait is crooked, one shoulder slightly slouched, and eyes I can only describe as longing. His ardent gaze scruples with what to do next. If he should come to me or wait for me to come to him.

The pause is momentary because determination sets in Andrew's eyes, and he takes his first step. Long strides, hell-bent on me.

When he reaches me, he cups my face and kisses me. It isn't fierce or desperate or even hasty. It feels like he's been on his feet in the most uncomfortable pair of shoes while braving a smile and acting as if he's completely fine, only to come home and take them off with a promise to himself that he's never going to put himself through that again. It's relief. There's reassurance and comfort in this kiss.

He pulls away and looks at me. A glance at my face and a quick scan over my body like he's checking on me. Making sure I'm okay. I almost hear it in his soft sigh, and I nearly answer with a weak no. I am most definitely not okay.

"I'm not him," he whispers.

"Wha—"

"I'm going to take care of you," he adds. "I *want* to take care of you."

I sigh, turning my face. "Andrew, I have some shit I need to work through, and it wasn't fair how I treated you. I shouldn't have kept you hidden from everyone. You deserve so much better than that."

"I know. But you were scared. And I need you to know I'm not him. I'm not going to be careless with your heart. I'm going to take care of it."

My chin trembles. "You are?" I ask tearfully.

He nods. Not a quiet, calm nod, but fast up and down bobs leaving little room for doubt. He kisses me again, letting his lips linger on mine. "I love you," he whispers.

I smile, loving the sound of those words from him. They sound safe yet profound. "I love you, too," I tell him, meaning it with every fiber in my body.

"I know."

"I really do," I add. "I'm so sorry I didn't say it before, but I do."

"I know."

This must be what it feels like to be cherished. Like I'm worth the time and energy and love. And none of it's a chore, it's an honor. It's an honor to love me. And the realization that someone would care enough about me to come all this way just to tell me he loves me causes everything to feel light. The shackles hooked to my heart are starting to disintegrate. And with time and patience, something Andrew is willing to give me, I can see them eventually disappearing, right alongside my past.

"Grace!"

We both startle. Andrew turns around to see we've drawn a small crowd. My parents, Jade, Trevor, and a sleepy Avery.

"It's so nice to meet you, Andrew." I hear my mom's voice croon and look just as she pulls him into an awkward embrace. "Grace has told us so much about you." I guess introductions are a bit redundant at this point.

I reach for Andrew's hand, and his eyes glisten with the knowledge that my parents know who he is. He isn't some strange man who crashed their party by bursting through the doors and kissing their daughter. He's Andrew Cohen, Grace's boyfriend.

"This is Jade," I tell Andrew, just as my eyes meet Jade's. "And her husband Trevor."

Andrew extends his hand to greet them, but my sister ignores the offer and hugs him the way my mom did, like how she embraces family.

The hubbub of Andrew's arrival dies down, and the dancing continues. My parents entertain their guests while Jade and Trevor call it a night with a fussy baby in their arms, and it's just Andrew and me at our table. There's scattered specks of confetti over the clothed tables alongside champagne glasses in various stages of fullness. We've managed to snag one of the last few slices of cake, and we're enjoying it with Andrew's arm draped over the chair behind me.

"Fifty years," Andrew comments. "That's a long life together."

"Mh-hmm," I answer.

"What's their secret?"

I shrug my shoulder. "My dad always does what my mom says. That might be a good start."

"Oh yeah?" he teases. He pinches my side, and it causes me to curl closer into him. "So happy wife, happy life?"

"Something like that."

"Hey, where's our son?"

I stifle a laugh, covering my mouth with my hand. "Our son?"

"What? I think I can call him that."

I tilt up to kiss his cheek. "He's staying the night at the kennel."

"A kennel?" he asks with deep disapproval. "No son of mine is going to be spending the night in a kennel."

His voice rises a few octaves, and I rush to cover his mouth, the laughter still bubbling up in my stomach. "It's a really nice kennel, and it's family-run. They even have a camera set up so I can watch him 24/7."

His fake indignance falters, and he covers my hand with his, placing a soft kiss into my palm. "We're picking him up tomorrow?" he asks.

"Yeah," I answer. "Bright and early."

"Good." He pecks my lips with a playful kiss and looks around, noticing the lively party that has yet to die down. "So can we just Irish goodbye this thing or..."

"Ready to go back to my room?"

He nods eagerly. "Please?"

"Come on." I lead him out the side exit where I noticed some of the wait staff coming and going. My parents might get upset that I snuck out early without the excuse of a fussy child or feigned illness, but I'll deal with them in the morning. Tonight, I'm making up for some lost time with my boyfriend.

Grace
EPILOGUE

"THE FLOOR LOOKS RECENTLY DONE."

I nod, taking in the craftsman-style crown molding and the alabaster white walls. I can smell the freshly dried paint fumes as we roam from empty room to empty room. Andrew struts in a wide circle like he's gathering the attention of a large boardroom using the technique of establishing dominance. Like he has something up his sleeve.

"And did you see the backyard?" he adds. "Buster would love it."

I swivel on my heels under the threshold of the master bathroom. "I did."

"So?"

"So what?"

Andrew points his index finger in the air and twirls it around like a lasso. "The house."

"What about the house?" I'm met with silence, forcing me to fill in the gaps. "For us?"

He smirks. "Yes."

"Since when are we looking for a house?"

Andrew shrugs as his arms wrap around my waist. "Since we saw the open house sign with a very charming realtor on it."

"Do you think those are veneers?"

"Possibly," Andrew answers, humoring me. "Or his teeth could naturally look like his gums are clamped on a large white horseshoe."

I avoid the segue, curiosity forcing our conversation back on track. He can't be serious. "Are we really considering this?"

"I mean, you've been saying you want to put your condo on the market. Put some feelers out to see if you get a bite."

"So I can get rid of the one my ex-husband was legally bound to give me. To have a fresh start," I argue, "not to buy a house. I can't afford something like this on my salary."

He lets go of me, running his hand over the marble bathroom counter. The one equipped with a double sink. Something that would be much more fitting to our bedtime routine on the nights he spends at my condo. "Or...we could get it together."

"You want to buy a house?"

"We've been talking about me moving in with you eventually, and maybe we can do this," he says. "It would be killing two birds with one stone. You get a new house, and I get to move out of my parents'."

I cross my arms and lean my hip against the same counter he seems to have a keen interest in. I eye him up and down, wondering if he's hiding a large cardboard check in his back pocket. "Did Ed McMahon pay you a visit?"

"Who?"

"Never mind," I say, shaking my head. "I forget that you're a practical zygote."

He scoops me in his arms, and I squeal when my butt lands on the cold surface. "Imagine us in that huge tub," he whispers, painting a tempting picture. He trails his nose against my jawline, and I feel it low in my belly. "I think it has water jets."

"I hear they're amazing for achy muscles and stress relief."

"*That's* what we'd use them for?"

I drape my arms over his shoulders, and he naturally closes the narrowing space between us. "Are you serious about this?"

"Why not?"

"Um, because."

"Because..."

"Because you don't have a job," I say as plainly as possible. I hate to point it out, but it's the truth. While he managed to snag an internship with The Hope Foundation seven months ago, shortly after he moved back in with his parents, it still remains an unpaid position. We hashed over whether or not he should take it, weighing out the pros and cons. Like if it would be worth him living off Top Ramen and asking his mom what's for dinner most nights to save a penny on groceries. But he didn't have very many options. And I'm so happy he did. While he's been chipping away at his savings after he cashed out what was left of his 401k, he's finally at a job he loves. He enjoys working with his boss. He's respected and appreciated. Valued.

"I have a job."

"I meant one that doesn't pay in Post-it Notes and paper clips."

"Ah, you mean actual money."

I pat a consoling hand on his bicep, offering a light squeeze to soften the blow. "I don't think the bank will take stolen office supplies as payment."

"Well, then..." His voice trails as if he has something hidden behind his words. Maybe this open house visit wasn't as fortuitous as I thought.

"What?" I tug at his secret, hoping he'd unravel it quicker if I pull at the thread and pop it open for me to finally see.

"It's a good thing I'm going to start getting paid real money."

My face lights up. "They offered you a position?"

He nods vigorously. "Just last week. You are now looking at The Hope Foundation's newest finance manager."

I kiss him, gripping his face with my fingers and hooking my ankles behind him. "I'm so proud of you."

The small room, normally echoey with the tiled walls and porcelain, grows quiet, the only sounds coming from our labored breaths and stifled moans. "If this is how you react to my news, what are you going to do when I bring home my first paycheck?"

"I think you're forgetting that I am a self-sufficient woman who does not love for money," I tease.

"So you'll put out even if I was a penniless intern?"

"Baby, I'd put out even if you had to sneak me into your parents' house at two in the morning again."

His warm hands travel up my bare back and tuck under my bra. "That was kind of fun."

"It was." I never thought at the ripe age of forty, I'd be sneaking into my boyfriend's parents' house to have sex with him on his childhood bed. But him fucking me with his hand clamped over my mouth was probably the hottest thing I've ever done.

Though, much like how his parents have been supportive of our relationship, I don't think they'd be opposed to illicit sleepovers considering he's in his thirties, well past the time for a talk about the birds and the bees. Especially now that their son may be leaving the nest once again.

"So?" Andrew asks, cutting into my amorous daydreaming. "Should we go for it?"

"You like this one?"

His eyes take an impassive shape. "Or another one. As long as it's ours."

"Really?" I run my hand down his chest. This is real. This man wants to be with me. He wants to buy a house with me. One with a backyard big enough for my dog to run around in. One where we can build a life and possibly grow old. And maybe, once we've outgrown our home through wrinkled skin and brittle bones, we'll somehow still end up side by side in the afterlife. Sharing a dance with him instead of sitting in a lonely seat at the singles table.

"Yeah." His soft voice is gentle and careful.

"Are you sure?" I ask. "It's a really big commitment. Not like leaving your Keurig at my place."

"I know." He tucks a strand of hair behind my ear.

I consider his proposition, but the usual conformist traditions start hacking away at my ability to jump headfirst into our atypical relationship. They turn my daydreams into a delusion, making me worry about my parents and his parents and everyone in between.

"Shouldn't we..."

"What?"

My eyes search his. I don't know how to do this, be with someone without all the conventional idiosyncrasies that make up a relationship. How did the rhyme go? First comes love, then comes marriage, then comes a baby in a baby carriage?

"I don't know," I answer, "be husband and wife or something?"

"Is that what you want?"

"I don't know," I tell him honestly. "I just think that's what people are going to expect. My parents, your parents—"

"Grace," he interrupts, "this is about us. We should be worried about what *we* want."

"And you?" I ask. "What do you want?"

"I don't care. As long as we're together."

"Me too." I've done the whole marriage thing. I walked down the aisle in a pretty white gown and posed for pictures. I celebrated anniversaries and birthdays. And I watched it all crumble alongside the hopeful person I used to be. But Andrew brought me back, and now we can do whatever the fuck we want.

I might've wanted the picket fence and two-point-five children at some point, all of it wrapped neatly with weekend soccer games and ballet recitals, but Andrew's shown me I don't need all of that to feel fulfilled. I can be happy with just me and him and Buster. We can fill our lives to the brim with whatever future we decide to write.

"So we're buying this house."

"Actually, can we maybe do some more shopping?"

"Okay," he says with an encouraging tone. "Why? Is there something about this one you don't like?"

"I *really* need a walk-in closet," I confess.

"It's just as well," he says, leaning down to kiss the corner of my mouth. "I think I can find Buster a bigger yard."

"So, what do you think?" Andrew steps away from me at the same time I hop off the counter. The realtor, who introduced himself as Dave, greets us with his blinding smile.

"It's very nice," I tell him with a grin, still on a high from this new development between me and Andrew.

"The bathrooms have been redone," Dave explains, "and the floors."

"Closet's a little small," Andrew comments. I stifle a giggle behind his arm.

Dave nods in agreement. "It's a good starter home."

Andrew leads the way back to the living room, and I follow with Dave trailing behind us. "Thank you for your time," Andrew tells Dave.

He hands Andrew his card. "If you're interested or are in search of an agent, feel free to give me a call."

Andrew tucks the card into his back pocket and flits his eyebrows in my direction. "Thank you."

We walk outside, leisurely making our way back to Andrew's car with a pep in both of our steps. I turn to Andrew just as he opens the door at the passenger side. "Did you want to drive around and look for more open houses?"

"Or we can go back to your place," he suggests with an implicit tone. "We can browse houses on Zillow from the comfort of your couch. Do other things too."

"Yeah," I whisper. "That sounds like fun."

He kisses me, pressing soft pecks to my cheek. He pauses, watching the late morning sun hit my eyes. I smile with something contemplative filling the creases around my mouth, making it twitch and quiver.

"What?"

I shake my head. "I *really* love you."

"I really love you, too."

"Let's go before they snatch up all the good houses," I say with a palm cupped to his jaw.

"Oh," he exclaims as I scoot into my seat, "can we find one with a theater room? I've always wanted one of those."

"As long as I get my closet, you can get whatever you want."

"Don't tempt me," he teases, his hand on the door, ready to close it behind me. "I might throw in an indoor pool."

I roll my eyes through a laugh. "Just shut the door so we can go home."

A Look at Book Three

THEY DON'T KNOW ABOUT US

This isn't the story of how they fell in love—it's the story of what came after.

Kendall thought she knew what forever looked like—James by her side, a family, a quiet kind of happiness. But a a tragic loss early in their marriage cracked something open. The grief stayed. Depression took hold. And even after the birth of their daughter, the distance between them never quite closed.

Now, the marriage they've spent years trying to hold together feels like it's barely hanging on.

Told in alternating timelines and perspectives, *For They Don't Know About Us* traces the beginning and unraveling of a love shaped by deep connection, silent pain, and the fragile hope that maybe—just maybe—what they had isn't gone for good.

Sometimes the hardest person to come back to... is the one you never really left.

AVAILABLE 2026

Acknowledgments

I'll make this short and sweet.

This takes a village. The amazing team at Love N. Books Press, my beta-readers, my PA Katy, my wonderful readers, my amazing author friends (especially my OC/LA author friends who are always a text message or DM away), my husband and my babies, and all the people in between. I would be nothing without each and every one of you. I always say this so I worry it may lose its meaning, but from the bottom of my heart, THANK YOU for being here.

JEANNIE CHOE
ROMANCE AUTHOR

Specializing in new adult contemporary romance novels, Jeannie Choe offers stories ranging from angsty and emotional to heartfelt and outright adorable. Because who doesn't love a happily ever after filled with squeal-inducing moments of romantic gestures?

Living off an endless number of paperbacks, cold brews, and 2000's rom-coms, Jeannie lives in Southern California spending her days with her family and two attention-seeking elder dachshunds.

www.jeanniechoeauthor.com